Death on the Learning Curve

Also by the author:

Playing Hurt: Treating the Warriors of the NFL

Death on the Learning Curve

Pierce Scranton

www.DeathOnTheLearningCurve.com

Elite Books

Santa Rosa, CA 95403

www.EliteBooksOnline.com

Library of Congress Cataloging-in-Publication Data:

Scranton, Pierce E.

Death on the learning curve / by Pierce E. Scranton, Jr. — 1st ed.

p. cm.

ISBN-13: 978-1-60070-014-9

ISBN-10: 1-60070-014-4

1. Residents (Medicine)—Fiction. I. Title.

PS3619.C74D43 2006

813'.6—dc22

2006028111

Cover design by Authors Publishing Cooperative

Typesetting by Karin Kinsey

Copyedited by Courtney Arnold

Typeset in Hoefler Text

Printed in USA

First Edition

10 9 8 7 6 5 4 3 2 1

CONTENTS

FOREWORD

There's a dark little secret that teaching hospitals across the country don't want you to know: Learning often comes at the cost of error.

July is an especially bad month to get sick or hurt, because that's when everyone moves up—med student to first-year resident, green resident to year two ... There is a vulnerable time of transition for bright, young doctors when all their medical school "book learning" crashes against the infinite variability of the human condition. There are so many ways to do things right, and *so many wrong.* Two patients with the same diagnosis might require entirely different treatments. If even a simple aspirin, given to the wrong patient, can kill, then imagine the possibilities when a new doctor takes up a scalpel.

The learning curve can be a moral and ethical minefield: Is an abortion a right or murder? Alone in an emergency room at two AM, should a doctor resuscitate a ninety-two-year-old, and possibly bring back a vegetable? Is collecting research data on a patient unethical? How about if the patient doesn't know it? Who draws the line in "turf wars" over different surgical services when doctors compete for patients in a teaching institution?

Every great doctor has had to face the learning curve. The path is marked by naïveté, well-intentioned ignorance, harm, and medical triumph. And somewhere along this path, every doctor-in-training has had to wonder whether decisions made would lead to healing or to greater harm. *Death on the Learning Curve* carries you right into the thick of it with a group of brand new doctors. You'll be there for every gut-wrenching decision and heart-breaking outcome, every life-or-death challenge and inspiring success. Can you imagine what it's like to lay awake at night, worrying that you might have killed someone? To watch the blood flow and the life slip away? Step onto the page with Dr. Ned Crosby and his cohorts, and you'll soon see that the learning curve never stops.

1

Cooling It

A trail of blood wound from an ambulance-docking bay, down the hall, and around the corner into Trauma Twelve. Two brand-spanking-new interns anxiously followed its path, drawn like hound dogs to prey. Ned Crosby and Eleanor Hazelette-Warner were the interns on this hunt, looking for their very first case. They passed the docking bay and the deserted ambulance with the red glare of revolving lights still strobing off the corridor walls. The ambulance doors hung open, and the empty space echoed static and police-band conversation.

It's like a surreal dream, Ned worried. Just last week he was a confident, new medical school graduate, ready to take on the world. Now, the reality of life and death decisions made him claustrophobic. He wanted to return to the easy comfort of looking at charts on the ward and leisurely planning treatment. Instead, here they were, ready or not, charging to answer this call.

Outside Trauma Twelve Ned saw a grief-stricken old man slumped against the door. He wore a rumpled brown suit with the left sleeve ripped halfway up the arm. He sat crying on the floor with his

9

arms wrapped around drawn-up knees, rocking back and forth. Two spindly legs with white socks and black wingtips stuck out below. As the gravity of this trail of blood and a crying old man struck Ned, he muttered, "Oh boy, Nedley, you're in for it now."

They pushed into Trauma Twelve and Ned saw Eleanor's eyes open in astonishment. Only minutes ago she'd been telling him how she wanted to go into Cardiology. Now they were looking at an elderly woman surrounded by a swarm of orderlies, nurses, interns, residents, and lab and x-ray techs. At her head was the chief resident, Neal Morgan. An ER intern was threading an Intracath IV up her right arm. On the left, a nurse started an angiocath. Ned watched as a radiology resident and an x-ray technician frantically pushed x-ray plates under the lady. They yelled, "X-ray!" and everyone including Ned hurried out the door or behind a lead screen. Then they rushed back to continue the resuscitation. But the chief resident and the tech were taking x-rays so often that no one could complete their tasks. Each time they cried, "X-ray!" fewer people moved from their spots. Some muttered curses, as though the swearing might be an antidote to the radiation. The resuscitation team finished threading IV lines into the lady's arms, they were taped securely, and Ned saw that Lactated Ringer's solution and fresh plasma were running wide open into her veins.

For a moment it was like shell shock for Ned: a trail of blood, the old man in the hall, this full-bore trauma resuscitation, and running out to escape the x-ray. He waved to catch Neal's eye, and the chief saw his two new interns.

"Hit by a truck. Eleanor! Go out into the hall, and get as much history as you can from the husband. You know, the usual: illnesses, medicines, and allergies, previous surgery ... whatever." As she turned away, he turned towards Ned, "Get in a Foley, please." He pointed with a finger, "There, in the cupboard on the right. Everybody here is doing something ... We could just use another hand."

Ned took two quick steps to the cupboard and rummaged through the packets. As he pulled out a number 14 Foley Catheter, the orderlies and another doctor finished cutting the woman out of her clothing with large scissors.

It's so incongruous, Ned thought. *One minute she's a nice, modest lady wearing Sunday-best clothes, and the next they just cut it all off!*

Dignity wasn't an issue in trying to save someone's life. As the clothes were pulled away, Ned saw that her left leg angled grotesquely, bent at the calf towards the middle. An orthopedic resident had helped in pulling the remaining clothing away. Then he checked the pulses, feeling with his fingers on top of the foot and at the inside of the ankle. He suddenly pulled the leg straight. They were startled by the crunch of grinding bone, and the woman on the litter gave a muffled shriek.

Morgan glared down at the resident, "For Christ's sake! If you're going to do something like that, please let her … let us all know!"

"Sorry, sorry … You're right." The resident held his arms up in mock surrender. He leaned over the woman. "Ma'am … Ma'am, I'm going to put you into a splint. I'm sorry for the pain."

The woman lay limply on the litter, breathing in rapid, shallow grunts. Her eyes swept nervously back and forth. A shock of gray hair ran down her forehead, pulled in disarray from the neat bun on top of her head. There was a smear of scrapes and asphalt streaks speckled with blood down her right cheek. She looked up, and with her free hand she reached and grabbed Dr. Morgan's arm. "My Andy's okay, doctor? Andy's okay? He's here at this hospital?"

Neil smiled down at her. "Ma'am, your husband's just fine. He's sitting right outside."

She didn't let his arm go, however. Instead, she gripped it even tighter and spoke softly, but firmly. "Now, you tell him I'm going to be fine. He's got a heart condition and I don't want him worrying."

Neal smiled down at her. "Ma'am, your husband's just fine. Right now he's sitting outside, waiting for us to help you."

Ned got a nurse to help hold out the patient's unbroken leg. He spoke to the woman on the litter, telling her that he was putting a catheter into her bladder. He did a quick prep, his gloved hands parted her labia, and he slid in the Foley. Bloody urine! *Did she have a ruptured bladder?* As he crouched down to hook the Foley to the drain bag, he looked up at her shivering body. Her pelvic area was distorted, bruised, and swollen. Her protuberant abdomen seemed to have ballooned up while he watched. Then he saw a large sandbag lying against her right ribcage. He guessed it was for broken ribs and a flail chest. The sandbag would act like a splint to help her breathe.

Morgan paused for a moment to organize the chaos of the crowded scene. "Okay, where are we? Two lines, right?"

"Right."

"Blood for type and cross, right? A CBC, lytes, and glucose, yes?"

"Yes."

"A Foley?"

"Bloody urine, Neal," Ned answered.

"X-rays? Where are the x-rays? Dammit, those guys got the films developed yet?"

"Here!" The x-ray technician rushed in the dripping films from out of the developing room. They were suspended on metal frames, pulled from the developing bath. Together, they held them up to the view box, one at a time.

Morgan flicked through them, scanning and grunting in approval or disapproval. The chest film showed multiple rib fractures, six through ten, on her right side. Her lung on that side had also collapsed. He grunted in disgust. "Damn, we'll need a chest tube." Her spine films showed no sign of fracture, but the pelvis was crushed on the right. A crumpled wing of the pelvis was pushed in like half of a closing book. Morgan cursed, "Damn! Look at that ileum. It's broken in pieces and folded. The symphysis pubis looks disrupted as well. Ned, you say she's got bloody urine? Let's check out her kidneys with an on-the-table IVP, stat." He turned to the x-ray technician. "Can we do it here?"

"Sure." The tech was anxious to please, and his answer was immediate.

Morgan shot the x-ray dye through the patient's IV line, and in a matter of minutes multiple x-rays were taken of her belly. After they were developed, the shadow of the kidneys suddenly appeared, and then the ureters. Ned was amazed. Things were getting done faster than he could even think of them! This wasn't like med school at all.

"Kidneys are fine, man."

"Let's do a cystogram and check her bladder, stat."

More x-ray dye was injected, this time right up her Foley catheter. The next x-ray showed the dye running straight up into the abdomen.

Morgan grunted, "You were right, Ned, she has a ruptured bladder."

"You gonna peridial her, Neal?" asked their junior resident, Sal DeLuca, a.k.a. Furball.

"No, not this time. She's got a ruptured bladder. We've got to crack her belly and clean her out. That urine can cause peritonitis like it's goin' out of style, particularly if she's got bugs in it!" Morgan's grin looked more like a grimace. "A peridial would just take more time; she might go into shock. Besides, I don't need to run saline in her belly and then suck it out again to check for blood. We already know it's going to be positive just from the bladder rupture."

Ned could almost see Morgan's mind ticking away methodically, planning ahead and fully in charge.

The orthopedic resident at the foot of the litter was looking over the patient's x-rays. "This is bad, Dr. Morgan. She'll lose at least a unit from the broken tibia ... a lot more from the pelvis. Let me get my team down here, and I'll put her in a full body cast. It'll hold these crushed bones still while you take care of her belly and minimize the bleeding."

Neal shot back furious daggers, incredulous. "Put a cast over her belly? Over my dead body! How the hell do you think I'm gonna operate?"

"Listen, we just put on a full spica cast, then cut a large window over the belly. It'll hold the pelvis still, and you'll still have plenty of access. I've read they're doing that up at King County in Seattle. They say it really works."

"Right! And the plaster dust just drips down into my belly! This ain't King County. Forget it!" Morgan hid his momentary confusion over this unrecognized form of treatment with derision. Besides, how reliable was the advice from a second year ortho resident he'd just admonished for crunching on her leg?

He turned away but the ortho resident persisted, addressing the comments to no one in particular, "Listen, you've got to hold that pelvis still. Let me cast her." Ned looked back and forth from him to Morgan.

But the latter's coal-black eyes bore through the both of them. "Ned, get over here. It's a stupid idea. I just finished two months on a pus service cleaning up after the damn 'Pods. No more infections! If you're gonna splint the leg, do it now, because in exactly ten minutes Mrs. ..." he glanced at the chart, "Mrs. Bernice Fanning is going to be in surgery."

The ortho resident looked incredulous, "I know, I know ... You're the trauma Chief! But when she bleeds out, don't say I didn't warn you." After a worried glance at Ned, he turned back to finish wrapping the Ace bandage around the plaster splints running down her leg.

They gathered up the lines, IV poles, chart files, and lab slips, and pushed Mrs. Fanning's litter into the hallway. A worried Mr.

Fanning rushed up and grabbed his wife's hand and kissed it. Ned was embarrassed and awed by this display of unrestrained affection. The man's meaty fingers gave a glimpse of their lives: the cracked calluses with ground-in grime, a broken fingernail, sun spots speckling the wrinkled backs, and a dented, golden wedding ring. Mr. Fanning cradled her hand next to his cheek. She turned her head to glance up, and as their eyes locked the pain in her face seemed to soften. "You'll be okay," he whispered.

"Andy," she murmured. "These doctors are going to take fine care of me, and we'll be going back home. You don't have to worry." She nodded her cleft chin firmly for emphasis, and wiped the wisps of gray hair from her eyebrow.

Dr. Morgan held up her hospital chart with the OR consent form clipped to the front. "Sir ... uh, Mr. Fanning? We need the consent signed before we can operate. I can't tell you everything I'm going to do, because ..." Neal shrugged, "because we don't know everything that's wrong inside her. So anyway, I've filled out the procedure as an emergency laparotomy. Okay? Whatever's wrong, we'll try to fix it."

Mr. Fanning didn't hesitate for an instant. He grasped the pen and signed the consent form without reading it. As they started pushing the litter down the hall, he walked with them to the elevator, still holding his wife's hand. He continued to whisper, "You'll be okay ... You'll be okay." He looked up at Ned, almost as if in apology, to undo what had been irrevocably done. "My hearing's not good ... too many years of farm machinery. Why are we here? I couldn't hear the truck. If only the humidity had been right for that second alfalfa cutting," he thought wistfully, out loud. Then the elevator doors closed, and the last thing they saw were his worried eyes still locked on his wife's face.

Neal turned to Eleanor. "Quickly, now, give me the history. What do we need to know?"

She took out a three-by-five card and began, "Bernice Fanning. Fifty-three years old. She's here with her husband for their silver anniversary. Down in Chinatown a truck lost its brakes, ran a red light, and hit them in a crosswalk. Her husband wears a hearing aid so he didn't hear it. She did and pushed him back. But she didn't make it herself. They've got a farm in Iowa. She's on digoxin, zero point 125 milligrams a day, for atrial fibrillation. She's never been in the operating room for anything. No allergies, no other medical problems. Anything else, chief?"

Morgan shook his head as the elevator doors opened. "Good work, doctor," he said as they wheeled the patient off the elevator. Frowning away her startled, involuntary, grateful smile, Eleanor turned quickly to file the paperwork.

An anesthesia resident met them in the holding area, and he took the chart from Morgan. He cracked it open and stuffed more laboratory data under the binder. "'Crit's 22, Neal, but the lytes are okay."

Morgan responded: "We'd better go straight to universal donor O-negative—we need the blood now. If we wait for a type and cross of her blood, it will take several hours." Sal DeLuca had run ahead of them, up the stairs, and he had already changed into scrubs. He stood, waiting at the main OR desk. Neal turned to him, "Sal, call down to the blood bank and ask for four units of O-negative blood. Ask them to rush the type and cross; and…also ask them how many units total of O-negative are available in the city."

DeLuca gave them a mock salute, "Roger, Chief." He was ambling over to the phone when he heard Morgan, who had paused in stride as if he had eyes in the back of his head. "Shake a leg," Morgan said to DeLuca without turning around. "This ain't the cushy University Hospital where people have time to ponder the situation." DeLuca blushed and broke into a run.

Ned and Morgan went to the surgeons' changing room, while Eleanor changed in the nurses'. When they met back in the hall, Mrs.

Fanning had already been wheeled into operating room number three. The anesthesiologist was busy hooking up the leads for the heart monitor, a blood pressure cuff, and a temperature probe.

"Why are we in three, Neal?" Sal wondered. "I thought I saw room one already open."

"Three's my lucky number. This case scares me. I want everything we got, any break going for us. That dipshit ortho resident got under my skin. I've never heard of putting someone in a cast and then operating, but I don't want any trouble. I've got a call in for the staff doc, Myron Nadler, to get here stat."

Ned laughed, "Even the attending guys come stat, huh?"

Morgan didn't crack a smile. "Stat may be the difference between life and death for this lady," he said grimly.

The anesthesiologist poked his head out the door. "Neal, she just ate some Chinese food two hours ago. Also, she's got a flail chest. What's the plan?"

"George, we don't have any choice. We've got to operate! Besides, with the abdominal trauma, her stomach won't empty anyway. Do a crash intubation, okay? Just shove it down fast. Then, stick a stomach tube down her and suck her out. We'll get DeLuca to stick in a chest tube to re-expand her lungs while we're scrubbing."

The anesthesiologist looked up at Sal, as he came over with a big grin. "Furball, is that really you?" As George pumped his hand vigorously his potbelly jiggled in synchrony.

DeLuca eyed him suspiciously. "How ya doin', Georgie? I haven't seen you since you threw up at my last party and passed out in the bathtub."

"You still havin' those wild sauna parties, Furball? Things are kind of slow around here." George rocked back and forth on his heels, eyeing the hair that covered DeLuca. It tufted out of his shirt, up his neck, and ran in patches over his fingers. Even his eyebrows joined.

"Naw, my liver couldn't take it. Besides, I'm married now."

"Married? The hell you say! Not Debbie ..." He leered salaciously and cupped his hands over his jiggling chest. "Oh, boy."

"Hey," DeLuca shot back. "Can it. Marriage is sacred," he glowered.

"Think you guys can stop yakking long enough so we can get this lady done?" Morgan shot out irritably. George grinned as he pulled up his mask, cinched the scrubs up under the potbelly, and retreated into the operating room.

"Eleanor, you and Ned go help move her onto the OR table. Tell George to put her to sleep on the litter. That way, when you move her, it won't hurt so much." Morgan turned to the scrub sink, scrubbing with diligence.

As Ned watched, he thought George was pretty smooth at anesthesia. Twenty c.c.s of Pentothal were injected intravenously, followed by succinylcholine to paralyze Mrs. Fanning. When her muscles stopped the macabre dancing, he quickly levered open her relaxed jaw. In one deft swooping motion, with a triumphant "There!" the intubation was complete. He greased up an NG tube with Vaseline, stuffed it down her nose and into her esophagus, and then began suctioning the stomach's contents.

DeLuca brought up a chest tube tray, opened it, and donned sterile gloves. He turned to the scrub nurse who had been busy setting up an instrument tray, and he introduced himself. "Hi, I'm Sal DeLuca. I need a number 10 scalpel blade and some zero silk on a cutting needle or a swedged-on, okay? Also, get the orderlies to bring in the suction bottles for the chest tube."

"Sure," said the pretty nurse with crisp authority. "By the way, since you're giving orders before introductions, my name's Anita Gandrelli." Anita looked slightly down at DeLuca. This was literal—she was statuesque, in comparison, at five-foot-eight—but it was figurative as well. She indifferently tossed the scalpel blade onto the chest tube tray as though to say, *You're on my turf, now, little resident.* "Anything else, just holler," she smiled, a little too sweetly. DeLuca blushed.

"You guys ready to move?" George had her tubes and lines secured.

Eleanor, Ned, and an orderly positioned themselves around the patient. "You all set?" Ned asked George.

"Ready to move." The masked anesthesiologist nodded back.

"Eleanor, take the feet, okay? Everyone ... on three."

At the count, they lifted Mrs. Fanning over to the operating room table. There was the sickening crunch, as her pelvic bones ground around inside her. "Jesus," Ned whispered. He looked over at Eleanor, whose face had turned ghost white. She still hung onto the feet, apparently paralyzed.

Anita hurried them on their way, shooing them from the room. "Interns, interns. Time's a-wastin'. You don't scrub, the case'll be over." Ned had been discreetly appraising her figure beneath the scrubs, but he lost interest with this bossy display. And he didn't see an ounce of warmth in her eyes. The circulating nurse started a brisk iodine prep of her belly, and, as they left for the scrub sink, Morgan passed them on the way back in, arms raised and dripping. From behind, they could hear Sal DeLuca grunt with approval as he slid in a chest tube.

Eleanor's anxious eyes peeked up from between the mask and cap, looking at Ned. He saw her hands trembling as she scrubbed. "I just don't know if I can handle this, Ned. I'm going into cardiology. I just ... I just don't want to deal with this kind of reality."

Ned continued to scrub before answering. "Eleanor," he said, arms raised and dripping, "no question, this is trial by fire. Hell, I'm scared, too. But right now our trauma team is all this lady's got." He held up his hand to silence her sudden response. "I know, I know ... we're interns, and we're lower than dog shit. But something we do, anything, could be the difference between her making it or not. Like it or not, you're on the team and we've got to see this through."

DeLuca came out. "Chest tube's in. Hurry up. The Immaculate Boss is ready to flash surgical steel. I'll scrub and catch up." From beneath the bushy eyebrows, he rolled his dark eyes in response to Ned's stare. "What're you looking at?"

"Furball, huh? So that's what they call you?" Ned's eyes twinkled.

"Hey! Neal'll furball your ass right outta here if you don't get in there and help!" They laughed, and even Eleanor managed a grin.

The abdominal prep was done, and Morgan and Anita Gandrelli were squaring off the operating field with draping sheets. Ned whispered to Eleanor to concentrate on the squared-off area, to think of it as a case. "This is the problem," he said, gesturing at her belly. "Right now, nothing else matters."

George looked up from the head of the table, "You know, Neal, she has a big cut on her scalp. You'll have to fix it when you're done."

Morgan nodded back, "I know. She was bleeding from it when they wheeled her in. Her skull films were okay, though. We'll sew it up when we got her belly in shape." His hand was poised, with the scalpel directly over the patient's belly. He looked up to the anesthesiologist, "Okay to cut?"

"Cut."

A thin ribbon of blood followed the knife down Mrs. Fanning's belly. His incision curved around her belly button, then straight down to just above the pubis. "Don't want to give her bladder another opening!" Morgan joked nervously.

"Her pressure's down Neal, really down." George looked up over the sterile drapes at them as the blood pressure cuff hissed in its release.

"Give her the O-negative blood." Morgan's eyes never looked up from the belly.

George looked around the room for their circulating nurse. "Get me a pressure cuff, Nancy. That way we can run blood in both arms under pressure." He looked up mischievously at Morgan, "Who knows, maybe I can catch up with these damn surgeons and get some fluids in the patient."

"Cut the damn chatter."

Mrs. Fanning's belly was open. Eleanor held on to a big-bladed, c-shaped Deaver abdominal retractor, and Ned, another. Urine and blood bathed the bowel and abdominal cavity. Morgan dumped in a liter of saline irrigation, and then sucked it out. Thick, abdominal laparotomy sponges were used to gently pull the bowel out of the way. "Moisten them with saline, please." Morgan said crisply.

"Yes, doctor." Earlier Anita may have been pushing people around, but now she seemed a model of efficiency. Her precision was a perfect compliment to "Immaculate." Every instrument on the Mayo stand was neatly in place, lined up for instant transfer to the surgeon. She watched the operating field like a hawk, her hand poised over the tray to anticipate his next move.

Morgan reached in and felt down in the abdominal cavity. "Jesus, there's so damn much swelling." He was searching with his fingers. "There!"

"What do we got going, Neal?" Dr. Myron Nadler, their supervising attending surgeon entered the room. He peered over Morgan's shoulder and looked into the abdomen. Morgan explained the patient's situation, and Dr. Nadler nodded and left the room to scrub.

"I think I found the Foley catheter tip that Ned put in." Morgan shifted around the retractors to the lower part of the abdomen. "Damn! It's so bloody and puffy ... I can't see anything." Neal struggled irritably with protruding bowel until he had it safely retracted out of the way. "There! I can see the hole in the bladder and the inflated balloon of the Foley! Anita, give me two Alyce clamps."

The blunt clamps were quickly passed over, and he reached down with long forceps and probed the distorted, swollen tissue. First one clamp, then the other was placed on either side of the lacerated bladder.

"Her pressure's really down, Neal." George's monotone drifted up from behind the drapes shielding him from the operative field.

"Damn!"

"It's 80 over 48. Her heart's really cranking at 125." The monotone hinted at some urgency.

"You runnin' in that blood?" Morgan spat out.

"Both arms."

"Can you get in a jugular line?" Dr. Nadler addressed them both as he strode back in the room, his arms aloft and glistening with antiseptic soapsuds. Curls of gray hair stuck out from the back of his cap. Ned thought he looked like a tired Mr. Magoo from the cartoons, with deep wrinkled bags under his eyes.

"I can try. Hang on a second." George rummaged around in the anesthesia cart like a big bear foraging through a garbage can. He pulled out a nineteen-gauge Intracath IV line. "Here goes! I'm going to tilt her head down." As George rotated the crank at the head of the operating table, Mrs. Fanning's head went down and her feet went up. The momentary increase in venous congestion distended her neck veins, and they bulged out, a deep blue. George felt for the carotid pulse in her neck, and then he ran a sharp Intracath into the internal jugular vein. A gush of dark blood ejected from the opening. "Great! Now we can monitor her central venous pressure, too ... make sure she's not in shock."

"Screw the CVP and all that technical jargon, Georgie, just catch up with her fluids."

Their circulating nurse hung another bag of blood while George hooked up the central venous pressure tubing. The other unit of blood in the pressure cuff was also empty, so George hung the last of the four units, and re-inflated the cuff. "She's had two units already, and two more are going in."

"Send for four more, please. Make it O-negative." The circulator darted out to phone in the order. Neil turned back to the abdomen and rapidly began sewing up the tear in the bladder. "Damn! It just seems like the swelling is getting worse; like her retroperitoneum, the whole bottom of her belly is filling with blood."

"It is. Her pressure's still 80 over 40." George's ethereal monotone drifted out again.

Their circulating nurse, Nancy, stuck her head back through the door. "Dr. Morgan, the blood bank's only got three units of O-negative left. They're still working on the cross match. What do you want to do?"

"Nancy, call the city's central blood bank. Tell them we've got a major trauma. We've got to have blood. Stat! Ask for four units, and have someone get those three units downstairs on the double! Make sure the orderly knows this lady is going to die if we don't get the blood. Tell him to run the tunnels. Don't wait for a damn elevator!" He finished sewing up the bladder and gave a satisfied grunt. Then he checked all four quadrants to inspect the spleen, pancreas, liver, and bowel. "There!" He looked up with the satisfaction at the completed task. "Nancy? Nancy!"

"She's out on the phone." Dr. Nadler offered.

"Oh. I wanted her to shoot in some saline through the Foley catheter so we could check on how tight the bladder repair is. How's her pressure, George?" Morgan's forehead was drenched in sweat. Anita turned her back towards him and told him to wipe the sweat off on the back of her scrub gown before it dripped it into the wound. "Thanks, Anita. Pressure!" he growled. "Dammit all, George, pressure!" He glared up at the head of the table.

"It's 70 over 40. Her pulse is now 145 ... It's thready, Neal. The CVP line reads zero." George's worried eyes looked up from the monitor. "We're way behind on fluids, Neal. She's going into shock. If we don't do something soon, she's gonna' cool it." There was an anxious edge to George's monotone.

Morgan looked across at Nadler, and then back into the patient's abdomen. He again quickly checked all four quadrants, and grunted. No bleeding. He ran the bowel. It took all of two minutes. The bowel now jutted out above the wound, pushed up from underneath by Mrs. Fanning's bulging retro-peritoneum. The back of her abdominal wall was like a balloon blowing up, filled with blood. Nancy rushed in with three units of O-negative blood. George hung them immediately.

"What're we gonna do, Neal? How can we close the belly?" Sal asked.

More of Morgan's perspiration dripped down and a drop splashed into the wound.

"Shit!"

"Here's a wipe, doctor." Nancy ran a dry towel across his forehead, carefully drying him without touching him. As the circulating nurse she was not wearing sterile garb and had to be careful around anyone on the operating team. To contaminate was to infect.

Morgan's eyes darted around the table. "We've got to do something. Dr. Nadler, what do you think? She must have lacerated an iliac artery or something. It must be pumping out blood underneath the lining of her belly. You can see we can't even close her belly. We've got to go find it, don't you think?"

Myron Nadler had a bewildered look across his sagging face, and he looked back at Morgan. "I don't see any other way, Neal. Her damn bowel's just sticking out in the breeze. I just don't see any other way."

Morgan used the large Deaver abdominal retractors and dampened sponges to pull the bowel out of the way. Ned and Eleanor hung onto the handles.

"Knife," he commanded. He made a small incision in the bluish-black peritoneum, staying on the patient's right side, on the same side as the broken pelvis. "We'll evacuate this clot, and then tie off any iliac feeder vessels." Gently, with abdominal Metzenbaum scissors, he extended the incision downward. Great gouts of reddish-black clots were removed. His fingers probed the distorted tissues, levering and tearing out the clots. "Jesus, we must have cleaned out three units, right there!" He exclaimed.

"Yeah," DeLuca chimed in. "And there's four or five left, all seeping through the retro peritoneum."

"Metzenbaum scissors." The brisk command was answered with the smack of the scissors in Morgan's open hand. His eyes never left the wound. Ned saw Anita smiling to herself behind her mask. This was a hot, aggressive team doing something important—and she was part of it.

"Careful. The ureter and iliac vein's over there, too." Dr. Nadler cautioned with a restraining hand.

"You think I don't know that?" Morgan snapped.

"Ease off him, Neal." Sal pleaded. "We're all just trying to help. It's so bloody, no one can see anything."

"Jesus Christ! What'd you guys do? Her pressure's 60 over zero! She's taching at 140." George jumped up and looked up over the drapes and into the wound.

"Nothing. We just evacuated a huge clot."

"You must have released a tamponade, because her pressure absolutely dropped out the bottom!"

"Goddammit!"

"Here's a wipe, doctor."

"There! I can feel it! I can feel the aorta." Morgan's eyes lit up. "Retractors! Easy ... easy ... there! Give me a vascular clamp." Anita slapped the Bulldog clamp neatly into his hand. There was a metallic grating sound.

George smiled. "Bingo! Her pressure's 90 over 60."

"Ya, George, but I had to clamp off her whole aorta. We'll follow it down, and quickly tie off any vessels." Morgan painstakingly dissected down through the clotted, edematous tissue, following down the right common iliac artery. "That's the internal iliac, posterior division," he announced. "Tie?" He held out his gloved hand.

"What kind?" Anita had in her hand three separate choices.

"Zero silk on an atraumatic needle. I'll pass it around the vessel."

"Zero silk it is." In a flash, Anita handed him the suture.

"One more, please." Morgan cut the first tie, and held out his hand again.

"Zero silk, doctor."

"There, a double-tie on the posterior iliac. Pressure!" He looked up at George.

"100 over 60." It was a non-plussed monotone floating up from behind the drapes, unimpressed by this encouraging sign.

The whole table murmured with relief. They looked around, and smiles appeared beneath their masks. DeLuca gave the "thumbs-up" sign. Morgan motioned absently to Ned, "Go ahead and start on that head laceration. Okay? Sal and I will look for any additional bleeders off the iliac. Then we'll get out of here. Eleanor, sweetheart!" She jerked her head up, startled. "No disrespect meant! Keep hanging onto those retractors, baby." Eleanor noticeably reddened, and she glared back across the table at Morgan. He laughed back, "Just trying to keep you awake, doctor, you looked kind of sleepy. That adrenaline rush of a feminist's rage reaction should help wake you up!"

Ned scrubbed out and went up to the head of the table. He put on a new set of gloves and carefully shaved Mrs. Fanning's head, removing the bloody gray hair from around her scalp laceration. *It wasn't too bad,* he thought. Especially compared to what they'd just been working on. He finished with the shave, and then scrubbed the ragged cut with Betadine solution. The laceration was only about an inch and a half long. It amazed him how much a person's head could bleed. This was the cut that had bled all the way down the ER hall. He re-gloved, put a sterile towel down to act as a drape, and began sewing up the wound.

"How's her pressure, George?"

"One-twenty over 73."

DeLuca gave a small whoop, and Dr. Nadler nodded approvingly to no one in particular. "Brilliant surgery, Neal. Really brilliant."

Nancy pushed through the OR doors again, her arms filled with more units of blood. "This just arrived, Dr. Morgan. It's the O-negative from the city's main bank. They said that's all they've got." She gently set the plastic bags on the anesthesia cart.

"What about our own type and cross?"

"I'll call our blood bank right now, doctor."

"Okay!" Morgan looked expansively around the table at their faces. "Georgie, you ready?"

"Yeah."

"I'm going to unclamp the aorta. You've caught up with her fluids now, right?"

George nodded his head. "Yeah, we're fine on the fluids. Three more units are hanging. Her central pressure's only three, but if you got those bleeding vessels tied off, we should be okay."

Morgan took off the vascular clamp. "Georgie?"

"One-ten over 70. Pulse is 80," a happy monotone drifted back.

"Let's get out. Stat! Anita, please give me zero chromic on a swedge." He turned to DeLuca. "Sal, do you mind if I close it? I just want to get the hell out of here as fast as I can."

"Hey! I'm with you, partner. Sew your little heart out!"

"Pressure?"

"One-ten."

Morgan quickly placed a suture at one end of the abdominal lining's retroperitoneal incision, and then continued sewing in a running fashion like a baseball stitch until the peritoneum was closed. "Pressure?"

"One ... 105 over 70."

"Okay, let's close the belly."

"Shouldn't we drain it?" Dr. Nadler's gray eyebrows twitched below his surgical cap, as he looked across the table towards Morgan.

"Uh ... good idea. Okay. Nancy, get us a half-inch Penrose drain. Also, some 18-gauge wire. Let's put some big through-and-throughs into her, right? Get out quick."

"Sounds good." Nancy ran to open the glass case holding suture packs.

Ned was amazed. In less than five minutes Morgan had closed the abdomen. White four-by-four gauze dressings were placed over the wound, and taped in place. Two rubber Penrose drains stuck out of the abdomen from under the dressings.

"Pressure?"

"One ... 100, or so ..."

"Okay. Let's move her." Neal glared at everyone around the table, "Is everyone ready?" They lined up on each side of the table. "One, two ... three!" They gave a heave and there was another sickening crunch of bones, Mrs. Fanning was lifted onto the litter.

George raised a hand. "Hold it a minute, before we take her to recovery, okay? I want to give her a little more oxygen, and also recheck her pressure." He bent down and pumped up the blood pressure cuff. "Ninety-four over 60. Pulse is 110."

It was like a clap of thunder after lightning. She was going back into shock!

Morgan looked at Nadler with a plea for help that was totally devoid of the earlier whiz-kid cockiness. But Dr. Nadler had no solace or wisdom to offer.

"I'm ... I'm surprised, Neal," he sputtered. "I thought things had been going rather well. I ... well, I just don't see pelvic trauma in my own practice. In fact, truth is, I've never seen anything like this in my life."

"Sonofabitch!" In exasperation, Neal Morgan turned back to the scrub nurse, "Anita, don't contaminate the instrument set yet. We might have to go back in. George, are you sure about that pressure? Check it again, please."

"Ninety over 60."

Morgan ripped off his gloves and gown, the frustration showing on his face. "Everyone stay put. I'm going to make a call. Please help get Mrs. Fanning back on the OR table." He raced out of the room and down the hall to the surgery desk, where he picked up the phone.

"One, two ... three!" Back over onto the operating table they lifted her. Again there was the sickening hollow crunch of pelvic bones, a grinding deep within Mrs. Fanning's body.

"Boy, you guys did it that time!" George looked up from the cuff. "Jesus, she's back down to 70 over 35."

Morgan rushed back into the room. In one sweeping move he ripped off her belly dressings and drains.

Anita was aghast. "Doctor, that is not the protocol in this hospital," she gasped.

Morgan just glared at her for an instant, his jaw muscles clenching and unclenching. Then he let out a deep breath to regain some composure. "Prep her, please. Open gown packs and drapes. We've got to go back in. Also, the instant you have time, Nancy, call the blood bank and get four units of platelets. I called Dr. Farnsworth and he said we may have diluted-out her clotting ability with all the blood we've given her. Okay?" He smiled reassuringly around the room at them, once more in charge.

"Yes, Dr. Morgan." Anita Gandrelli was flustered. Protocol in her neat little OR was evaporating. With it went her confident sense of authority. Technique was being broken, as sterility and most procedural pathways had either been violated or were in doubt. Nervous perspiration soaked her scrub suit. She seemed to be sulking, but her eyes stayed meekly glued to the instrument tray.

"What'd he say, Neal? What'd he say?" Eleanor, Ned, and DeLuca were all looking at Morgan as they frantically scrubbed outside the operating room.

"He said I should have tied off both posterior iliacs, because they communicate. He also said to watch out for DIC."

"What?"

"DIC ... disseminated intravascular coagulopathy. Some ... some bullshit clotting disorder." Neal waved his hand absently in the air, dismissing them. "You know, the patients keep bleeding because their clotting mechanisms get all out of whack. The last thing he said was to get an on-the-table arteriogram to look for more bleeders. If we find any, we'll get some clot and grind muscle up with it and shoot the whole gob into the bleeder to clot it." Morgan's sweat-streaked face struggled to compose into a mask of calm and control. He had his little battle-plan ready, and he was still in charge. He was going to do something that mattered, something, by God, that would save this woman.

They rushed back into the room, hurrying on with the gown and gloves. Ned looked over towards Eleanor, but she was staring vacantly at the ceiling, her eyes glassy and unfocused. Once gowned and gloved, she kept her arms up, and mechanically went over to her side of the table to wait.

It was now two in the morning.

When phone calls for their team came from the ward, the ER, or the ICU, those inside this tense, spotlighted room shouted instructions for Nancy to relay over the phone. Packets of blood, like soft little red eggs, arrived from the blood bank, and Morgan yelled, "We've got to have more blood and platelets."

He took some sterile wire cutters in his hand, and glared around the room. "This patient is going to be fine!" Then the cutters dipped to rapidly snip the eighteen-gauge wire. Mrs. Fanning's bulging, glistening bowel again extruded out of the swollen cavity.

"Sweet Jesus!" He gasped. The abdomen was full of blood. "Suction, please."

"What d'ya think? Three units?" DeLuca wondered out loud.

"At least." They sucked out the blood, down to the retroperitoneal incision. "It's bulged up, leaking ... but it's holding. Let's go over to the other side. If I take out my first closure again, maybe I won't be able to sew it back up. The tissue won't take all those needle holes. Pressure, Georgie?"

"Sixty over zero! She's going into shock."

"Goddammit! Retractor. Moist laps, please. Hold this ..." Morgan's eyes were wild and he worked like a demon, possessed with the desire to save Mrs. Fanning. He pushed furiously, pulled, and prodded at the tissues. He dissected sharply, then bluntly, and with his fingers probed down from the left, down to the throbbing common iliac artery. The rasping sound of the vascular clamp grated though the room. This was answered by Georgie's mechanical ventilator as it sighed and heaved, breathing for Mrs. Fanning. Ned looked across at the tired, gray-headed Myron Nadler. He stood hanging onto a retractor like a passive intern.

"She's 80 over 40," George's voice floated up.

"Come on, baby, get up there!" DeLuca looked heavenward for an instant, and then he made the sign of the cross over the wound. Suddenly he looked up at everyone, self-consciously.

"Hold the abdominal retractor here. Not there! Here! Come on, Eleanor, wake up!" They'd followed the opposite iliac artery down to the posterior vessel. Morgan passed two more sutures around this collateral artery, ligating the vessel.

"So what's happening?" All eyes went to George at the head of the table.

"Hold on. I'm taking her pressure now." The hiss of the blood pressure cuff blended in with that of the automatic respirator. "Ninety over 40."

There was absolute silence in the operating room. Then the Ohio respirator kicked in again, to take another breath for Mrs. Fanning. "We've ... we've got to think of something." Neal looked around.

"Shit Neal, what'll we do?"

He looked up; "We're going to do an on-the-table arteriogram, to find the bleeder."

"What bleeder? You've tied them all off!"

"Sal ... so why's she goddamn bleeding?" Morgan snapped back. "She's goddamn bleeding to death, and we've got to find it and stop it!"

"But ..."

"But what! Is she bleeding?" He stared around the room. "Is she bleeding?" There was absolute silence. No one returned his gaze. "All right, then, let's move these retractors back! Nancy, get some Fogarty vascular catheters, and ... and call x-ray."

The Ohio respirator sounded with a clunk and a hiss, as it took another breath for Mrs. Fanning. It took its programmed "sigh," since George had it turned on automatic, to slightly over-inflate the lungs, mimicking a yawn or a sigh.

A sleepy radiology resident stumbled in wearing a wrinkled scrub suit, and he took his place at the head of the table. Morgan was back thrashing around in the belly. More swollen, bloody tissue welled up, and blackened clots spattered onto their gowns and the floor. He had succeeded in finding the aorta again, and they threaded a catheter down it, to just above the bifurcation where it split into the two iliac arteries.

An x-ray tech had pushed a portable x-ray unit into the room. Sterile, blue surgical drapes hung over the tube, which in turn hung over the patient's abdomen. It looked like a floppy, blue preying mantis, poised over the patient. Morgan had Nancy open a large 50-cc glass syringe, and he filled it with x-ray contrast dye. The radiology resident grunted as he knelt and crawled under the drapes, pushing a large x-ray plate under Mrs. Fanning.

"We're going to release the vascular clamps, shoot in the dye, and then take a picture. Is everyone ready?" Morgan looked around the table at them. Eleanor's head bobbed and drooped as she hung onto the retractor. It was 4:30 in the morning.

"Okay ... clamps off. Here goes the dye." Morgan pushed on the large syringe with all his might. When it was half empty, he yelled, "Shoot it!" and the x-ray was taken.

"Got it."

"Good."

"Quick, put another cassette in!" The radiologist cried.

"What for?" Morgan grumbled.

"I wanna see something." The x-ray tech quickly dove under the drapes and slid another cassette under Mrs. Fanning.

The radiologist cried, "Shooting ... Got it!" Then the tech pulled away the overhanging x-ray machine, and they returned to the wound.

"Pressure's 80 over 30."

"Give her more blood. We're almost there, George. As soon as we find that bleeder, we'll clog it with clot and ground-up muscle. You ready with that muscle, Sal?"

DeLuca had been mincing and grinding up a small piece of intra-abdominal psoas muscle that Morgan had harvested. It was mashed up with clotted blood, and he'd stuffed the mixture into another 20-cc glass syringe. He hooked the syringe up to the Fogarty vascular catheter, and gave the plunger a little squeeze. Burgundy-colored ooze squeezed out from the catheter tip. He looked up at them, his glassy, red eyes blinking and smiling. "Lookin' good, Neal. Find that damn bleeder and we're in like Flynn!"

The technician returned with the two developed x-rays, and the radiology resident grasped them and explained, "The first shot is the arteriogram. If we've got a bleeder here, we'll see it."

They clustered around the view box, clasping their hands in front to avoid contamination. They looked like a praying choir bathed in a mysterious holy light. The resident thrust up the first of the films onto the illuminated view box, and secured it under the clamps. They'd gotten a perfect arteriogram.

"Nice shot, Neal."

The team echoed DeLuca's cheering.

It showed Mrs. Fanning's aorta, where it split at the bifurcation, the superior iliac vessels, and even the two "nubs" where the posterior vessels had been tied off. There was nothing else to be seen. The radiologist then hung the second film.

"I didn't know if I'd catch it or not. It was strictly a luck shot, as far as the timing. If we were down in the x-ray department, I would have guaranteed it." He looked confidently around the room and smiled. The hollow boasting was wasted on an exhausted team.

"Anyway, we got lucky. This second shot shows the venous return. Look at the tremendous haziness in the pelvis. Your patient's pelvis is smashed, Neal, and it's pouring out blood from bone marrow veins, not arteries. I'm sorry, but I don't think there's anything you guys can do. There's no bleeding artery here to inject and clog with a clot. All you can do is pray." He pulled down the x-rays. "Do ya' mind if I take these? I've got to dictate on them, and I want to show them to my staff doctor. Jesus guys, tough case!"

"Neal," George was squeezing the pressure cuff, forcing the last of their units of blood into Mrs. Fanning's body. "Her pressure stinks. I've only got one unit left. What are we going to do?"

Morgan was numb. He was still looking at the empty x-ray view box. Sal DeLuca sat down and absently stirred at the muscle-clot mixture that was congealing on a sponge. "Put her in Trendelenberg," Morgan murmured "Tilt the table so her head's down and her feet are up."

"She's already in Trendelenberg, Neal."

"We ... we've got to close her up, I guess. Sal ... Sal, help close, please? Dr. Nadler?"

Myron Nadler shrugged, exhausted, and stepped forward to help in the closure.

They worked on in silence, listening to the respirator and the heart monitor. There was a small hiss from the sucking chest tube, and from her nasogastric sump suction. They drove the eighteen-gauge wire again through the abdominal wall. Neal Morgan's hands mechanically placed the suture, bringing each wire down in a perfect square knot. Ned watched the little light on the heart monitor flipping faster and faster. Red rubber cushions were slid onto the wires to protect the skin and prevent chafing or scraping. Antibiotic gauze was placed over the wound, then four-by-four sponges, and a thick, absorbent ABD pad. This was protocol. The monitor's beeping noise was now continuous.

"V-fib, Neal. Should we call a code?" Morgan glanced back at George with glazed eyes, and shook his head.

The respirator continued to chug and puff on automatic, and Mrs. Fanning's chest tube hissed as it sucked her lungs into expansion. As they dressed her wound, the harsh tearing sound of adhesive tape broke the stillness of the room. No one could speak. Then, with the shrill, insistent sound of the heart monitor, Mrs. Fanning flat-lined, her heartbeat slipping away forever along with soft summer nights on a porch swing in Iowa, fireflies in the dark, and the love of her husband. Neal Morgan took off his gloves and mechanically stepped out of the gown, letting it fall from his body. He stumbled over it as he walked towards the door. "I'll talk to Mr. Fanning," he murmured.

George switched off the heart alarm, and shut off the Ohio Respirator. He picked up a small flashlight, and flashed the beam into each of the patient's pupils. They were fully dilated, and unresponsive to the light. "Five-oh-eight AM, July third, 1971— the time of death. Is that right, Anita?"

"That's what time it is, doctor."

Ned walked around the table and put his arm around Eleanor's shoulder. He reached behind her, and pulled at the string ties on the cloth surgical gown. He stripped it away, along with her gloves. She seemed stiff, unresponsive and glassy-eyed. "Come on," he whispered. "We've got to make rounds. We've got the other patients to take care of."

Silent tears welled in her eyes, spilling down in wet streaks on the front of her scrub suit, as they strode, stiff-legged and sore, from the operating room. As Ned approached the surgeons' locker room, he heard racking sobs coming from within, and whispers and muffled cries running beneath the door. So he continued on past, and crept down the rusty back stairs to be outside in the new day's misty early dawn.

In a quiet corner, in the morning light behind the alleyway of the hospital, he wept for Bernice Fanning, their case for that day.

July 3, 1971, 6:10 AM

That morning, rounds were very subdued. Neal Morgan meandered down the hall like a mechanical man, asking for temperature, crit, and vitals. A smear of black stubble underscored his stress-marked face. Sal DeLuca smoked a cigarette under a "No Smoking" sign. Furball's stubble went nearly up to his eyes, under his chin, and down his neck like a rolling crop of dark grain. All of them stunk with the nervous perspiration of continuous stress. As they stood at the head of each new patient's bed, they shifted from foot to foot, relieving their swollen feet that had been abused by standing all night.

"Jesus, Cros', it's like a morgue in here," said Blade Blackston. "What happened?" They were trudging up a back stairwell from the ICU to Four North.

"We lost one last night, Vernon. Shit, my first night on call, and we lost one. It was awful."

"I guess it was bad, Ned; you called me Vernon. But how bad is bad? Before this is over you'll find that people cool it in this joint all the time."

"This one was special. She was a farmer's wife from Iowa, a really sweet lady who had just saved her husband's life." He whispered in Blade's ear. "I don't know what happened, but we may...we may have killed her. Every time we moved her on the table there was this terrible crunching of bones. She got every unit of blood the city had, and we still couldn't keep up with the bleeding. This ortho resident said to put her in a body cast ... I wonder if he was right."

They heard brisk footsteps behind them and a harrumph. Ned twisted to see who it was, "Oh, Doctor Farnsworth." The troupe stopped in the hallway to face the hospital's Chief of Staff.

"Gentlemen, gentlemen," said the dapper Dr. Farnsworth. Bright intelligence flashed in his eyes and his hands fluttered.

Ned looked across at him in dread. Dr. Farnsworth stopped directly in front of Morgan, but addressed them all. "I've heard about your, your tragedy, last night. I want you to know that these things are never easy for any of us." His back became rigid, as he looked straight at Neal Morgan. "Neal, in massive pelvic trauma, the mortality rate exceeds 50 percent. No other hospital in our city will even handle these cases. In another hospital, most likely she would have lain up on the ward and died. At least, you tried. These cases are terrible. At this present state of our knowledge, there are no rules, only judgment calls. You're going to be one of the finest chief residents we've ever had at the General. There is nothing to dulcify this tragedy other than the knowledge that I know everyone here did the best they could. You've got the patients of our entire service counting on you to continue to provide them with good care. And so, carry on."

He pivoted and strode a few steps down the hallway. Then he turned, his hand contemplatively fingering his chin.

"I know these are complicated cases, Dr. Morgan, and one can only second guess in hindsight." His bald head was cocked inquisitively. "Dr. Morgan, you did consult with a specialist, didn't you?"

"Yes, sir."

"You talked with him ... but did you listen?" As he moved off, he left the question floating in the sunlit corridor.

Morgan started with an angry scowl. His glassy, red-rimmed eyes surveyed the team. "Well ... what're you all standing around for? Let's go."

But they waited until he was a solitary few paces ahead before they roused their exhausted bodies to follow.

*   *   *   *

Ned Crosby looked up from his diary, closing it momentarily. Here he was, twenty-five years later, sitting safely in the sanctuary of his den, reading about a tragic episode that occurred during his internship. Amazing, he thought. If I hadn't come home in time, I would have lost this book in a junk pile my wife had put out for the garage sale. *He would have lost his history, his memories of the naive learning curve he went through, learning to be a doctor. He reflected on the tragic episode he'd just read. He himself bore no guilt for the death of Mrs. Fanning. But he still felt a deep sorrow for the misguided, well-intentioned team. In later years, his surgical training saw an amazing evolution in the management of severe pelvic trauma. Farnsworth was right, no hospital wanted massive pelvic trauma, because if you put them in a pelvic sling they'd probably die, and if you operated they died. Nevertheless, surgeons tried more aggressive treatment, but the frantic abdominal laparotomy in the face of a crushed pelvis was shown to increase, not decrease mortality. So the standard of treatment swung towards immobilizing a patient's pelvis in huge plaster body casts or "G-suits." This treatment gave way to the insertion of special stabilizing "pelvic rods"—an external frame. A few short years after that, there was a return to the laparotomy with immediate internal fixation using special Swiss plates and screws. He knew it was only a matter of time before that, too, yielded to further technological advances. What was "state of the art" now soon became archaic. MRIs and CAT scans didn't even exist back then.*

He looked down at the diary's pages, and then poured himself a small brandy. But he frowned as he saw a slight tremor in his hands. Mrs. Fanning still had him shook up! Ned reached out and grasped an imaginary scalpel in the air. With a mock cutting motion his sinewy tendons, a few knobby knuckles, and a web of veins congealed into a surgically precise cutting machine, a deft instrument to repair or heal damaged tissues or bone. With a grunt of satisfaction, he took a measured sip of brandy and turned back to the diary. He'd pulled the book to safety, and just started browsing right in the middle.

Everything had a beginning, and so did this. Oh that auspicious beginning! What was it like, that first day? Ned fingered the yellowed paper, turning to the diary's very first page.

2

In the Beginning

July 1, 1971, 7:00 AM

As Ned Crosby and the other new interns trooped into the auditorium of the General Hospital, he looked up to see a handyman perched high above them on a twenty-foot ladder, changing light bulbs. On this hectic and portentous day, Ned wondered what he and his fellow interns must look like from up there, moving nervously down the aisle. *I'll bet we look like a bunch of crazy white blotches,* he thought.

Yesterday he'd arrived at the hospital all full of himself, only to be greeted by a bored receptionist and given a mimeographed list of where to go and what to do: his assigned room, the auditorium, Central Supply, an so on. He'd wandered around the bustling hospital, impressed by the obvious friendliness of the employees. But he also sensed a reticence, an undercurrent in their recognition that he was one of the oh-so-new interns. They were sizing him up, too. Would he be easy to work with, or would he be a supercilious snob impressed by his commanding position?

The emotional high from Medical School graduation was just a memory. M.D.! This soon evaporated as June's brief vacation with

41

anxiety and foreboding. He worried about beginning a new life as a doctor. He had heard of the pressures of internship. And now another unknown, as he traveled across the country to a new home in a strange city. Where could he get a cheap, reliable used car? Where should he bank? Could he get a nearby apartment? No longer a student, he would now be on call for life-and-death decisions at any time of the day or night. Was he going to measure up? A thousand gremlins of anxiety gnawed at his brain.

He remembered blurting out these fears to the preceding intern, who'd taken him around when he interviewed for the position. That intern had laughed and pointed towards Warren Childress, the same handyman on the ladder, who was then pushing a laundry bin down the hallway. "Whenever you need to know something around here, just ask Warren," he'd said. "Warren's spent twenty years in this hospital, watching over each batch of interns like a mother hen. He runs the physical plant of the hospital, but he can help you over the rough spots in getting settled in."

Now in the auditorium, Ned saw the handyman pause and smile down at the bright, shiny new faces. And because, in fact, Warren had helped him find a cheap, convenient apartment nearby, Ned smiled back appreciatively. Their eyes met, and Ned thought that the handyman was sizing up the rest of this new group, too.

Below this man on the precarious ladder, the interns giggled and gestured, a mix of nervousness and pride. They were dressed in ill-fitting, baggy, white pants and smocks which signified their status: Doctors at last! No license to practice independently, yet, but still they had new rank. No more medical school drudgery.

Warren had handed out those same white uniforms to Ned and the rest of the interns only yesterday, in the laundry supply room.

"Waist?" he inquired. "Shirt size?"

Ned had watched him politely wait for an answer as though it mattered, as though he wanted the new doctors to remember that he had personally bestowed upon them the proper clothing, emblematic of their new status. It was sort of a baptism, Ned had thought.

And then, without seeming to check, Warren grabbed the topmost pair of whites from the stack and pushed them through the window's opening.

"Be jus' right for you, doctor. You adjust the buttons at the waist."

Blade Blackston, Ned's new roommate, had protested. "Warren, could you at least try to find me the largest size?"

Blackston unfolded the white cotton pants. He held them up to his waist, revealing that they were at least two inches short. The waist could be made to fit by moving the straps that caught in the two buttons that regulated circumference. But there was a sharp contrast between these baggy, ill-fitting whites and Blackston's stylish, cultivated attire. Later, in the locker room, the interns struggled in frenzy, fiddling with and adjusting their new clothes. They could barely suppress their grins as they changed into this uniform of official, new doctors. Like butterflies emerging from cocoons, they left the changing room and strutted proudly to join the throng.

Until that moment there had been an unspoken awareness of their inadequate medical student status. They had been patronized during their clinical work, and treated to instruction in small groups, sort of like an after-thought. They had always felt ill at ease, not really part of the diagnostic and therapeutic team—unnecessary, but tolerated. In fact, their instructors were often interns. But the great wheel of karma had turned, and now was their moment; it was they who would lead and instruct. They would be interns.

Today forty white, baggy blotches streamed into the auditorium and clambered down the ancient rows of folded wooden chairs. Ned waved up at Warren high on the ladder, "You best be careful up there. You just might be my first patient!" Warren laughed back.

Ned and Blade slid awkwardly down the narrow row of seats, banging their knees on the protruding wooden armrests. The battered arms, in use for decades, had a few carved obscenities attesting to the fact that they were the original chairs, in place since the hospital had been built and dedicated as a WPA project in 1937. Sunlight streamed through the windows, lined by limp, burgundy drapes reeking of mustiness. There was an occasional subtle waft of the acrid smell of antiseptic, drying on the worn tile floor. As Ned and Blade scooted in and folded down their seats, they saw that the chair bottoms were plastered with a pastel mosaic of stale blobs, several decades of deposited chewing gum.

Depressed by this seediness, Ned reined in the excitement boiling below the surface of his seemingly placid exterior. Beneath the calm were the burden and the knowledge that in joining this grand tradition of medicine, he was following in the footsteps of his recently deceased father.

Now, God help me, it's my turn to start the journey, he thought, *the transition from medical student to healing physician.*

He ran his hands nervously through his curly brown hair, trying to smooth a part in the chestnut mop that Blade sarcastically referred to as "somewhat Romanesque." Last night as they'd unpacked in the apartment, Blade had said he reminded him of a tightly wound pocket watch with a tooth or two missing in the cogwheel. In the middle of a sentence, he'd suddenly jump from thought to thought, slipping into animation and excitement. Then, he'd realize Blade hadn't understood a thing he'd said because he hadn't completed a single idea! Blade called him, "guarded-frenetic."

Ned looked past Warren's ladder and surveyed the paintings that hung on the walls of the auditorium. Distinguished, bearded portraits returned his stare. Some subjects were thoughtfully posed, holding eyeglasses or stethoscopes as they directed noble gazes into the distance.

"Probably administrative types," Blade ventured. He cuffed Ned's shoulder and mocked his serious concentration. "If they painted down low enough, you'd see they were playing pocket pool."

Ned looked incredulous at the blasphemy, but Blade laughed and cuffed him again.

At the podium in front stood a perspicacious looking bald man, fidgeting with some papers. He swallowed nervously, and his navy and red polka-dotted bow tie bobbed between his protuberant Adam's apple and white coat. Stenciled on the coat's breast pocket, above the emblem, *Where Knowledge Heals,* was the name and title *L. Farnsworth, M.D., Chief of Staff.*

He probed the entering group with rapier-like eyes, and it seemed as though he was judging each of them, too. The left side of his forehead was balder than the right, revealing a dent of shining asymmetry in the skull. A contracted, white craniotomy scar gleamed back at the interns and it pulled his eyebrow up into a perpetual sideways question mark.

Ned had heard the rumors of what had happened to Dr. Farnsworth: As a surgical resident, he had been attacked with a hatchet by a berserk patient. Farnsworth had come into the emergency room to work up an assault victim, not knowing that the man was a psychotic paranoid schizophrenic who'd heard voices whispering that the next man to enter the room was going to kill him. He'd hidden a small hatchet at the small of his back. Fortuitously, the attack occurred right next door to the trauma room. In a matter of minutes, Lloyd Farnsworth had had large bore intravenous lines inserted into the veins of his arms, a Foley catheter up in his bladder, and skull films. The doctor had become the patient on a litter, and he was rushed to the operating room for a decompressive craniotomy.

Farnsworth was right-handed, so the left-sided assault injured the brain's cerebral cortex, which controlled voluntary right-sided movement. The neural damage did not impair speech or thought, but it ended what had been predicted to be a brilliant surgical career.

However, his cognitive functions were as sharp as ever. Many an intern, and even the more practiced residents, had felt the sting of Farnsworth's acerbic barbs during his teaching rounds. Regardless of the history, Blade summed it up best, "Ned, for the next year, that man up there is God."

Farnsworth harrumphed. "Doctors, please be seated as soon as you can." He gestured expansively towards the chairs, and his fingers fluttered like erratic butterflies.

Ned's eyes danced approvingly. *Doctors,* he thought. *Why not?*

It was hard to put into words what it was like enduring four years of painful learning, ignorance, and belittlement—of knowing how little you actually knew. Now, at last, a little respect: *Damn right, Doctor!*

A stocky young man squeezed past Blade, stumbling over Ned, who smiled and looked up, pulling his feet out of the way.

"Excuse me."

"No problem, man," said the intern as he deftly twisted his girth into the seat. He stuck out his hand. "Jones is the name. Everett Jones."

Ned pumped the hand vigorously. "I'm Ned Crosby. And this is Blade, er, I mean, Vernon Blackston. Warren found us an apartment last week and we're rooming together."

"No problem. Hi, Vernon, or is it Blade?" Everett Jones stared awkwardly adjusting his thick eyeglasses wrapped in gold wire rims.

Blade had chiseled features and piercing, gunmetal gray eyes. He had high cheekbones and a sharp nose that seemed carved from granite. This contrasted with a generous expressive mouth. He had "presence"—a buoyant personality that attracted attention, and an infectious smile that could levitate the entire surgeons' lounge. Later Ned would discover Blade's womanizing faults, but he would also find him to be a loyal friend, a hard worker, and an entertaining companion.

"Blade's fine, Everett." Blackston laughed, and he shook Jones' hand, "Where you from?"

"Me? U. of A. Med., Arizona," Everett smiled, revealing bright, crooked teeth.

They were suddenly interrupted by the commotion of a man and woman hurrying down the aisle.

"David, I told you we'd be late," carped the wiry little woman. "I just knew when you took that wrong turn onto 45th we'd get stuck in the one-way traffic." Her pursed red lips pouted toward her companion.

"Eleanor, we're just fine. Nothing's started yet, so stop the griping."

The David they were eyeing looked like a flower child straight from Woodstock. His bushy pate resembled a collection of exploded birds' nests, complete with droppings. Patches of premature gray hair stuck out everywhere.

His mate wheeled and gave a stern look that stopped all conversation in the auditorium. She directed him like a child down one of the rows of seats.

"They may not have started, but you haven't finished," she hissed. "For God's sake, button the fly on those ridiculous new whites!"

Ned almost stood to crane his neck, looking at this couple on the opposite left aisle. *What would possess someone to berate their spouse so loudly that half the auditorium turned to listen,* he wondered? *Jeez, here's a real ball-breaker, that one.* As though she could read minds, she turned, and caught him staring. He sheepishly sat back down.

There was more scurrying as another tardy intern ran down the aisle, stumbled into Ned's row, and flopped down. "Damn, damn, damn! Am I late, or what?"

"No. Why? What's wrong?" asked Everett.

"I can't believe it. I just put on these whites, see? So I'm trying to pick up a quick cup of coffee when this wino asks me where the ER is? Hell, how do I know? I just got here. So I turn to ask a passing nurse. But before I realize it, the guy blows lunch on my pants!" He gave them an exasperated sigh. "Just look at the mess!"

Ned gazed down at the stained pants. "Looks like just a little spray, was he far away?"

"Maybe three feet, but you can see the spatters."

"It's not too bad; will it wipe off?" Ned surveyed the greenish-brown spots nervously, twisting at a tuft of hair.

"Yeah, I used three towels."

"What's with the shoes?" Ned's gaze shifted from the stained pants to his shoes.

"Oh, these?" The intern grinned. Each shoe had a large, red, oversized tongue that flopped out over the laces. Above the tongue were two crossed eyes and a bulbous nose. "I got 'em yesterday, downtown. Figured they're so bizarre that people will think I'm a cool dude instead of someone scared shitless!" He stuck out his hand; "I'm Dave Lefke, Columbia."

Ned shook back. He started to introduce Everett and Blade when Dr. Farnsworth addressed them.

"Gentlemen ... gentlemen," he flashed a mechanical administrative grin, "and ladies, too. Doctors, I should say! I begin with felicitations. We're delighted ... delighted to have you here, and to welcome you to our staff. You'll be pleased to know that you are the select of the select." He beamed and the bow tie bobbed congenially. "This year our institution processed a record 2,021 applications."

The crowd of interns murmured, and Farnsworth hushed them with hands pressing downward.

"By our forty-fifth round, we had selected our forty interns. You gentlemen, and, ah ... you, young lady ..." he smiled at the only female

48

intern in the group, "represent the crème de la crème, as it were. This may be the finest group of interns we've ever had at the General."

A rising murmur of excitement rippled through the crowd. *Crème de la crème, eh? By God, yes!* Ned could sense everyone's chests swelling with pride. "Damn right!" he whispered.

He remembered the anxiety of the match. He'd had to choose an internship, but the hospitals got to put down their choices, as well. On that portentous day, many disgraced fellow medical students had failed to match any hospital at all.

"Yes, well, that's enough self-satisfied burbling," said Farnsworth. He mopped at his dented forehead with a handkerchief and grinned, "Try not letting the self-love get out of hand. As time goes by, you young doctors might do well to dip into the writings of the Eastern philosophers, who knew that the way to enlightenment is through humility." He punctuated the "mil" in "humility" with an index finger in the air and a jump of the bow tie.

The group blinked uncertainly at this display of pedantry. What did Far-Eastern philosophy have to do with anything? There was a moment of awkward silence. Out of the corner of his eye, Ned saw a dark-complexioned intern with an elegantly turbaned head and fierce mustache rolling his eyes and chuckling while he whispered to his neighbors.

Dr. Farnsworth suddenly swung his attention down to his papers and pressed on. "I was about to say, we should now proceed with the drawing." He looked around the room. "As you know, this hospital has one of the last, classical, rotating internships in the country. Twenty of you are rotating medical, and the other twenty are rotating surgical service. With all the various services: cardiology, urology, pulmonary medicine, and so forth, each of you will draw for the right to select the rotations, depending on your interests, from these large boards behind me. In each of these two bowels," he grinned, "excuse me— bowls—are twenty numbers."

They tittered at his crude play on words as if on cue.

"Everyone will come up and draw a number. The number you choose gives you, in order, the right to pick a slate of rotations."

The titter turned into loud rumbling.

"And doctors," Farnsworth held up a restraining finger for emphasis, "good luck."

Ned was aware that there was more to this ceremony than met the eye. The surgical interns had to choose nine months of surgical rotations and three months of medical. The medical interns the converse. But the right to choose first, and to choose the order, could mean the chance to gain or lose a career. If you were interested in orthopedics, but drew a low number, you might never even get on the rotation, let alone get on soon enough for the ortho faculty to get a look at your ability. Someone else who made a good impression would get your chance to apply for the residency.

Farnsworth's mechanical smile disappeared in momentary alarm as the interns swarmed en masse around the bowls labeled "Medicine" and "Surgery." Only the turbaned intern approached serenely. His ramrod posture in the baggy whites gave him a commanding air. Some actually made way for him in awe, as though he should not be denied. Others were too busy groaning and gasping at the numbers they had drawn.

Blade reached into the surgical bowl, his eyes flashing with expected recognition, as though good luck for him had been preordained. He let out a little whistle and announced. "Numero uno! Nedley, I say, I say, number one!"

He put a fatherly hand on Ned's shoulder and magnanimously gestured towards the bowl as though to say, since number one's taken, you should draw number two. Instead, Ned drew number seventeen. He slumped dejectedly.

The interns milled about the rotation board each waiting his or her turn, some beaming and others with gloomy faces, watching their slots disappear from the board. Above this grumbling din, Farnsworth shouted to be heard.

"Doctors ... doctors!" He nodded approvingly at the sudden silence. "Now don't forget that for each slate of the twelve rotations you draw, you can trade individual rotations with the other interns."

There was momentary silence, and then a collective gasp of relief. Then, with a sudden roar, all forty interns went crazy, parlaying and trading as if they were on the floor of the Chicago Commodities Exchange. Everyone was frantically trying to dump unpopular rotations for ones they preferred. They still had to have the prerequisite nine and three, but now the options had broadened. And amid this stockyard braying and clamor, the turbaned Indian intern was repeatedly shouting, "Yes! Yes! Most certainly, yes. Yes!"

Though Blade had chosen the very first surgical slate, even he wound up having second thoughts and replaced urology with "plastics" courtesy of a medical intern who was interested in kidney disease ("I'd rather work on noses and boobs than somebody's plumbing!" he said with un-salesman-like candor). Ned surprised himself with the fervor of his own wheeling and dealing. When they were finally seated, flushed with the excitement of bartering, every intern in the room seemed content that they had screwed someone else with an absolute dog of a rotation.

"What'd you get ... whatever your name is?" Blade peered around the turban at the index card in the Indian's hand.

"Holy shit," cried Blade. His gray eyes sparkled in amusement. "Look at his card! He's got eleven months on the hepatitis service and one month of general surgery! Now how could he do that?" The dark-complected Indian merely smiled his dazzling white smile, introduced himself as Ramamurti Singh, and glided away.

Ned beamed at anyone and everyone. He had parlayed his rotation into the first month on trauma, then one month on OB, then two months on the extremity service, then back to trauma, two on neurosurgery, two on orthopedics, two on medicine, and one in the emergency room.

Back in their seats, Blade nudged him in the ribs, "Not bad, Nedley, eh? Just look at this crème de la crème of an internship." He gestured benevolently around him. "We've got Mr. Everett Crooked Teeth on the right, Dave Lefke on the left ... behind us is some turban-head from God knows where, and to wrap it up a freaky flower child 'mit shrew." He leaned back, smiled expansively, and slapped Ned on the back. "Yes sir! Stick with ol' Blade, Crosby. We'll have women by the dozen and the world by the short hairs!"

Ned grinned back, "Only one problem, Blade."

"Huh? What's that?"

"I've checked it out. There are no nursing students in this hospital. They're all across town at the university."

Blackston pouted all through their coffee break and into the next session.

* * * *

Following the portentous drawing for rotations and a brief break, they were lectured by monotonous administrators, a sugary-sweet nursing supervisor, a droning city councilman who welcomed them to his "fair city," and finally, again, by Farnsworth.

"A reminder," he warned, his darting laser-beam eyes fixing on each of them. "The decisions you make, the orders you write, the clinical signs you miss, and the incisions you make ... they can be the difference between restoring life and causing a precipitous death."

He paused for a moment, inhaling deeply and rocking back and forth on his heels. He flashed an index finger momentarily in the air.

"They say that July is a bad time for a patient to get admitted to a teaching hospital. But not here, doctors ... not here."

There was a long silence, and it seemed that he had finished. They began to leave, but he suddenly raised the admonishing finger again.

"One last thought, doctors. With the indigent patient population we have, much of our care is ameliorative, not curative. Never forget: Care for the patients you care for."

They adjourned to an afternoon welcoming picnic. The Class of '71 interns played a game of softball against selected staff and administrators. It was an informal chance to get to know one another. But no one could relax or focus on the game; they were too scared. It was like walking around in a crowd, knowing that someone had pulled a pin on a hand grenade, carefully holding it out of sight. Anyone there could be the idiot to cause the harm. And no one knew if it might be them.

David Hazelette-Warner limped off the field, dejectedly throwing his baseball glove on the ground.

"I've failed, I've failed."

They stared incredulously as he actually slumped down and began to weep. Failed at what, Ned wondered?

"They're watching us, you know," Hazelette-Warner muttered to no one in particular. "They're watching and sizing us up...looking for the weaknesses." He rubbed his reddened eyes. "I dropped a fly ball. How could I be that stupid?"

Blade, who'd made a spectacular barehanded catch without thinking about it, stared in amazement at this display.

They took a break from the barbecue and Blade filled in Ned on more gossip. Blade had the skinny on everyone. Everett's nickname was now officially "No Problem" ("He's always saying, No Problem, Ned!"), and Blade had christened Dave Lefke "Lunch." It was bad enough that a wino barfed lunch on him, but at the picnic he had spilled an entire bowl of baked beans on his shirt! Finally, the married couple was David and Eleanor Hazelette-Warner. They had been married in their final year at Harvard Medical School. He was the son of a rich oil magnate, and when she snagged him, all of her college loans suddenly disappeared.

* * * *

Amazing, Ned thought as he fingered the diary's pages. Twenty-five years ago, they had been a collection of bright whiz kids, the "crème-de-la-crème" as Farnsworth had said. And yet Ned reflected that they had been so ignorant that they really didn't know what they didn't know. It was sort of like some guy reading about how to use a chain saw, passing a written test, and then being told he could go cut down trees! They had no idea how stressful it would be, transitioning from the "book learning" of medical school into actually taking care of sick and injured patients. In fact, one of them would not survive the year.

Ned found his place again, and returned to where he'd left off with the trauma team.

* * * *

July 2, 1971, 6:20 AM

After the Bernice Fanning tragedy it took them three hours to get through rounds. It was difficult psychologically to get ready to immerse themselves into the violence of their service. There were forty-five patients in all: thirty on the main trauma ward, Six North, and fifteen others spread out in the surgical ICU, orthopedics, and neurosurgical wards. It wasn't so much that forty-five patients were a lot for seven doctors (four interns, two junior residents, and their chief); it was the magnitude of what was wrong with them.

These green interns were unprepared for the horror and violence of a big city trauma service. Some injuries were accidental. Ned's first assigned patient had a broken tibia from a bullet shot from a thirty-eight-caliber revolver that he had inadvertently discharged while cleaning it. He was on the trauma service because the mushrooming, hollow-point, lead slug had blown out the main artery of his leg after it shattered the tibia. Pins had been driven through both sides of the broken bone (courtesy of ortho) and incorporated into a plaster cast to stabilize the fracture. The leg's popliteal artery and vein had been grafted. The cast had a "window" in the back to allow for the wound's dressing changes and an eventual skin graft.

Some of the violence was self-inflicted. In the surgical ICU lay an Asian woman whose family business had been threatened by escalating extortion from a Triad gang. Rather than dishonor the family name, the matriarch, Mrs. Chu, attempted suicide. She had thrown herself from the roof of their second-story apartment. When she struck the roof of a passing truck, she fractured both of her heels and received a compression fracture of the lumbar spine. Then she ricocheted off the truck and landed on a parking meter, which lacerated her liver. On the second day after surgery, foul drainage from her stomach tube was discovered, and the nurses reported that her temperature had spiked to 104.6 degrees. That was when they discovered that Mrs. Chu had drunk sulfuric acid before she leaped.

"That wasn't a gesture, man," a Blade whispered grimly. "She intended to check out, ticket punched all the way to the end."

Now Mrs. Chu lay on a respirator in the surgical ICU with a tracheotomy, arm restraints, and foul smelling abdominal and thoracic drains.

Some of the violence inflicted by one person on another was hard to believe. A robber in a Catholic sacred candle store had splashed hydrochloric acid in the eyes of the clerk so that she wouldn't be able to identify him to police. But he'd left his fingerprints on the beaker, so they got him anyway. A mugger had become enraged at only finding two dollars on his victim, so he emptied a nine-shot automatic into his abdomen. Gang members, in an effort to "send a message," beat the father of a rival sixteen-year-old gang leader senseless with hatchets.

Then, of course, there were the junkies: They were hurled from buildings for non-payment of debts. They jumped for their lives from rooftops in drug deals gone sour. They shot while committing robberies, and were, in turn, shot themselves. They were slashed, knifed, clubbed, and beaten. Besides these junkies, there were fifteen gunshot patients, five knifing patients, three motorcycle victims with fractures and internal injuries, and six auto accident patients. Finally, there were six attempted suicides.

There was a hodge-podge of bizarre injuries. An executive, while hunting in the mountains, had the defective magazine of his rifle explode when the shell misfired. The magazine was next to his cheek, since he was aiming the weapon at the time, and the explosion blew off half his cheek and jaw. The carotid artery was transected. If it hadn't been for the quick action of a companion who applied pressure properly, he would have died on the spot. He was rushed to their trauma team. Two gay men were experimenting with a Coke bottle when misadventure occurred. The trauma team triumphantly retrieved the bottle in the operating room. But the patient's lower intestine had been lacerated and he now lay recovering from a colostomy. By the end of rounds, even—and perhaps especially—the new university residents were in a state of shock.

Ned was sure he could find the words "dirt" or "smell" somewhere in Stedman's Medical Dictionary. But reading those words could not prepare a new intern for the experience of rancid, purulent pus. They stood at the bedside of an alcoholic gunshot patient. The stench of his open abdominal fistula draining blood-flecked, yellow stool into a leaking colostomy bag, in combination with his alcoholic breath and cigarette smell, was actually smothered by two putrid feet sticking out of the sheet. They were covered with weeping athlete's foot fungus and an infected ingrown toenail. Peter Castleford, their other first-year resident, had turned slate-gray. DeLuca whimpered that he hoped Ned could help take care of these people. Eleanor mechanically thumbed through her cards, barely awake on her feet,

"Gunshot, gunshot, suicide, gunshot, liver laceration ... My God! How ... how can people behave this way?"

"Welcome to the real world, Sunshine," Morgan volunteered sarcastically. "Let me offer some advice." He held up a cautionary hand, ignoring a startled gasp from Eleanor, and looked them all in the eye. "I know, I know ... you'll think I'm being cynical. But you've got to realize that you won't 'make it' if you personalize these people. I'm not asking you to stop being a human...just to hide part of it away. Look at what happened last night. We did all we could, but sometimes the world grinds you up. When you throw into this the fact that many of the patients at this hospital are here because they did this to themselves, so self-destructive, you can't empathize."

As they moped down the hallway, Peter Castleford started fumbling with some sort of philosophical objection. But before he got two sentences out, an angry Morgan cut him off.

"Look, deal with it, or it'll deal with you."

"No problem, man," said Jones, trying to defuse the tension.

"Everett, that reminds me." Morgan thought for a moment. "You never seem to have a problem, do you? Call this coin in the air."

The spinning silver flashed in the air briefly before he caught it and smacked it on the back of his hand.

"Heads."

"Ned, what's the intern's motto?" Morgan cocked a mischievous eyebrow.

Crosby groaned and offered the slogan. "Life's a stacked outhouse."

"There it is," said Morgan smiling triumphantly. "You, sir, won the right to take out stitches and check wounds in the trauma clinic with Eleanor."

"But ... but, no one asked me," whined Eleanor. "I ... I ... After last night ..."

Morgan absently clipped his fingernails. "Sleep for swamis doesn't count, Sunshine. Especially, hyphenated swamis."

Eleanor acidly shot back, "I'm a doctor, if you please, just like you!" She glared at Morgan, stiffening her five-foot-two-inch posture, erect and bristling.

Morgan smiled back coldly. "Er, sorry ... *Doctor* Sunshine." Then he pivoted on his heel, and left the ward.

Blade turned to muffle a snorting laugh with a cough, and Eleanor simmered furiously at them all. "Damn him! And, damn you all! Just like my idiot husband. Says something stupid, and turns and walks away!" She stalked down the hallway, rifling through her cards, muttering.

"Interesting little hellcat," Sal volunteered.

July 16, 1971 4:25 AM

Two weeks roared by and Ned was called to the emergency room for a consult. Dave "Lunch" Lefke was on his Emergency Room rotation, and it was his call that brought Ned down to the ER.

"So what gives?" Ned asked, eyeing Lunch's cross-eyed shoes.

Lefke rubbed at his burr haircut, and motioned for Ned to follow him. "I got this drunk, see. He's in congestive heart failure, and we're going to admit him to the medical service. In fact, he's all "tuned-up," you know. The IV is in, bloods are drawn, medicine given...but, for a big gash on his forehead. The chief on medicine asked me to sew it up, but I don't think I can do it. Shit, Ned I'm going into dermatology. Can you help?"

They walked into the examining room. Sprawled on the litter like a Raggedy Andy doll, the drunken patient was sound asleep. His alcoholic snores blasted them with the smell of stale gin. He was in a fresh hospital gown with an IV running into his arm. A wad of bloody four-by-four sponges was taped over his right forehead.

"He looks filthy ... Got any fleas or lice?" asked Ned.

"Naw. I checked. He's clean."

Lunch absently began to scratch and check himself for fleas. The drunk snored louder.

"What's his name?"

"James Heffernan."

"Simple as that, huh?"

"Well, he answers to Whitey, but otherwise he's apple pie and motherhood," Lunch offered with a whimsical grin.

"He blow lunch on you?" Ned shot him a malicious grin.

"Naw, but he knocked over the bedside urinal. Lucky I can jump."

"Doesn't look like you jumped high enough."

Telltale yellow streaks stained Lunch's cuffs. Lunch looked down again, saw the streaks, and cursed.

"Mr. Heffernan? Mr. Heffernan?" Ned shook the patient's shoulder. The drunk sputtered and coughed, and in a rasping, gravelly voice he growled an answer. Ned told him that they were going to look at the cut on his forehead, if he didn't mind.

"Suit yourself," Heffernan grumbled. He picked at his ruddy, bulbous nose. "Just wake me for breakfast." As he slumped back he wiped his finger on the sheet, rolled over, belched, and broke wind.

Ned rolled his eyes at Lunch, "Apple pie and motherhood, huh?"

He peeled away the gauze, and stared down at a ragged, swollen, stellate laceration. The cut looked like a bloody spider, about an inch and a half in diameter, smashed above the drunk's right eye. Its ragged, torn legs stretched-out in all directions.

"Looks like someone mugged him. Maybe he was hit with a baseball bat or a two-by-four," Ned thought out loud as he picked at the wound edges with a cotton-tipped swab.

Heffernan winced and groaned.

"We figured the same," Lunch offered. "He didn't have a wallet on him when the meat wagon brought him in. What do you think?"

Ned studied the wound. "I think we'll have to cut out all the dead tissue, mobilize the good stuff, and then I'll let you go ahead and close it up."

Lunch's face suddenly twisted nervously, "Unh, Ned, you're the expert, you know." He gestured meekly towards the wound.

"Expert, my ass! Two weeks on the trauma team doesn't make me expert in anything, except that I'm beginning to know how much I don't know."

"Two weeks, huh? Time flies. How's it going?"

"It was pretty rough at first. But I got this little oriental lady who tried to commit suicide ... now she smiles when I come around." He shrugged. "There are trade-offs. How about you, Lunch? You getting into the groove?"

Lunch looked for a moment as though he was suppressing flatulence. Then his pained expression cleared.

"I like the intellectual aspects of medicine," he said resolutely. "How about, like listening to an S-4 gallop, a heart murmur disappearing after you digitalize someone and push 20 of Lasix IV? You know...get them out of congestive heart failure. Now that's medicine! These surgical things ..." he gestured absently. "I have...maybe just a little more dexterity than an elephant threading a needle."

Ned had a wry look on his face, "I think I'd bet on the elephant." He ignored a raised middle finger. "Get a suture set and let's get started. I've been watching everybody else operate for the last two weeks while I haven't been able to do a thing. Mr. Apple Pie and Motherhood will do just fine as my first patient!"

They infiltrated the wound with one percent Xylocaine and epinephrine. As Ned started injecting the anesthetic, Heffernan awakened with a yelp. But once the wound was anesthetized, he flopped back and went soundly to sleep. Ned was just starting a gentle Betadine scrub when two heads popped through the drapes. The nursing supervisor said she wanted to introduce to them a newly arrived, foreign medical student from Holland.

A pale, gangly, mustached man with sandy blond hair tentatively entered the room. "My name is Johann Drinker," he said, grinning self-consciously. He shook Dave Lefke's hand. Ned held out his sterile-gloved hand, and they pretended to shake in mid-air. Drinker laughed.

"It my pleasure. You do surgery, yah?"

"Yah," Ned grinned. "We're going to try, anyway. Kinda' early for you to be up, isn't it, Johann? We don't get too many visitors in the ER at four in the morning."

"Yah, yah. I fly all night. Back home now ... now, how you say...apres-midi? No! Not French. It almost afternoon in Holland! I so excited, coming here, my first day at a new American hospital, I not wait. Come now." He grinned. "You want smoke, yes?" He pulled open the coat lapel of a green and brown hounds-tooth sport coat.

"Hold it, hold it, Johann. We got to operate. Operate, first. Then smoke," Ned motioned for him to close his jacket.

Johann blushed. "Sorry. I hear custom in America, offer smoke, and make happiness. I fucked up."

Ned and Lunch laughed.

"Whatever. Maybe we'd better get started before the anesthetic wears off."

They squared-off the wound with sterile towels, isolating the laceration in a sterile working field. Ned went to work with a scalpel, cutting out the crushed, dead tissue. He kept cutting and debriding, until nothing but pink, healthy, bleeding tissue was left. He and Lunch looked down on a large crescent hole, the top margin twice as big as the bottom. The smashed spider had been cut out, but a distorted, blood red crescent moon now swung over Heffernan's eyebrow.

"Jesus, Ned, how're you going to close that?" asked Lunch. "The upper margin is twice the length of the lower. They won't match up and you'll have loose flaps or dog ears."

Ned could almost hear Lefke thinking, *Damn, I ask this guy to help me and instead he screws things up even further!*

Ned looked thoughtfully at the gaping, crescent hole. "Hmm, you know. I just kept debriding the dead tissue. I didn't realize that the edges would get so out of sync." He shuddered. Was his eagerness to finally do something turning into folly? Was it his turn to screw-up?

Johann from Holland looked over at the hole and his sandy eyebrows flicked inquisitively. "Excuse me, I just exchange student, but you fuck up, yah?"

"Er ... yah, Johann. Just a little, just a little. Let me think."

"What's cookin', Ned?" Sal DeLuca poked his head through the drapes.

Johann stuck out his hand. "I Johann Drinker, from Holland. How you do?" Authoritatively, with a flourish, he waved his hand towards Ned, "This Doctor ... Doctor Ned, he just fuck-up a little."

DeLuca burst out laughing. He shook hands in return. "Sal DeLuca."

"I say something funny? A little, yah?"

"No," DeLuca answered. "Actually, you're right on the money." He turned to Ned, "How ya doin', hotshot? Any idea how to close that hole?"

"Right on money ... hotshot?" A mystified Johann looked for translating help, frantically leafing through his English/Dutch dictionary.

"I don't know, Sal. Give me a second." Ned made some drawing motions with his hands. Then he stopped, closed his eyes, and concentrated. "Okay. I'm ready. Where'd I put that scalpel?"

"Scalpel? Haven't you cut enough already?"

He answered authoritatively, "Scalpel." They watched Ned cut out two, pie-shaped wedges from the upper crescent border.

Johann Drinker looked down at the wound. His eyes got big and he gasped. "What you do, Crosby?"

"Let me see," DeLuca looked at the wound. "Jesus, Ned. It looks like you cut the top half of a star in his head! What're those points for? Shit! Look at all the blood! Why didn't you get Plastics here?"

"Watch." Ned brought down the borders, closing with sutures the upper "points" of the star, which sucked up the discrepancy in the lengths of the upper and lower edge of the wound. Suddenly, the laceration looked like a thin curved line with two lines poking up where the points had been.

"Jesus. Well, will you look at that!" DeLuca muttered.

"It looks gorgeous, Ned. I can't believe it. I thought you were mutilating him," Lunch Lefke beamed.

"Gott domn! Dat's good! You got a gift, Crosby, a real gift."

Ned finished putting on the dressing, then stood and removed his gloves. "My pleasure, Johann. We've got to run. Hope you enjoy the General."

"I never seen no'ting like dat! Here." Johann opened his sport coat and pulled out not a cigarette, but a fat stogie. "You like, yah? My happiness."

DeLuca's eyes got big. "A Monte Cristo! Havana! Ned, I haven't seen a Cuban cigar for ten years. Not since the Bay of Pigs! And then, dammit, I was too young to smoke!"

"You want one too, yah?"

"Please, oh, please give me a cigar," DeLuca went down on his knees and raised his hands to beg like a dog, his tongue panting. With a ceremonial flourish, like a priest giving communion, Drinker inserted the cigar in DeLuca's open mouth.

"Herr Doctor Lefke?"

"Bitte, Bitte!" Lefke knelt and received his benediction as well.

In a flash, three Cuban cigars were puffing behind the drapes. Neal Morgan, looking for his team, flung the curtain open.

"Cuban, Neal! Cuban!" DeLuca puffed away, actually inhaled, coughed, and sighed ecstatically.

"Cuban, huh?" Morgan rolled the cigar in his hands. "I don't even smoke ..." He lit up with the rest of them. "Hmmm ... kind of mild. Rich ... Real smooth ... I like the flavor. Is that a hint of rum?" He puffed again.

The curtains parted again, and Eleanor's curly head poked through. In the two weeks on the trauma team, her coy girlishness had vanished. "Phew! This smoke ... what's going on?" She waved the smoke away with her hand.

"Cuban!" Sal was jubilant. "Cuban!"

"Cuban?"

"Here, take a puff."

"Sal, I don't even smoke!"

"You're one of us. You're one of us! Smoke, Doctor!" Morgan jammed the cigar in her face.

An emergency room nurse named Kathy and an orderly holding a fire extinguisher ripped the curtains apart. "Sweet Jesus, I might have known!"

"Cuban, Kathy!" Neal exclaimed as though the word itself was absolution.

"I Johann Drinker, medical student. You remember, yah? Dat Crosby, he fuck up just a little ... then, win. Right on money, Big time! We celebrate."

* * * *

Ned lowered the diary and chuckled. Cultural changes, political correctness, and the now ever-present threat of malpractice suits had ended episodes like that. In the first place, in the sixties and seventies, everyone smoked. In fact, if you didn't people thought you were odd. The idea of smoking now, let alone cigars, in a smoke-free hospital ... Ned laughed at the indignant rage. Times change, *he thought,* but sometimes for the better.

Secondly, Ned had "flown blind," using instinct, intuition, and innovation to dramatically correct a disfiguring facial laceration. The orbital nerve was nearby. If he'd gotten it, in today's world he probably would have been sued. He would be unable to answer the lawyer's question. "Dr. Crosby, tell the ladies and gentlemen of the jury (sweetly sneered), your qualifications to practice plastic facial surgery ..." In today's world anyone venturing outside a prescribed specialty, no matter how noble the intent, was inviting a lawsuit.

* * * *

July 23, 1971, 9:40 AM

"Suck, Ned, dammit!"

"Sorry."

"Watch what you're doing," Morgan grumbled.

"Sorry."

"Is that all you can say, Sorry?"

"Sorry, Neal."

"Here hold this."

In his third week they were in the middle of a "lap," an abdominal exploratory, looking around to correct possible internal injuries. The peridial had been positive for blood in the belly, so in they went. Sal was working on a different patient in OR Two with Eleanor assisting. An attending surgeon was "riding herd," supervising Sal's surgery. Ned and Neal's patient was a male pedestrian who had been struck by a car in a crosswalk in a hit-and-run. His face was a mass of bloody lacerations. The plastic surgery service had come down to handle the cosmetics, while the trauma team made sure the belly was okay. It was what they now referred to as Morgan's patented "slash-and-dash" procedure. Within two minutes the belly was open. In another two, each quadrant had been checked. Finally, Morgan ran the bowel.

Suddenly, he stopped in the middle of the frantic pace and looked across the table at Ned. He grasped Ned's hands, and put them into the belly. "I want you to try it once. Don't handle things a lot, but get the feel of checking the quadrants, then run the bowel. Tell me what you find, what you see."

Ned peered over the edge. Using damp abdominal laparotomy sponges, he gently pulled the bowel away from the left upper quadrant. It kept oozing back, but he patiently packed it off and checked the spleen. The gray-red organ had a small bruise, but it was otherwise normal. Next, he went to the liver, first one lobe, then the other. There was a small laceration, maybe a half an inch long, but not very deep. He checked the "gutters," and then followed the bowel.

"What do you think?" Morgan had waited patiently, but he instantly began the grilling when Ned's hands came out of the wound.

"He seems okay, Neal."

"Okay?" he snorted. "Did you find anything?"

"Just a small liver laceration, not too big. No active bleeding, and a bruise on the spleen. It's probably why our abdominal peridial was bloody."

"Right. Good work. So ... what do you think about general surgery, Ned?"

Morgan's eyes were friendly, but they were also very serious. Only three weeks into the internship and Neal was asking Ned about the career that he, Morgan, had chosen for his own life's work. He offered, "You know, I know I seem little hard-edged at times. But I've wanted to be a surgeon ever since I was a kid, watching Ben Casey on television. This is a tough program, and I knew that the only way I'd survive was to be hard as nails. I never take anything for granted. Eventually it's become a way of life. Maybe I'm too hard." Neal shrugged, "I don't know. But I do know that there are twelve guys that started this program with me five years ago who are no longer here."

"Well, I ... well," Ned stammered, trying to stall and think of some diplomatic response. He now had a question and a soliloquy to respond to.

"Say, you guys wanna see this up here?" The plastic surgery resident at the head of the table motioned them "This is the only thing keepin' this thing alive! Look," he said. He grasped the man's nose and swung it off. Only the nostril's right nasal alar fold was intact. The resident actually swung the nose off like opening a book. "Isn't that amazing? The only thing keepin' this patient's nose alive right now is the right alar artery!"

Their patient's face was transformed into a bloody, black hole with sinuses and green mucous, staring back.

"Jesus!" Ned turned white. "Sonofabitch! I ... I gotta sit down." He rushed over to a stool, and sat. Then he doubled over and took great gasps of air. "Shit! I think I'm either gonna barf or pass out."

"Breathe deep, Ned. Breathe deep."

After awhile, Ned calmed down, but he refused to look up towards the head of the table. "I don't know what happened, Neal. I ... I wasn't ready for it. He should have warned us."

Morgan laughed. "Ned, welcome to the club. Everyone's got their weak spot. Me, it's eyes. I get sick if I see someone sewing on an eye. I can't take it and I have to leave. You're still white as a sheet. Get the heck outta here, and I'll close."

Ned fought his way out of the room, but the vision of the bloody, black abyss wouldn't leave. He lurched into the surgeons' changing room, found the toilet, and threw up.

"Flu," he muttered to the orderlies smoking in the lounge.

July 31, 1971, 11:47 AM

"We got two!" Morgan yelled above the din of the ER. Trauma rooms eleven and twelve were both open. It was an auto accident. The driver had been thrown from the car; his girlfriend had rolled with it. She was in Trauma Twelve. Eleanor Hazelette-Warner and Sal DeLuca were busy in the room. It was the usual orderly chaos: IV lines, catheters, x-ray, and ortho, all flailing away.

"Shit, Crosby, where were you?" Morgan's irritation seethed under the surface.

"Sorry, Neal. I got the runs so bad couldn't get off the john. I've been sick the last week with the crud."

"Listen, this is bad," Morgan said. "The guy in eleven's dead. He was thrown from the car, but he hit a rock with the back of his head. He's the son of a city councilman. They've notified his parents, and they're on their way. You gotta' do something, you know, clean him up, whatever. We got a real mess next door, but Farnsworth personally called me to make sure this boy is made presentable to his family. City council votes next week on the hospital's budget. Nothing gross, okay? If it's bad, pull a sheet over his head, and don't let them look! Everything in his girlfriend is either broken, punctured, or bleeding, but we've got a chance to save her."

Ned was in a daze. *Dead? Why did he have to get stuck handling a dead body?* "Can't Eleanor ..."

Morgan responded tersely. "Ned. Clean him up. Talk to the family ... I can't wait any longer!" He tore down the hall after the patient on the litter, which trailed a crowd of nurses and doctors holding up lines, lab work, and x-rays.

Ned entered Trauma Eleven. In the middle of the room, on a litter, lay the body of a man in his early twenties. At first glance there didn't seem to be an obvious injury, and he looked like he could be sleeping. But a pool of blood drenched the sheets behind his head. Ned got a towel, soaked it in warm water, and wiped the man's face and neck clean, removing some grass stains and mud. He found a six-inch roll of soft Kerlex gauze, and wrapped it like a dressing around the head to hide the crushed area in back. *Goddammit, why am I the one to tend this guy?*

The body didn't have the signs of stiffness or rigor mortis yet, though his skin color was a kind of a whitish blue gray. Ned noticed that the guy seemed his own age. Damn, the same eccentric chestnut tufts; he even parted his hair on the same side!

There was a tentative knock at the door. "Excuse me ... Excuse me?"

A diminutive, middle-aged, round-faced woman in a navy and white polka dot dress entered the room. Despite of her small size, her head was erect and her carriage was confident, a presence used to being in the public light. She had early streaks of gray showing in her brown hair. This was tucked under an old-fashioned, Mamie

Eisenhower black pillbox hat. Her eyes inquisitively darted around the room, appraising everything.

"Yes?" Ned started across the room. *Was she family? Did she belong in the room,* he wondered?

Her demeanor was inquisitive. "I don't know if I'm in the right spot. I'm looking for my son. He was in an accident ..." Her hand came up to her mouth suddenly, as she saw the face of the body on the litter. "Oh ... oh my. That's my boy, Johnny."

"Oh ... oh, Jesus. Excuse me, ah ..." Ned straightened his posture and tried to meet her eye directly. "They did all they could. He's passed away." He reached for her arm.

"No ... no, I'll be okay." She patted his arm to reassure him. "I promise. Please, I just want to say good-bye."

"Well ... sure. Do you want me to leave?"

"No, no. It's okay." She turned from Ned, walked tentatively over to the litter, and grasped her dead son's hand. She stood quietly for a moment, and then smiled down to him. "Hi, Johnny. It's Mom. Trying to hurry home again, weren't you?" She smiled as her eyes filled with tears. Then she shook the hand in a scolding fashion. "But it's okay, Johnny, because you know that your father and I always insisted that you to be responsible for yourself." She sighed, "Sometimes, Johnny, sometimes ... things just don't work out. You're here, lucky ... at peace. The rest of us will just have to go on, and try to put things back together."

She shuddered and silent tears ran down her cheeks. She leaned down and put her arms around the body, holding it gently. She gave his cheek a kiss, and then said, "Goodnight, Johnny." She turned to Ned and said, "Thank you for your help, and for your patience." Then she tiptoed quietly out of the room.

3

Fireballs of the Eucharist

August 1, 1971, 7:00 AM

Rounds on the next rotation of obstetrics were scheduled for seven the next morning. Crosby's nascent life as an obstetrics intern would begin when he joined the new residents from the university. But they had left a message with the paging operator that they would make their own preparatory rounds with the departing team, and catch him later in the cafeteria. Remembering back to that first day on the trauma rotation, he was leery, twitching nervously in the cafeteria, listening to the monotonous voices of the paging operators tracking down other lost doctors for their next rotations. It sounded like the drone of the announcer at a horse race. The General's OB ward was on the third floor of the North wing and immediately adjacent to the delivery room. It turned out that his partner assigned to OB was Lunch Lefke.

Lefke still had sleep-puffed eyes and a pillow-creased face. He'd been on call the night before, just like Ned. Two blossoming, red razor cuts added to the pockmarked landscape on his cheek, dabbed with bits of torn tissue paper that stuck to the blood. Ned stole a glance under the table and smiled at the ever-present cross-eyed shoes.

71

Lefke was a will-'o-the-wisp six feet, with a round-back slouch hunching over a sunken chest. He looked like a walking question mark. His dark brown hair was cropped close in a burr cut with a cowlick in the front. Ned noticed that Lunch seemed to ooze a nonchalant, relaxed confidence. He'd shift his head to the side and nod knowingly, as if whatever it was, he'd already heard it. But Ned saw his nervous eyes dart furtively around the room, and he noticed that Lefke's fingernails were bitten to the quick.

They finished eating, and Lefke clasped his nervous hands to hide the tremor.

"I don't know, Crosby," he said unevenly. "I don't know if I can take this." His voice broke even more than that time together with James Heffernan in the emergency room. "I didn't want this obstetrics crap from the start. In fact, I didn't even want this internship! If it weren't for my Dad, I wouldn't be here. But he was here in '41 ... Said it'd do me good!" Lefke absently bit at a nail. Suddenly he locked eyes with Ned's. "Listen, man, no way I'm delivering a baby. You think I'm delivering a baby? Christ, I've never even done a rectal, let alone deliver a baby! For the last two years of med school I've been on a fast-track for dermatology."

Ned, startled out of his own sleep-deprived anxieties, focused glassy eyes on Lunch's frightened features. "Lunch, how could you possibly go through medical school without doing a rectal? Excuse me if I don't believe the 'no rectal' story!"

But Lunch's face masked solemn seriousness. He leaned forward and whispered, "Listen Cros, I mean it! In med school I mean, I faked it. I dodged, slipped away ... you name it." He sneaked a peek behind him to make sure no one was listening, and bit at another nail. "There's just ... just something incredibly revolting about feeling around inside someone's rectum. No patient ever complained that I didn't do a rectal. In fact, if you think about it, nothing good ever goes in, and for sure nothing good has ever come out!"

Ned was skeptical. "So why didn't you just trade rotations?"

"I tried," Lunch shrugged helplessly. "I pleaded with that Ramamurti guy. But he wouldn't trade one damn hepatitis rotation for OB. Dammit, Ned, I'm stuck."

For Ned, this was like finding a little toy boat containing a diamond, floating on the sea of anxieties. A project! The terrors of trauma were gone. Now it was just babies ... and something to focus on and distract himself. *No siree!* He pontificated to himself. *No dermatologist should ever have to suffer the indignity of performing a rectal exam. Not with Nedley around!*

"Listen, Lunch. We've got just a month, see—four weeks or twenty-eight little days. It'll be a snap, and I'll help."

He clapped his arm around Lefke's shoulder, and playfully ruffled what there was of his cropped hair. Lunch shrugged glumly, but then he looked at Ned like a puppy that had piddled on the floor and discovered he wouldn't be smacked with a newspaper. His eyes brightened with the recognition of conspiracy, and he wistfully scuffed his cross-eyed shoes together.

"The truth is I know no one here at the General but my best buddy, Blade. Heck, our call is staggered so I hardly see him," Ned became animated and assumed a benevolent, pontifical air. "People cope in different ways, you know."

Lunch looked mystified.

"Cope?"

Ned leaned forward conspiratorially, "I'm a methodical plodder nourished by a rich interior life."

"A what?"

"Lunch, this is my own deep secret. You ever hear of the Phantom?"

"The what?"

"You know, The Phantom! The Ghost Who Walks ... Uncle Walker?" With still no recognition, an exasperated Ned explained,

"Come on, Lunch, where you been? You mean you don't read the comics?"

Lefke rolled his eyes and shrugged.

"Listen, Lunch, I live to see the daily paper so I can keep up with the Phantom's exploits. You get me a paper each morning and I swear I'll keep you out of rectals!"

"Uncle who?"

"Never mind. Just get me the damn comics every morning in the paper, and ... well ... rectal, smectal."

The wall clock over the cafeteria door showed seven AM, but still no OB residents. So Ned insisted they get proactive. They trudged up the stairwell to Three North, and there they found the new team. Introductions were made, and rounds began. There were only ten patients on the service. The first room had a patient who was a prima gravida—having her first baby— at thirty-two weeks gestation, with her pregnancy complicated by threatening symptoms of severe preeclampsia. This was a dangerous condition in which the pregnant woman's kidneys started to shut down. Fluid retention and blood pressure problems could become lethal. Her weight gain was estimated at 45 pounds, her blood pressure 170 over 110, and her renal studies confirmed two-plus protein in the urine. So far, fetal monitoring had been satisfactory. She had been admitted as an emergency the day before, right out of pre-natal clinic on her first visit.

"Some mother, huh?" Ned had whispered, trying to hide his dismay.

"Get used to it," their chief resident, Fred North, responded. "Most of our patients are unwed and have had no prenatal care. They're scared, they may not speak English, and it's safe to assume that any known complication in medical history can happen."

"So how come the ward's so empty with only ten patients?" Lunch asked.

"You gotta be kidding," The chief laughed. "What woman in her right mind, with insurance, would come to a teaching hospital for elective gynecological care?"

Lunch shrugged, eyed for a moment a delectable fingernail to bite, and then nervously stuffed his hands in his pockets.

Dr. Fred North was a sallow-faced, bent figure with muddy brown hair. His slouch was worse than Lefke's! But in spite of the spindly physical appearance, his eyes radiated authority. Piercing, narrow-set eyes contrasted a flattened, broken nose. The more cynical Blade had nicknamed him "Roadkill."

Ned glanced at the residents' faces. They were creased with fatigue and their hollow eyes surrounded by worry-lines. The residents were only a couple years older than Ned, but their faces were filled with so much stress that they practically looked middle-aged. They returned Ned's glassy stare. He mused to himself; there was a hardness and desperation in their faces that came from having to make fateful and painful decisions. *I won't get like that,* he told himself. *I'm going to care, to learn and be a good doctor, but I'm not going to let it grind me into the ground.*

The group continued rounds. Two women were in active labor; the uterine contractions were coming every five minutes in one patient, and every three in the other. There were no signs of fetal distress, and the vital signs for both the mothers and their unborn infants were stable. Another groaning patient was being checked in by the nurses with the telltale, slick, bloody-wet stains of a broken water bag down her nylon stockings. She wasn't in labor yet, but she complained of severe lower abdominal cramping.

Dr. North swung around and crooked a bony finger toward Lunch Lefke, "You and I have clinic today, Dave. I'll leave Larry and Crosby to be on call tonight." As they parted ways, Ned saw his slouch suddenly stiffen, and he glimpsed the terrified look in Lefke's eyes as he disappeared down the stairwell.

"Crosby?"

"Yes."

"Larry Margolis."

They stuck out their hands and shook. Margolis had light blue eyes and a friendly smile. The unshaved beard stubble betrayed the fact that he, like Ned had also spent last night on call. Ned stared at his crushed fingers after they'd shaken hands.

Margolis laughed, "Sorry. Four years at West Point. You either salute, or if it's a civilian, shake hard. You know, keep the civvies in their place" The muscular forearms and the sandy flattop hair cut started to add up. "Ever caught one?"

"Yeah, I've delivered a few," said Ned nonchalantly. *An Army schmuck, huh?* "Maybe ten ... all uncomplicated. No forceps."

"Hoooweee. Hot stuff," grinned Margolis, who laughed sarcastically, like ten deliveries was but a day's work.

Ned knew he was being teased, and he blushed. "No, I just liked OB, and I happened to hang around and got lucky when some women went into labor." Ned could imagine the wheels turning in Margolis's mind.

"You got a residency, yet?" Margolis absently massaged the back of his neck.

"Nope. I'm wide open." This was the professional equivalent of flirting. Ned had learned early in medical school that things went easier if one professed an interest in the specialty at hand. It was only natural; if you were interested in them, they'd be interested in you. In any case, it was true that Ned really didn't know what area of medicine he wanted to enter.

"Just want to go through these rotations and hopefully go into something surgical."

Margolis gave Ned an appraising look. "Well, Ned, we'll spend a little time with you here, and see how you like delivering babies. It's the greatest profession in the world."

As Margolis and Ned finished their verbal sounding of each other's career plans, the nurses announced that the other gravida-two patient was now in hard labor and approaching eight centimeters' dilation. Two additional patients were coming up from the ER, one in early labor, and one with ruptured membranes. Both were prima gravidas, neither had received prenatal care, and one was hysterically screaming in Spanish. To make matters worse, the pre-eclampsia patient they'd just seen earlier broke her waters. As they scrambled to organize this chaos, the ER called yet again to announce that a gravida eleven had just walked in to declare the start of her labor. They were rushing her up because she'd told the nurses she generally "went" in about a half-hour.

When they'd arrived that morning, Ned had thought the quiet ward seemed like a good place to catch up on sleep. He suddenly got an ominous feeling that a hurricane was approaching. The floor's nurses and aides swarmed into action, preparing empty beds, getting the delivery rooms ready, and checking that adequate supplies were readily available.

While they made preparations, Lunch Lefke and Chief Resident North returned. They'd made quick work of an OB clinic that had only a handful of patients in it. The new patients from the ER arrived in labor, and Fred North made a quick division, assigning four to Ned and four each to the rest. The nurses, aides, interns, and residents all pitched in, timing contractions and checking fetal hearts with the fetoscope. With Ned in tow checking vital signs, North moved from room to room, performing vaginal exams, ordering medication, and monitoring their progress.

"How'd clinic go, Lunch?" Ned laughed after almost locking fetoscopes as they ran out of separate rooms and into each other.

"Er okay, Ned."

"Any rectals?" Ned grinned.

"Up yours." Lefke bit at a nail. "It was a small clinic. Dr. North showed me around, introduced me to the staff, and we just checked some girls, talking to them about nutrition and a prenatal delivery class that the clinic puts on."

At that moment Ned felt the gaze of a troll-like, pregnant apparition standing alone in the middle of the hall. She was wearing a ratty, gray, woolen coat and carrying a battered shopping bag. Her pockmarked face featured a large, hairy nose, a hanging proboscis drooping over coarse lips. The upper lip sported a scab from a healed split. Vein-streaked cheeks were framed by stringy gray hair that ended at buffalo-humped shoulders. For a moment, Ned was convinced he was still dreaming in the on-call room. He imagined this bizarre apparition would snap her fingers and disappear in a clap of thunder. However, her dark eyes twinkled as she flashed him a broken-toothed grin. She gestured upward with her arms like a conductor addressing the orchestra, "Well?" she rasped.

"Er ... well, what?" Lunch looked at her in disbelief.

"Well, you want me to drop this damn kid on the floor here, or what? Those stupid people in the ER were taking too long so I just walked up. This kid is number eleven you know!" She grunted dramatically once, and clutched at her abdomen.

Fred North popped out of a room and stared with an open-mouth, "Well I'll be ... Rosie, for God's sake! Rosie Delaney ... it's you again!"

Rosie flashed a broken-toothed grin, "Northie, you've rotated back to the General! This'll make three catches for you now, won't it?"

North, still numb in disbelief, nodded mechanically.

"Northie, you know I ain't never lied, don't you?"

He nodded again.

"In that case, get off your ass, and let's get this kid out! I figure I got ... maybe ten minutes at most."

Dr. North blanched, "She's not kidding. Quick Lefke, start scrubbing. Mary, open up in Delivery Two. Crosby, get an IV going ... lactated Ringer's."

Rosie protested, "Northie, what for? Why you gonna let some damn intern stick me?"

Ned blushed, but North squared his jaw and stood firm. "Rosie, no arguments. This may be number eleven for you, but I'm still the boss. Lie down like a good girl, and get that IV in so we can get along with the delivery."

Grumbling, she started to waddle into an empty room with Ned in tow when she suddenly wheeled, glared, and pointed a finger in his face. "You get one shot, buster. One is all! No 'pin-cushion Rosie' for you to learn on, see!"

Ned started to stammer an answer, but she wheeled away with a grimace as a labor pain made her flop down on the bed. She motioned to the metal dressing cabinet along the wall, while she grunted with a new contraction.

"Get me my gown, please, Mr. Intern. They're in the middle drawer."

Ned handed her the gown and started to pull the privacy curtain around the bed, but she growled out in a gravelly voice, "Oh, why bother?" As she removed her wool coat Ned saw that, underneath it, she was stark naked! He stifled a gasp as he looked up and down at the fat, stretch-marked body. Her stumpy ankles bulged over shoes with burst, blue-veined varicosities. Sagging flesh drooped everywhere. Pendulous, purplish breasts with hairy, dark aureole pointed down to bizarre stretch marks mapping her protuberant abdomen. Folds of limp, yellow, fatty flesh hung from her upper arms and inside each thigh. She grunted again as she flopped into the bed, flinging her hairy legs up on the sheets with shoes still on.

"Let's go Mr. Intern, or did you get too excited, seeing so much of a woman?" She grunted again and laughed harshly.

At first Ned was shocked by her grotesqueness. As he gazed at this fecund contradiction to his perceptions of femininity, he realized his preconceived stereotypes were altered forever. He couldn't be sure, but he also thought he saw the glimmer of a twinkle in her eye. So he kept his disgust and confusion to himself.

The nurse's aide brought in the IV tray, and Ned expertly slid in a 19-gauge, plastic-tubed Angiocath IV. He flushed the tubing, and secured it with crossed adhesive strips. Rosie looked down over her smashed nose at the IV needle and flexed the fingers slowly, like a gunfighter, admiring her hand. She cursed, and then spat on the floor.

"Hate damn needles ... Hate 'em!" She eyed Ned caustically. "You weren't so bad though. Better'n the last. That bozo took three shots at it, 'til I kicked him in the nuts."

Her eyes twinkled again, and Ned couldn't tell whether she was telling the truth.

"How many tries would I have got?" he asked, trying to muster a wry expression to match hers.

"I like your dark eyes and those curls, bozo, but I hate needles. Don't press your luck. Let's go." She grunted again, grabbed the IV bottle out of Ned's startled grasp, threw herself of the bed, and started to waddle out the door.

Ned lurched after her, "Wait! I haven't checked you, yet. I didn't get your vital ... I didn't check the baby."

Rosie laughed and kept waddling down the hall with her exam gown flapping open in the back, flashing her blue-mottled, sagging buttocks to the world. She sniffed the air like a dog scenting the wind, then selected a door and pushed her head through.

"You guys ready, or what?"

Ned was rushing up a litter when she pushed into the delivery room, and waddled over to the table. With a disdainful flick of her wrist she dismissed the open-mouthed anesthesia resident.

"Let's go Northie, before I drop this kid on the tile." She heaved her bulk onto the delivery table with a grunt, "Come on ... come on." She gestured impatiently to the nurses as they scurried to get the stirrups in place. She was now grunting and sweating profusely. Dried yellow mucous hung from her bulbous nose. She sniffed, blew it into her hand, and wiped it on the table.

Ned started to follow her, but the doors swung back open, and the delivery nurses in scrub suits, with cool, appraising eyes and amused smiles, laughed at him, "Better get into some scrubs doctor, or this baby comes into the world by itself!"

He laughed good-naturedly at himself, and turned to race for the doctor's changing room. Stumbling out of his clothes and frantically kicking off the pant legs, he chided himself: *You're still green, green, green! One month on trauma, and you forget a basic rule: Get into a scrub suit. I've got to get better, to settle down and think ahead.* Moments later, with fresh scrubs, a surgical cap, and mask on, he was inside the delivery room.

Dr. North had seated himself between Rosie's legs. Lunch, who had already changed and scrubbed, stood outside her left leg to first-assist the delivery. This was exactly how Ned remembered his obstetrical deliveries in medical school.

"You ready, Freddie?" Rosie looked down at them and laughed at her rhyme.

"Ah ... yes, fire away."

Now the whole room laughed.

She gave a giant grunt and then bore down. Flatulence escaped. "Just blowin' you a kiss, Freddie."

Lunch Lefke rolled his eyes. Rosie's knuckles turned white as she squeezed the grasp handles on the labor table and let out a guttural growl. It looked as though her protuberant, contracting abdomen was standing up on end. A white, balloon-like bubble appeared at her vaginal opening.

"Garrummpht!" Out came another deep animal growl.

The white bubble expanded from the size of a tennis ball, to an orange, then to a grapefruit, and then to a basketball. It was eye-level with Dr. North, and he gasped in disbelief.

"Gaaarrummpft!"

He quickly grasped a hemostat and stabbed the white amniotic sac bubble on the left side. A jet of amniotic fluid shot out and drenched Lunch Lefke, who looked as if he would either vomit or faint dead away. North quickly grasped the emerging infant's head and controlled the rest of the delivery. "Almost got you, didn't I Doc?"

North sighed at Lunch, who was looking down at his soaked pants and cross-eyed shoes, and then looked up with a facial contortion that seemed to suppress a retch.

Rosie was eyeing them both. "You two done lollygaging' down there, or what? Get that damn placenta outta there, Freddie so I can go home!" North started to massage her abdomen.

"You there," said Rosie. She reared up and looked over her legs at Lefke. "What's your name?"

Lunch started out of his catatonic coma in alarm.

"Yeah, you, Mr. Bozo intern doctor. What's your name?"

"Be nice, Rosie," interrupted North. "It's his first day." He kept massaging her belly as he pulled out the placenta.

"It's Lunch, ma'am ... er, ma'am, I mean it's David Lefke." Lefke's eyes darted nervously around the room, searching for an escape route from this new source of humiliation.

"Well boys," said the patient, "Rosie's in a good mood. Just to show my appreciation to Freddie North and Dave Lefke, this baby's going to be named Frederick David Delaney." She paused for a moment, thoughtfully picking at her smashed nose before she turned to the nurses. "Yeah, I like that! Write it down on the certificate because that's what it is, Frederick D. Delaney."

North looked up from between her legs and raised an inquisitive eyebrow. "Only one problem Rosie," he said. "It's a girl."

"A girl? Damn!" She reared up, hockered, and spat on the floor again. "Another damn girl!" Then her face lit up. "Northie, that's no problem. Fredericka Davidia Delaney!"

North looked up at Dave Lefke and Ned with a quizzical look not dissimilar to that of a brook trout that has just discovered that the tasty meal he just swallowed had a barb in it. "Sometimes you think you've lost, and sometimes you win big. It's all in the eye of the beholder." He gave a sheepish shrug, "By the way, where are those pediatricians?"

"Comin' through, comin' through ... pediatricians comin' through." Two masked and gowned figures entered through the swinging doors.

Ned blinked in surprise, "Blade ... er, Dr. Blackston. What, for God's sake, are you doing here?"

"Peds, my man! It seemed like a good idea at the time, but in the end that Ramamurti guy wouldn't switch. All our staff is tied up in an ICU emergency, and they asked if I could show this ever-so-lovely medical student a well-baby check."

He and a trailing young woman looked with distaste at a bleeding vaginal laceration from the baby's rapid birth.

"Uh ... you are going to fix that, aren't you?" he blurted out, and then winked at Ned.

Dr. North was not amused by Blackston's unprofessional glibness, and he stared him down. "Please examine the infant, doctor," he said sternly. "Dr. Lefke and I will finish here."

The scrub nurse had prepared absorbable chromic two-aught gut suture, and she handed Dr. North the loaded needle holder. North looked up at Lefke.

"You've sewn these up before. Haven't you?"

"Uh, ya ... sure," Lefke lied insincerely.

"Well, I'm going to do this one, just to make sure you see how I want it done. As the time goes by, we'll put you to work. You know the old saying, Lefke, 'See one, do one, teach one.'"

Ned and Lefke laughed. After Dr. North had infiltrated lidocaine anesthetic into the laceration, he cut out the ragged edges from the vaginal wall. Layer by layer, the reconstructive episiotomy was closed tightly. Lefke followed him alertly, snipping the sutures after the knots were tied. As he watched, Ned started to feel less incompetent. There was nothing new here, just a routine vaginal laceration repair.

While he watched Dr. North put the finishing touches on the vaginal episiotomy, out of the corner of his eye he saw Blade Blackston suddenly dart across the room. The baby in the bassinet had turned blue. In a quick, athletic leap, Blackston sprang over to the instrument table, deftly grabbed the red rubber suction bulb from it, and then leapt back to the baby. The medical student stood by meekly, wide-eyed and paralyzed. Carefully holding the dusky infant in one arm, head down, Blackston suctioned a glob of mucous that had blocked its airway. The baby responded with shrieks and wails. Its color immediately pinked-up and it waved its little clenched fists defiantly in the air. It had happened so fast, it made everything in the room seem as though moving in slow motion. The baby responded, and they let out a collective sigh. Blackston held the baby aloft for those in the room to see.

"Some day," he announced to no one in particular, "Some day, maybe you'll be a strong little fighter, maybe even a doctor!" He was absorbed in what he'd done, but when he looked around to see their stares, he meekly replaced the baby in its bassinet. He winked at Ned. *Was this a show for the student,* Ned wondered?

Dr. Blackston finished up with the baby's neonatal physical. "Estimated Apgar score is nine. The baby's hips are located, and there's no evidence of a clubfoot. No heart murmurs." He turned to Ned, "No meconium with the delivery, was there, Ned?"

Ned shook his head.

"See ..." Blade turned back patronizingly to his medical student protégé, "a non-stressful delivery. A well baby." He smiled his best Adonis smile. "We'll take this 'well baby' down to the nursery to do a heel stick for a hematocrit, and then bag her for urine."

No question, Ned thought, *the hunt is on!*

August 2, 1971, 8:17 PM

The obstetrics team worked like demons as their day crept into dusk. The ward clerk called down for food to be sent up from the cafeteria. The pre-eclampsia patient went into labor, and her eclampsia symptoms became worse. Her blood pressure skyrocketed to 220 over 115. With the increased intra-cranial pressure, she became delirious. Dr. North ordered a mag sulfate drip to run in her IV, but her eclampsia symptoms didn't change. He then ordered the "old stand-by," an eclampsia medicine Ned had never heard of, called Gartrone. But it didn't help either. Then the shrieking patient started projectile vomiting, a sign of a Gartrone overdose. Signs of fetal distress became apparent, with the baby's heart rate alternately racing to 190 and then plunging below 100.

After consulting with the staff doctors, they decided to perform an emergency cesarean section. The surgery was difficult. It was hard to control the bleeding, and North, Lefke, and the staff obstetrician were in surgery for hours trying to save the mother and the baby.

Ned lost another coin flip, and Lefke was supposed to be off call. However, they all wound up staying there that night. Ned and Margolis stayed out of the section to care for the remaining women in labor.

It was dark out, and Ned was amazed when he saw Blade Blackston back in delivery again with the medical student. Blackston was giving a baby oxygen, and even briefly, mouth to mouth resuscitation.

"I didn't know you could do that, Blade."

"Smedley, there's a lot you don't know about me." He winked back at him as they rushed the baby from the room.

In the meantime, more women were admitted in labor, and Dr. Margolis and Ned were the only doctors available. Cries of women, panting in labor, echoed down the hallways. Ned's arms were chafed beet red from repeated scrubbing, but he no longer felt like such a bumbling idiot. He was so busy trying to take care of people that he didn't have time to worry. He felt like a pinball, flipped from bumper to bumper, reacting to the emergencies: ruptured membranes, heart rate of 160, and cries of pain.

"Are you worried about fetal distress?"

"Damn right!"

"Some episiotomy! Can you sew it up? Where are those damn pediatricians?"

This went on into the wee hours of the morning. Ned delivered ten babies himself, as many as during his entire three-month OB rotation in medical school. A total of eighteen women were delivered that night. He and Margolis lurched from room to room like drunken ghosts, continuing the monitoring, checking dilatation, and listening to fetal heartbeats.

At five in the morning Ned was surprised to see Warren Childress, from Central Supply, poke his head into the delivery room as they were wheeling out another delivered patient.

"You Crosby?"

"Huh?" Ned's glassy, red-rimmed eyes peered back over a face full of dark stubble. His teeth felt scum-coated, and he sniffed a revolting whiff of fetid nervous perspiration—his own. He had no bubbly emotions left; he was just trying to survive.

"Just checkin'. Where yo' wallet, Crosby?"

"Damn!" Ned staggered from the delivery room and raced to the changing area. His pants were sprawled inside out, on the floor, right where he'd kicked out of them that morning. The pockets were empty. For shit's sake! He rubbed at his sleepless face in frustration. First day on a new rotation and here he was a stupid, bumbling, country bumpkin, an easy mark in the big city! Sonofabitch!

"This yours, Crosby?" Warren held up a worn, black leather wallet. Ned snatched it from his hand and searched the recesses. Everything was there!

"Warren ..."

A sardonic smile appeared on Warren's face as he held up his hand. "Don't ask! Ever since my mother got me a job in da kitchen in '53, I take care of things 'round here. I spoke to a friend of mine. We don't like anyone stealin' from the General's doctors. I tell 'em to stay 'way from you".

Warren started to turn away, but Ned grasped his shoulder. "Warren, I mean really, thanks."

A glimmer of warmth shone in Warren's eyes and his gold tooth flashed with his smile.

"You still new here, right? Don't leave no temptation around. 'Sides," he cackled, "you didn't have no money in it, anyhow!"

Ned laughed, "Isn't that the truth! Well, anyway, Warren thanks. I owe you. I won't forget. Really, I won't."

Warren flashed Ned a smile. "Some day, I gonna' pick up the newspapers, an' read about something famous, one 'a you doctors done. But you know, it'll be about one a my doctors ... one 'a mine that I watch over."

With that he disappeared through the electric doors.

* * * *

87

Ned paused as he realized that if ever there had been a pivotal moment in his internship, it might have been here. In the midst of the seedy dregs of humanity, in a decrepit, charity county hospital, an old black man had cared for them all as though they were his own children. Warren gave without asking in return. In that small episode Ned had found a grain of perspective that changed the way he approached every patient from that moment on.

* * * *

August 16, 1971, 9:45 PM

After the demands of the killer trauma rotation, Ned discovered that, occasionally, the General's young doctors actually did have free time! Not every day continued the hectic pace of that first. The interns met evenings at the Lakewood, a dingy bar in the heart of the surrounding slum. The sinister streets of this neighborhood were dangerously dark, with streetlights smashed by bullets or rocks thrown by vandals. Menacing alleyways held tramps and desperate junkies lurking in the doorways. But the neighborhood residents took a protective attitude toward the General and its doctors and nurses. The young men and women at this local watering hole might be the only thing between them and death on some lonely night.

"They's our doctors," the denizens of the Lakewood said with pride. And the owner was tolerant about the tabs they ran, knowing that few of them had much money to spare.

Legend had it that in 1952, an intern, hurrying to morning rounds, was arrested for speeding. The judge in court had pronounced the sentence: fifty-dollar fine or two days in jail. But the intern had stammered back, "I guess I'll have to go to jail, your honor."

He explained to the astonished judge that the General paid no salary, and after eight months of internship he had no money, couldn't get a loan, and that his parents were dead. This led to an emergency session of the city council. It was immediately voted to offer interns at the General the salary of fifty dollars per year. This was immediately paid to the speeding offender.

Since then, salaries had risen—but not by much. Residents were paid more than interns, because a starving resident was also a licensed physician. He might jump into general practice out of desperation to support his family and curtail the residency. Poor interns fit right in to the poor neighborhood, seediness or no.

The Lakewood Bar stunk of stale smoke, greasy fries, and sweat. An acrid urine odor drifted from the "Gents" room, where a slanted open trough ran into a rusty pipe at the end of the wall. Graffiti scrawled on the wall suggested that the pipe ran straight back to the draft beer tap.

Ned, Blackston, Lunch Lefke, and Blackston's medical student, Beth Williamson, were crammed into the corner behind the jukebox. In this second month of internship they'd discovered this was the "in" place to be. As an extra inducement, Blade had informed Ned with a somewhat crooked smile that some really nice "talent," some available nurses, hung out there, as well.

As they sipped their draft beers, Blade bemusedly surveyed Lunch Lefke, asking what had happened to his cross-eyed shoes.

"What was it, Lefke, all the barf, the broken amniotic sacs, or what? I can hardly recognize you without those shoes."

Ned looked under the table to inspect Lefke's new, conventional, burgundy penny-loafers.

Lunch stared glumly into his own half-drunk beer, drumming his bitten fingernails against the rim. He sighed and turned; "You can't believe what happened." He absently bit at a fingernail and then continued. "I know it sounds kind of dumb, but with those crazy shoes, people seemed to open up more. It was sort of like, maybe this guy is kind of casual, and maybe the expectations weren't so high. In fact, that pre-eclamptic we sectioned on our first day actually laughed every time she saw my shoes."

"So what happened, Lunch?" Beth inquired. She hung affectionately on Blackston's biceps.

Despite her physical familiarity with him, there was an air of patrician indifferent aloofness that was driving Blade wild. "This one's going to be tough," he'd confided to Ned.

Lunch rubbed his face with his palms. "Hell, you all know how much I hate this rotation and how nervous I am." He struggled in thought and then transformed, sitting straighter in the booth. He shook his finger for emphasis, "But, Ned, you've got to admit I spin crits, dip urines, and take the residents' shit with the best of you. Whenever Margolis is chewing out my ass because I forgot to pull the packing from some infected vagina, I could take it because I'd look down and see my cross-eyed shoes looking back, saying, 'Roll with the punch, Lunch.'"

They all smiled, except for Blackston, who was impatient to get to the crux of the story.

"Well, what happened, for Chrissakes?"

Lunch flinched. "Okay. Ned, remember that little prim-ep, two days ago, the seventeen-year-old with her first baby?"

Ned nodded.

"She was just seventeen, and she turned down an abortion because she believed that taking the baby's life was wrong. I mean, jeez, she wasn't even Catholic! So after fifteen hours of hard labor this little girl had only dilated to six centimeters at zero station. Man, she was hurting. But the baby's head kept slowly progressing, and North didn't want to C-section her. I was wolfing down supper in the locker room, gone maybe...maybe twenty minutes at most. I thought the fetal heart rate was kinda high, and I told North. He said, 'Finish your sandwich, and keep monitoring.' So after I wolfed down the rest of supper, I came back, and ... and the baby was dead."

They gasped. Lunch's eyes watered and turned red, but he continued in a cracking voice. "She delivered a stillborn that was alive before I went to supper. When it came out ... that's when we saw the cord wrapped around the neck. If I'd a stayed there monitoring, maybe it would've had a chance."

He drained his beer mug, shrugged dejectedly, and looked around at the group.

"I went to see her the next day, you know, because I wanted to say something supportive. So I tried to tell her that she had her whole life ahead of her, and that ... maybe her little baby was somewhere in heaven. That's when she looked down at my cross-eyed shoes and started screaming."

He looked around the table at them.

"The shoes weren't funny anymore. In fact, none of this is funny."

"Ease up," said Ned, giving Lunch an affectionate pat on the shoulder. He paused. "Before my dad died last year, he told me how tough the internship was going to be. He was an old-time family doctor. He said there was what he called a learning curve, you know. Each of us is learning from patients, how to diagnose, and how to treat. And he said that, since we interns and were at the start of the learning curve, we'd make mistakes—and even though we didn't mean to, that we might hurt people." He clamped his arm around Lunch's shoulder. "You're doing the best you can, Lunch, and that's all any of us can do."

When Ned was through, Blackston winked at him and cackled, "Besides, Lunch, no one said dermatology was going to be easy! Anyway, don't forget I've got ten bucks riding on you-know-what. Don't let me down now."

In spite of Lefke's secretiveness, the word had leaked out. There was an unofficial pool floating through the hospital, on whether or not Lunch could escape OB without doing a rectal exam. All bets were posted down in central supply, where Warren Childress kept track of the money.

Beth shushed Blackston's cackling and changed the subject. "So what is it that you want to be, Ned Crosby? I hear scuttlebutt among the nurses that you're really good. Do you like OB?"

Ned blushed, but before could answer, Blackston interrupted: "Well, I'm cutting on someone. Just what it is I'll be cutting on, I don't know." His fiercest steely gaze confidently swept the table like a scythe.

Ned ignored the impetuous interruption and smiled back at Beth. Her aquiline beauty was dazzling. Rich, shiny, blond curls spilled onto her straight, delicate shoulders. Fragile collarbones led to a thin pulsing vein on each side of her neck. She seemed so soft, so feminine, that he could see why Blade couldn't resist her. Her aristocratic face was a mixture of soft beauty with blue-gray eyes that matched the intensity of Blackston's. Ned had seen the entire hospital cafeteria become quiet when she entered. Everything was understated, from the slightest trace of pearl pink lipstick to a hint of perfume. She wore a soft, pale, washed-out denim shirt that had been thrown on carelessly. Was the second button accidentally opened, hinting at the swell of her breast, or was it on purpose? *No question,* Ned thought, *Blade was overwhelmed.*

"I don't know, Beth," he shrugged. "Almost for sure not OB. I just had all my old-fashioned notions of femininity and motherhood blown away by some lady named Delaney who's getting rich off the state, pumping out welfare babies. Now, as for delivering babies ... Mother Nature, God—or somebody—has worked it out so smoothly that all we doc's do is catch 'em. Whatever I do, I want to do something where what I do really matters." He sighed, "It's pretty confusing. Some of the people we see are pretty hard to care for, and besides, they don't even care for themselves."

Blackston was getting bored. "For Chrissakes, guys, lighten up. How complicated can all this be? Ned doesn't want to hurt anyone, and Lunch doesn't want to do a rectal. Lunch, you've been on OB two weeks now, and you've still avoided the dreaded deed, haven't you?"

There was a conspiratorial flash as Lunch met Blackston's eyes. Blackston threw a crumpled five-dollar bill out on the table.

"Well ... two more weeks of dodging, bobbing, and weaving, and here's five more that says with Crosby running interference, you're home free. Money on the nose for Lunch Lefke, to win."

August 23, 1971, 9:23 AM

Dr. North announced that they would use a Pfannenstiel approach.

"She may be crazy," he said, "but we should at least give her a cosmetic scar."

The Pfannenstiel approach was an abdominal incision, transverse across the belly, just slightly above the mons pubis. It was a standard Cesarean section approach. It was also referred to as the "bikini" approach, because the scar was cosmetically nice and wouldn't be noticeable on the body of a woman wearing a bikini.

The bikini approach in this court-ordered "therapeutic abortion" seemed incongruous to Ned. He idly twisted at a tuft of hair while he gazed down at the icy, distorted face of the woman twisting and struggling in arm restraints. He'd tried to read up something in the textbooks to describe therapeutic abortions, but there just wasn't anything written. He thought back in contrast to the tears of joy that he'd seen in the eyes of new mothers when they first saw their newborn child. This lady gazed vacantly at the ceiling while her lips mouthed unspoken words. He tried to introduce himself, to establish some kind of rapport.

"Ma'am, ma'am?" He touched her shoulder. "I'm Dr. Crosby."

She started and glanced coldly at his touching hand. Then a multitude of incongruous emotions suppressed by drugs rippled across her face as she turned back to a noiseless conversation with the ceiling.

"I've got to listen to your heart and lungs, ma'am, take your blood pressure ... you know, to make sure everything's safe before surgery."

Crosby glanced at the transfer sheets in her chart. This patient was a psychotic schizophrenic, and committed to the state insane asylum. An orderly had raped her while she was drugged on a tranquilizer called Stelazine. It wasn't until she began to show that the staff launched an investigation, uncovering the rape. Her enraged parents filed a lawsuit against the asylum, and obtained a court order for a hysterectomy-abortion.

Ned glanced at the official transfer sheet: "In the Superior Court of ... so and so ... whereas ... so ordered." Stamped and notarized with the seal of the state of California. The chief resident, Dr. North, had merely shrugged to the group and said, "Let's look at this as a teaching exercise, an anatomy lesson." Inwardly, Ned had chafed at this. *If this woman's parents heard him, what would they think?*

Ned carefully examined her, listening to her heart, percussing the chest, and taking her blood pressure. With each maneuver, he explained to her what he was going to do and why.

Her lips continued to silently mouth words, but once she spoke up gaily, "Lettuce is green, lettuce is green." Then half her face frowned and she began arguing with herself.

Unnerved, Ned found himself speaking louder and louder in an effort to communicate. Suddenly she turned her head abruptly towards him, and for a moment her hazel eyes cleared.

"You don't have to yell."

As their eyes met, Ned was astonished to see a young woman staring back with a seemingly cognitive, "normal" face nestled in the cacophony of scattered wisps and clumps of stringy hair. Then the vacant glaze filmed over her consciousness, and she sank back to resume the conversation in her own mysterious world.

Ned and a nurse wheeled her into the operating room. Her hands twitched rhythmically as a side effect of the high blood levels of Stelazine. Out of curiosity he checked her reflexes with a small rubber hammer, and her knee and ankle jerks kept vibrating for several beats after each blow. *Wasn't the medical term for that "clonus?"* he thought. She had probably been overdosed to keep her sedated; but the twitching continued, even after they gave her 75 milligrams of Demerol and two milligrams of Valium.

While they were tying her arm restraints to the operating room table, Ned felt her squeeze his hand. As she squeezed it, his eyes locked cognitively again with the young hazel-eyed woman who lay rhythmically twitching.

Is this what medicine is about? Ned wondered.

He tried to smile reassuringly, but realized he was wearing a surgical mask. He hoped she could see the crinkles of his smile-lines at the eyes, and he squeezed her hand back. The anesthesiologist emptied a syringe full of pentathol into the IV, and with a sigh, the young woman's eyes glazed over and she slipped into unconsciousness.

The operating room and scrub area were curiously quiet. The surgeons and interns were wrapped in their own thoughts as they scrubbed and stared off into space. Nurses and orderlies quietly glided around the room. Lunch Lefke hummed a few bars of "Beautiful Dreamer," which had become his habitual way of relieving anxiety. He'd sworn off biting his fingernails. He and Crosby now scrubbed less diligently; their frequently scrubbed arms were lobster-like, wrapped in a cherry red rash way up to their elbows. Instead of brushing hard, they each gently caressed the skin with antiseptic soap.

"I won't have any skin left," Ned muttered. With arms upraised and dripping with suds, they entered the room.

The neatly rounded abdomen stared up at them. The curving mound glistened with orangish-brown Betadine scrub solution. It seemed so smooth, such a gentle roundness, that it invited their hands to gently touch and feel it. Life was inside. They squared off the belly with draping towels, and then threw on the larger top sheets. Finally, the scrub nurse pushed up to the operating field with the Mayo stand filled with scalpels, clamps, and scissors.

"A teaching exercise, right?" North's eyes moved from face to face as he looked at Lunch, Ned, and Margolis around the table. "A little anatomy today."

Lunch shifted nervously. North glanced up at Ned.

"You've been with us on at least ten sections, haven't you?"

Ned nodded.

"Wanna do the approach? You should know the Pfannenstiel by now, don't you?"

Ned paused. *A case! Christ, Jesus Christ, what every intern in the hospital was dreaming of! A case!* He'd only gotten to watch on the trauma team. He knew the muscle layers, the rectus abdominus, and the external and internal obliques ... but after that he wasn't too sure. North handed him the knife, which carried a large, number 20 scalpel blade.

Ned gazed down at the blade, eyeing the surgical steel. It reflected the overhead operating lights, shining back into his eyes. The razor-sharp edge looked lethal, and he realized that he was holding in his hands an instrument with great power to harm or heal. In a dark alleyway, this would be considered a weapon and he could be arrested. Here, he was a surgeon. He looked down towards the draped abdomen. *Where to cut?* The pubic hair had been shaved, and now he'd lost his bearings. The small area of draped abdomen seemed as large and formless as the Sahara desert! He felt beads of sweat forming on his forehead. The knife felt clumsy in his hand. He looked up at North, and a strangled "Where?" escaped from his throat.

North's eyes crinkled with a smile, and he steadied Ned's hand. "Ned, don't worry. This is a teaching hospital. Today it's your time, so take your time, okay? No one's in a hurry." He picked up a hemostat and stuck the instrument's point twice on the abdomen, making two small indentations. "Connect the dots," he chuckled, and winked at Margolis, who was standing across on the other side of the operating table.

Ned screwed up his courage and passed the scalpel across, between the indentations. In a panic, he quickly looked for the blood to follow, but there was none. *Damn! I must not even have gotten through the skin!* He'd been afraid to cut. North reassured him, saying it was far better to be cautious than a "slasher." Ned tried to cut again, and a ribbon of bright red blood followed the scalpel across the abdomen. *Holy shit! She's bleeding!*

Sponges dabbed up the blood before he could say anything, and North cauterized the little pumpers with a Bovie cautery. Acrid, bluish smoke from the burnt flesh drifted across the projecting OR lights. Ned finished cutting through the skin this time, and the reddish-blue muscle fibers below the fat twitched and went into spasm as the scalpel raked across them. Then they danced and wiggled madly, like a nest of worms, as the electrocautery cooked more bleeders. For a second, Ned thought he was going to pass out.

Self-retaining retractors were placed into the wound, but Dr. North didn't like the exposure. He replaced them with two four-prong rakes, and placed Lunch's hands on the handles.

"Ah ... for you, suh," he pronounced, with a mock British accent. "The famous intern's pose: holding a retractor."

Lunch grinned sheepishly as he looked around at their faces.

Ned was sweating profusely, so he asked the circulating nurse for a wipe. Beads of sweat congealed on his forehead, and ran down to his mask. *Mustn't let them fall into the wound and contaminate it,* he thought. He'd always thought surgeons needed a wipe because they were working so hard. Now he knew better—they were scared shitless! No mistakes, please ... *No perspiration to contaminate the wound.* A nurse tapped on his shoulder, and he turned so she could wipe his forehead with an alcohol-soaked sponge that would help evaporate and cool.

She smiled into his eyes and murmured encouragement. They were all rooting for him. However, the alcohol fumes almost blinded Ned, and he turned away quickly, shook his head, and blinked.

"Smarts, huh?" North grinned. He ran a hemostat across a muscle. "What's that layer?"

"Uh ... external abdominal oblique."

"Good. Keep cutting."

There was dead silence in the operating room. The hiss of the anesthesiologist's gasbag made the only noise.

"Stop."

Ned's hand froze.

"What's that?"

"Er ... peritoneum. The abdominal lining."

"Right. Lift it up with your pick-ups, and make a small nick with the scalpel."

Ned made a small incision and gazed into a black hole. North grabbed one side of the peritoneum with another pair of pick-ups.

"Now I'll hold the other end up, and carefully cut some more." He suddenly slapped Ned's hand. "Don't cut the bowel or bladder!"

North and Margolis chuckled and grinned at each other.

Ned ran the scissors across the peritoneum. Abdominal retractors were inserted, and they gazed down on shiny loops of bluish bowel surrounding a bulging, grapefruit-sized, pink, pulsating uterus. Ned eyed the open abdomen. The hole seemed giant, bottomless. Deep within were the terrors of bladder, uterus, arteries ... blood! His head swam; these were structures he could harm. More beads of sweat formed.

"Well, Doctor?"

"Uh, I ... I've got to stop, Dr. North. I'd be in over my head."

98

Ned placed the scalpel on the Mayo stand and rested his hands on the table to hide the tremor.

North grinned. "You passed."

"Passed what?"

"I wanted to see how far you'd go. The worst surgeon in the world is someone who never asks for help, who thinks he can do it all. You, Dr. Crosby, knew when to quit."

Passed what? Ned repeated to himself. His eyes were still glued to the bottomless hole, and he hadn't heard a word Dr. North had just said.

North laughed and grasped some elongated Mayo scissors. "Don't worry about it Ned, just watch. Lefke, hold these retractors. Crosby's done for the day."

He moved in saline-dampened abdominal laparotomy sponges, and used them to push the patient's bowel out of the way. Gaseous bubbles of bowel billowed out, and North chuckled and pushed them away.

"Foul humors, U.B.F.s of the abdomen ... be gone!"

"U.B.F.s?" Lunch asked.

"Unborn farts, stupid." He turned to the scrub nurse, "Kelly clamps, please."

The scrub nurse handed two clamps to Dr. North. He dissected out and isolated a large ligament on the right side of the uterus. He put both clamps across it, and then cut across the middle between the clamps. He held out an empty hand, "Tie, please."

"Zero silk, doctor?"

"Zero's fine." He grasped the suture and tied it around the base of the tissue on each side of the Kelly clamp.

"Again."

The process was repeated: clamp, cut, and tie. Clamp, cut, tie.

"What was that, Lefke?"

"Uh ... round ligament?" Lefke ventured nervously.

"You asking or answering?" North admonished.

"It's the round ligament."

"Right."

The procedure continued: clamp, cut, tie. Clamp, cut tie. Suddenly, within the uterus, there was movement. A nurse gasped, and for a moment they seemed frozen in time.

Then North, like nothing happened, announced, "And as we continue this teaching exercise, as I cut down, here's the cervix, only from the inside."

He sewed the opening off with an inverting suture that kept the wound as sterile as possible, avoiding bacterial contamination from the outside vagina. Then he over-sewed the peritoneum. He glanced up at Ned, whose eyes were glued to the cavity.

"Cat got your tongue, Crosby? I haven't heard a peep from you."

Ned had remained standing, like a statue, as North worked his way around the entire uterus. As the last two clamps squeezed shut with a final, metallic, grating rasp of the catch mechanism, Ned looked up at the others and whispered, "It's dead now, isn't it?"

"What? What's that, Ned?" Dr. North was absorbed in tying down the last suture.

"I said, its dead now, isn't it?" Ned eyed him meekly from across the table.

North was handling the swollen uterus to the nurse, to remove it from the room. Then he sighed and continued to work, daubing, sucking, and cauterizing bleeders. He grunted in approval as he finished the belly's irrigation with sterile saline. Finally he turned his narrow-set, fatigued eyes across the table towards Ned and they locked.

"You think I like this?" he asked. "You think this is fun, killing babies?"

"Jesus, man. I didn't mean …"

"Well, listen. I don't damn like it!" He glanced up to Dr. Margolis and nodded down at the wound. "You'll close, won't you? I need a cigarette."

Fred North wheeled from the operating table and strode calmly from the room. But the operating room doors swung closed with a loud clap.

Ned looked around the room nervously. "Shit, I didn't mean to make a moral statement. I was thinking, you know … I guess I just wondered if it was a boy or a girl, or since the mom's crazy, who would mourn it … I guess I just said what popped into my head. I'm sorry I was stupid."

"Forget it, Ned," Margolis looked across the table at him. "It was on all our minds. We just didn't say it. That's one reason Fred made it a training session for you. I think he wanted to take his mind off of what he was doing. Last week, his wife had a miscarriage. It was her third."

"Shit!" Ned slumped down on a stool in disbelief. *How could I be so stupid?*

Margolis smiled over at Ned. "Okay, you got us into this mess, asshole. Now stand up and get us out!" He handed him the suture and they started sewing.

Ned stayed with the patient until she awoke in recovery room. Even in her sleep her rhythmic twitching had never stopped. Suddenly, she gasped in pain and clutched at her abdomen. Ned grabbed her arms while the nurse retied the restraints to the bed rails. They were afraid she might tear off her dressings, so they gave her intravenous Thorazine and Demerol to sedate her and control the pain.

Ned tried to capture her gaze again, to reassure her. "It's okay, it's okay ... Everything's going to be okay."

But her stony face was a mask of disconsolate agony. She lurched up, zombie-like, against the restraints, and gasped out with a feral shriek. Then she twisted her head away from him. Ned wrote orders for more pain medication, but when he returned she was calmly, silently mouthing words again. And as he leaned closer, he could hear her whispering, "Baby gone, baby gone, baby gone ..."

* * *

Ned would never forget the conflicting emotions of that first "case." There was an innate instinct he had to overcome, to not cut into or harm someone. He could never imagine being in a knife fight. How horrible, to actually be trying to cut or kill another human being. But here, in the surgical suite, was the intellectual knowledge that in the cutting was the healing. In later years, any time he attempted a new procedure, the old fear always came back: Am I going to hurt this person?

* * *

July 27, 1971, 2:00 AM

When the phone suddenly rang in the on-call room, a startled Ned sprang up, lunged, and knocked it off the metal nightstand. He cursed and groped on the floor in darkness for the receiver.

"Hello?"

A nurse's voice answered, "Dr. Crosby? Dr. Crosby?"

"Uh ... yes," he rasped.

"Dr. Crosby, this is Kathy in the ER. Dr. Margolis wants you down here, stat."

"Stat?" Dream-filled sleep still fogged Ned's brain. He desperately wanted to return to its soothing balm.

"Yeah, you know, 'stat' as in, like, pronto, or get your ass down here, right now!" There was a laugh as the line clicked dead.

Ned fumbled with the covers, flinging them away. In the blackness of the on-call room, his stocking feet sought his loafers on the floor, finding one still tangled in the phone cord. He didn't turn on the lights so as not to awaken Blade, who was also on call. He checked to make sure that nothing obscene was hanging out of his green scrubs, and then thought about dragging a comb across his head. That brought a laugh. Then he struggled to get into the sleeves of his white jacket, which carried his name badge, stethoscope, oto-opthalmoscope, and patient cards.

Stat, stat, stat! Why doesn't anything in this hospital happen on regular time? Ned wondered. As he stumbled from the on-call room and began to close the door, the wedge of light caught not one but two forms in Blackston's bed. *Crazy bastard,* he smiled.

There was the usual milling confusion in the ER, and Ned blinked sleepily as he shouldered his way past the mob in the waiting room to the triage station. He tugged at the sleeve of the nurse who had called him. She was checking in a drunken patient, whose throat had been superficially slashed with a broken beer bottle in a brawl.

"I'm Crosby, what'd you want?" He tried to straighten-up, to appear alert.

She continued filling out the admission sheet without looking up at him and pointed down the hall, "Trauma Twelve."

At this indifference he turned to shuffle down the hall, then suddenly remembered who this nurse was. Blade had strongly recommended a "new find" in the ER. *Check out the one named Kathy,* Blade had said. So Ned twisted to look back at her, pretending to adjust his white jacket. But he blushed in embarrassment as he turned, because she had straightened up from filling out the forms, and was staring right back at him. As their eyes met, he walked smack into an empty IV pole and knocked it over. "Idiot," he mumbled as he stooped to pick it up. But he noted the warmth in her smile, at least, as she laughed at him. His parting memory, before he made his flustered way into the trauma room, was of mysterious, dark eyes and long lashes.

The trauma room was always set up for rapid patient resuscitation. Prepared IV trays were ready, and bottles of lactated Ringer's solution hung from IV poles, with the lines hooked up and poised to give life-saving fluids or medication. An x-ray unit hung from the ceiling, and other sterile set-ups were ready for any emergency procedure—thoracotomies, laporotomies, tracheotomies ... Outside Trauma Twelve was a middle-aged woman in a white blouse and a dark green, pleated skirt, weeping uncontrollably. A well-to-do, grim-looking, gray-haired man in a business suit had a comforting arm around her shoulder. Ned avoided their pleading eyes and gingerly eased into the room.

As he pushed open the trauma room door, a putrid, suffocating, sweet-smelling odor swept over him. Like rotten peaches. Nurses, interns, and ER doctors, in a beehive of activity, surrounded a young woman who lay on a litter in the center of the room. IV lines penetrated both of her arms, and nasal oxygen had been attached with a strap to her nose. An intern rushed in and yelled, "Crit, seven. Gram positive rods in the smear!" to no one in particular.

"What? Seven?"

"Seven, man."

"Damn! I've never heard of anyone alive with a hematocrit of seven. She almost doesn't have any blood in her. The bacteria must be destroying her blood cells."

Ned pushed into the crowd to look down at the patient. She appeared to be a teenager at most. Her face was the color of ashes in a misty dawn, and her breath came in deep, ragged gasps over dry, cracked lips. Ned looked closer, and she twisted towards him and fought restlessly against wrist restraints. *What is this,* he thought, *another crazy lady?*

Margolis was standing on the other side of the bed, and he looked over and caught Ned's eye. His lips mouthed the words, "Feel her belly." Ned reached in and placed his hands on her protuberant abdomen. He gasped. Crinkles, like spongy bubbles, could be felt underneath the skin. Open, bubbly sores protruded from her swollen vaginal lips. The sickening-sweet odor was suffocating. Streaks of grayish, bulbous tissue extended up her body to the thorax. *She has gas gangrene,* Ned thought. An orderly rushed in with packets of blood, which were hung immediately from each IV pole.

"O-negative?"

It was Neal Morgan! Ned caught his eye, but Neal was occupied and, as usual, all business.

"O-negative."

"No time for a crossmatch?"

"You kidding? Her crit's seven."

EKG lines were attached to the patient, but the tracing on the heart monitor was almost unreadable. Her heart rate was up to 220 beats per minute.

"Ten million units of penicillin in each IV, stat. Give it all at once, a bolus push," Neal ordered.

David Hazelette-Warner was on his ER rotation, and his nervous hands fumbled, drawing up the medicine. The empty bottle broke on the floor as he frantically flung it out of the way.

"Turn up the oxygen to twelve liters per minute, and careful throwing those damn bottles. Someone'll get cut!"

"Roger."

"This ain't no submarine."

"Screw off."

The team's mock glibness belied the grizzly scene. *That's how they cope with it,* Ned thought.

The patient's labored respirations were at 56 per minute. An anesthesiologist at the head of the litter was forcing blood into her veins through both IV lines, using a pressure cuff on each of the bags of blood. Neal moved up to the head of the bed, where he was attempting a subclavian vein stick with a large-bore Intracath needle. He was trying to get in a central heart line. Neal cautiously slid the 18-gauge needle under the clavicle, searching under the collarbone in her chest for the subclavian vein, which led straight to the heart. As he carefully advanced the needle, he sucked on a syringe that was attached to it. He was hoping to see it fill with blood. Instead, the syringe suddenly filled with air.

"Damn!" he cried.

"You've punctured her lung," the anesthesiologist admonished.

"Goddammit! Why don't you announce it to the rest of the hospital! Get me a chest tube! We've got a pneumothorax, here."

"Do you want a chest x-ray, doctor?"

"I already know I collapsed the damn lung," he spat. He kept probing with the needle, his eyes unfocused as he felt under the clavicle.

"There!" Blood spurted into the syringe, and he frantically fed the IV line down the metal Intracath collar, through the vein and into the patient's heart. "Now we can monitor her central venous pressure." Morgan gave his patented authoritative nod to the entire room.

"The chest tube set is here, doctor." An ER nurse ripped open the sterile cover on a chest tube tray.

"Give it to me."

"Scalpel?" she asked in a monotone.

Like this happens all the time down here? Ned wondered

"A number 10 blade."

In one swoop Morgan stabbed the scalpel blade straight down onto the patient's right ribcage into her chest wall, ignoring her cry, and then stuffed the chest tube into the opening. He glanced down at the connector, "Is this that new Heimlich tube they've been telling me about?" No one answered. The EKG alarm suddenly sounded, and the monitor screen showed ventricular fibrillation. The patient's overwhelmed heart could no longer beat. The machine's red warning lights flashed. Morgan cursed and finished hooking up the chest tube, frantically sewing it in place. Up at the head of the bed, the anesthesiologist levered the girl's head back and intubated her.

"Give her 25 milligrams of IV lidocaine," Morgan ordered.

There was no change in the EKG after they finished injecting the medicine.

"Stand back!" Morgan approached her with two paddles covered with jelly, lines running to a defibrillator unit. "Everyone, stand back!"

The swarm of doctors suddenly shrank fearfully away from her as he placed the paddles across the patient's chest and pushed a button with his thumb. Her body jerked spasmodically as 400 watts of electricity surged into her.

"Any change?" Morgan looked up.

"Still V-fib," the anesthesiologist answered.

"Let's hit her again." He hit the button and her body jerked stiffly a second time.

"Still V-fib."

"Shit." Neal astonished Ned when he suddenly brought his fist crashing down on her left anterior chest wall, just above her breast. "Any change?"

"Nothing. She's starting to flat line."

"Two amps of bicarb IV, then intracardiac epinephrine."

A nurse gave him a giant needle on a syringe. Morgan felt below the patient's breast, between her ribs, then grunted and plunged in the needle. Blood returned into the syringe.

"I'm in the heart," he announced to no one in particular. He pushed down on the syringe's plunger. "Anything?"

The others shook their heads.

"More epi."

Neal Morgan looked desperately around the room. His hands trembled as he again stabbed into her chest wall with the second ampoule of epinephrine. Ned thought that his orderly, precise movements seemed to have purpose, but nothing positive was happening to the patient. Gas bubbles crinkled in the grayish tissue under Morgan's hands as the gangrene continued to climb the chest wall and claim this young woman. Ned could see Neal's hands involuntarily pull back, trembling over the spongy tissue.

This is macabre, Ned thought. There was nothing he'd learned in a medical textbook to prepare him for this.

Morgan was visibly frustrated that the patient was failing to respond to his commands. He suddenly jumped onto the bed, straddled her body, and began closed cardiac massage.

Larry Margolis reached up and restrained him. "You've done everything you can, Neal; it's time to let her go."

For an instant, Morgan's wild, black eyes stared defiantly back; then they registered recognition and, finally, resignation. His erect, martial posture slumped in defeat.

"Goddammit, you're right, Larry," he muttered. "We can't save her." He glanced around the room at the trauma team, gesturing absently with his hand. "You've all done well, we did everything we could; she was just too far gone."

The alarm from the EKG machine was still sounding, and he wheeled and kicked at it. "Shit! Not a damn thing worked!" Then he meekly turned to the nurses and aides in the room. "Uh ... could you clean her up, please? I'll do the hard part and go tell the parents. Anyone who touches her wear gloves; and remember, that gas gangrene is still active. We'll have to call Path, warn them, and let them figure out how to handle the body." He slipped off his bloodied gloves and turned to Margolis and Ned. "Sorry to wake you. I thought you might be able to help." He shrugged, "Guess I was wrong."

Ned came around to the other side of the litter next to Margolis. "Jesus Christ! What was that all about?"

Margolis' eyes were staring off into space, "I ... I just saw her this week in OB Clinic, Ned. She was sixteen years old and two months pregnant. I told her to tell her parents, but she wouldn't. I couldn't force her, you know. You're looking at the results of an illegal abortion attempt."

Ned slumped down on a stool and gathered his knees up in his arms, rocking back and forth. "I don't believe it," he muttered. "First there's the crazy lady ... now this." Confusion crossed his face as he looked up at Margolis. "I thought obstetrics was about babies, about bringing new life into the world. Instead, all I'm seeing is death. First we kill a crazy lady's baby, and then we see another one who kills herself trying to kill the baby."

Larry pulled up a stool and sat down beside him. They stared glumly up at the young girl's dead body. Masked workers, double-gloved and covered with gowns and hoods, were cleaning up the body, pulling out the chest tube, and wiping at the bloodstains. Bubbly, squishing sounds could be heard as they washed the dried, reddish-black blood from her chest and her flaccid, discolored breasts. Ned heard a woman's shriek out in the hallway, followed by hysterical sobbing.

Margolis rubbed his stubbly face with both hands, and threw his arm around Ned's shoulder. "Ned, you know, there's not always an obvious reason for everything that happens." He waved absently in the air. "Try not to think about it. Sometimes you just try to help people the best you can. Never look back, and never ask why."

* * * *

Ned put down the diary and shifted positions in the easy chair. He mused over the revolutions and evolutions in health care. In today's world a post-menopausal grandmother could bear to term her barren daughter's fertilized egg, delivering in the end a healthy baby. In spite of these technological marvels, the moral issues that had plagued Ned then still had not been resolved. In fact, the extremes of opinion were more polarized than ever. The court-ordered therapeutic abortion performed on the psychotic woman seemed to Ned morally wrong, yet it made perfect legal sense. However, the right-to-lifers of today would have called it a legal prescription for murder. To deny the right to abortion for an emotionally immature, unprepared teenager would still today lead to the desperate catastrophic response of the "back-alley" abortion, and to the sanctimonious wringing of hands by the zealots.

* * * *

August 31, 1971, 8:51 AM

On the last day of the obstetrics rotation, Lunch Lefke was directed by Fred North to teach a group of second-year medical students the proper technique for a pelvic and rectal exam. Lunch's hands were actually sporting fingernails again, but he stuffed them into his pockets to hide his temptation to bite. He whistled "Beautiful Dreamer" as he descended the stairwell to the obstetrics' clinic.

"I'll stall," he confided to Ned. "I'll be so thorough teaching the other stuff, that we'll run out of time and they'll never realize that we missed the rectal."

Ned gave him the thumbs-up sign with an encouraging grin. Lunch had worked hard and had never shirked responsibility, no matter how tired he was or how messy the job. *The guy deserves a smooth entry into dermatology,* thought Ned. Later, he drifted down to the clinic to see how it went.

Lunch entered the obstetrics clinic suite in high spirits. Only two hours were left, and he would be home free.

Two anxious medical students slouched on folding chairs in a corner. The third fidgeted on an exam table, nervously swinging his feet. He was stocky, with freckles, curly, red hair, and a brand new white coat sporting the name "J. Nilsson III. S-3."

Ned went over to talk to the nurses at the workstation, but he saw the students brighten as Lunch entered. Lunch had caught twenty-four babies, and Ned could almost swear that his slouch had disappeared. He had been on call every other night for a month. The resultant stress and haggard look gave him authority that no bright-eyed, cocky, book-learning medical student could match. Furthermore, the clinic nurses liked Lunch, and they had told the students he was good with the patients. They would learn a lot.

Lunch was nonchalant and shook their hands brusquely. He quickly began moving from room to room, drawing curtains and donning sterile gloves. He patiently took patient histories, questioned, and thoroughly examined their abdomens or healing episiotomies. There were clever asides and double-entendres to the students that seemed to zip over Nilsson's head, which was just fine with Lunch. The freckle-faced, stocky guy seemed like kind of a blockhead. Each of the medical students got to listen to a pregnant belly with the fetoscope. They giggled at each other's appearance with the awkward contraption on their heads. Lunch lectured them on post-natal care.

"How long before an episiotomy is ... er, ready for action again?" Nilsson asked, his pudgy hands fumbling with his glasses.

Six wide eyes and three open mouths gaped back. Without changing his demeanor, Lunch paternalistically pulled Nilsson out into the hallway and discreetly chewed him out about his gaff.

"Try to show a little sensitivity," he admonished.

Nilsson returned, red-faced with his eyes downcast. Lunch Lefke was behind him, confident and with a ramrod posture.

I'm on top of these bastards now, he thought.

He looked at his watch: a half-hour left, and one patient to go. She was a new patient, a fifty-five-year-old lady who was five feet one inch and weighed 255 pounds. "Portly" was a polite term for Mrs. Gloria Richmond. She gave them a ready smile, but beneath it they could see the apprehension as her eyes darted around the young, staring faces. The female medical student grabbed Dr. Lefke's sleeve and whispered insistently about the pelvic and rectal exams. Another one chimed in, "Yeah, Dr. Lefke? Tomorrow we're supposed to be doing them."

Nilsson twisted his hand in a strange gesture unknown to Lunch, but all the medical students nodded knowingly as though great concurring wisdom had been confirmed. This unnerved him.

He smiled nervously toward the patient, and introduced himself. He introduced the medical students, and then asked Mrs. Richmond, "Ma'am, how can we help you? What brings you to our clinic today?"

Mrs. Richmond rolled her eyes and grabbed at her belly. "Doctor, I do'an know the term, but I needs he'p. I got fireballs a' da Eucharist! That doctor at the free clinic done sent me here." She nodded sternly for emphasis.

Dumbfounded, Lunch Lefke rummaged frantically through her chart's paperwork. The students murmured among themselves. *What, for God's sake, were fireballs a' da Eucharist?* Lefke quickly scanned the free clinic's referral slip: An abdominal exam had revealed a moderately tender mass in the right lower quadrant. It was firm, and believed to be protruding from the right lobe of the uterus. The tentative diagnosis was fibroids of the uterus.

Lunch's slump quickly straightened itself, and he smiled condescendingly towards the medical students. "What she means, students, is fibroids of the uterus, a benign tumor."

"That's right!" Mrs. Richmond beamed back.

Lunch grasped Mrs. Richmond's hand. "Ma'am, we need to examine you. If you don't mind, these young doctors need to learn about examining women, and since I have to check you, would it be okay if they observe? We'll be gentle, and very appreciative of your cooperation."

"I do'an know," she said, glancing apprehensively at the group. But her eyes fell on the female medical student, who smiled encouragingly, and so she shrugged, "Why not?"

Lunch showed the students the three sizes of speculums. He showed them how the protruding paddles would spread with the grip, and how to lock the paddles in an open position with the flick of a thumbscrew. Before using the speculum he did the pelvic exam manually, and described to the students what he felt. Gentle pressure on the abdomen with the opposite hand helped his Vaseline-coated fingers define the shape of the pelvic organs. This was the essence of pure teaching, using a cooperative, tolerant patient in the most intimate of personal space. Each student carefully and awkwardly took a turn. Nilsson's beet-red face was beaded with drops of sweat and his glasses fogged. Lunch apologized to Mrs. Richmond for any discomfort, and then selected a speculum. More Vaseline was applied, and he easily slid in the speculum. In and out, he showed the students the entry, the spread, and the lock. The reddened cervix stared back, and Lunch reached for the specimen stick to get a cervical swab when flatulence escaped.

He flushed, and his pimple scars turned purple. "Well—ah, yes ma'am. All of us have seen what we needed to see. Er, obvious fibroids ... Uh, I ... I'm sure they don't need surgery." He turned to the medical students and brusquely said, "You've seen how to do a proper pelvic exam, and now you can each do one." Suddenly he brightened and cackled, "See one, do one, and teach one!" Then he began to walk out.

However, Nilsson's pudgy arm shot out and grabbed at Lefke's sleeve. "What about the rectal exam, Dr. Lefke?" he whined. "What about the rectal? We don't have a clue." He turned to their patient and pleaded, "Please, Ma'am. Is it okay? We need to learn, and we've never done one."

The students' eyes were all on Mrs. Richmond, so they couldn't see Lunch staring dejectedly at his shoes shaking his head no. Looking back at Lefke, she smiled brightly and said, "That's okay, you nice doctors!"

Their heads swiveled towards Lefke. He grimly stripped off one glove, and carefully selected a big fat fingernail to bite on. The one on his index finger looked just fine; why not? His enlarging eyes seemed to be straining out of their orbits, and his contorted grimace looked as though he was trying to suppress a diarrheal movement. Nilsson moved behind him to see better, and the two others flanked each thigh.

No one was really sure what had happened. For a moment it looked like Lefke was a bloated bottom fish yanked from the ocean's depths, mouth open and gasping for air. Lefke's hand darted in and out so fast, with a flapping tremor, that he became entangled with his own tie. In his nervousness, he'd bitten off a fingernail, but he'd forgotten to re-glove. There was a muffled cry, and then a snip of bandage scissors. Shell-shocked, he stumbled from the room, his tie cut off, and his bandage scissors lying on the exam room floor. Later, Fred North and Niilson were seen leaving Warren's room in central supply with a pocket full of money. Another legend was born at the General.

4

Pus

August 31, 1971, 8:30 PM

lade Blackston stretched across the sofa like a languid cat
lounging on a sunny porch. Kitty-corner, sharing the reading
lamp, Ned's wiry frame collapsed like an accordion into an
armchair with one leg draped over the armrest. He hardly looked
up from the Sunday comics as Blackston "alley-oop'ed" him a can of
cold beer. He popped it open with a hiss of wet spray, and Blackston
chuckled at his best friend's amusing, eccentric obsession.

The Phantom was holding off a gang of evil, cigar-chomping
thieves who had kidnapped a princess and stolen a mythical Kingdom
of Jjomba's priceless treasure. No way was Ned going to miss an episode from the comic's exciting conclusion. It had taken a month of
Lefke's purloined newspapers to get Ned to this point in the story.

But Blackston broke Ned's concentration with an exasperated
"What do you think, Ned?"

Ned raised an eyebrow his way with a frown, but didn't lift his
head from the paper. "Think about what?" he mumbled.

"Life, Nedley, life." Blackston reached over and pulled down Ned's paper.

Ned laughed as he took another swig from the beer, "Not much life, here, Blade. Ol' Farnsworth said that on call would be every third night. So how come no one got the message on the trauma team or OB? Two straight months ... I'm on call every other. That nurse in the ER you said to check out? Kathy? Whatever? I've never even had a chance to say hello." Then he raised an inquiring eyebrow. "Peds, on the other hand, can't have been too bad. To the establishment's astonishment, not only did you actually save a few lives, but also you seemed to have a little extra energy left to perform in the on-call room? Yes?"

Blade rolled his eyes in mock embarrassment, "So sue me if I got lucky." He drained his own beer and belched. "Peds was drudgery. The only good thing was that the pediatric chief resident watched me start some IV's on little preemie babies, do a couple of cut-downs, and finally, I did a spinal tap or two. On my last day she said, 'Dr. Blackston, you've got good hands, but ... but, you just can't keep them to yourself!' She was kinda pissed that I nailed two of her nurses." As Blackston wiped the foam from his mouth, his eyes steeled. "The only good thing on Peds was meeting Beth."

Ned stared thoughtfully at his own beer can, crushed it, and arced a lazy hook shot into the trashcan. He sighed and looked at his friend. "You see? You see? Two months of busting ass, and still no idea of what I'll do in medicine. Worse yet, there's not a woman in sight. The Blade, though, The Blade knows he's cut from surgical cloth, and scores with Beth."

But Blackston waved a cautionary finger in the air. "Smedley, Smedley, now don't go jumping to conclusions. That little episode in the on-call room wasn't Beth. Speaking of which," he said, looking at his watch and springing up from the couch, "I gotta run. Dinner with Beth." He swaggered out the room, mimicking a bullfighter. "Toro, toro."

September 1, 1971, 6:45 AM

It was Ned's first day on the extremity service. He and Everett "No Problem" Jones had drawn another rotation together. Jones was hunched on the plastic cafeteria chair, absently fiddling with his French toast. Earlier, he'd almost knocked over the table, sawing at the toast with his knife and fork. The interns had started a rumor that the cook mixed either latex or cement with the batter. As he was sawing, Jones opined that it was probably both.

Ned sipped at his coffee, shivered, and arched his back like he'd just swallowed acid. "Jesus, the coffee here has such a bitter edge, I'll bet it could cut your toast."

He bent furtively down and drank the remaining milk in his cereal bowl. Then he looked across the table, noticing Jones' thick body and muscular neck. The poor guy was already beginning to lose hair. Some thin wisps of blond fuzz stuck out like outposts on a desert frontier, barely enough to drag a comb through. Delicate wire rim glasses provided an interesting contrast to his bull frame, square jaw and deeply cleft chin. He had a ready smile with teeth that were like a row of piano keys gone awry. This made the "No Problem" nickname even better. Jones radiated the quiet confidence of a stocky man who had found peace with his five feet six inches—no Napoleonic complex.

"By the way, I've got bad news and good news." Everett mumbled.

"What's that?"

"Neal Morgan rotated off trauma, and he's the new pus chief. You and I got Immaculate again." Everett ignored Ned's gasp. "The good news is I called him last night. He has to wait for a new University resident to show up, so we meet them on the floor after breakfast, not before."

Ned sighed. *It wasn't all that bad,* he thought. Morgan was demanding, but he was a known commodity. He was fair. You knew

117

what was expected of you. Other than his fastidious drive for perfection, there were no bizarre personality traits. At times, Ned actually admired Neal's confidence and skill. Neal had told him one day, "If you're going to actually cut people open, then you have to believe in yourself, to have confidence." So far, no other surgical intern besides Ned had put his hands inside an open abdomen. That flattery, itself, counted for something.

The team met on Two North, referred to as the pus ward. With Neal was a new resident named Hal Tipton. Harold. Hal was a distinct contrast to Neal's precision appearance. His whites had probably been taken straight out of the dryer and donned on the spot. The rumpled cuffs ended at a pair of sneakers, which were clean but sported several broken shoelaces, tied together up the lacing. Ned could have sworn that Neal ground his teeth when he saw Tipton's makeshift laces. The team moved down the ward with Neal leading the way and assigning patients.

Rapping his pencil nervously on the clipboard, Morgan began a recitation of each patient, the diagnosis, hematocrit, infecting organism, and so forth.

"Crosby ... you ready?"

"Yes, sir."

He entered a room and gestured towards the patient. "Brown, Anthony. Twenty-seven years of age. A black male, skin-popper. Cellulitis, left arm. Crit, thirty-seven. Malnutrition, iron deficient. He's been afebrile for thirty-six hours. Organism: Staphylococcus aureus and Streptococcus, Type B. Dakins solution soaks, qid. Ten million units of penicillin, two point five, IV, every six hours. Got it?"

"It's on the card, got it."

"Jones?"

"Yes, sir."

"MacNulty, Albert. Fifty-seven years of age. Forty-five percent, full-thickness burns. Twenty-five percent, second degree. He's a bridge troll, living under a bridge, who was set on fire by fellow drunks. Last night his temperature rose to 102.4 degrees. Crit, 32. Chronic, iron-deficiency anemia and burn drainage. Organism: Staphylococcus aureus and a Pseudomonas superinfection—see that greenish color?" Inquisitive eyes scanned Everett's for any sign of acknowledgment or nascent intelligence. "Penicillin, two point five, qid, and gentamicin. Watch his kidney function and ears, will you? No deaf trolls on our service!" Morgan chuckled to no one in particular, and then his eyes lit up. "New treatment! Beginning today, we start Phisohex soaks, damp-to-dry, with four-by-fours. I read that that new acne treatment kills staph. Got it?"

"No problem."

"Crosby?"

"Yes, sir."

On and on they went, moving from one isolation room to another. Since it was another new rotation, Ned couldn't help looking enthusiastically at each new patient as a challenging problem to solve. However, the litany of putrid pus and self-destruction seemed endless. There were thirty isolation rooms in all, each occupied by an infected patient with stinking sores, black limbs, or weeping pus. Twenty-three of the patients were addicts with life-threatening infections secondary to drug abuse. One of the heroin addicts was a white, male, twenty-three-year-old going on fifty-something. He had a blackened, shriveled hand suspended over his head in pin traction. Two stainless steel pins skewered his metacarpals and elbow, attaching the blackened hand to the traction hanging above him. He was a hardened drug addict with no veins left. In his desperation for a high, he had injected heroin directly into the radial artery at the wrist. The speared artery had spasmed and then clotted shut. The junkie awakened from his narcotic euphoria to excruciating spasms and pain while the muscles, tendons, and finally, the whole hand slowly necrosed. He had been hanging in traction to control swelling and cellulitis. They were waiting for final demarcation of what

119

tis-sue would live and what would die in his gangrenous hand. Then, appropriate amputation flaps could be fashioned.

To hide his horror, Ned gave him a reassuring pat on the leg. He leaned closer when the addict motioned with his good hand. *Jesus,* he thought, *this guy's two years younger than me and looks old enough to be my dad.*

"Incredibly bad scene, man. Can you give me anything for the pain?" The addict started to tug at Ned's sleeve, "Shit, man, can you do something, or what?"

But Ned recoiled.

"Man, if you can't help out a guy with pain ... what kind of bullshit doctor are you, anyway?"

Neal Morgan indifferently interjected that all addicts on their service were on Methadone, and that no pain medication of any kind was to be prescribed.

"Keep an eye on that guy, Crosby. He's so hard core he might get someone to inject heroin into his subclavian line."

"Yes, sir."

Of the remaining non-addict patients, two were burn victims, three were diabetics with infected feet or amputation stumps, and two other patients had draining abdominal wounds from gunshots. Each patient was isolated, and elaborate masking, gowning, and gloving procedures were necessary just to enter each room. At the end of rounds, Morgan's eyes swept across their dejected faces. He gestured down the hall with open palms like Jesus Christ to the multitudes. "Gentlemen, welcome to the pus bucket of General Hospital. Questions?"

They were speechless. Hal muttered a half-hearted grunt. Such self-destruction hadn't been mentioned in medical school training at the university. Half the patients had called out for narcotic medications, expertly naming brands, nicknames, and dosages. "How about some Percs, doc? Any chance for some Darvocet or Diazepam? Come on, man ... just five milligrams?" The whining and pleading followed the interns up and down the hall. "Any uppers, man? Say, come on. How 'bout a blue? Just one? Pleeaase? You goddamn doctors!"

Ned forced a mechanical grin. "Well, hard to do more harm to these people than they've already done to themselves." He gestured down the hall, "Is this all we get? Infected addicts?"

Morgan thoughtfully stroked his chin and shook his head. "Nope. We scavenge. Any open infection in the hospital is ours...if we want it. The only limitation is bed space, and right now our ward's full." His black eyes beamed. "In fact, we're always full! On this service I see maybe five consults a day, all of them infections."

"So, is our extremity service only junkies?" Jones wanted to know.

"These are the sickest. They've got open draining wounds, abscesses, they're septic or they're near death. If I didn't get them away from the damn swamis, they'd probably never make it." He rolled his eyes, "You know the swamis, and they'd still be scratching their heads, checking cultures, quoting literature, and repeating the serum potassium!"

The interns smirked knowingly, having already been educated in the derogatory term for medical docs or internists. The surgeons were always lampooning their cerebrated, mystical diagnoses, and the quoting of articles in obscure medical journals. They liked to think that it took a man of action, one of their ilk, to step in and truly treat someone. The surgeons, in turn, were figures derided by the internists as crude "sawbones" or slashers, though this was not often spoken within hearing distance.

Morgan's name sounded metallically on the overhead page, and he smiled at Ned and Jones. "Gotta' go. Oh, and by the way, tomorrow we have teaching rounds with Dr. Farnsworth. They're for your benefit ... supposedly." His caustic blackness bore into them. "He likes to teach, and he's really good. But you'd better make sure you know every troll on this ward like he's a relative, 'cause if you make me look bad, I can be very unpleasant." He absently bit at a nail edge. "Know the numbers, boys. Get every dressing changed, a note in every chart ... and get these trolls in shape. You interns want better patients, make these better and get rid of them." With that, he pivoted on his heel and left, his false crocodile smile their last lingering memory.

"What an asshole!" Ned muttered. He'd forgotten how Neal could turn into a prick whenever he got a bee in his bonnet. "Must've had a bad night on call," he muttered.

"No problem, really," said Jones. "Just keep your eye on the big picture."

"What do you mean?" Ned asked.

"Well, this is the last service with Immaculate, right? For one month we're partners again. We'll cover for each other. Just like before. Take better care of these trolls than they've ever dreamed. You might even see me waxing the floors and polishing the brass." Jones broke into a crooked grin as he polished his wire-rimmed glasses.

"Only one problem, No Problem."

"What's the problem?"

"Its two months of pus, see, not one."

"Now that's a problem."

They divided the patients, separated, and worked through the morning. Outside each room, the ritual of donning a gown and gloves was repeated to prevent the spread of infection from one patient to the next. Dressings were changed, and as Ned pealed away the bandages, old pus, dead skin, and scabs were stripped as well. Whines and muffled curses echoed down the hallway. The addicts gasped through gritted teeth, gripped their side rails, and cried out in pain. Ned combed through each chart, carefully updating the progress notes and checking out the lab data.

"Now here's a problem." Jones stood in a doorway, absently fingering the cleft in his chin as he flipped back and forth through a patient's chart.

"What's that?" Crosby slipped a gown off as he stepped out of a patient's room.

"It's cellulitis, see? This guy's been here for a week. The bacterial organism is Streptococcus, sensitive to penicillin. This guy's last white count was eight point five, with a normal differential. I took down his dressing, and jeez, the wound looked good! The guy's an addict, and Immaculate wanted me to change antibiotics to Methicillin after a re-culture because his temperature keeps spiking as high as 102.4 degrees."

Ned frowned for a moment, and then his eyes snapped brightly with intelligence. "To coin a phrase, 'No Problem.' Let's take his temperature now, but after you stick in the thermometer, come out."

They trudged down to the nursing station, grabbed a thermometer, and returned to the room. Jones donned his mask and gown, knocked on the door, and administered the thermometer. Then he returned to Ned.

"So what now, genius?"

Ned did not answer. He was looking at the second hand of his watch when he said "Now!" And, without putting on a gown, he quickly entered the patient's room.

"Hey! What the hell happened to privacy! Doesn't anybody know how to knock? You damn interns can't barge into my room like this!" The red-faced patient stared at them defiantly, his tattooed arms crossed.

But Ned grasped the addict's hand, which had disappeared, under his armpit. "Et voila! Une cigarette lighter, monsieur." He presented it with a flourish to Everett, "Pardoning the poor French ... As I said, No Problem, no problem." Their patient sat sullenly cursing them in his bed.

"What do we do?" Jones absently flicked the lighter on and off.

"We, partner, don't do anything" said Ned. "We're interns, remember? Like, lower than scales on a snake's belly in a rut? Morgan does the doin'." He beamed with satisfaction, "You know, I think I found two malingerers myself. One guy's got a coat hanger hidden between the mattresses and springs that he actually digs into his infected wound to make it look worse. I asked him why, he said he's got no home, no money, no job, and the General's the best thing that ever happened to him. Three squares a day, a bed, and a roof. The way I see it, we got three less junkies."

The addict glared up at them from his bed. "Hey man, you ain't thinkin' a dischargin' me, are you? I'm a sick man!" He yelled after them, "I'm sick, goddammit! I'm sick an' I ain't goin'!"

They continued rounds into the late morning. By lunchtime the service was spiffed up. More importantly, all the patients' three-by-five cards were in order.

As they pushed their cafeteria trays down past the racks of food, Jones kept wiping his hands and looking at them. "I feel dirty, Ned. Like some of that pus is still clinging, waiting to infect me."

Their second year resident, Harold Tipton, had overheard them as he joined their table.

"That's not all, boys," Tipton said. "In addition to all the pus these addicts carry, they share needles. Like ... hepatitis anyone?" Tipton laughed as they grimaced with distaste, and even eyed the food suspiciously. "And don't forget how virulent some of those damn bugs can be."

Ned shuddered, telling them the story of the abortion patient he'd seen on OB with gas gangrene. Tipton matched this with one of his own—necrotizing fasciitis, a type of Streptococcal infection that produces gas and runs up a patient's body, eating up the muscle while you watch. It's just like gas gangrene, guys."

"You're kidding," stammered Jones. "I thought Streptococcus was a simple bacteria, and easy to kill."

"I've never seen it myself," said Tipton. "But I've heard of it. You'll think I'm lying, but this is the God's truth." He stared around the table. "There was a case here at the General, in the early forties, before the time of antibiotics, okay? This guy caught his dork in his zipper, and—search me how it happened—but he got the foreskin infected. He came into the ER with gas bubbles in his groin. By the time they got him to surgery, he was dead." The interns squirmed and felt discreetly between their legs to make sure their own equipment was intact.

"Zipper, huh?"

"God's truth."

"That why we all got buttons on our whites?" Everett wanted to know.

Tipton grinned. "You'll have to ask Warren that. Anything worth knowing in this hospital, he knows it."

He swept his hair back from his forehead. It was combed straight back, and reminded Ned of an Italian stud in a foreign movie. Tipton had a pencil-thin, striped tie that was ten years out of style, and his worn sneakers suggested that he had slept through the dawning of the Age of Aquarius.

He saw Ned checking out the wrinkled whites, "That's what they make scrub suits for, Ned. They're always in style."

Ned noticed corded forearm tendons rippling out to sinewy tendons. Had he worked construction, Ned wondered? Tipton said he'd grown up pitching hay bales on a Nebraska farm. With a wink, he added that a close match with Dan Gable in the Big Eight championships might have had something else to do with the forearms. Wrestling would also explain the cauliflower ear. Ned also noticed a facial tic that belied Tipton's easy-going manner. His eyelid twitched. It seemed like maybe farm-boy had his own demons he was wrestling with.

"So what's the poop on that burn patient, MacNulty?"

Everett had been cleaning his glasses, but he replaced them and dug into the stack of three-by-five cards. Then he brightened, "Oh, him. He's actually an interesting guy—a logger from Alaska."

"A logger? Down here at the General?"

Jones scanned MacNulty's three-by-five. "That's right," he fired back. "You know, this guy fascinated me. He said he was a choker-setter, a chaser, and a rigging slinger ... whatever the hell those are. Frankly, his face is like a boiled lobster that's been run through a grinder. He's a wiry old cuss, but he's got these bright, sparkly-blue eyes that look like you can see the sky in them."

Tipton glanced up from wolfing down his hot turkey sandwich, and smiled as Jones went on.

"He came down here with his buddies on a binge, drinking during the Fourth of July camp shutdown. After drinking for a week, he was blind drunk when they left him. Then he got rolled while sleeping under a bridge. He says he doesn't remember much until he awakened, hanging in traction, with burns over forty-five percent of his body. He was probably in an alcoholic blackout."

Tipton leaned forward and grabbed the patient's card, quizzing Jones like a patronizing schoolteacher. "No cheating, and what is his status now, doctor?"

Jones hesitantly tried to peek at the card, but he wouldn't budge it, so Everett had to search his memory. "Let's see...just before we rotated on the service, MacNulty came out of DTs."

"Good," said Tipton with a nod.

"Another alky, huh?" Ned said absently. He glanced over to the corner of the cafeteria where that ER nurse, Kathy, was lunching with her colleagues. His pulse quickened when she turned his way, saw him, and smiled.

"No, *was* an alky ... Was." Jones seemed offended. "I like him! He didn't whimper once when I changed his dressings. His burns have got good granulation tissue, and if we clean up that damn staph infection, he could get skin-grafted."

Ned's heart was pounding. Kathy and the group of nurses had stood up to leave. She had yawned and stretched, and Ned couldn't help noticing the curvy silhouette beneath the nursing uniform. A cute nursing cap sat on luminous brunette hair, which cascaded over her shoulders. Even the baggy, royal blue ER scrubs couldn't hide her pleasing proportions. Ned was in his unconscious, dumb staring act again as they walked by, and suddenly Kathy looked over.

"Hi," She smiled. Her whole face seemed to light up. Ned blushed and attempted to lift his hand in a feeble wave. They disappeared out the cafeteria's swinging doors.

"... All he wants to do is get back to the woods," Jones was saying. "MacNulty was clenching and unclenching his hands today, just checking his grip strength. He gave me a wink and said he'd stoop even lower than an intern, and go back and set chokers."

Tipton pushed back his tray and stood, "You do those Phisohex dressings like Morgan wanted?"

"Yep! And they looked good, too. Those wounds get cleaned up, skin graft him ... it's back to the woods for MacNulty." Everett's crooked piano keys flashed with a piece of turkey hanging in them.

Hal heard his name over the hospital intercom. Getting up, he tossed a coin onto the table. "I'll check in with Neal while you two decide who's on call tonight."

Jones and Ned scrambled for the coin. By the time Jones had flipped the coin three times, and beaten Ned every time, Tipton had returned.

"Hey, perk up," he told Ned. "Let's hit the ER. Neal's found us a little work." He winked. "Jones, you get to see these consults." He handed over two additional three-by-five cards to Jones' stack.

"What are these?" Jones looked through his wire rims like an owl that had gotten goosed.

"Consults, Jonesy. Cases we ambitious young surgical studs have poached from other services. Pus for you to debride, suck, squeeze, or whatever you want." Tipton ran his hand through his ebony hair. "Neal's already written the chart note, just go to the floor and follow whatever orders he's written."

As they left Everett, Ned offered him a parting shot. "I'll bet our pus is better than your pus!"

Jones saluted them, discreetly touching his forehead with his upraised middle finger, and they scooted down the hall double-time.

"So what's cooking?" asked Ned.

"Neal says we got an acute abdomen in the ER."

"Er ... what's that to do with us? I thought general surgery would get the patients like that."

"Guess you don't know Neal yet." Tipton rolled his eyes. "Some guys get to be chief resident by being smart. Others get there by methodically covering all their bases. Neal does both. In addition to that, as you already know, he's aggressive. Any chance he can slip in front of someone else, well ... what they didn't know didn't hurt them." He winked, "Actually he's going to be a really good surgeon. They all say he has great hands."

They rounded the corner to the ER's swinging doors. Ned was hoping to see Kathy again, but they spotted Morgan across the milling confusion. A drunk sat in the middle of the floor with a red blossom on a bloody bandage wrapped around his head like a turban. He was kicking at an intern who tentatively tried to help him onto a litter. Morgan looked up from his clipboard. "She's in room eight, Crosby. Please do a physical, and then report back to us."

Ned nodded and held out his hand. "Gotta card? I'm out again." Morgan ground his teeth and groaned, fishing out several. "Just keepin' you happy, boss," said Ned with a grin.

He entered room eight saw a woman lying on the litter, moaning and running her hands up and down her abdomen. When Ned approached, she jerked her hands out defensively.

"Don't touch me ... please? Don't touch! Oh Jesus, Jesus, Jesus ... I must be dreaming. In a minute I'll wake up."

She moaned again. Her eyelids were puffy and red, and her cheeks were tear-streaked. The chart said her name was Bonnie Joe Maylath, thirty-eight and single. She had a pert, dishwater blond hairdo, kind of like a Doris Day cut. Her horn-rimmed glasses were slightly askew, with gold beads leading back to little golden hoop earrings, dangling from tiny earlobes. The left one was bent.

"I'm Ned Crosby." He stuck out his hand.

"Amazing. A real person. Not 'doctor' this or 'nurse' that ... Ned Crosby, huh? You a real doctor?" She looked skeptically up at him.

He held up his hand and laughed. "I'm an intern, but honest to God, interns are real doctors. I am an M.D. Help me a little, and tell me why you're here. What's going on?"

She stifled a sob, then let it out and clutched at her belly. "Damn! Y'all have heard, 'it only hurts when I laugh?' Shit! I can't even cry!" Ned smiled down at her while she tried to compose herself. She let out a sigh, and Ned looked again at her chart: The vitals showed that she was five feet three inches, 145 pounds. Her pulse was 92 and regular, respiration's were 44 and shallow. Ned found her blood pressure to be 184 over 82, and her temperature was 102.2 degrees. Allergies, none. Medications, birth control pills.

As he lowered the chart, she gestured with her hands and spoke. She stopped once to sniff, and then bit her lip fiercely and started again. "I'm a secretary, see? Just a plain lil' ol' secretary in this two-bit restaurant supply company—Ajax Restaurant Equipment." There was a definite Tennessee twang. "There's just ten of us and the boss. Why, we had a bang-up year, and when the sales figures came in the boss, Mr. Colville, he says, 'Hey, we deserve a party!' So we all go out for a smash-up dinner, and afterwards to his place for drinks." She wrung her hands and clutched at her abdomen. "Shoot, doc, I really don't know what happened. People were leaving ... and, and I wanted to leave, too. But Mr. Colville says, 'Hey, Bonnie, one little nightcap. Come on, be a sport!' Well darn it, I didn't want more to drink, but it was the boss and all ... and I wanted to be nice." Tears welled in her eyes, "I kinda remember him pawing at me. The next thing I knew, I woke up, naked and in his bed. I felt horrible. I was embarrassed ... I had a horrible headache, and my belly hurt. Why, by the time I snuck out of there with my clothes, I could hardly stand up with the pain. I drove right over here." She clutched at his arm and began weeping bitterly. "Doctor, for God's sake! What's happened to me? What did that man do to me?"

Ned Crosby patted her arm. "Listen, Miss Maylath, don't worry. We'll find out what's wrong, and we'll take care of you."

The snap and mischief in Ned's dancing eyes had disappeared into an ominous hardness. He locked eyes with her to let her know how serious he was.

"I promise."

He went through the standard medical questions, but discovered her entire background was healthy. He went over her again, checking her blood pressure, pulse, respirations, and temperature. Her temperature was now 102.8! Her lung fields were clear. She had a normal heart and breast exam, but her abdomen was absolutely rigid. She pleaded with him not to press on her abdomen, so he jiggled the bed instead. She said that even that hurt a lot. *Positive rebound,* he thought. He listened to her abdomen. There were no bowel sounds, but he heard a curious whine. He shook his head once, and swiveled the stethoscope to a different setting. The whine persisted.

"Ma'am, I've got to do a rectal exam."

130

"Please ... please don't," she pleaded with wild eyes. "Why, I ... I can't even lift my legs it hurts so much."

"I've got to ... Here, I'll help." Ned had already donned a rubber glove and squeezed some Vaseline onto his right index finger. With his left hand he pulled up her right leg, and gingerly inserted a finger. She cried out as he probed. She pleaded for him to stop, then shrieked with pain when he probed further. When he withdrew his finger there were bloody streaks on it.

"My God," she panted. "Please don't do that again." She fumbled with a box of Kleenex and pulled one out to blow her nose.

He wiped the tears from her eyes with another. "I'm sorry. I had to check. It's my job." He turned to leave, "Miss Maylath, I'm going to check on your lab work. I'll be back."

Outside the examining room Morgan and Tipton sat on an empty litter. Their legs were idly swinging over the edge while they were in deep discussion. Morgan thrust some Xeroxed sheets of lab values towards Ned, which he stuffed into the lab section of Bonnie Joe's chart.

"Did a rectal, huh?" Neal commented. "I could hear it. I know it must not have been fun, but I like your thoroughness."

Ned surveyed the lab values: Her electrolytes were normal, but the white count was elevated at 21,800! There was an 85 percent left shift. *Christ,* he thought, *this lady was in trouble!* Her blood level was 39. An electrocardiogram and chest film looked normal. Ned held up her abdominal x-ray, and saw free air under her diaphragm in the abdomen. A perforated viscous! But where? His eye wandered down the x-ray to an ill-defined, oblong, tubular density. "Jesus Neal, what's that?"

"You tell us, Doctor Crosby. What do you think?"

"I don't know. I've never seen anything like it. Is it an artifact? Did they screw up the x-ray?" Ned searched their faces. Once again, nothing he'd studied in medical school had prepared him for this.

131

Morgan smirked, and his black eyes probed. "Put it together. Remember her history, doctor."

"She said she was at a party. The boss pawed at her, and she passes out ... Jesus Christ!" Ned looked up at them in surprise. "That guy slipped her some kind of Mickey, and stuck this ... whatever this thing is in," he gestured at the blurred x-ray, "and he perforated her rectum! Jesus! What a degenerate sonofabitch!"

"What do you think, Hal?"

"Well," Hal offered, "contrary to popular opinion, I think an intern is capable of learning."

Morgan went on, "In my four years as a general surgery resident I've fished out coke bottles, light bulbs, golf balls ... and, even a small Mason jar from where the sun doesn't shine. You can't believe what weird things people will stick up there. But this will be my first electric dildo."

"Yeah Neal, but that guy drugged her and then raped her," said Tipton. "She's got peritonitis. In fact, we could take great care of this lady, and in spite of it, she could take a turn for the worse and die."

Morgan nodded, holding his hand up in restraint. "You're right, you're right. For that reason, let me be the one to sign off on her physical. No sense in having your names on the chart for lawyers to subpoena. That's not an intern's job." He took the chart from Ned. "While I'm writing, get an IV started, okay? Lactated Ringer's. Run it at 20 drops a minute. Pass an NG tube down to suck out her stomach, and bring her up to surgery, stat. We're gonna lap her as soon as you're done."

"Should an acute abdomen go to general surgery?" asked Ned.

Morgan's demeanor stiffened, and his narrow eyes flickered Ned's way. "Why shouldn't we do a little extra work if we're up for it? I just happened by the ER as her x-rays came out. It is peritonitis, Mr. dog shit intern, or do you want some more junkie pus?"

Ned thought about that for one half of a millisecond, grinned, and shook his head.

September 1, 1971, 4:17 PM

They used a standard, midline, exploratory laparotomy incision on Bonnie Joe Maylath. It stretched ten inches, exactly down the midline except for where it curved around her belly button. Morgan performed the surgery. Tipton first-assisted, and Ned hung onto the retractors in the well-established "intern's pose." There was a quick flash of steel, instant Bovie smoke, and with a swiftness that took Ned's breath away, they were staring into the belly at inflamed, fatty omentum—the thin, veiled sac that stretched over the abdominal contents.

"Interesting, don't you think, how that veil of fat comes down to protect and seal off the injury?" said Morgan. "God's given us an amazing machine."

The fatty sac was slightly inflamed, but it had moved down to cover the injured lower quadrant of Bonnie Maylath's belly.

"What's that?" Morgan's eyes darted over to Ned as he lifted up the abdominal wall and pointed with a hemostat.

"Um ... inferior epigastric artery?"

"Say it like you know it."

"I hate to bullshit."

"I don't want you to bullshit. I want you to know it." Morgan's eyes grew distant and unfocused as he carefully felt with his hand inside the abdomen. Suddenly they brightened, and he pulled from her open belly a plastic vibrator, the motor still furiously churning.

"Er ... what should we say? Takes a licking and keeps on ticking?" He looked around the room mischievously.

"Jesus, you're sick," said the scrub nurse, giving Morgan a dirty look.

When he asked for the Mayo scissors, she slapped them into his palm with a snap that made him jump.

"All right, all right," he whined. "Only trying to inject a little humor into a bowel situation."

The scrub nurse's scowl and blush could be seen under her mask. Morgan raised his arms in mock self-defense.

"Don't hit me!"

After a moment's thought, Neal riveted his attention on Harold Tipton and his nonchalant demeanor grew sharp. "Okay, Hal, it's quiz time. Where do we go from here? What's next?" His gaze glowered over his mask and across the table.

Tipton glanced up nervously. "Uh ... I think we should run the bowel. You know, make sure that stupid dildo didn't perforate something else. We gotta irrigate with antibiotics, and maybe do a colostomy on the way out to rest her colon and let it heal from the perforation. Then, close over drains."

He set his chin affirmatively and looked up around the table for approval. Ned noticed Hal's facial tic flipping away, betraying his inner anxieties.

"How about it Crosby? Any lucky guesses? Or is Hal right? Give us your best shot."

Now Neal's steely black gaze bore into Ned as he started, looking up from the retractors.

He shrugged off the fact that Morgan's had pitted him against the second-year resident, thought for a while, and answered. "Listen, Neal. I'm no surgeon, and all I can remember is what I saw on the surgical rotation in med school. I'm only guessing, but I believe we need to close the perforated rectum."

Tipton rolled his eyes in exasperation. He'd forgotten about the perforation.

"Then, we need to irrigate the belly and run the bowel." Ned went on, "Finally, wouldn't a colostomy be near where her rectum is perforated, and maybe a set-up for adhesions? How about a cecostomy? Would it be just as good? It's on the opposite side. Then, close her over drains."

Morgan looked across the table at him, wide-eyed. "Holy shit, Crosby! What are you, some kind of freak intern? I hope you're going into general surgery, because that was good!" His dark eyes suddenly leveled with Tipton's, "Too bad this is a pyramid program, Hal. Nut-cutting time's gettin' closer for you second-year residents. You, buddy, have got to get your act together."

Tipton stepped back and asked for a forehead wipe. He looked flushed, and as if trying to control the muscles of his face. The silence in the room was deafening.

Morgan proceeded with the case. In a matter of minutes the lacerated rectum had been expertly and securely closed. Antibiotic irrigation was splashed into the open belly, sucked out, and then they ran the bowel. There were no other lacerations, and only one small contusion. Ned was fascinated, watching the efficiency of Neal Morgan. *He might be compulsive immaculate, whatever,* he thought, *but he's damn good!* His authority and confidence absolutely dominated the room. Morgan's razor-sharp mind seemed always to be one step ahead of the case, reminding the scrub and circulating nurses of things they would need for the next stages of the operation. Soft, rubber Penrose drains had been pulled out of stab wounds in all four quadrants of her belly. Sterile safety pins were clipped into each drain so that they couldn't disappear back inside. Crosby was deep in thought about the drainage of the gutters when his hand was slapped with scissors. He looked up at Neal in surprise. *Huh? Could eyes that cold actually smile?*

"So, Mr. Miracle Intern. Wanna do the McBurney approach for the cecostomy? Come on. I'll waltz you through it. Your first case."

Ned's eyes scanned the team. He met Morgan's stare, then saw Hal Tipton's eyelid twitching with the involuntary tic. He looked back at Morgan, and then down into the wound.

"I don't know how to do it, Neal. I wouldn't feel right. I've never cut on anybody in my life."

Morgan was bored now, and he shrugged with indifference. "Suit yourself." He turned to Tipton, offering the scalpel, "Hal?"

Morgan handed a beaming Hal the knife and they proceeded. Ned was quizzed about each muscle layer, but he knew them all. Finally, Morgan gave up his interrogations, and they concentrated on the cecostomy. They closed the central laparotomy incision with 20 gauge, stainless-steel wire. Then they partially closed the cecostomy wound. Betadine was slopped over the belly for infection control, and finally, with Bonnie safe in the recovery room, Ned was seated and writing orders.

Morgan left them to see yet another, and he told Tipton to stay and supervise Ned's orders to manage the nasogastric suction and cecostomy tube. Tipton and Ned sat together in the recovery room, in the midst of sucking sounds from respirators, hissing oxygen, and the cries of patients in pain.

"Thanks, man," said Tipton. Sweat drenched the front of his scrub suit.

"Thanks for what?"

"You know damn well for what! You gave me a chance to come back. When a resident gets on Morgan's bad side, I've heard that he never lets him back up. I was almost down for the count until you gave up the approach."

Ned looked across at him, but he didn't answer. He continued to write orders.

"Cecostomy to gravity, right?"

Tipton nodded.

"What about a Foley Catheter? She's gonna hurt so much, she won't be able to get up and pee. Let's give her a break for a couple of days. Besides, we can monitor her output better."

"You're really something, aren't you?" Tipton smiled.

Ned smiled in return. "Listen, Hal. This is just between us, okay?"

Tipton nodded again.

"I don't really know that I want to prove myself in general surgery. I'd like to become some kind of surgeon. But just look at our chief! This kind of uptight life isn't for me—but don't tell Neal, okay? People are nicer if they think you're interested." He turned back to writing orders.

"You're kidding," said Tipton incredulously. "You're good! You could be a good surgeon!"

Crosby shook his head, "It's like this: I've seen what a pyramid program can do. When I was back at Cincinnati, they had a six-year surgical program. It was on call every other night, in a program where only four out of the sixteen that started actually made it to be chief. Some of the stuff those guys pulled on each other was pretty brutal. They actually caught one guy infecting his rival's patients' wounds. I don't want to be a surgeon so bad that I'll screw my buddies. What I'll be, I don't know yet ... but a general surgeon, I ain't." He grinned and slammed the chart shut. "Looks like we've now got a chance to eat supper."

Tipton hit the wall switch to activate the electric doors of the Recovery Room. As they passed through, a squat man with a bald pate and heavy sideburns straightened up from the wall and caught stride with them. His was wearing a blue three-piece suit. He pulled at Tipton's arm, "Ah, excuse me. You're ... you're Dr. Tipton, aren't you?"

Tipton stopped in mid-stride and pointedly disengaged his arm. "Yes, and who are you?"

The man's eyes flicked evasively between Ned and Tipton, like a snake testing the wind. *It was curious how some people never made eye contact,* Ned thought. He surveyed his frayed cuffs with cheap, rhinestone cuff links.

"I'm related to Miss Maylath. I'm inquiring after her." Still his eyes danced back and forth between them. "What's her condition?"

"Oh, you're her father?" Tipton asked.

A nervous chuckle escaped the man's throat, and his pursed lips twitched above a sweaty double chin. They started to form a yes, and then quivered into, "Er ... hardly. The nurses, you know, in the emergency room said she had a ruptured bowel. Is she okay? I'm representing her interests."

Suddenly, Tipton grabbed the stained lapels of the man's suit like an accordion, his sinewy forearm muscle and tendon gathering in the cloth. Tipton snarled: "I'll bet you're the greasy slime ball that stuck the electric dildo up her, aren't you?" He shot a quick look at Ned, "Quick, call security."

The man's shoes were nearly off the ground. For a moment his bulging eyes were even with Tipton's as he struggled in the vise-like grip. "If you don't let go of me, I'll have you arrested," he spit venomously. "Arrest ... hell! I'll sue your ass for assault, infliction of trauma, humiliation ... you name it!"

As Tipton disdainfully released him he straightened his coat and tried to become an inquisitor.

"Now, Dr. Tipton, to make things easier you will please answer my questions. What kind of device was this you found? What any other form of evidence present? Did this woman say anything of an accusatory nature? I ... I demand to see my client!"

But Hal's bulk blocked him from the recovery room. He eyed him like a predator stalking game, eyes locked on the target. His soft, direct speech betrayed a methodical wrestler's frontal assault and simple Nebraska roots.

"You're not her lawyer." It was not a challenge, just laid out as a statement of fact. "This woman's never heard of you! In fact, our patient doesn't even know what happened!" He shook his fist in the lawyer's face. "You get your ass outta here, you scum-sucking ambulance chaser, or I'll give you something to sue about, right now." His eyelid twitch motored up to full throttle as he advanced towards the lawyer.

Sensing that Tipton was now on the edge of losing control, the man cringed and looked wildly at Ned for help. "Jesus, man, he's threatening me! Help!"

Ned looked at both of them, not knowing what to do. Where was this covered in medical school? No one moved for a moment, and then the lawyer began to back down the hall.

"I'm not done here; and I'm not done with you either, Mr. Fancy Pants Intern. After I see my client, I'm gonna see how you'd like your ass subpoenaed in court!" And with that, he wheeled around and was gone.

Ned let out a breath in relief, but Tipton was still in a loose martial arts pose, his eyelid twitching. He turned to Ned.

"Did you hear what he called me? Did you hear what the little shit said?"

Ned looked at him with blank look.

"He called me an intern! I'll sue his ass for that insult—loss of consortium ... the whole nine yards."

They broke into laughter. It became infectious with the release of tension, and soon they were leaning, weak-kneed, against the wall.

Ned slapped Tipton on the back, "Scum sucking ... a scum-sucking ambulance chaser."

"Did you really like it?" Hal was wiping his eyes.

"It was outstanding."

"My version of Marlon Brando's movie, *One-Eyed Jacks*. The only thing that was missing from our scene was a chair to throw."

Hal threw his arm around Ned's shoulder and they walked down the hall, with their shadows following along the wall in the evening sunset.

Ned gave him a nudge in the ribs, "One problem with you, Tipton."

"Huh? What's that?"

"You're too nice to be a general surgeon ... scum sucker!"

September 2, 1971, 2:44 AM

In spite of the hour and the darkness, Ned Crosby lay wide-awake in bed. At 5:30 AM, three hours from now, he would rise to make his solitary rounds in the dark, stripping dressings, recording temperatures, and satisfying Immaculate Morgan's demands. However, in the bed across the room were muffled grunts and passionate moans, mixed with the sucking sounds of sweating bodies moving against one another.

Earlier, Blade Blackston had tiptoed in with his shoes off, with an amorous companion tittering behind. He had whispered that the "coast was clear," but she had reluctantly squeaked in return, questioning the bundle in Ned's bed.

It's only Crosby," an insistent Blade had whispered. "Sleeps like the dead ... We been friends for years ... slept through a house fire, once."

"Really?" she whispered, giggling as Blade greedily pulled her down beside him on the bed. Ned had glimpsed her silhouette when she entered, and he saw by the frizzy hairdo that it wasn't Beth. In the dark Ned heard them quickly stripping out of their scrub suits, and falling into a passionate frenzy. A half an hour later they were locked in a second wild embrace. The bedsprings were squeaking, covers flapping, and their bellies were lustily smacking together.

God grant me the serenity to be quiet, Ned prayed. He thought about their frenzied thrashing, and his mind wandered to the drugged and raped Bonnie Maylath up on the ward. Or ... good Lord! What about that Gravida Eleven welfare baby-factory, Rosie Delaney? How could anyone ... Never mind! *Where was the sense in it all, he wondered?* Here was damn Blade Blackston, acting like a rabbit. Yet when Ned saw him with Beth, it seemed all he could do was stutter and blush. Then Ned thought about Kathy, and for a moment his own lust ran wild. There was a muffled soprano gasp, a shuddering grunt, followed by a frantic whispering, "Jesus, Jesus, don't dig your nails all the way through to my spine!" Then, silence. Ned rolled over and made some coughing sounds, and sneezed once to encourage a departure. Twice, he could handle. Three times? No way!

The furtive sounds of kicking covers quickly followed. Ned heard a woman's insistent whisper, but Blade appeared to stretch out lethargically, ready to drift off to sleep. The muffled whispers in the darkness grew more insistent, and the rustling of covers more frantic. Finally a voice spoke rather firmly, "Vernon, I can't find them. Give me a hand!"

Without really meaning to, Ned stretched out both arms and began to applaud vigorously. She squealed in dismay, threw on her scrub suit, grabbed her shoes, and charged from the room. Ned buried his head in the pillow to muffle the laughter, but he heard her departing screech, "Sleeps through fires, huh? You bastard!" Then the door slammed shut, and peace and quiet returned to the darkness of Ned's on call room.

September 2, 1971, 7:30 AM

Dr. Farnsworth had four medical students in tow this morning as they entered the Two North extremity service. Ned and No Problem Jones had their little patient cards ready and in order by room number. Morgan's pressed pants looked as if they could stand up and conduct rounds on their own. Even Hal Tipton had attempted to clean up his scuffed sneakers beneath the baggy, rumpled whites. It occurred to Ned that there might actually be something to that rumor he'd heard that Neal had actually bought Hal a pair of new, whole shoestrings.

Farnsworth was pleased to see them on time, ready and waiting, and he gave Neal Morgan a little mock salute. "Good morning, Dr. Morgan?" The eyebrow crawled inquisitively up the forehead.

Ned wondered how you could ask "good morning" as a question, and understood why Farnsworth had been nicknamed "The Inquisitor."

"Good morning, sir!" Ramrod straight. Neal's reply was brisk and affirmative. He smiled back confidently.

"Let us proceed," Farnsworth gestured down the hall with a flourish of his hand, and they began rounds.

As they stopped at the first patient's room, Morgan's gaze swept knowingly over to Everett like a master signaling a well-trained dog. He said, "Dr. Jones?" and nodded towards Dr. Farnsworth, indicating that Everett should recite the particulars of the case.

"Mr. Julio Sanchez, sir." Everett pulled out his three-by-five card, "He's a twenty-nine-year-old male, admitted with cellulitis of the foot. He has juvenile diabetes, onset at age twelve, and is now insulin-dependent. Toes two through five have black tips, two open sores, plantarly, culturing staphylococcus, klebsiella, and some strep, Group D, sir."

Jones flipped the card over and began to recite additional information when Farnsworth's hand magically appeared in the air to silence him.

"Thank you, doctor." His eyes gleamed, and the bow tie bobbed on his Adam's apple. "Let us enter the room ... Oh, oh," he held up his hand, "not all of us." A condescending smile swept over the medical students. "Students look in. Doctor Everett Jones and I will gown and glove."

After the donning of protective apparel, they entered. The four medical students craned to see in, while Morgan paced and twitched nervously in the background. Everett peeled away the gauze, layer by layer, down to the inflamed, black and red foot. A putrid odor drifted to the doorway, and several medical students twitched their noses, looking at each other in disgust. Farnsworth looked the consummate academician as he surveyed the limb. His hands fluttered up and down the extremity, feeling Sanchez's pulses, and checking with the back of his hand the temperature comparison from one leg to another. Then he grabbed one black toe and wiggled it, grinning up at the patient, "Esta mucho dolor, aqui?"

"Feels fine, doc! Can't feel a damn thing down there. Nada." said Julio Sanchez. One of the medical students giggled at Farnsworth's gaffe. The patient lay propped up on one elbow, stroking a wispy black mustache, surveying his foot and enjoying the attention. He'd never seen so many doctors in all his life.

"Oh, you speak English. Splendid," said Farnsworth, affecting not to notice the error. He sat down. "Mr. Sanchez, how long have you been a patient here?"

"One week."

"And your diabetes ... Dr. Jones said since age twelve, right?"

"Right." Sanchez nodded his head. He had sallow cheeks, and his dark eyes flicked back and forth from the medical students to Dr. Farnsworth.

"How much insulin do you take?"

"When I get it from the free clinic, 40 of Lente insulin, and 20 of regular in the morning. Sometimes, I forget," Sanchez shrugged. "Sometimes ... sometimes when I'm in the orchards, picking ... well, you know if I run out, then ... nada!" He grinned.

143

"How do you check yourself?" Dr. Farnsworth asked.

Mr. Sanchez looked befuddled and then shrugged. After a pause, Farnsworth stuck out his hand and a surprised Sanchez regarded it for one confused moment. Then he reached up and they shook. Farnsworth gave him a fatherly pat on the shoulder.

"Mr. Sanchez, my friend, you'll have some hard choices to make soon. As the head of this hospital, let me reassure you, you'll get the best of care." He glanced up at Everett. "Redress the foot, please." Then they left the room.

The group moved down the hallway, out of earshot from Julio Sanchez. Dr. Farnsworth surveyed the group and his eyes settled on Hal Tipton. "Now then, Dr. Tipton. What do you think about this patient, Mr. Sanchez? What does our extremity service have in store for him?" The bow tie quivered.

Their eyes swiveled to Hal, but he held up under the stares and mimicked Neal's air of confidence. Without hesitation he said: "Obvious cellulitis, culturing staph, strep, and klebsiella. We got his diabetes under control with insulin, a sliding-scale urine check every four hours, and a finger stick for glucose every morning. He's on 10 million of penicillin per day, and 80 milligrams per kilo of gentamicin. His creatinine's two point two." He looked triumphantly at Farnsworth. "No ear symptoms. When his toes finish demarcating, I think localized amputations will be appropriate. Maybe in two or three days we can operate." He scanned their faces, looking towards Neal for approval.

Farnsworth's eyes darted back and forth among the group, probing and measuring. He inhaled a slow, deep, sucking breath, and rocked back and forth on his toes, almost as though he was chanting a mantra. Then the eyes fell again on Tipton, boring a little deeper into his soul.

"How are his pulses, Dr. Tipton?"

"Er ... uh, I guess in a twenty-nine year old they are okay, sir."

"Really! Do you know? Or are you just guessing?"

Hal's eyelid began twitching, "Uh, I didn't check, sir."

The bow tie bobbed. "Well now, Doctor Tipton. What about some of the signs of vascular insufficiency? What are they? Please address the medical students here." He gestured towards them with his hand, "What should these bright, new doctors be looking for in vascular insufficiency?"

Tipton sighed once, and put some new scuffs on his tennis shoes. "Well, sir ... I suppose ... uh, pulses, like you said. Then, um ... then ... hair. Yes! Hair, sir!" He blurted out, "If they don't have hair on the legs, it's a sign of vascular insufficiency!" He beamed, ignoring a bead of perspiration, which dripped from his nose. His beefy hands were clasped behind his back so hard the knuckles were white. His eyelid tick began to flutter so fast Ned thought Hal might go airborne.

"Yes, hair." Farnsworth's bow tie was in a low quiver. "Now, our Mr. Sanchez, Dr. Tipton. Tell us about the hair on his legs?" His left eyebrow seemed to arch even more inquisitively, running up his forehead onto the elliptical, shiny scar.

More perspiration flowed down Hal's face, and he wiped his forehead with his sleeve. "I don't know, sir. I don't know."

The bow tie nearly leapt from the Adam's apple. "Don't know? If you had been less meretricious and more propitiatory towards your team, you would learn about your patients." Dr. Farnsworth turned towards Jones, "Doctor Jones, can you tell us about the hair on our Mr. Sanchez's legs?"

Everett nodded. "He doesn't have any, sir."

"And what does that mean to you, Doctor Jones?" The Adam's apple quivered again.

"That he's got a significant compromise in his blood supply to the legs, sir. It's simple: No hair, no blood supply."

"Right!" The bow tie bounced affirmatively, and the rocking mantra slowed down.

"Of course," Everett thought out loud, "he's Mexican, and sometimes people of indigenous ancestry don't have any hair on their legs, anyway."

Farnsworth flushed beet red, and the bow tie jerked furiously. "So we've read up on people of indigenous ancestry, have we? Good. Very important. Each of us must be prepared to look at the whole of man, the True Man as the Taoists might say. Western Medicine can be so very ... so very ..." and here he paused and looked at a bewildered Jones, as though Everett was eagerly waiting with the answer on the tip of his tongue. "So very one-dimensional!" Farnsworth sighed, the rocking mantra now in a four-four rhythm. "So tell us, Dr. Jones, what should help us to determine the circulatory status of our poor Mr. Sanchez?"

No Problem slouched against the wall. "Well sir, like you said, pulses help. But in a young diabetic, there are probably good pulses anyway. He won't have atherosclerotic plaques at that age. Besides, diabetes is a small vessel disease. The bigger arteries aren't affected. I'd expect good pulses, and in fact, Sanchez is two-plus from his femoral artery on down, except for one-plus at the dorsalis pedis artery. He's got no hair, but he doesn't remember if he's ever had any. Both legs, though, seem very cold."

The bow tie settled into a low satisfied vibration, and a stationary Dr. Farnsworth smiled to the medical students. "Now students, write this down. Pulse strength, loss of hair, and surface temperature of the extremity," he flourished with his hand, "all are signs of limb viability—or the lack thereof." He glared over at Tipton, "There's more. Sensation! Sometimes diabetics lose sensation ... get diabetic neuropathy. Tipton?" The eyebrow quivered sideways at Hal.

"I don't know, sir. I thought his foot was painful. I didn't check."

Farnsworth snapped back, "He said, 'Esta no dolor, aqui,' doctor!"

Tipton stared at the cracks in the floor.

"Jones?" Farnsworth's eyebrow crawled the other way towards Everett.

"He couldn't tell when I put a tuning fork on his foot, sir," said Jones. "He couldn't feel the vibration."

"So!" Farnsworth surveyed the group. "We've got a juvenile diabetic with diabetic neuropathy who has black toes. He had no hair and cold extremities, right Jones?"

An affirmative nod.

"Tipton here ... excuse me," Farnsworth arched his back and raised an admonishing finger, "Doctor Tipton here, says in a few days we can snip the tips. Ha! Ha! Snip the tips!" The bow tie oscillated sideways, seeking a victim. He squinted at Ned's nametag. "Doctor ... Doctor Crosby! What do you think of that, Crosby?"

Ned shuffled nervously. "I haven't seen the foot, sir. Close up, that is. It's just our second day on the service. But the klebsiella makes me worry. It's an anaerobic organism. That means pus, er ... excuse me, infection, sir, in a closed space. A deep infection in his foot."

Farnsworth's eyes flashed around the room, and the Adam's apple and bow tie nearly ejaculated from his throat. "Yes! Yes, yes, yes, yes! Now let's ask our Doctor Tipton, what about Klebsiella, and lopping off little toes? What do you think, Doctor Tipton? Still ready to 'nip-the-tips' in two days?" He flashed a grin to the group, but his steely gaze seemed to pierce Tipton's brainpan.

Hal's eyelid had reached fibrillation, and now flat lined in a sideways quiver. "Well, sir, perhaps the klebsiella is a contaminant. It doesn't make sense, a bowel organism in the foot. I, I'll stand by, 'amputate the toes in two days.'"

"Anyone else?"

The bow tie darted around, but there were no takers. The eyebrow crawled back down to flutter over Farnsworth's eye. No one wanted to guess. Dr. Farnsworth let out a sigh, and clucked his tongue.

"Tsk, tsk. So much to learn ... so little time. Gentlemen ... er, doctors. The patient has gangrene. He had small vessel, peripheral vascular disease, which is secondary to diabetes. He is growing klebsiella. I repeat he is growing klebsiella. I mean you doctors cultured it, not me! He has a cool leg, no hair, and by tomorrow, Dr. Tipton," Farnsworth's posture arched erect and his voice raised several octaves, "I want Doppler readings on this diabetic's pulses, I want a discourse from you on the four fascial spaces of the foot, and I want your selection and reasons for why our Mr. Sanchez should have either a Syme's-type amputation, or a below-knee amputation! Is that clear, Doctor Tipton?"

Hal Tipton stammered and nodded, his eyelid twitching wildly. Lloyd Farnsworth and the awestruck medical students wheeled to depart. No Problem Jones shrugged sympathetically and looked at Tipton, who refused to return anyone's gaze.

Out in the hall, Farnsworth suddenly stopped and raised an index finger. The medical students trailing after him stumbled and collided into each other.

"Oh, and two more things. Did anyone notice that I sat down with Mr. Sanchez? Why did I do that?"

There was an awkward moment of silence.

"Well, I'll tell you," he glared. "It's a lot nicer to sit down with someone and demonstrate a little concern when they're going to need a significant amputation, than to stand impersonally and lecture. While the scholarly intellect may be able to analyze, only the soul can sense the deeper bonds that people may need. So read your Chang-

Tse! Secondly, Dr. Morgan. Your team needs more of your propaedeutic measures ... their failure falls on your shoulders."

And with that, they left.

To break the tension, Jones whistled through his crooked teeth, "Whooee!" He turned to Morgan. "Well, boss, what now? And what's propadeu ... propa ... whatever?"

A furious Morgan ground his teeth, and faced the group. "Propaedeutic. It means to give instruction. I need to teach you better. I had to look it up myself my first year of residency after Farnsworth had finished with me. What it means is that we all help Tipton," he hissed through pursed lips. "We finish rounds, see, then you and Hal go to the Library to study amputations, while Crosby and I do the Doppler studies." Morgan's granite visage stared down at them. "This surgical department may be a bitch of a pyramid program," he said looking at Ned, who flinched, "but we'll look after our own on my service."

Their remaining rounds were subdued. The shaken interns quoted their numbers, the bacterial organisms cultured, and the temperatures reported. Each patient's wounds were exposed for Morgan's approval. He liked the appearance of MacNulty's burns and requested that Jones continue the Phisohex-soaked gauze sponges, qid, or four times a day. He was even more impressed with the discovery of the three malingerers, and he curtly dismissed them from the hospital with a curled lip. He told them to "find a hotel in some other city."

Ned trudged off to find the Doppler device. He took a deep breath, and then sighed to release nervous energy. Jesus, was that teaching? It was a brutal game of one-upmanship, a game of ignorance and knowledge. *How much do you know? I know more! Oh, no you don't! Yes, I do!* It reminded him of his father's spankings which were always "going to hurt me more than you." Ned had been through eight years of higher education, and right now he felt like an idiot. Tipton had two more years than that, and yet he'd just been castrated in front of them all. *Why couldn't we just learn, without having to suck so much shit?* Ned wondered.

September 2, 1971, 5:27 PM

It was late afternoon. Everett "No Problem" Jones and Hal Tipton had returned from the library. The four of them were seated in Two North's small conference room. They went over the literature, which had been gleaned for pearls about Syme's ankle amputations, and below-knee amputations. Tipton had dug up an article by someone named Burgess who'd written about posterior-flap amputations and immediate prosthetic fitting. Morgan wrote down the data on Mr. Sanchez, and told the group about the patient's Doppler arterial pressure studies. They concluded that a below-knee amputation would be best. Tipton showed them a picture of a cross-section of a foot that illustrated four separate muscular compartments. He guessed that in Sanchez one or all of the spaces could be abscessed. If they were going to amputate, they'd better do it soon before the infection spread higher. Cutting the foot off might work, but going below the knee would be safer.

As the sun was setting, Morgan suggested they make "spot rounds" to check on the sicker patients, and to make sure everything was covered before morning teaching rounds again with Farnsworth. After their team's brutal first learning experience, Morgan wanted to batten-down the hatches, as it were.

Everett's favorite patient, the logger, MacNulty, kidded the doctors that he was teaching them everything they knew about burns. Morgan admired the pink granulation tissue on the burns, and announced that, in two days, skin grafting would be performed. MacNulty's eyes beamed over his vein-streaked, smashed nose. His gravely voice proclaimed that soon he'd be leaping over beds dragging a "training choker," getting back in shape for the woods.

As they wandered down the hallway, Ned heard Bonnie Maylath's voice rasp out from inside the room.

"Who are you?" Her throat was still raw from the anesthesia resident's less than skillful intubation.

Tipton opened the door. "Well I'll be damned!" he cried, and he darted into the room. There was a scuffle, a shout, and suddenly that same balding lawyer in the blue suit, who had confronted them outside of the recovery room, catapulted headfirst from the room. He tripped and struck his head on the chart cart. His scalp cracked, and a red blossom of blood flowed freely from a small cut, matting his sideburn. He seemed dazed for a second, and then whitened at seeing his own blood. He fumbled in his pants pocket for a handkerchief to compress the wound.

"This ... this is outrageous!" He hissed. He glared at the open-mouthed team. "He assaulted me, by God! I've got you as witnesses, and I, I'm ... I'm going to sue."

Hal stared calmly at him from the patient's doorway, cold eyes hooded like a cat eyeing a crippled bird. Only the clenched jaw muscles betrayed any tension. He coolly wagged a finger in front of the lawyer's face.

"No, no, no. What we saw, all of us," and he gestured around the hallway, "was you, tripping to hurry from the room when you discovered you weren't gowned, masked, and gloved. You hurried because you didn't want Miss Maylath to sue you for contaminating her wounds."

The stumpy floor nurse, Hilda, had come up to see about the commotion.

"Nurse, please call Security," Tipton told her. He turned in a ready stance back towards the bleeding attorney, arms loose in a martial state of readiness. The lawyer wilted. "Security is going to take you to the emergency room, since you accidentally tripped in our hospital. But if I ever see you on this floor again, I'll have you arrested ... but only after I help you back up a couple of times after you trip again."

Two burly guards with nightsticks arrived, and Hal asked them to escort the man to the emergency room. But when he was safe from Tipton, he twisted in their grasp and spat on the floor. "I wouldn't let Jesus himself touch me in this cesspool of a hospital!"

"Suit yourself," said Tipton. He gestured to the guards, "In that case, throw this jerk out. But get his name and first file a report for trespass."

Curiously, throughout this confrontation, Neil Morgan seemed passive, almost awkward, as if afraid of personal confrontation. His domain was the power of intellectual academics. He dominated by overwhelming his opponents in knowledge and skill as a surgeon. Hal Tipton's power had been man-to-man in the real world.

September 3, 1971, 10:10 AM

Teaching rounds went smoothly the next day. They got through fourteen patients in an hour before Farnsworth gave his mock salute, signaling the end of the day's lesson. He'd been impressed with the handling of Bonnie Joe Maylath. He quizzed the medical students, and they took turns listening with stethoscopes to her belly. There were good bowel sounds, and her cecostomy was functioning. They removed her nasogastric tube. The group decision to perform a below-knee amputation on Mr. Sanchez was approved by Farnsworth, who agreed that the operation should be performed no later than the following morning. He had never heard of posterior flaps or a Burgess approach, however.

"Use the standard 'fish-mouth' incision, please, Dr. Morgan." Another mock salute. "A very nice erudition for the team ... You are to be commended."

An amputation was also scheduled for the heroin addict with the blackened hand, and Dr. Farnsworth agreed that, as the wounds were clean, skin grafting could be performed the next day on MacNulty. As he departed, however, the flourishing index finger was raised again, with more stumbling of the trailing medical students.

"Something about that Phisohex ...," he muttered. "Something makes me worry about that."

"Kills all staph!" Morgan's dark eyes beamed enthusiastically.

"Yes, yes, yes ... But I feel uneasiness, like I'm forgetting about something. I'll get back to you."

September 10, 1971, 1:03 AM

It was another night on call. Ned looked wistfully out the window, gazing at the flickering, warm glow emanating from the rows of lighted homes that lined the darkened streets stretching across the belly of the inner city. The soft haze of the streetlights diffused through a surrounding fog outside Two North, the pus service of the General.

Each illumination represents someone's happy home, he thought. The people outside this hospital were healthy, safe, and sleeping in their beds; they were warm and cared for by someone. It was one in the morning, and, inside the General, Ned had just finished changing Albert MacNulty's dressings. Tomorrow was graft day, and he'd promised Jones that the granulation tissue would virtually gleam, sans pus. He was astounded as Albert kept moving his arms around in their pins. He knew it had to hurt, and yet Albert continued twist and turn in an effort to help.

"In Alaska, doc, you learn fast: never watch another man work. You always help."

Another night in Hell, Ned mused, *doing what no one else would, saving the putrid lives and limbs of self-destructive people who didn't know how to care for themselves.*

MacNulty was a friendly oasis in this desert of self-destruction. Ned gravitated towards his warmth. Albert had become the ward pet: irascible, crafty, mischievous, and irrepressible. Earlier in the day, the floor nurse, Hilda, had run shrieking from the room. She'd terminated MacNulty's bath abruptly when, in spite of his traction pins and open burns, he'd managed to pop up an erection.

"Almost couldn't find enough blood left in me, doc!" he cackled, winking.

Ned liked to listen to his logging stories of Alaska. He had a way of "yarning," a mesmerizing voice that kept his audience spellbound. The end of the tale usually had some bizarre, obscene twist, followed by an eruption of bawdy laughter. Those eavesdropping outside joined in, because no one could resist a MacNulty yarn. He told Ned a simple tale of how he'd struggled in the rain for hours one day, changing the oil on a yarder that half hung out over a cliff in a logging camp. Even the other junkies kept quiet. *Now, how on earth could changing the oil in some damn machine be that interesting,* Ned wondered? And yet, he'd hung onto every word, just like the rest of them. It was a gift. Hilda had crept back into the room after MacNulty promised that his blood would "stay in his other head." The other nurses finally dragged her out for evening report at the change of shift.

Ned and MacNulty talked far into the night. He told Ned about lying on his back in the woods on a soft bed of moss, watching floating eagles, lazily riding the evening thermals. The raptors' musical cries echoed down to their young in rooks on dead hemlock snags at the ocean's edge. He described a breaching humpback whale crashing in the sound, throwing up salt spray with a million diamonds of reflected light.

"And the salmon, doc—blood red in their spawning colors ... so thick you could walk across the water on them."

The sounds, smells, and colors were painted so real that Ned could almost grasp them. He was never quite sure where truth ended and fiction began.

MacNulty winked, "Listen, lad. You know, they say the eyes are the window to a man's soul." His finger hanging in traction swung and pointed for emphasis. "That's the God's truth. Everyone knows, a man's a liar, and you can see it in his eyes." He winked again. What I seen, all those beautiful things, they was the food for my soul." He gestured with his arms, still hanging by the speared, antiseptic, steel pins. "Money ... I got none. But I'm rich, lad. What I seen, what these windows to my soul have gathered ... Ain't hardly another man so rich!" He sighed contentedly. "So tomorra', I gets some new skin. You snot-nosed interns gonna' learn some more off ol' MacNulty. Get some sleep, lad, and don't ever forget, find some time to feed that soul."

September 16, 1971, 1:27 PM

The days slipped by, and MacNulty's open burns were now covered with mesh-like webs of skin graft. Strips of his skin had been harvested from his thighs, run through a mesher, and then sewn onto the burns. His arms still hung in traction to prevent an inadvertent slough if a bed sheet were to rub against the grafts. Everett Jones painstakingly removed dressings, daily. He used Q-tips and peroxide to carefully tease the gauze away without disturbing the grafts. As he peeled away the bandages, he could hear the *thump, thump, thump* of Mr. Sanchez on crutches, hopping up and down the hall. Bonnie Joe Maylath was now walking with a nurse on either side, crouched over slightly to protect her still-tender abdomen. As she hobbled past, she gave Ned a brave smile, murmuring that she'd "kill for a shampoo or a bath." Ned laughed and gave an affirmative nod to the nurses. They settled for a sponge bath in her room and a shampoo in the sink.

Criminal assault charges had been filed against her employer. He had been arrested and posted bail. An assistant district prosecutor, who seemed about Ned's age, interviewed Miss Maylath and photographed her healing abdominal wound. He'd taken the "device" from the pathology lab as evidence. Ned had to go over the chart with the young prosecutor, explaining the medical jargon in lay terms to describe her injuries. He asked about the obnoxious lawyer, but the young prosecutor just shrugged.

"It's interesting. It turns out he's the brother of Miss Maylath's employer. He claims his intentions were the best, only to express concern and offer help. However, trying to get her to sign a release from damages isn't so innocent, and we may have a trip to the disciplinary section of the Bar Association for Mr. Colville's brother. He's been warned, and as long as he doesn't do anything further, there's not really much that we can do."

Bonnie chimed in that she never wanted to see this Toby Colville "ever again in a million years." But she also asked the prosecutor if she should get a lawyer and file a lawsuit against the employer himself. Yet another stranger had come by offering to sue him for her, leaving his card.

"Like buzzards circling meat," he scowled. "For now, let's press the criminal charges on your boss. Once he's convicted, you'll have plenty of time to decide what you want to do in civil court. Three years, in fact, according to the statute of limitations in this state."

Days, then a week went by. The addict with the amputated hand was discharged, and Mr. Sanchez's wound on the amputation stump was healing nicely. A prosthetist had come by to fit him with a trial limb. More addicts were admitted with infections, cellulitis, and dead fingers. Two patients with perirectal abscesses had been drained and packed.

MacNulty's skin grafts had an 80 percent "take." His blue eyes sparkled when he was told in the morning they'd have the traction pins removed. He was going to start physical therapy so he could learn to walk again. Ned and Everett Jones beamed. "You ever heard hay wire singin' down a bull block after a road change, boys? That's what I'm doing now. Singin'." MacNulty winked at them. They didn't have a clue what haywire or a road change was, but the way McNulty looked, it had to be good.

Ned noticed that the new horror stories on rounds didn't seem to bother him anymore. He and Jones had become immune to the self-destructive behavior, the whining, and the addicts with stinking pus, dead limbs, and tears of self-pity. He was reminded of a Zane Grey paperback he'd read long ago, about a cold cowboy on a horse in a snowstorm. The cowboy found refuge from the blizzard by finding a warm spot, deep inside himself, and concentrating on it to shut out the frigid environment. He likened himself to the cowboy. The horrors of the pus service were like the inconsequential stings of pelting snow. Deep inside, he concentrated on Miss Katherine Anne Lindstrom, of the ER. He'd shyly asked her, with his heart pounding in his throat, to have a beer down at the Lakewood. He could remember every word she said.

"What do you want to be?" she asked.

"Good."

"Good, at what?"

"I want to learn to help people, without hurting them. That's the first rule, you know. First, do no harm." Ned sighed. "Probably, I'll do something surgical. Just what, I don't know yet. How about you?"

"I'm already good." Her eyes flashed, accented by light blue mascara. Her smooth, graceful arms radiated health and youth. He wanted to run his fingertips over the curve of her shoulder, down her arm to linger, and touch her fingertips that gestured excitedly as she talked

"At ... at what?" Ned stammered.

"That's for me to know and you to wonder about." Her eyes flashed again flirtatiously. She pulled distractedly at a delicate white earlobe, and Ned resisted the immediate urge to bite it.

"I was being serious." Ned had a pained, intense look.

"So was I."

157

She threw back her head, and ran fingers through her luxurious, shoulder-length hair. Her eyes mocked him, and she furrowed her brow, mimicking his anxiety with a laugh. Then her gaze steadied, and as Ned slowly began to sink into her brown eyes, Freddie shook his shoulder and reminded him that it was two in the morning. They wouldn't mind leaving, would they, while Freddie closed up the bar?

Ned shook himself from this reverie, and began working-up another addict. Later, when he was finished, the team gathered in the conference room to review the day's cases.

Everett Jones burst in, "Somethin's up, man, I don't like what's going on with MacNulty. He's not right."

An annoyed Morgan glanced up, "What're you talking about? He's great! The pins come out tomorrow."

The look of fear in Jones' face was a long way from his No Problem demeanor. He grabbed Morgan's arm as he sat down to explain. "I don't get it. I went in to talk to him, but he was talkin' to himself. At first I started to leave, you know, figuring maybe he was dreaming or something. Hell, I didn't want to disturb him. But the jabbering didn't make sense, and so I kind'a shook his shoulder, you know, so's if he's having a nightmare, or something, I'd wake him. Man, MacNulty turns towards me, and his pupils were like pinpoints, teeth chattering and he's whispering through clenched teeth. He says, 'Get the bugs off of me!'"

Morgan dropped the chart work, stood, and paced back and forth. "Now wait a minute, Everett. MacNulty went through DTs over two weeks ago. Patients don't go through DTs twice! Let's have a look."

Their chairs screeched as the group bolted en masse from the conference room. They quickly gowned and gloved. Inside, they could hear the chattering of teeth while MacNulty's gravelly voice muttered and moaned. There was a metallic vibration from the bed-springs, jiggling steel pins, and the overhead traction. As they entered they could see that the covers had been kicked away. MacNulty lay naked on the bed, his pale limbs trembling like willow branches in the wind. Blotches of fresh blood and plasma were smeared where some of the skin grafts had rubbed off as his arms slapped together. A pungent, yellow stain of urine spread slowly from his groin. They gazed in disbelief and, finally, Morgan stammered, "Jesus Christ, get the floor nurse, and get some Valium. Get them stat!"

Ned raced down the hall for help.

"Get his blood pressure and pulse, Jones, I'm gonna' try to talk to him." Morgan shook his shoulder, "Albert! Albert MacNulty! Wake up; you're having a bad dream!"

MacNulty's head was arched back, his eyes rigidly locked towards the ceiling. He looked like a vibrating, pithed frog. A froth of spittle dribbled down his gray-whiskered chin as his vacant pinpoint pupils drifted herky-jerky around the room. He muttered a rhythmic, raspy chant to the ceiling through clenched teeth, "Bugs, bugs, bugs, bugs ..."

Ned returned with a syringe containing Valium. He set it on the nightstand as Morgan gingerly held onto MacNulty's trembling arm, trying to avoid dislodging any more skin grafts. Ned stuck a needle in a vein and drew blood for electrolytes, glucose, and a hematocrit. Through MacNulty's IV, Morgan injected two point five ccs of Valium. The same rigid tremor persisted, so he gave him another two point five. After two minutes MacNulty still hadn't stopped vibrating, so Morgan gave him the rest as a bolus push. MacNulty sighed, letting out a deep breath, and the tremor seemed to stop. Ned raced out to run the tube of blood to the lab for stat analysis.

"Jesus Christ," Neal muttered, "I've never seen DTs twice in the same patient! What's his blood pressure?" Morgan had tried to cover up MacNulty's nude body, but then he remembered the urine-soaked sheets so he pulled them back and turned to Hilda, "Can we get some clean sheets, Hilda? We can all lift him, and help clean this mess off the bed."

Everett was shaking his head. He'd taken the blood pressure once, but blew up the cuff again for a recheck. "I don't get it. Its 250 over 118. He's always been low. Yesterday he was 105 over 75."

"Why's he hot?" Morgan said as he withdrew his hand from his forehead.

"He hasn't been. Jeez, Neal, he's been afebrile for the last six days!"

The two nurses were now outside the doorway, and one of them produced a thermometer while Hilda brought in clean sheets. They took a rectal temperature while MacNulty babbled on incoherently.

"104.6 degrees."

"Christ on a crutch ... 104.6?" Morgan nervously rubbed his eyes with his palms, almost hoping when he opened them again, like magic, this problem would disappear.

"You got it, 104." No Problem looked around grimly at the group.

Suddenly the overhead traction jerked and rattled as Albert MacNulty had a grand mal seizure. As the pin in his right hand ripped out of the bone, his traction weights swung and clanked together, crashing to the floor. Hilda had to dodge to keep from getting hit by the swinging weights. Blood-flecked slobber oozed from MacNulty's purple lips as he clenched and unclenched his jaw. He began grunting and gasping as he chewed on his tongue. Morgan forced his mouth open and placed a twisted washcloth across it to stop the chewing. Putrid, brown, runny stool oozed from his rectum onto the bare mattress.

"Goddammit, Neal, what's going on?" Everett cried in a broken voice. He was near tears. His wire-rimmed glasses were askew as he held onto MacNulty's free arm, trying to protect the remaining grafts. Many had torn loose with the thrashing, and blood flowed from torn-out pin-sites in his hands and elbow.

"Maybe it's hypoglycemia! Nurse! Hilda! Jesus Christ, hurry, please. Get us some IV glucose, stat!" Neal's face was a collage of bewilderment, frustration, and the need to act, to do something, anything, to regain control

Ned returned on the run. He skidded around the corner, hanging onto the doorknob to stop. "Neal, you won't believe it. His glucose is 860! His potassium is five point five ... and ... and the rest is normal."

Morgan looked around and ground his clenched teeth. "Shit! It doesn't make sense. Get me another amp of Valium, and you'd better get some bicarb, too. Hilda! Make it insulin, not glucose! I don't know what's happening. And, and ... goddammit, call the swamis. Call the goddamn swamis! We need help. Jesus Christ!"

Another grand mal seizure started, and Morgan climbed up on top of MacNulty, straddling his chest to hold him onto the bed. He held the twisted washcloth in MacNulty's mouth while the jerking continued. Ned struggled to get in more Valium, but the tetanic contortions had ripped out the IV line. Suddenly MacNulty stopped spasming, and began deep breathing great gasps of air. Then he stopped. Ned could never have imagined that the act of dying was so simple. One minute he sucked in a great gasp of air, and then it just simply leaked out. They called a code, and in a matter of minutes the hall was filled with the sounds of alarm and running doctors. The Two North "crash cart," with its EKG monitor and defibrillator, appeared as puffing orderlies wheeled it into the room. Morgan was on the bed, pumping on MacNulty's chest until they got the EKG leads on. An anesthesiologist stumbled through the crowd and intubated him from the head of the bed. But the code didn't work. For a split second MacNulty's eyes went pinpoint and then they dilated. In agonal incoherence he seemed to lift his head once, and as his head rhythmically jerked, his eyes swept around the room, settling on Ned. They went pinpoint once again and finally dilated for good.

Everett Jones sat in the corner in a state of shock. He kept picking up pieces of skin graft from the mattress and trying to smooth them out. The skin lay in a pile at the bed stand like a maca-bre, wrinkled, pink butterfly, crushed on a piece of sterile gauze. The EKG alarm sounded as a flat line ran on the strip. In spite of the code, the injected medicines, and the doctors' resuscitation attempts, they could not bring him back. He was pronounced dead at 4:47, pupils staring, open, fixed, and dilated to a shining light. Ned slipped in-between the crowded code team, reached down, and with his fingers, closed MacNulty's eyes.

Morgan was muttering and cursing, kicking through the strips of EKG paper and discarded ampules and syringes. "It just doesn't make sense," he muttered. "It just doesn't make sense. He was doing so well!" he pleaded, to no one in particular. The overhead page operator called his name, but he seemed to be unaware of it.

Ned wanted to get away from the horror of this event, so he crept down the hall to the nurse's station, and dialed the page operator.

"Call Dr. Farnsworth, stat. That's all the message was, doctor." The line clicked dead.

Crosby dialed the number to take the message, and Farnsworth's voice crackled over the phone. "That you, Neal?"

"Ah, no sir. Neal's tied up, and this is Ned Crosby. I just called to get his message."

"Oh, you! Good fellow, there, Crosby. Listen. Something's been eating at me about that burn fellow up there. I finally remembered an article in a medical journal I've just read. The authors reported that Phisohex, placed directly on a burn or on a mucous membrane, will be absorbed and go straight to the brain. The FDA is going to take it off the market. Too much absorption, it can kill you. You tell Neal to stop those Phisohex dressings, Ned. We want to help people around here, not kill them. Okay?"

"Yes sir, I'll tell him," Ned said numbly, and he hung up the phone.

* * * *

Ned closed the diary, and got up to stretch his sore back. Twenty-five years later, he still hadn't gotten over that one. A deep sense of guilt and betrayal probably still resided in every member of the team. Phisohex, in the late sixties, was used by millions of Americans. Every high school or college student with even a hint of acne or a zit laboriously scrubbed their faces day and night to rid themselves of the disfiguring, embarrassing blemishes. It had been marketed as an external soap, and thus, no one had asked the question, What happens if you use this, NOT as directed? *Like the drug Thalidomide, which produced deformed babies, there was no way the FDA could have predicted every conceivable use and misuse of a drug, given the infinite variations in human behavior. They focused on and tested drugs on the basis of what the drug was designed to do, not always on what it wasn't supposed to do. Who knew how many people had died or been harmed by misapplication of Phisohex on an open burn? Ned shuddered.*

As for Bonnie Maylath, she fared better than MacNulty. She recovered from the assault, and one month later had the cecostomy portal closed. Eight months later she testified in court against her employer, as did Neal Morgan under subpoena, regarding her injuries. He was convicted of first-degree assault, and given one to five years in the state penitentiary. Bonnie Maylath also prevailed in a civil lawsuit against him, but it was a meaningless victory because his brother had filed for Chapter 11 bankruptcy protection.

5

The Bridge Troll

October 1, 1971, 5:43 PM

"Nedley, my man. You're roomin' with a real surgeon ... a man of action." A magnanimous goodwill radiated from Blade Blackston. It was almost a palpable aura. He held his hands up to the light, peering at the fingertips, and then flexed and extended them. He experimentally wiggled a pinkie, and then used it to pop open a beer can. "These hands of magic performed surgery today. Did a hernia, that is, as in skin-to-skin!"

"Way to go, Blade!" Ned smiled at his friend's pride.

"My first case ... a reward for the work of two months on general surgery. The staff doc took me through it."

"I should be so lucky," said Ned with a sigh. "My reward has been to skin graft a junkie."

"Listen, Ned. When I first started cutting, I felt lost. But, as the layers of anatomy unrolled and I got over the heebie-jeebies of seeing someone bleed when I cut them, all of a sudden, I was, hell, I knew I was helping someone!" The Blade waved his arms wildly, "It was

165

almost ... almost better than sex!" Then the arms hung limply at his side. "Well, not quite that good, Ned. But you get the picture."

Ned laughed. *Ah, Blade,* he thought, *a man-child in an Adonis' body, motoring through life in conquest-mode.* He was nowhere near as lazy as someone with his looks and charm might be tempted to be. Ned had heard the rumors about how hard Blackston worked, and how he literally lived in the ICU for three straight days, pulling through an elderly, Polish immigrant with a ruptured aortic aneurysm. Blade had just refused to let him die. First the "save" on Pediatrics and now the aneurysm patient. Next, his first hernia operation. Blade was approaching legendary stature for an intern.

"Now tell us about Miss Beth, oh expansive, great surgeon," said Ned. "Are you still bedding every other woman except the one that makes your little heart go pitty-pat?"

The Blade's cheerful mood was punctured. "Miss Beth wants to play hard to get," he said crossly. "To show her the meaning of hard to get, this boy has been performing overtime." His full grin came back for a fleeting moment, then pursed and vanished. "Can't say it's been all work and no fun."

Ned turned back to the morning comics. The Phantom had just shot the guns out of the hands of the cigar-chomping thugs, rescued the Princess, and was accepting the village treasure to build an orphanage in Jjomba. Life was good.

October 2, 1971, 10:30 PM

The two residents were arguing in the emergency room. It was 10:30 on a Monday night, and their voices began to raise an octave in frustration and anger.

"It's a dump! You're dumping this nauseating, disgusting patient on us because your delicate internist's nose can't stand the stench!" Neal Morgan was bristling with a seething, barely concealed rage.

166

"A dump? No, Dr. Morgan, a patient is not a dump!" Dr. Sylvia Brigham's shrill voice patronizingly trilled back. She was the chief resident on the medical service (The Head Swami, in Morgan's derisive lingo). Her thick tortoise-shell glasses didn't obscure closely set, glaring, blue eyes that bore back at Morgan. Ned thought they looked like fighting bandy roosters, circling angrily and ready to charge in and peck. Sylvia had close-cropped ebony hair, stood six feet even, and wrapped her considerable girth in tight black skirts that swished as she stormed around the hospital in tan Hush Puppies. She reminded Ned of the proverbial class brain, the obnoxious fat girl in the back of every high school class that always had her hand in the air to answer the teacher's question.

Morgan glared and spat back, "This is straight medical, and you swamis don't have the guts to handle your own damn problems!"

"Problems? I'll ignore your derisive little nickname for an honorable profession, and remind you that gross cellulitis with a temperature of 102 is somewhat more than a medical problem! It's a problem, all right ... a problem for the extremity service!" She folded her arms in finality.

"One hundred and two, my butt!" exclaimed Morgan. "It's at 102 because he's in DTs; he has congestive failure, and pneumonia. That little red rash on his leg is peanuts compared to his medical problems."

Ned Crosby sat on a litter, bemusedly swinging his legs and enjoying this contest of wills. Next to him sat David Hazelette-Warner and Dave "Lunch" Lefke. Lefke had been discussing his interpretation of the international classification of erections. Across the emergency room, on a litter, lay the inebriated, insensate object of this quarrel. He was a bridge troll, brought to the hospital by a police paddy wagon and hastily dumped at the ER entrance. They were termed trolls, grooms, gomers, or PPP (piss-poor protoplasm) ... eventually they all found their way to the interns of the General.

The departing police, who were originally going to bust the troll for vagrancy, had quickly changed their minds. They told the admitting nurse they estimated he'd been drinking wine under a bridge for at least two weeks. Finally, they thought he'd been lying in his own feces and vomit for at least three days. His salt and pepper beard was matted and filthy with dribbled red wine and green bile. His tan work pants were board-like, smeared with an aromatic, brown, caked stool.

Two orderlies had been sent out with a litter. But after a tentative, nauseating look, they scurried back into the emergency room to don gowns, masks, and gloves. The troll muttered and gasped as they maneuvered him onto a litter and wheeled it into the ER. Cries of disgust followed the fetid odor as he wheeled past the triage desk and into the main ER. The man's breath came in shallow, ragged rasps. A cloud of lice and fleas hopped over his face, crawling down his eyebrows, and leaping like broad jumpers onto his matted beard. The orderlies used large bandage scissors to cut him out of his stiff, stinking clothes. These were thrown in a plastic bag for incineration. A portable, stainless steel bathing tub had been wheeled up. They filled it with hot water and a flea-killer called Kwell to scrub the patient down and destroy the lice and fleas.

Dr. Brigham suddenly settled the dispute by doing an abrupt about-face, walking out of the room, and declaring to no one in particular: "The patient has an infected leg and will not be admitted to the medical service. Dr. Farnsworth will be notified if this patient's infection is not taken care of."

Morgan stared at her retreating figure and yelled in a rage, "Goddammit, come back here and argue! I'm not done yet!"

David Hazelette-Warner slid off the litter, scratched his bird's nest head, and flashed a relieved Cheshire cat grin at Ned. "Guess that solves my problem for the night. My condolences, doctor Crosby." He turned to run after his chief, breaking wind in stride.

Lunch Lefke skipped gleefully after him, also grinning sheepishly back at Ned. "Cheer up, Ned. Things could be worse. You could be stuck on a medical service with an intern from Harvard who farts all the time." He tried to smile sympathetically and added, "Well, look at it this way. Sometimes you lose," he said, gesturing towards Hazelette-Warner's disappearing back, "and sometimes you lose big!" this time gesturing toward the bridge troll. He broke into a malicious cackle and glided out the door.

Ned saluted back with his middle finger, and shook his head in disbelief. He couldn't believe their pus service was getting the dump. Here was a guy in obvious congestive heart failure, probably going into DTs, and the medical resident had simply walked away.

"Just like my damn wife," Morgan came up and muttered. "Try to discuss something intelligently, and she makes some irrational statement and leaves." He glared over at the troll, his fists clenched in frustration. "Hmmm. Ned, I've got some bad news for you."

"I know, I know. Life's a stacked outhouse." Ned looked askance.

"You got it." Neal tried to suppress his grin.

The lice and fleas had crawled up and hopped onto the troll's head, which was the last part of his body above the Kwell bath. The orderlies cursed, slapping the fleas off their gloved hands and arms. They shrunk away from the troll, shedding their gowns and gloves and throwing them into the Kwell bath as well. "Nuff 'a that shit!"

The troll's breathing became even more labored now, broken by phlegm-racked coughing fits. Suddenly a glob of phlegm caught in his throat and he choked, turned blue, and sank beneath the Kwell suds.

"Holy shit!" Ned's eyes grew big as he jumped up off the litter.

"Somebody grab his head." Neal thundered.

"Grab it yourself, man!" The orderlies slunk away.

"Sweet Jesus, call a code."

The alarm for the code rang, and footsteps sounded as nurses, an anesthesia resident, and two unwary ER interns came running to help.

Ned had grabbed the troll's stringy beard, and pulled his head out of the bath. "Ah, Christ," he muttered. He reached in a finger and manually cleared a glob of phlegm from the man's airway. Fleas and lice started hopping up to escape the deadly bath, and crawled onto his hand. He looked around helplessly at the group. "Shit, can't someone get a tube ... pleeaase? Can someone get a tube?" He quickly switched hands, and with a vengeance, plunged the first one with the fleas on his fist under the Kwell bath. "Die, you bastards!"

Gloved hands tentatively approached. Extending from them was a laryngoscope and tube. A grim-faced Morgan guided them. The anesthesia resident sat dumbly on a stool, white-faced and frozen, looking wide-eyed at the hopping fleas. He kept muttering, "No way, man. No way."

"Hold him up, Ned." Morgan eyed the gaping mouth lined by yellow, broken teeth and ulcerated gums. Escaping fleas hopped over to the tube. "Goddammit, shit." Morgan concentrated on the patient's epiglottis and larynx. "Hold him still ... hold him, hold him ... there!"

With a quick thrust, Neal shoved the tube down his windpipe. He quickly inflated the cuff on the tube to seal it inside the trachea. In one sweeping motion he put two wraps of one-inch adhesive tape around the troll's head, with a doubled loop around the tube. The airway was now secure. A ventilation bag was attached, and Morgan squeezed it a couple of times and breathed for the patient. He looked over at Ned, who was still hanging onto the matted beard. Their eyes met with instant recognition of the same thought. "Why not?" They both grinned in unison. They covered the troll's mouth and nose, and plunged his head under water. Now only the tube stuck out. Two fleas hopped up to the top of the tube, but Neal flicked them vehemently into the Kwell bath.

He grinned again at Ned. "Helluva way to make a living, huh? The noble pursuit of medicine, and all that. Uh, Ned, this patient we're caring for, he does have a pulse, doesn't he?"

Ned wasn't sure if he should be smiling or crying. He nodded, and a bitter chortle escaped as he plunged his other hand back into the Kwell bath. "Never, Neal. Never did I think, in a million years, that I'd see you slip a tube down a flea-ridden bridge troll's throat."

"Yeah, so what," said Morgan. "Anyway, don't forget that life's still a stacked outhouse for interns. This is a hierarchy, and you, as the low toadie, are ordered to mind this troll as if he was your best friend." Morgan paused reflectively for a minute. "However, that's not the kind of healer I am. Nope. You and I are going to bring back this troll together. We're gonna' trim the beard, balance the electrolytes, clean the stool, and hydrate the dehydration. We're gonna' groom this guy if I have to spend every night up with him for the next week." Neal had a far away look in his eye. "Yep, that's what we're gonna' do."

"But why?" asked Ned, unable to keep the skepticism from his voice. To his mind there was an incongruity here. Neal ran a tough service, but an altruistic Albert Schweitzer he wasn't.

"Because," said Morgan, his eyes aglow with mischief, "when he's better I'm gonna' walk him up to that damn swami, Sylvia Brigham, and we'll have him say 'thank you' to Miss goody two-shoes Swami for refusing to take care of him!" Flickering behind Morgan's mischievous eyes was a steely, determined look that suggested the execution of pent-up vengeance.

They dragged the troll from the bath, and the sheepish orderlies returned to help. Ned drew blood for laboratory analysis and inserted a Foley catheter up his penis. A urinalysis showed concentrated urine, suggesting dehydration, but a chest film showed pneumonia with an enlarged heart and signs of congestive failure. Ned started an IV with D5 and quarter normal saline with 40 milliequivalents of potassium. He also gave the man an intravenous bolus of digitalis to help strengthen his heart. Neal suggested that 20 milligrams of Lasix be shot into the IV, to dry out his lungs.

Ned looked up from the lab data that a nurse handed to him. "Neal, his liver enzymes are off the chart!"

"What'd you think?" Morgan snapped. "His liver is five fingerbreadths below the right costal margin."

"His crit's 32."

"Chronic iron deficiency. Severe malnutrition."

"Albumin is one point one."

"M. O. S."

"M. O. S.?"

"More of the same, stupid."

"Oh."

They cranked the head of the litter upward, propping the troll's head on pillows. Orderlies and nurse's aides dried him off, thoroughly cleaning his beard and matted hair. He lay wheezing on the bed like a drowned rat in its last, agonal gasps. Ned tied leather restraints to his hands and feet, but as the man had regained consciousness, he twisted agitatedly against the ties.

"Easy, fella'. Everything will be just fine. You gave us quite a scare. Don't struggle now, just relax."

Ned tried to comfort the troll, but he wheezed and kept pointing at the tube down his throat with one hand in the restraints.

"Oh, you want that out?"

The troll nodded fiercely, his bleary eyes tearing over vein-streaked, ruddy cheeks. Ned stuck a syringe on the suction tube to deflate the inner cuff, pulling the tube out as the troll hacked and coughed. He spat out bloody phlegm. Ned used a towel to wipe the spittle from his chin. "Easy now. My name is Crosby. Doctor Crosby. What's yours?"

The troll lay for a moment, sucking in weak, panting gasps of air into lungs that sounded like gravel, rattling before answering. His voice came out in a rough whisper. "Jesus Christ ... Where am I?"

"This is the General, sir. What's your name?"

The troll's blood-shot eyes darted around the room suspiciously, peering out from under shaggy, gray eyebrows. He rubbed at his runny, broken nose, which bent towards his left vein-streaked cheek.

"My name," he wheezed, "my name is Bernard Kingston. Bernie. You can just call me Bernie."

"Bernie, listen. You're at the General Hospital. You've been on a drinking binge, living under a bridge for quite awhile. Sir, how long do you think you were under there?"

The troll held up a tremulous, gnarled hand, flexing wiry tendons under wrinkled skin, and shakily grasped Ned's sleeve. "What's the date, doc? What month are we in?"

"It's October, October the second."

Kingston sighed. "I been under that bridge since August eighteenth, the day I lost my bakery. I been living under that damn bridge for almost two months!"

"What've you been eating?" Ned asked.

"Eating?" Kingston grunted petulantly, laughed, and then coughed up more phlegm. He leaned out over the bed rails and spat on the floor. "I been ... gettin' by." He winked and touched his broken nose.

Ned groaned. Two months! Jesus! They were in trouble for sure. This man was probably far sicker than they realized. Who could guess what would happen: alcoholic DTs, congestive failure, a seizure from electrolyte imbalance? They could all occur in the near future. Damn that Sylvia Brigham! Ned remembered someone saying that the mortality rate from delirium tremens was around ten percent. He rapidly questioned Kingston about his health history and performed a physical exam. When he was done, he scrubbed the man's infected right leg and dressed it with an antibiotic ointment. He decided to gently wrap the spindly but puffy limb in an Ace bandage for some therapeutic compression. Then he started nasal oxygen at three liters per minute. As a precaution, he threaded a large Intracath IV line up the right arm vein for a central venous pressure line. He added multivitamins and thiamine to the IV bottle. And finally, he double-checked the restraints on all four extremities. There was a little slack, but they could be tightened further if and when DTs occurred. Ned felt like a ship's captain battening down the hatches in front of an on-coming gale. Mr. Bernie Kingston was calmly snoring when the orderlies took him up to the extremity ward for admission.

October 4, 1971, 11:12 AM

Acrid, bluish smoke drifted up and across the operating room spotlights. Hal Tipton's nervous eyes darted up to Ned, and then back into the wound. They'd been working for an hour. Immaculate Morgan had poached another case. It had happened this way: Drifting through the ER, he'd overheard the triage nurse directing a patient to the appointment desk for the general surgery clinic. A quick investigation led to the discovery that the patient had chronic drainage from a pilonidal cyst. Standard procedural channels were bypassed, which was normal for a poacher like Morgan. The patient was admitted to the extremity service for an "emergency" debridement of the "infected" cyst. Morgan was merely taking care of his own. He'd thought that Hal Tipton would enjoy the opportunity to do an elective surgical case other than another skin grafting or an abscess popping in their junkie population.

Their patient was a twenty-eight-year-old white man, intubated, and lying prone with his chest propped up on pillows on the operating room table. His buttocks were squared-off with operating drapes, centered over the pilonidal cyst. An earlier injection of the cyst with x-ray dye had showed multiple channels, honey-combing the sacral region above his buttocks in an area about three by five inches.

Immaculate had warned Tipton regarding the high rate of recurrence in cyst excisions. "Get it all out, Hal," he had said, smiling encouragingly. "I'm going to see some consults and prepare for grand rounds at the university while you and Crosby do the surgery."

That had been an hour ago.

"What do you think, Ned?" Tipton's anxious eyes peered over the mask across the table.

Ned gazed down into the hole of the resection. It was an elliptical wedge, now about seven inches long and three-and-a-half wide at the base, going straight down to the spinal sacrum. They shuddered when they heard a clunk, as an Israel retractor Ned was holding touched solid sacral bone.

Ned shrugged insecurely.

"I don't know, Hal. I've never read about or heard of a resection of a pilonidal cyst before. I can tell you one thing for sure, though."

"What's that?" Tipton's eyes flicked up nervously.

"Don't cut out anymore. Jesus, what a hole! You've gone right down to his sacrum. Did we cut any sacral nerves? Do you know if his flexor bendus will still become a dingus maximus?"

"Very funny, smart alec. Those nerves are all on the inside, anyway. At the worst, he'll have a numb butt." Tipton buzzed another bleeder with the cautery.

Ned looked at the hole and shuddered involuntarily. "Jesus! This guy's first bowel movement is going to be murder!"

They started to close, but the tissues seemed so stiff and woody that the gap wouldn't come together. The smaller gauge sutures kept breaking each time they tried to tighten the knot down. Tipton asked for number one silk. "Might as well get 'El Ropo,'" he grinned. They each started to sew at opposite ends of the fish-mouth incision, where the wound wasn't quite as wide. The thicker sutures helped to bring the skin margins together, especially when Ned pushed on the sides of the wound while Hal tied the knots. In the middle, the bleeding gap remained.

"Let's pack it open," Tipton ventured. "We can come back at a later operation if we have to, and pull things together even more during the week or two that it'll take for healing to occur."

"You know, you might need a Plastic Surgeon to help close this, Hal," said Ned grimly.

Tipton didn't answer, but continued stuffing four-by-fours down the wound. Ned saw Tipton's eyelid twitching again. They sealed the wound with two-inch strips of adhesive tape, turned the patient over onto a litter, and waited for the anesthesiologist to extubate him.

Ned was busy writing orders, but Tipton just stared off into space. He sighed and muttered unintelligibly as he rubbed at a two-day growth on his beard-stubbled face.

"What's up?" Ned asked.

"Oh ... I don't know. Maybe I'm just too tired." Tipton's smile showed through the fatigue, but his fingers drummed nervously on the desk. "Listen, Ned. I'm outta here. I was up most of last night, and it's time for me to go home."

"I know the feeling," Ned grinned. "There've been times when I would have killed for some sleep, but I had no choice except to stay awake. The next day I'm up all day doing scut rounds, and finally, when I collapse on the bed, I'm dying for sleep. The only problem is, I'm so wound up with anxiety, and my mind is whirling along at ninety miles an hour. I keep replaying everything I've done that day. I wind up dreaming all night about complications because of some imagined screw-up. Then I wake up exhausted. Take Dr. Crosby's feel good cure, Hal: go home, have a double scotch and you'll be out like a light."

"You've convinced me," Hal grinned. "See you on morning rounds." He walked out, stiff-legged with rummy, glazed eyes, ready to find his family and to seek dreamless sleep.

For Ned, though, that entire night was a nightmare. It started out quiet, and he hung around the ER, hoping for a chance to talk with Kathy. She brightened when she saw him, and as soon as she had helped a patient into the x-ray department, she came over with a big smile. Ned was hoping that she was interested in more than idle talk. He liked to tease her about her worries on patient care at the General, even though he shared them tacitly.

"What inhumanities inflicted on patients have you witnessed this evening, Miss Clara Barton?" he chided.

Kathy smiled, "Nothing that an alert nurse couldn't step in and prevent." Her brown eyes twinkled. "And what has the great healer been up to?"

Ned stiffened his posture with mock self-importance. "Not much. I've just been helping Hal Tipton on a life-threatening pilonidal cyst resection." He caught sight of his sleepless face reflected on a metal tray at the nurses' station. "You know," he said, "if I ever manage to scrape off this stubble and clean up a little, do you think you might consider going out with me?"

Kathy's twinkle had started to turn into a more serious look when the ward clerk called her for another patient. He heard her casually toss over her shoulder as she left, "Yes ... well, we'll see." But before she was out of sight she turned again just to see if he was watching her, and to throw a final barb. "Surgery on a pilonidal cyst won't exactly win you the Nobel Prize in medicine."

Their banter was interrupted as an ambulance screamed in with a forty-two-year-old, gay male in shock with gram-negative sepsis from an ischio-rectal abscess. The patient was delirious with a temperature of 105 degrees. It looked like a giant, ripe grapefruit was growing out of his buttock.

Ned frantically did the history and physical as they wheeled the litter up to surgery. A crash intubation was followed by Morgan's immediate number 11 scalpel stab in the buttock. This resulted in a gushing jet of gray-brown pus. The stench was overwhelming.

While he and Morgan evacuated the abscess and irrigated the wound, a nurse wearing a mask poked her head through the door. "Is there a Dr. Crosby here? Oooh ... nice smell!"

"That's me, boss," Ned smiled up at her over his mask. "Just suckin' on pus and hopin' for a call."

"Real nice. Uh, well your very own pus floor called. They asked me to tell you that patient with the pilonidal cyst excision? His dressing is drenched with blood. His heart rate is 110."

"One-ten." Ned thought for a minute. "What's his pressure?"

"Just a minute." The nurse disappeared, and then her head poked back around the corner of the door again. "It's 106 over 65."

Ned looked up from the rectal wound. "Tell them to reinforce the dressing with ABD pads, and wrap a six-inch Ace bandage around his waist. I'll be up in a bit, and spin a crit. If his pressure goes below 100, call me stat, and start two units of plasma."

Morgan had finished irrigating the abscess hole near the patient's rectum with antibiotic solution, and he was now stuffing large gauze packing up the abscess space. "What's that all about?" he asked irritably.

"Oh, it's that pilonidal cyst patient you poached for Hal from the ER," said Ned. "I guess he's bleeding from the wound. I'll check him when we finish up here."

"That damn Hal," Neal muttered under his breath. "He can't seem to get anything right." Ned got the impression the words were meant for him to hear. "How old is that guy, Ned?"

"Twenty-eight."

"Be careful." Morgan grimaced as he felt around inside the patient's rectum to make sure there hadn't been a rectal perforation.

"Why?"

"In a young guy like that, he's sure to have good, pliable blood vessels. If he bleeds a lot, those vessels can contract down, and keep his blood pressure up. His pulse'll be a little high, but you'll think that since the pressure is fine, why worry? All of a sudden, crash. He's bled into shock. His pressure drops like a ton of bricks, and you're in trouble. Shock city."

"Guess I'd better get up and see him." Ned started to step away from the operating room table as the final dressings were placed over the wound.

Morgan took off his mask and grinned his patented crocodile grin. The lips were up in a smile, but you knew nothing nice was going to come out of the mouth. "Yeah, you should. But after you write the orders on this case, and after you dictate the operative report," he snipped back to Ned in a falsetto, "handle the scut, doctor; handle the scut." He gave him a wicked grin.

The phone rang again in recovery room. Their ward clerk called over to Ned to pick up the phone. Now head nurse Hilda on Two North reported that the patient's pressure had dropped to 94 over 60. His pulse was 136, and his respirations were 46. Jesus! The guy was going into shock!

Ned raced up the back stairs to the second floor. Daily rounds with Immaculate had strengthened his legs, and he arrived at the top barely breathing deeply. The night nurses, Hilda and Charlene, met him at the entryway to the ward. They were pacing nervously at the stairwell doors.

Ned had developed a soft spot for the stumpy, gray-haired Hilda. Her face was a landscape of wrinkles contoured into smile lines around a perpetual, wry grin. Her common-sense approach had already helped him out of many a jam. Ned figured that Hilda had probably forgotten more about patient care than he would ever learn. She would pretend to think out loud, questioning the intern's treatment possibilities in a noncommittal manner. Somehow Ned had caught on that she was actually helping them stay out of trouble, as she pretended that the young doctor had thought up the new orders. Whenever Hilda called, Ned knew he'd better listen. She was a lifer in the General with a heart of gold.

"What kept you?" she scolded.

"I ran all the way!"

"I guess I still get jumpy," she apologized. "Ever since Mr. MacNulty, well ..." she pursed her lips and sighed. Ned knew what she meant.

"Come you gabbers, let's get going!" Charlene grabbed Ned's arm and marched him down the hall. She was a wizened, silver-haired nurse also nearing retirement. As she pushed him down the hall her skinny, arthritic knock-knees churned to keep up with his longer legs.

They swept into the patient's room, for once not bothering to gown or glove, since he didn't have an infection. Ned glanced at the chart. Kasperson, Steven J. Twenty-eight years old, and, amazing for the General, no major medical problems. The wispy goatee made him look like a young, redheaded Uncle Sam. Ned thought all goatees looked bizarre, but who was he to critique the appearance of a prize, non-junkie patient with no pus?

"Mr. Kasperson? Steve Kasperson?"

Kasperson groaned and rolled his head to turn and look back at Ned. "That you, doc? Sorry I can't move. My ass is killing me!"

He lay on his side, curled fetally, facing away from them. He was panting. The reinforcing Ace bandage was drenched with blood, which seeped down from it and onto the bed.

Ned eyed the bloody, dark red dressings, and looked back at the nurses. Hilda had already hung a bottle of plasma, which was running wide open. "Let's draw blood for a stat type and cross, and I'll do a finger stick for a hematocrit, as well. Give him 12 milligrams of morphine, I.M., because I want to undo the dressings and look at the wound."

Hilda and Charlene darted out of the room. Almost like magic, Charlene reappeared with a finger-stick kit, syringes, and test tubes for the cross match.

"Steve, give me your hand." Mr. Kasperson rolled over onto his shoulder, and stuck out his hand. Ned grasped the index finger and poked, "A little stick."

"Ouch!" Kasperson complained.

"Sorry ... okay. I know fingertips are sensitive. Uh, Charlene, give me a tube."

While squeezing a drop of blood from the finger, Ned placed a capillary tube next to it and the blood rose straight up the tube. He squeezed again to get a back-up second tube, in case the first one broke in the centrifuge.

"Got that tourniquet?" Ned turned again to Charlene for a large rubber tourniquet, which was wrapped around Mr. Kasperson's arm. "Hold still, please?"

"Damn! You guys are turning me into a pincushion. Why'd you stick me twice?" Kasperson tried to smile bravely, but there was an undercurrent of anxiety and annoyance flickering in his eyes.

"I didn't. That was once." The syringe filled with blood, so Ned pulled the needle from the vein.

"Yes you did—once in the finger, and once in the arm." Hilda grinned knowingly at Ned across the bed, as if to say touché.

"Er ... well, you're right. But ... but we needed different tests and that's why the two sticks."

"Oh."

"In fact, here comes a third stick. Hilda's going to give you some morphine in the butt, so it won't hurt so much when I look at your wound.

181

Hilda's eyebrow was raised skeptically at Ned, but not so the patient could see. Then she was all business as she plunged the needle into his lateral buttock and injected the morphine.

"Ouch!" he cried again.

"Steve, I don't know why you jumped," kidded Ned. "That didn't hurt me a bit."

The patient's angry, confused look dissolved into a smile at his wry comment.

Ned sprinted down the hall to the little lab on the ward. He placed the capillary tubes in the centrifuge and turned it on. While it was spinning, he paused to reflect. Really, the patient and Hilda had been right. Kasperson had been stuck twice, unnecessarily. In fact, if he'd planned it right, the three sticks could have been one. Ned could have drawn the blood from the vein, getting extra for the capillary tube hematocrit, and the morphine could have been injected intravenously at the same time. Instead, Ned had hurt him needlessly. Damn! Were all the other interns making the same stupid mistakes he was? When was he going to get some common sense? The timer on the centrifuge stopped, and Ned lifted the cover. He lined up the tubes, one at a time on the little paper scale with a grid to measure the hematocrit. Eighteen! Jesus, the guy had bled out at least six units!

Two at a time he leaped down the stairs. Down into the bowels of the hospital he ran, clutching the tube of Kasperson's blood protectively to his chest. On the B floor, he entered the dank hallways of the hospital tunnels. Huge pipes carrying gas, steam, and water stretched down the darkened corridors, clanking and hissing in an eerie disconcerting symphony. Dusty yellow strips of loose insulation hung down from the ceiling. There was a scurrying scratching sound as a small shadow disappeared into a darkened corner. No wonder the nurses hate these halls, Ned thought.

Down the corridor he ran until he reached the blood bank. Breathing hard, he passed the tube to the attendant. "Careful with it please," said Ned, trying to keep the panic out of his voice. He also tried to appear in control, trying to convey enough urgency and authority to produce quick results. "I need four units, type and cross, stat. I'll take whole blood, preferably, but I'll take whatever you've got! Stat! Okay? Stat!"

Next, it was sprint back up the stairs. It was four flights from the bottom, and by this time Ned was gasping. Hilda and Charlene were waiting at the doorway again, and without saying a word, Hilda opened up some sterile gloves, and Ned put them on as they marched back down the hall.

Steve Kasperson was having a great time! His respiration was still labored, but he didn't really care. Wonderful stuff, morphine ... Ned asked him to roll onto his belly. Charlene had giant bandage scissors ready, and with a flourish and a swoop, Ned cut through the Ace compression wrap. He peeled off the layers and gazed down into the bleeding hole. There were no pumping arterial bleeders! There was nothing but red ooze, everywhere.

"Damn! I was hoping I could find something to cauterize or tie off, and presto, that's the end of the bleeding problem!" Ned complained out loud. "Uh ... maybe I'd better call Neal."

Ned told Morgan over the phone that the patient had lost lots of blood, but he couldn't find anything actively bleeding. Morgan sounded annoyed as he said, "Listen Ned, there's an old surgical saying: 'All bleeding stops ... eventually.' Pack his wound back up, reinforce the dressing, and get him to lie on his back to help put extra pressure on it. Give him the blood when it comes and you'll be okay." Now his annoyance increased, "What the hell kind of hole did Tipton put in him, anyway?"

Ned laughed nervously. "Uh ... let's just say the Grand Canyon's reputation is still intact." Ned chuckled again, this time with relief. "All bleeding stops, eventually. What'll they come up with next, Neal?"

There was a sudden anguished shriek on the ward, so loud, that even Neal heard it over the phone.

"What was that?" he barked. Ned turned a questioning look towards Hilda.

Hilda, in turn, looked to Charlene, and she ventured, "It sounded like it came from that new patient, Bernard Kingston's room." Another anguished shriek sounded.

"Oh, shit."

October 18, 1971, 8:31 AM

Lloyd Farnsworth's bow tie was dancing around the semi-circle of people standing outside the patient's room. They were in the usual "choir" formation, with medical students in front, then the interns, and as usual, Dr. Tipton and Immaculate pacing on the periphery. Farnsworth conducted: "Now students, delirium tremens can be very dangerous. There are several stages of DTs." He surveyed the group. "Dr. Crosby?"

"Yes, sir."

"What's the first stage?"

"Well sir, I guess an alcoholic, when taken off the booze, will seem alert but agitated. He'll get quite irritable and real shaky. That's the first stage."

"And our Mr. Kingston, Dr. Crosby? When he was admitted, what stage was he in?"

"That first stage, sir."

"What then, Dr. Crosby? When that first stage is confirmed, what does it adumbrate?"

"Sir?"

"Foreshadow, doctor. What does it foreshadow?"

"The next stage is alcoholic hallucinosis, or, basically, hallucinations. That's what happened to Mr. Kingston at about 11:30 last night. He accused us of sending in a large orderly to kill him. He was

184

still restrained, but he began screaming and struggling to get out of bed. We gave him IV Valium to calm him down."

"Very good, doctor. Now students, does anyone know what 'rum fits' are?" The bow tie bobbed inquisitively.

A freckled medical student meekly raised a hand, "Er ... seizures, sir?"

"Very good ... that's Heinz, isn't it?"

"Yes sir."

"And how about full-blown DTs? Delirium tremens?" The bow tie flicked back and forth, from face to face.

"The most dangerous part of alcoholic withdrawal, sir," Ned volunteered. "Agitation, confusion, hallucinations, seizures, tachycardia, and sweats. The mortality rate can be up to ten percent."

"Ah ... Dr. Crosby. Have you applied for a surgical residency yet?" The high-handedness of this digression from teaching students left Ned reeling. This naked display of power in front of students, peers, and the residents seemed inappropriate. Ned saw Tipton's eyelid twitching out of the corner of his eye, and he flinched with embarrassment.

"No sir," he mumbled through gritted teeth.

"Come see me before you decide," said Farnsworth. He turned back to the students, "By the way, we get the sickest patients, and so the mortality in our institution has been as high as twenty percent. A reflection of the indigent, severely ill, patients we get, students; not a reflection on the type of care." Farnsworth's smile seemed to solicit a laugh, and several in the group dutifully came up with a giggle.

They entered Bernard Kingston's room. He was strapped down onto his bed. The consummate teacher, Farnsworth turned to the students as he gestured towards the patient.

"Now here we have a case of full-blown delirium tremens. Notice the patient's tremor."

That was an understatement. Bernie's body was vibrating like a dried reed in the wind. His knees and hands flapped and slapped against the bed. Pipe stem arms with sagging, sallow flesh struggled and writhed against the leather restraints. His chafed wrists and ankles were rubbed raw and bleeding, in spite of the protective padding in the restraints. His body was bathed in sweat, and his breath came in ragged gasps.

"Mr. Kingston? Mr. Kingston?" Farnsworth deftly leaned over the patient in a brief interval between violent tremors.

Bernie twisted towards the sounds of the call, then screamed and cringed away from the group. Farnsworth jumped back, startled as well.

"Get away from me!" Bernie hissed. "I know who you are ... and you're not going to get me!" His stringy hair and beard were matted with sweat. His yellow, blood-shot eyes rolled wide with fear like those of a bawling calf.

"Who am I?" Dr. Farnsworth smiled reassuringly with a knowing look at the students.

Kingston's glassy eyes rolled. "Ha! I ... I know who you are. You think you can pull that crap with me? No sirree! Not on ol' Bernie. You think you're gonna' get me, but you ain't!" He grimaced at Farnsworth, and snarled like a mad dog; then he whimpered and cowered before unseen demons.

"Notice the rapid speech through clenched teeth, students. I don't know why, but it's characteristic. If you're treating a suspected alcoholic and they start talking rapidly through pursed lips or gritted teeth, push the Librium or Valium and get some restraints ready, because DTs aren't far behind."

The group collectively sighed as they departed, moving on to the next room.

"Do we need gowns for this next patient?" Dr. Farnsworth turned to ask Morgan and Tipton.

"No, Dr. Farnsworth," answered Morgan coolly. "Dr. Crosby?" he raised his authoritative eyebrow at Ned, prompting him to give the history.

"Mr. Steve Kasperson, sir. He's a twenty-eight-year-old male with a draining pilonidal cyst. He presented yesterday with ..." Ned ran through the history, the surgery, the episode of shock, and the resuscitation with two units of plasma and four units of blood.

"What's his hematocrit, now, Doctor Crosby?"

"Uh, it's 32 this morning, sir."

"Let's see the wound."

They filed into the room. Dr. Farnsworth shook Mr. Kasperson's hand and introduced himself and the students. He sat down at the bedside, and made small talk, his bow tie bobbing congenially.

Mr. Kasperson's eyes lit up with the concern and attention. "I was kinda' scared last night," he said, "but Dr. Crosby took good care of me, and I feel better this morning." He looked over at the medical students. "Hope none of you get pilonidal cysts!"

They laughed nervously, though Ned saw two of them discretely feel their backsides.

"Now, Mr. Kasperson, would you mind if we checked your wound?"

"Gosh, no, doc. Just don't hurt me, okay?"

Dr. Farnsworth smiled reassuringly, and gave him a friendly pat on the shoulder. He then looked over at Ned. "Dr. Crosby?"

Ned produced some bandage scissors from his jacket pocket. After the patient had rolled onto his belly, Ned cut through the Ace bandage. He then donned some sterile gloves and pulled away the ABD pad and the four-by-fours. Soon they were gazing down into the sacral hole.

Dr Farnsworth's eyes dilated, his nostrils seemed to flare for an instant, and his mouth dropped open. The bow tie seemed to arch out over the wound and drooped down his Adam's apple. He nodded curtly and turned to the students.

"A healing pilonidal cyst excision, students. Not much to see, really. Very uncommon, though. Rarely need excision. That'll be all for today. Students, meet me tomorrow on the medicine ward at 7:30." He shooed them from the room. Then he turned to Morgan and spoke curtly, "I want you and your team in my office in twenty minutes." He abruptly wheeled and left.

Tipton looked around at the group, white-faced with his eyelid twitching on high flutter. "What's up? What'd ya think, Neal?"

But Morgan looked grim. "Just what he said, in twenty minutes. Get the wound covered up, Ned, and let's finish up."

They sat nervously in Dr. Farnsworth's office. Morgan and Tipton sat in the paired chairs in front of his walnut desk. Ned and "No Problem" Jones stood behind. They'd been waiting for over half an hour. Perspiration ran down Morgan's and Tipton's faces, and the latter's eyelid twitched continuously.

"What d'ya think's up?" Jones whispered.

"I don't know," Ned whispered back, "but Farnsworth sat down again with the patient. Whenever he does that, somebody's screwed up."

Dr. Farnsworth burst through the swinging door, white coat flapping, and his distracted face seemingly preoccupied with a thousand and one thoughts. He pursed his lips, sat down behind the highly polished walnut desk, and made a cathedral out of his fingers. Sunlight streamed through the windows, reflecting from the ellipsoid scar on his scalp.

"Now then, doctors." The bow tie bobbed up, and he smiled congenially at Ned, the rapier, for the moment, hidden. "Doctor

Crosby, can you tell me what you think about our pilonidal patient, Mr. Steven Kasperson?"

Ned looked around the room. "Well sir ... uh, I really don't know. I've never been involved in resecting a pilonidal cyst, before. I didn't even know what they were until yesterday. I'm sorry I let him bleed down into shock. I didn't know ..."

Farnsworth grimaced and waved him quiet with an impatient hand. "Doctor Morgan," There was a pregnant pause.

"Uh ... Yes, sir."

"Where were you during surgery?"

Morgan shifted uneasily in his chair. "I was seeing consults, sir."

"Busy poaching, again, Neal?"

"No, sir."

Farnsworth shifted quickly in his chair, his fluttering fingers drumming on the armrests. "I really don't know quite how to say this. I've been out walking ... walking and thinking. I've been trying tai chi, to find my center, to compose myself if you will, so that I don't lose my temper. My teaching rounds are deliberately acerbic. People under stress can learn better than when no expectations are placed upon them. In a teaching institution I expect everyone to have foremost in their consciousness that I'm watching, that I'm going to challenge them, and that I'm going to always be ready to force them to account for their actions."

Several jaws clenched tighter as he went on.

"I have just witnessed a great travesty ... the mutilation of a human being, done innocently in the name of medicine."

There seemed to be an infinity of silence for about 45 seconds.

"Doctor Tipton."

"Yes sir." Tipton's voice was hoarse, as though he could hardly get out the words.

"Why did you operate on that man if you didn't know what you were doing?"

"I ... I don't know, sir. I guess ... I guess I thought I could do it."

"Do it!" Farnsworth exploded. "You cut out half his back, right down to his sacrum! Do you know what you've done?"

Tipton's eyes were downcast and he was incapable of responding.

"Good Lord! We're going to have to get Plastics to close this man's sacral area, and hope they can do it without swinging a large skin graft. You cut right down to his damn sacrum!"

Farnsworth's cathedraled hands spread and he rubbed his face. His hands pressed at his eyes and he then pulled his palms away, appearing startled, almost as though he expected them to have vanished. He turned to stare at Morgan. "Doctor ... Doctor Morgan."

"Yes, sir."

"We've always given the chief resident on my service the judgment call on whether or not to bring in an attending staff surgeon. This is a lugubrious task for me, but as of this moment, you will never poach, never steal another service's case. Your rounds and your consults will be confined to the extremity service, and, you will use an attending surgeon for consultation, for the duration. You will supervise any and all surgery in the operating room. Is that clear?"

"Yes, sir."

October 27, 1971, 5:25 PM

They were at the beach. Ned had wanted to go jogging, to let off some steam. The ever-present stress, the constant needling, and the testing by Morgan and Farnsworth, let alone the incessant subordination to the residents, or the whining, irritating demands of the self-destructive addicts had finally begun to wear him down. Kathy had suggested Kamiakam State Park, twenty miles north of the city.

"It's peaceful, and at this time of the year, no one's there," she smiled.

Miss Katherine, as he now called her, had made it clear that she disliked traditional movie-and-dinner dates, and that suited Ned just fine.

He left her spreading a blanket behind some boulders on a grassy slope, while he went exploring. The park brochure claimed the south shore had an excellent three-mile sandy beach, "suitable for all ages and activities." Ned kicked off his shoes, and began to run along the beach in a sweatshirt and swim trunks.

It was a large lake. A brisk north wind had kicked up, creating small waves, and Ned found the blasts of air exhilarating. As the waves crashed, spume and the freshwater smell of the lake blew in with the on-shore breeze. Sea gulls mewed and cried overhead, swooping and wheeling in the wind. A Kingfisher hovered momentarily in the air before it dove like a rocket for a fish. He felt like he could run forever. He wanted to fly, to leap to freedom, and to leave the burden of the General behind. The brisk autumn air was exhilarating, and it seemed to be mainlining power into his churning legs. His feet smacked and splashed on the firm, damp sand as he ran, dodging driftwood and rocks, running up the shore. After twenty minutes, Ned came to a flowing creek that entered the lake, and so he reversed directions and ran back.

Kathy had curled up out of the wind, nestled in between some boulders, where she was reading a book and catching the last warmth of the late afternoon sun. She waved her book as she caught sight of him returning, and he waved for her to get up.

"Oh, Miss Katherine ... Miss Katherine?" Mischief danced in his eyes.

She closed the book carefully, marked her place, and jogged out, keeping pace with him as they ran along the sandy beach. An auburn sheen streamed out behind her in the wind, as the sun flashed on her chestnut hair, rippling in the on-shore breeze. Her face was alight, and her dark eyes flashed. They dodged in and out, running around pools, galloping and playing. The mist from blowing lake spume caught on the soft down of her cheek.

Kathy seemed an unnerving bundle of attractive contradictions. One minute she bossed Ned abruptly around the ER, and the next, when they were alone, she seemed a vulnerable little girl. When the on-call phone rang at night, she never gave him the chance to question sleepily or argue about the need or wisdom of coming down to see a patient. "You're needed in the ER, stat!" Click. "There's a patient here who must be seen, stat!" Click. "ER, doctor. Stat!" Ned could never argue with a dead phone. Aloof and all professional at work, she was invitingly warm off duty. He felt like he was being toyed with, and yet he found he was reluctant to be drawn into the shallow pattern of romance and desire that had betrayed him in past relationships. He wanted some control, to not hurt or be hurt.

The snappy autumn air and the joy of physical exertion had cleared Ned's mind, and the furrows and worry-lines seemed to fade from his face. He was flushed with excitement, and he shouted as a wave smacked into their legs. Kathy giggled as he stumbled in the lake, and he fought to keep his balance. He kicked foam and lake water on her in retaliation. His lungs burned from the extra exertion, but the crisp air made him feel almost like he could fly. Electricity surged in his veins. He strode out, stiff-legged, and pretended to glide past her effortlessly. Spray clung to her tee shirt, revealing her to him. She laughed and pushed him as another wave hit their knees. He stumbled again, but caught the water with both hands, and threw it over her. She shrieked with laughter, kicking water back at him, and then another wave caught them and they both fell. One minute they were both having a furious water fight, and suddenly, in the next, they were locked in a frenzied embrace. She suddenly sprang up, aware that they were in a public place, and made him stop. They walked back to the blanket.

At the boulders they basked in the last rays of the setting sun flashing on the western horizon. Kathy shuddered once, and pulled Ned's right arm around her tightly.

"You cold?" he asked.

She looked up, and Ned could see her eyes glistening. He let himself be drawn deeply into her gaze.

"Not cold, Ned, just happy," she smiled. "I don't mind telling you, Ned Crosby, I've fallen pretty hard for you. You've ruined my ER, which I've always run with an iron fist! I can't think or concentrate, anymore. Each time an intern comes down through the door in those damn, baggy whites, I think it's going to be you. And when it isn't, I keep seeing you, or wishing it was you. And I know I shouldn't be saying this, Ned, that I should be acting lady-like and all that, playing hard to get, but I guess I just can't help how I feel."

She wiped the tears away from her eyes and looked away, embarrassed. Ned was embarrassed too, but he pulled her chin back towards him, and kissed her tears, holding her and not saying anything.

During the ride home, she looked over at him, smiling quizzically. "Well, aren't you the quiet one," she commented.

"Sometimes it's better to not say anything," he ventured, rubbing his jaw thoughtfully. "I have a long and distinguished history of saying some really dumb things.

She looked over at him, a frown forming on her delicate brow. "Maybe I'm the one who just said the dumb things."

He laughed, and her frown faded a little. He wanted to say something witty, not something intimate that could be misconstrued and lead to pain. She seemed precious to him, and he did not want to hurt her.

As he turned off the highway, he tried to sound cheery but noncommittal: "For now, I think I'm content to just enjoy being with you, and to not be saying too much. Is that okay?"

"Well, Chatty Kathy," she chided herself. "I guess that's the way it's supposed to be nowadays. On the other hand, I'm not sure you're cute enough to spend the sexual revolution with."

He wanted her to explain herself, but instead of responding to his query, she hummed along with Seals and Croft on the radio, singing "Diamond Girl." Each time Diamond Girl sang, she giggled and pointed to herself. Ned drove on in a thoughtful silence. He parked in front of her apartment.

"Well, I guess I ain't much of a revolutionary, depositing you at your door with nothing but a peck on the cheek." He leaned over and his lips tentatively brushed at her cheek.

A rosy color crept up her face, but she pulled away to look him directly in the eyes.

"Listen, Miss Katherine," he murmured. "I mean it. I can't put into words yet how I feel. I'll just screw things up if I try. But the fact that I care about what it is I say to you must say something."

October 30, 1971, 9:10 AM

Ned, No Problem Jones, Tipton, and Morgan sat in the cafeteria.

"You got it?" they asked, looking to Jones.

"Got it, right here." Everett held up a large, department-store shopping bag.

"Will it fit?" they interrogated.

"It'd better. Otherwise, we're all out some money," Jones shrugged.

They continued eating breakfast. It was their last day on the extremity service.

Ned looked over at his chief. "Listen, Neal. In case I don't get a chance, the way things sometime get so damn frantic around here, uh ... thanks. I never dreamed I'd learn so much on a pus service. I know that sounds funny, but I really mean it." Ned stuck out his hand and they shook.

"Ditto, from me, Neal," Jones grinned, "Stick out your paw like a man and shake."

"No problem," Morgan grinned back. They shook hands around.

Warren came up to the group, and stuck his hand in as well. "Since you doctas is all shakin' hands, I figure I might as well join in. There any money in all this?"

The group broke up in laughter.

"I want to thank all of you, too," said Tipton with a formal air.

"Us?" said Ned. "We're only toady interns."

"No, I mean it."

They looked at him now.

"Starting tomorrow, I've resigned from the Department of Surgery. Effective from that day, I'm going into anesthesia."

"No!" Morgan wiped at his mouth.

"You're bullshitting!" said Jones flippantly, trying to cover the group's confusion.

Hal Tipton's face was calm, and Ned noticed that his eyelid was no longer twitching.

"No, I really mean it." He looked solemnly around the table. "I woke up at home last Sunday morning. My wife was still sound asleep, so I lay there in bed, listening to my kids in the living room, playing on the floor and watching cartoons on the TV. I realized that I hardly saw them anymore. They were going to grow up and not know who their dad was." Suddenly he grinned. "And it came to me. I got this great gestalt of myself, no longer as a surgeon, but as an anesthesiologist!" He turned to Ned. "You'll laugh, but it was your idea. You know you and that damn comic strip of yours: *When the Phantom hits them, they stay asleep for a long time!"*

They laughed at the ridiculous statement.

"I love surgery and surgical procedures. I could never be a swami. But ... but, I just don't have it in me to cut on people. You guys helped me realize that. So anyway, I called the anesthesia department, and since one of their guys has come down with hepatitis, they accepted me on the spot. I told Doctor Farnsworth yesterday." Tipton grimaced and rolled his eyes. "Man, did he fly into agitation. But then he suddenly said, 'Hal, perhaps this is propitious after all.' So that's me—propitious!" He surveyed them, a quiet, serene smile on his face. "The only thing is ... I've got to get a dictionary to find out what propitious is!"

They all laughed.

Morgan looked like a silent croaking frog, visibly restraining himself from speaking. Ned vowed to compliment him later on preserving the camaraderie of the group's last day. It was well known that Morgan believed those individuals not in surgical specialties possibly represented lower, subhuman forms of life. Neal glanced at his watch, then stood, and gave his patented, "We go," to no one in particular.

On cue, Jones and Ned raced out in front of him, sprinted up the stairs, and were both waiting, combing their hair in the fire hose glass case when he arrived on the second floor.

"Cute," He mumbled sarcastically. "Very cute."

The ward clerk brightened to see them, and the floor nurses came out with them to make rounds. Everyone knew it was their last day for the rotation, and for all their struggles, this had been a well-liked group. When they came to Bernard Kingston's room, Ned knocked on the door.

"Just a minute," came a nurse's reply. "We're applying the final touches." As they waited, Neil Morgan paced, ground his teeth and muttered. From behind the door came the "snip, snip" sound of scissors. But soon they called out, "Okay ... we're ready."

They entered and saw Bernard Kingston sitting on his bed, alert and clean in his hospital gown. Flanking him were Charlene and Hilda. Barber scissors and a comb lay on the nightstand. The wrinkled fireplug Hilda was combing his hair. It had been ten days since the delirium tremens had stopped. Kingston had been on hyperalimentation. It was a relatively new technique for the General, and was supposed to be reserved for malnourished patients with abdominal fistulas, vomiting disorders, or general emaciation. Morgan had been itching to try it out on someone. Over the last ten days, through a subclavian line, Kingston had received high doses of intravenous proteins, carbohydrates, and vitamins. He had gained twenty pounds. His sallow, vein-streaked cheeks had filled out, and robust energy radiated from a face that looked twenty years younger. With his gray hair carefully brushed and his beard and eyebrows neatly trimmed, he looked like a distinguished author or senior partner in a law firm. He grinned up at them with clean teeth and a sparkling smile, courtesy of two of the General's more enterprising dental students.

Jones stepped forward with the shopping bag. Out came a three-piece suit, a clean, white shirt, and a fashionable wide tie. They'd all chipped in to buy the clothes. When he'd finished putting on the clothing and stepped out of his room onto the pus ward, Bernard Kingston looked like an investment banker who had just made a killing in the stock market.

"Now you're all set, aren't you?" Morgan held him by the shoulder as they walked to the elevator.

"The Social Worker's got it all set up, doc. When I leave here, I go straight to the airport. My sister will pick me up when I land in Des Moines. She's already got a job waiting for me at a bakery."

"You don't mind doing this last thing for us, do you, Bernie? It's kind of—well, we here at the General want to make kind of an example of you, you know, to show other parts of the hospital the good work we do," Morgan patiently cajoled him.

Bernie flashed them a wide grin. "You boys helped me so much, I'm lucky to be alive. Just saying hello to some other doc is okay by me. Doesn't begin to pay you all back for everything you've done."

They climbed onto the West Wing's elevator, and, after it ground to a halt, all five of them stepped off onto the medical ward. Dr. Sylvia Brigham was in the middle of teaching rounds. Lunch Lefke and David Hazelette-Warner were presenting cases. Medical students listened attentively, and, in the background, Dr. Farnsworth interjected a point or two.

There was a sudden hush at this invasion of the surgeons. It almost seemed like a tightly formed naval formation of white coats had maneuvered in to offer a broadside blast. Sylvia Brigham turned her closely set eyes to determine who was intruding on her domain. She squinted suspiciously through thick glasses at the surgeons.

"Yes, Dr. Morgan? What can we do for you?" It was polite, but with a subdued shrillness.

"Ah, Dr. Brigham. I've brought you someone special to meet."

She eyed the gentleman in the gray, three-piece suit. "A guest professor? How nice. I'm Doctor Sylvia Brigham, chief of medicine." She extended her hand.

Bernard Kingston extended his, and they shook. "Bernard Kingston, ma'am." He gave her a deferential bow.

"Doctor Kingston ... Doctor Kingston," she muttered. "I don't remember a Doctor Kingston on our schedule as a guest professor ..."

"Er ... No, ma'am," said Bernie with an embarrassed chuckle. "I'm a baker by trade. Gettin' ready to go back home. These doctors just wanted me to meet you."

Morgan broke in: "Yes, we wanted him to meet you again before he left."

"Again? Meet me again?" Her suspicious eyes scanned Morgan's face through thick glasses. "Neal ... uh, Dr. Morgan. Kindly explain this interruption of rounds. I don't ever recall meeting this gentleman." Her voice had raised an octave or two, but still remained slightly below that of a blaring submarine's klaxon.

Morgan's black eyes bore through her like cold laser beams. He paused theatrically for a moment, letting his gaze sweep across their gathering. "Oh, but you did, Doctor Brigham. Oh, but you did! Mr. Kingston came in through the emergency room precisely two weeks ago in congestive failure, with pneumonia, dehydration, delirium tremens, and with cellulitis of the leg. You refused to take care of him. Through our care, Mr. Kingston here has recovered."

Sylvia Brigham leaned over and peered closely at Mr. Kingston's neatly trimmed beard and face. A flicker of recognition suddenly shown in her eyes, and her hand came up hesitantly to stifle a comment.

Mr. Kingston perked up, assuming that he'd done his duty, and said brightly, "Goodbye, ma'am." He looked at the group expectantly, his eyebrows bobbing as though wondering if he should ad-lib a few lines.

But before he could say a word, Morgan tapped his elbow and the group was on its way back to the elevator. As the elevator's ancient brass doors creaked shut and they descended, Ned rolled his eyes and whistled, "Immaculate, you drew blood, man. You drew blood."

Morgan's eyes narrowed. The forbidden moniker had been used. But the moment was too sweet to dwell on an ignorant intern's impropriety. Dr. Neal Morgan grinned a deep, satisfied grin.

"Poaching just has too many advantages to ever really give it up," he said. Then, watching the astonished look on Ned's face, he added. "Don't worry, Ned, I've absorbed the lesson of the last rotation. Maybe for now on we'll just poach medical patients."

October 30, 1971, 10:10 PM

Sal DeLuca had finally weakened. After the constant goading from his fellow residents, on top of the pressures of his own residency, he announced that the hospital's first EADR party (end of another damn rotation) would be that night at his house. Xeroxed announcements had appeared all over the hospital, and DeLuca's place was jammed.

Ned was sleep-deprived and rummy. The bubbles rising in a glass of sparkling burgundy mesmerized him. He peered at the bubbles, first from one angle and then another. He knelt down and squinted through the glass, catching the overhead ceiling lights. A driving bass rhythm vibrated though the house. Cigarette smoke swirled around writhing, dancing bodies. Nursing caps bobbed, stethoscopes swung, and residents and interns dressed in green scrubs and hospital whites lurched, danced, and clung to their partners in the pandemonium of the party. Sal DeLuca had squeezed-in every nurse, divorcee, graduate student and doctor that the house could hold. Dancing consisted of frantic jostling in the crowd, bumping, feeling, and insincere apologies.

Beer spattered the gyrating throng after a new keg was tapped, releasing a jet of foam. DeLuca nodded approvingly at some soggy blouses. "Just like skiing, eh? Keep them tips up!" His Italian wife's dark eyes flashed in anger and she kicked him hard in the shins.

DeLuca declined all their questions as to where a starving resident got the ability to afford a house with a pool and sauna in the back. Maybe he married it? Who cared? They were glad to enjoy a taste of the good life to come. There were squeals and cheers as familiar faces reappeared. Ned was becoming used to the transience of relationships in a teaching hospital. One could be a part of a team that endured very intense stress for one or two months, only to have the doctors disappear as the group dissolved into the next rotation. It was common to hear someone ask, "Whatever happened to ... what's his name ... you know, that guy who was on neuro with us?" Nevertheless, the forgotten residents who had come and gone wouldn't miss a chance at one of Sal's sauna parties. They were legendary.

DeLuca himself was in an outrageous, 1920's baggy, knee-length bathing suit, with huge orange and purple stars on a black background. A gold crucifix nestled on his chest like a baby golden sparrow nesting in a giant matte of black hair. He was drinking sparkling burgundy with the trauma team, and smoking another Cuban cigar. Johann Drinker, the Dutch medical student, had been true to his name and now lay spread-eagled on the couch, his mind somewhere on the fringes of consciousness. "Furball! Furball! Furball!" the chant came from the swimming pool.

"They love me!" DeLuca grinned at his skeptical wife.

Ned sighted him through the Burgundy bubbles. "We all love you, Furball."

DeLuca swung dramatically around the kitchen table and stood at the sliding glass door that opened onto the pool deck. He had the cigar in his mouth, and his arms upraised in a V for victory. There was a raucous cheer as his squat, hairy body tore across the patio deck and flung itself into the center of the pool. There were squeals of delight and dismay as poolside onlookers were deluged. He came up with his arms still in a victory V, the champagne bottle in one hand, and the droopy, watery cigar in the other.

Eleanor Hazelette-Warner was still wearing her scrub dress and white coat. David was on call, she explained to Ned and Katherine. Their apartment was a mess, and she'd spent the entire day shopping for groceries and cleaning. She was so engrossed in the trials of being a wife, housekeeper, and doctor that she was too late to notice DeLuca's sneak from behind. With a triumphant Tarzan yell, carrying the bottle of champagne in the crook of one arm and Eleanor in the other, he leapt and splashed back into the pool. They took turns with the bottle.

"Miss Katherine," Ned said dreamily. She gave him a kiss goodbye. She was wearing her nurses' uniform complete with cap and white hose stockings. She was due back at the General on night shift. He gave her a bleary smile. "I wanted to be more alert for you, but I was up all night," he sighed.

She whispered, "I wish I could spend this time with you. You look like you need looking after." She scolded him, "Now don't go throwing up in the house. I can't have you making a spectacle of yourself."

Ned lurched for her. "How about at least throwin' a nice kiss?"

She gave him a quick, teasing kiss. "I'm already late. For God's sake, Ned, have fun. Goodbye."

He stared wistfully after her parting form. He thought of her eyes, and her hair, and of the way she could light up the room with a smile. *She is too beautiful, too fragile to be alone in the ER,* he thought. In the ER was nothing but blood, bums, and danger. He wanted to be back there, to protect her. *Jesus,* he thought, *I'm getting screwed up from this booze.*

Friendly hands slapped him on the back and tousled his hair. Someone kissed him, and felt his crotch. *Was that Anita Gandrelli?* He staggered out the sliding glass door and onto the patio overlooking the pool. "Sauna, sauna, sauna ..." sounded a chant. *Maybe that's it,* he wondered. *I need to sweat out this damn alcohol, and sober up a bit.* He drifted over to the deckhouse and opened the entry to the sauna.

"Close the door, asshole!"

"Don't let the heat out!"

"Come on, man!"

Ned turned to face a swarm of stark naked nurses and doctors. In the middle was a mass of hair. "Fur ... Fur ..." he choked.

"You crazy, Ned? Get outta' your clothes."

"Huh? Oh ... ya, ya, sure." Ned staggered over to lean against the cedar wall.

"Yah, yah, Ned. You tink you fuck up in here, too?"

They howled at Drinker, whose mantis-like, spindly legs were draped over three women as he reclined against the wall.

"Come, Ned," Furball pronounced like a choir director, head uplifted on high.

"Come on," Drinker feebly waved him on.

"Come on, man!" came a chorus of encouragement.

Ned struggled out of his clothes. He hopped and stumbled around to their laughter, almost falling flat on his butt except that a hoard of helping hands reached up and steadied him. He stared up at a mass of bodies, and nowhere to sit.

"Room for one more up here."

"Huh?" Ned spun drunkenly to look for the voice.

"Get that little hard butt up here."

The group howled. It was Eleanor. She was naked, and leaning on DeLuca's hairy shoulder. She was wearing only a happy grin and a robin's egg blue hair ribbon. Wet, dark curls of hair drooped over her forehead. Ned saw two empty champagne bottles in the corner. He struggled up over the bodies to get to the second level, where they sat.

"Oops."

"Excuse me."

"Thank you!"

"Come again."

"I haven't come yet!"

"Hi, Eleanor."

"Have a seat."

"No room."

"Lap."

"Eleanor ... I'll crush you."

He was pulled down. The room seemed to swim. Glistening, dripping bodies were lathered in sweat. DeLuca told jokes, and many of the old tales of the General were told and retold. Then they made a mass charge at the pool, disturbing two people in a passionate embrace at the far end. There were giggles and curses. They moved en mass—red toes, bunions, runny noses, hairy butts, penises, and pink, flopping nipples—like a giant, pink and white, many-legged centipede back to the sauna, stumbling, laughing, bumbling, flesh smacking, again, into the cedar-scented heat. More lore and legends were passed around. There were wild tales of Farnsworth as a junior resident, caught with a surgical nurse in the on-call room by a jealous telephone operator who herself was trying to track him down. On the second mass exodus to cool off in the pool, Ned didn't leave. He was exhausted. He looked around to see Eleanor sprawled on the cedar bench boards, laughing. He staggered over. "You okay?"

She looked up at him, giggling, then suddenly drew his head down and kissed him deeply. Her mouth tasted of salt as her tongue flicked and probed between his lips. Beads of sweat dripped down from his chest, onto hers. He looked down at her small, wet, glistening breasts with jutting, little, pink nipples, and then back into her eyes. "You're ... you're married."

She firmly pulled his head back down with both hands, and kissed him again, hard and breathlessly. "You're ... getting bigger."

He looked down in dismay. "Eleanor, no. I ... I mean, we ... we can't do this. It's not right! How could you face David?"

She waved a hand in disgust. "David, Shmavid. Who cares? This is now. I need this." She looked down at him again. "I can see," she smiled, "you do, too."

He backed away, reaching down to grab up his trampled, soggy clothes, still crumpled in the corner. "Eleanor, it's no good. You're

204

married. It's ... I just don't do that. I really like you but ..." he gestured around, "this just isn't right."

Eleanor lolled back on the cedar bench. She smiled at him again, but this time it was with hard bitch eyes. "See ya' later, sunshine."

6

Only Fools and Duck Hunters

NOVEMBER 9, 1971, 7:27 PM

"Have another beer, doc."

A rheumy, cavernous, black socket squinted at Ned in the early evening darkness. Like an apparition, a beer can wavered in the air next to the remaining bloodshot eye.

"Jesus Christ, Blinky! Will you get the damn patch over that hole! You'll shake the doc up so bad, he won't be able to shoot."

Neal Morgan's father, Carl, groped across at Blinky from the driver's side. He tried not to take his eyes off the road as he twisted the eye patch strap around Blinky Walters' empty socket. There was some sputtering and unintelligible cursing while Blinky swatted away the helping hand. With a flourish, he adjusted the eye patch himself. In the back of the station wagon, a black Labrador broke wind and whimpered in the Port-a-Kennel at the sound of his master's voice.

"Shaddup, ya' damn dog!"

Ned mournfully reflected that this was possibly going to be one of the stupidest things he'd done in his life. Impossibly, they were on their way to hunt ducks, driving a shiny new station wagon, purloined with a lot of pleading and sweet-talk from Neal Morgan's wife. Morgan had gotten a chief from the university to cover for them, and then convinced Ned to come hunting with his dad and a guide. This meant using up one of the intern's seven precious vacation days. They were all packed up in the "frou-frou duck mobile," as Blinky had christened it. They squealed out of the ER's parking lot and headed east. Loaded with shotguns, a dog in a Port-a-Kennel, and beers bristling, they drove to renew the ancient, manly bonds of the hunting pack.

"You won't believe it, Ned," an enthusiastic Morgan had told him. "The northern ducks are down. Thousands ... no, hundreds of thousands! Big, fat, grain-fed mallards, all squawking and quacking, wheeling ... and then *blam!*"

Ned felt like a naive freshman during fraternity rush. Morgan's hunting invitation was part of Neal's persistent campaign to get him to commit to the general surgery residency. Ned was surprised and flattered by this "charm offensive" by a not-too-charming individual. He finally broke down and said yes.

Would the Phantom have been ungracious? Ned thought. *Never! But does the Phantom hunt ducks?*

Hours later they were crossing the mountains in a station wagon with a farting canine in the back and a broken-down, half-crazy, one-eyed duck guide in the front. Madness! He thought wistfully of what it could have been like to have a whole free evening with Katherine.

Blinky Walters was into his second set of yarns about duck hunting. The string-bean guide sprayed beer from a popped can, as he gestured and boasted about winning the 1967 state duck-calling championship. He derisively referred to his vanquished rival as "Big Dick" McFarland. "Ol' Big Dick tried this ..." and, "when that didn't work, Big Dick tried that ..."

"Blinky ..." Morgan reached over the front seat and grasped the wiry man's bony shoulder. "Blinky," Morgan insistently called.

"I thought he was tall an' his name was Dick," Carl added.

"Naw, his name was Ron ..." answered Blinky.

"Blinky!" Morgan's bark interrupted their cackling.

"Er ... what, doc?" Blinky twisted around, and fixed his single orb on Morgan. "I'm in the middle a' the state championships, see. Ducks is all around ... an' I got 'em comin' in with my feeding chuckle. Their wings is set, an' they're comin' round to land."

The older gray-headed clone of Neal Morgan, with a razor part on his balding pate, chimed in, "Keep 'em coming, Blinky. Keep 'em coming!"

Neal blurted out in exasperation. "Blinky! For Chris sake! You're spraying beer all over my wife's new wagon. She's going to kill me! Puleaaase! I promised her I'd return it to her in the same condition it was on the day she bought it. Now all this beer ... and even that damn windy dog of yours ... the smell is already atrocious." Neal looked out the window in disgust, muttering to himself, "So much for the new upholstery smell."

Blinky touched his nose, and flashed a yellow-toothed grin back. "Not to worry, doc, not to worry. Ol' Blinky'll be more careful." He slurped his beer and chuckled towards Carl Morgan, "Can't speak for ol' Magic, though."

More throaty cackling erupted from the two cronies up front.

Morgan glanced nervously over at Ned. "Elly will kill me. Damn, I can feel it coming ... death by strangulation." Then he grinned, "But what the hell. I've been wanting to do this ever since my dad took me, way back when I was ten years old." He shrugged in apparent resignation. "You got another beer in that cooler, Blinky?"

The dog let go again, and whimpered even louder.

"Sweet Jesus, Blinky! That one singed my nostril hairs!"

They rolled down the windows, and a freezing wind roared through the station wagon. Shivering, they rolled them back up as soon as the acrid smell had left. Carl Morgan grimaced over at Blinky, wiping his eyes. "You think we ought to stop and maybe let Magic sort of air out a little?"

"Naw ... ol' Magic is just fine. He always starts whimperin' when he knows we're goin' huntin'. Gets kinda' excited, you know. 'Sides, if we let him out here, he'll jus' shet on the car wheels. When Magic's doin' his business, he kinda likes to back up to somethin' and let her go. Never have figured that dog out."

Blinky chugged the beer, crushed the can, and threw the empty onto the floor. Neal Morgan winced as if he'd been stabbed in the back. He ground his teeth.

Blinky remained in his high spirits. "You docs lissen, now. You all know that highfalutin' scientific stuff on how to treat sickness and death at the hospital. What ya' don't know is that a patient might need a little friendship at home. A Labrador can ... a lab can add quality ta yer life. Cheer ya' up! Don't matter how bad the day's been, those dogs are always there, a waggin' their tails ta greet ya, wantin' to play, an' ta be your friend. Why hell, if it hadn't been for ol' Magic, I'd be a ruint man."

Morgan groaned. "I suppose if we don't ask, Ned, we'll hear about it anyway ... Now how's that, Blinky?" he trilled in a falsetto. "How was it you was almost ruint?"

"Funny you should ask, Doc." A single orbed, Cheshire cat grin floated back. "It were seven year ago. I still had my other eye, then." Blinky twisted around in the car seat to turn and talk to Neal. "Deep in love, I was. Like a fool ... Magic was just a pup, then, an' I didn't know 'bout his peculiarities, like, you know, needin' to back up onta somethin'. So I'm all set ta pop the question, right? It's a sunny day an' we got a big picnic basket in the park. Magic's rompin' around and retrieving sticks. Hell, ol' Laura an' me comes back from a walk fer to eat, and there on the basket, Magic had backed up and let her rip! God's truth, that damn girl lets out a shriek, an' then she kicked Magic right in the you-know-whats ..." Blinky solemnly raised a hand, like a Chief Justice administering the oath. "An' that, docs, was the end a' that!"

Ned decided it was best to try to drink himself into unconsciousness. Morgan, who crumpled in an exasperated heap, also chose oblivion.

* * * *

"Wake up, doc. Wake up. We're here."

Ned groaned and yawned. "What time is it?" he asked, crawling out of the backseat, stiff-legged. He stretched and twisted his stiff back. "Musta slept funny," he muttered. He almost tripped over Magic, who was busy wolfing down dog food in a bowl by the back bumper of the wagon. The dog growled at his leg, but its grizzled, gray snout never left the food in the bowl. "Do we hunt soon, or what?"

Blinky laughed. "Carl, we got to learn yer son an' his friend 'bout huntin'."

His arms were full of duffel bags and shotguns, and he struggled and stumbled with the awkward load, moving towards a small cabin. His eye patch was twisted off again, and in the darkness, Ned saw the black hole turn towards him.

"It's 11:30, doc. At night you drink, at dawn you hunt. Right now the darkness is a strong clue."

Neal's father put an arm around each of their shoulders and steered the sleepy doctors up a gravel road towards a large lodge. The parking lot out front was bathed with a flashing, red neon sign that spelled "Daisy's Resort." Hunting rigs, beat-up cars and rickety pickup trucks surrounded it. Painted below the sign were black, rusted letters on a sheet of steel proclaiming: "World Famous Hunting Resort. Waterfowling, Fishing, Guided Excursions. Cabins for Rent. Earl and Daisy Murdoch, Proprietors."

Carl Morgan gave Ned a pat on the shoulder and chuckled, "Boys, since its 'World Famous,' I think we should go in."

They wound their way through the parked rigs, and stepped inside to the cacophony of a raucous, red-necked, hunting bar. This isolated little "watering hole" was filled with a swirling crowd of ranchers, farmers, hunting guides, and tipsy hunters all looking for a place to celebrate Friday night. Country and western music blared. Like a crazy carousel, people were dancing and bobbing in pairs around the floor in battered, straw cowboy hats, camouflage vests, and "Can't Bust'em" denim work shirts.

Ned stepped hesitantly into a palpable wall of odors: stale beer, cigarette smoke, the wood-smell of a sawdust floor, and rank sweat. Blinky came up from behind and pushed them into the crowd. As they prodded and slid their way through Ned noticed that the walls were lined with wide board-and-batten planks, onto which were painted various hunting scenes: On one, a covey of frightened quail exploded from under a pointing dog; on another, ducks landed upwind in a blustery November marsh, and a majestic elk in a dark forest warily sniffed at danger. The artistry had an expressive, sensitive touch, Ned thought. You could see the fear in the quails' eyes. The artistry seemed kind of a surprise in a noisy, swinging Friday night joint like this, a touch of class.

Blinky's arm snaked out, and he caught a pretty barmaid, pushing through the crowd with a pitcher of beer in each hand. "Skippy, darlin', tell us where Earl is. I gots two young docs, needs their huntin' licenses."

The young barmaid flashed a shy smile, and then nodded her head towards the rear of the room. "Earl's in the office, Blinky. An' try an' keep that damn patch on this time, huh?" She got right in his face, sticking out her chin and glaring. "Last week when you were drunk, you started dancin' round without it. It was so gross, hell; I figure I lost a hundred dollars in tips, 'cause people took one look or got sick an' left!" She swept her appraising green eyes up and down over Ned, and then plunged into the crowd, pushing the pitchers ahead of her.

212

Blinky pushed them through the patrons. The tables were full so they settled in at the corner of the bar. Blinky disappeared into the back office for a second, only to emerge with the owner, Earl Murdoch. Earl loomed ominously over them, a giant of a man with a swarthy face, a huge, grizzled head of deranged hair, and a full beard sporting streaks of gray. His shirt was unbuttoned and open down his chest, which bristled with salt-and-pepper hair. Ned gaped. Earl Murdoch made Furball look like a gentile, fair-complected WASP!

Carl Morgan and Earl vigorously shook hands and traded back-slaps. Then the latter's dark eyes drifted over to Neal and Ned.

"Well, well, well. So Carl's brought the cub, huh?"

Neal Morgan squirmed.

"And the other one?"

Ned stuck out his hand to shake, wincing in the expectation of a bone-crushing grip from Earl's big paw. Ned had to open his hand all the way just to get around Earl's. "I'm Ned Crosby, sir, nice to meet you."

Earl's meaty hand was surprisingly gentle. The hairy mitt then drifted over and playfully cuffed Neal Morgan on the cheek, a cuff that, Ned thought, didn't seem quite so gentle.

"So! Carl's all proud ... An' he should be! Damn near ready to hang out a shingle. A surgeon, huh?" Murdoch's bushy eyebrows crinkled with a smile as he turned towards Carl. "Hell, Blinky, I can remember when this one sat with us in a duck blind ... an' with only a BB gun!"

He clapped Neal on the shoulder, eliciting a nervous laugh, almost a giggle. *Chief resident at the General? Now he was a cub.* Ned perked up; suddenly he was beginning to enjoy the trip. Earl gave them each state license papers to legalize their day of hunting. Carl whispered to Earl that the cost was on him. Then he asked where they could get the necessary federal duck stamps.

"What the hell you think this place is?" Earl roared. "A damn post-office?" With a twinkle in his eye, he reached around behind the bar and pulled out a postal worker's hat. "Actually, boys, it is." With a cackle, he opened a small metal box and extracted two stamps. His meaty paws delicately separated them, a little pink tongue darted from the black forest of a beard and licked them, and then he glued them to the back of Morgan's and Ned's hunting licenses. "Now sign in ink across them, docs, an' yer legal." He glanced up over the crowd. "Skippy! Skippy, honey. Come on over here."

It was the blond barmaid Ned had seen earlier. Her straight blond hair was damp, and her flushed face was streaked with sweat. She wore a full-length, flowered smock, tied narrow at the waist with a colorful crimson belt.

"Skippy, you remember Carl ..."

She rolled her eyes as if to say, *Dad, come on. You know I know Carl.*

"An' this is his boy Neal, and Neal's friend, Ned. They're doctors!" Earl gestured with a meaty paw. "Could you bring 'em a beer, hon'?"

Skippy ducked behind the bar, and drew four drafts. "You want one, too, dad?"

"Naw. How 'bout some black coffee? I gotta' do the books." His coal black eyes wandered back to Ned. "So what d'ya think, doc? Ever hunted before?"

Ned shrugged noncommittally.

"Don't worry, boy, er, doc. No better guide around than Blinky. He can call ducks so well, he'll make 'em land on yer gun barrel, and pull the trigger for ya!"

Blinky preened in the praise, suppressing a guffaw.

Ned tried to be polite and join in the conversation. "I really like your place, Mr. Murdoch. Whoever did those hunting scenes on the walls is a real artist."

Earl clapped his arm around Skippy's shoulder as she shyly looked up and blushed.

"See, honey, I tol' ya' they was good. Now here's an educated doc sayin' so, too."

Her face nearly disappeared in his beard as he gave her a peck on the cheek. Then he turned away to talk to Carl and Blinky, catching up on old times.

Neal Morgan was out of his element, and he looked it. Neatly pressed pants, shiny shoes, and smart answers weren't exactly what Daisy's was all about. In fact, Daisy's was about escaping the rigors of modern professional life that Neal was trying to excel in. He looked around glumly. There was no one here he could impress. He downed his beer in a gulp, and spun off his stool.

"Ned, I'm turning in. Stay as long as you like, because we can sleep on the way home after the hunt." As he started to shoulder his way out through the crowd, he suddenly stopped and turned, raising a finger and mimicking Farnsworth in a falsetto. "Er ... ah, don't forget, gentlemen: after we return, life once again is a stacked outhouse."

Ned laughed, raising his beer mug in a mock salute as he saw his chief resident, now a cub, wander through the crowd and disappear. *Should he follow,* he thought? He spun back to the bar on his stool, downing the remaining beer.

"Did you really like them?"

Another mug full of beer sat on the bar in front of him. Perched next to him on a barstool, Skippy drained her own beer and clasped her hands, resting her chin on them.

"I really did ... er, do!" he stammered. He held up the draft, and nodded thanks.

Her eyes were downcast again, and he shifted nervously. She shook out her luxurious blond mane, then almost self-consciously, as though to hide the rich beauty, pulled it back into a plain ponytail. The exotic beauty of her prominent cheekbones struck Ned, framing high but almond-shaped, green eyes. Her lips were finely etched, underscored by a dimple. As they talked, her facial expressions were a collage of constant shy animation, with an occasional penetrating stare. *Who really resided behind this shyness,* he wondered. Ned drew her out before she realized it, and for a moment he had her exchanging teasing barbs and blurting answers even before the questions were asked.

"What did you like about the pictures?" she asked, pouring another beer. "Tell me." She smiled, but Ned saw a new thread of intensity in her eyes.

Jesus, he thought. *Now, what the hell do I say?* He looked around self-consciously. "Ah, Skippy ... I truly don't know much about art, except ... except that some things I like, and some things I don't. But these paintings on the planks? I like. They seem so real, and the balance and color are very good."

"They were real." She set her chin matter-of-factly. "I was there."

"No kidding?"

"That pointer after the quail?" She pointed across the room.

"Yeah?"

"That's Dodger, our Springer spaniel. Course, he's dead, now," she shrugged. "But see how his ears are perked an' his eyes are lookin' right at us, not at the quail? It's cause that's the way I wanted him to look at me from the wall. You know, we could never take a photo of him. Lord knows why. He was shy and he'd always draw his ears back and slink away when someone pointed a camera in his direction."

Ned finished his beer, fascinated. "I suppose each of these pictures has its story, am I right?"

"Damn straight! Oops!" Her eyes sparkled like a mischievous girl with her fist caught in the cookie jar. She wiped the beer foam from her mouth. "Sorry, I cursed doc."

Ned laughed. There was another draft in front of him. *Now what the hell was going on?* Another beer, he didn't need. The room began to swim a little, to sort of vibrate. He excused himself from Skippy, and staggered to the john.

People he didn't know laughed and clapped him on the back. "Shoot'em up, doc." He was giddy. He slurred out a thanks. "Go get'em, boy. Don't let ol' Blinky bullshit ya' too much!" What could he say? It was obvious that a proud papa Carl had been bragging around about his son, Neal.

After he was finished, he nodded amicably and stumbled back to his barstool and crawled back on. The full beer was still waiting for him, dripping with condensation onto the bar. Skippy had left to make another beer run, this time carrying two pitchers in each hand. Her lithe, white arms were tensed under the load, and she deftly dodged grasping hands with downcast eyes as she wound her way through the crowd. Her square jaw was clenched as she returned with a load of empties.

"What're they doing?"

"Huh?" Skippy shook her hands and massaged her fingers from the strain of carrying so many pitchers.

Ned gestured towards the crowd. "What's that dance? I've never seen people dancing like that."

"Where you from?" She wiped a wisp of hair from her forehead. She held a red barrette in her teeth for a moment while she tossed her blond mane back again, gathering it again into a ponytail.

"Cincy. I mean Cincinnati. Er ... that's where I was from before I came here to finish my training." He watched her downcast eyes as she washed the pitchers.

"Figures ... an Easterner." Mock derision filled her green eyes, transformed into impish teasing. "Doc, that's the two-step. Some people from Texas call it the Texas Two Step, but anybody who knows country, has known the two-step for years."

"Is it hard? To dance, I mean?" he stammered.

She gave him a dower look, "Now how hard can a two step be, doc?"

"You can call me Ned."

"Let me get these pitchers filled up, and I'll show ya." She grunted as she lifted another load, flexing her arms and locking her elbows.

"You want some help?"

"Sure, doc ... I mean, Ned." She rolled her eyes, "Just what I need. A doctor, bartending in my dad's joint." Her look of dismissal made him want to crawl under the stool.

The two-step, he thought. *Damn.* What appeared to be a milling crowd actually had a pattern, gliding around the floor, circling counter clock-wise, a big bunch of farmers and cowboys, wearing work boots, or their best Justins or Noconas, moving lightly on their feet, hats pulled low, twirling their girls. Two slides to the left, one to the right. There was a lot of whooping and hollering. The two-step. Would Ned suddenly awaken in an on-call room and discover that he'd been dreaming? The beer looked real and he chugged it. No ... this was real. He could see how they did it, could feel the rhythm in his legs. Could he match their light grace?

"You gonna jus' sit there and bob all night, or you comin' out?"

Skippy was in front of him. Now her blond mane flowed down over her shoulders, framing her almond eyes and delicate cheeks. There was a scared look in her eyes. She forced a smile and took his arm. He noticed for the first time that she seemed to walk with a limp in her gait. He'd thought she had been just adjusting her stride to the loads of beer pitchers that she carried.

"Hold me proper, now," she scolded. She raised her dimpled chin aristocratically and guffawed.

"Oops, sorry. I've had too much to drink."

Her graceful neck arched up. His right hand lightly grasped her surprisingly narrow waist through the flowered shift. His left held her hand out, and they slipped into the crowd. There wasn't a lot of room.

"If I stumble, it's 'cause someone bumped me, see?"

He grinned down at her through glazed eyes, fighting to stay sober. For a moment she seemed distracted, embarrassed that she was with him. An Easterner, huh? They began to dance.

"You'll do fine, Mr. Doctor, sir. Ned. Hell, whatever," she giggled.

A kaleidoscope of emotions crossed her face: fear, pride, exhilaration, anxiety ... He was mesmerized: Who was really beneath the facade?

"On the downbeat, I'm gonna twirl. Hah! You act like you know what you're doin'."

Her eyes flashed, and she threw her head back in laughter. The smock flew out in a swirl of blurred colors; she flew back into his arms, light as a feather. He fingered the small of her back. On the next downbeat, he surprised her and twirled her, himself. The sexuality of the dancing, their touching, and the effects of the alcohol made him want to pull her closer, to breath in her smell and to feel her next to him.

"Lot a leg action in this dance, Ned." She seemed to be reading his mind. "My bony knees might hit somethin'."

A wry smile crept over her face, and for a moment her green eyes locked with his. His cheeks flushed as he gazed back, beads of sweat ran down his forehead, and they surged on, riding the crest of the rhythm. His pulse throbbed as music coursed though his veins.

He twirled her again, and suddenly she grimaced and bit her lip.

"What's the matter?"

"Oh, it's nothin' ..." her words trailed off, and she studied him. They danced a while in silence, and then she said. "Why you think they call me Skippy, anyway?"

"Huh?"

"Thought you knew. Don't you doctors know everything?" She arched a sullen eyebrow as she mocked him. "I was born with it, I guess. They call it a clubfoot ... talipes ... somethin' or other. Daddy says old Doc Edwards casted my foot when I was a baby, to straighten it. But after that, he said there was nothin' to be done. Anyway," she tossed her long blond hair, "I get by. Just bothers me once in a while. See?" She twirled again and smiled. "All better."

She seemed to have closed the subject, but Ned wanted to at least say something educated while swimming in this sea of inexperience. "I don't know much about it, Skippy, but I know that sometimes surgery can help."

"Really! Now why would little ol' me get an operation when I'm doin' just fine?" She smiled brightly, waving at friends.

Ned tried to hide his defensiveness and embarrassment. "Really. I said I didn't know that much about it. Okay? It's just something I heard, is all. I don't really know much about foot surgery." He missed a beat and they stumbled.

She lurched to a stop, stone cold in the middle of the floor. "Well if you're so damn smart, then why don't you look at it and tell me what to do?"

Ned stopped in his tracks. "Skippy, honest. I don't have my ... I'm only just learning. "

"Well, couldn't ya' just look?" she accused.

"Right here?"

"Honestly!" She grabbed his hand, and they marched through the crowd and out the screen door. She yelled back for another barmaid to watch things, and she took Ned's hand and dragged him down the gravel path. "Daddy gave me the first cabin. Look at my foot there if you're so damn bashful!"

The outside air was ice cold, prickling Ned's skin and giving him goose bumps. His breath steamed out in front of him. A brilliant, night sky was filled with stars, stretching overhead.

Skippy suddenly stopped, craned her head towards the south, and pointed. "See that?"

Ned squinted into the starlight. "See what?"

"Orion, Ned. You know, the constellation, Orion. The three stars of the belt, and the three of the scabbard?" She leaned over and pointed up into the night. "Look."

"Uh huh, yeah. I can see it."

"Follow Orion's belt out and up to the right, about eight belt-lengths. Some people have a lucky star. Me, I got lucky stars. You can see the little group 'a stars there, shaped like a kite. Every time I see it, it's good luck."

"Orion's kite, huh?"

"No, stupid. Skippy's kite."

"Isn't it Taurus, the bull?"

"Taurus, smaurus! It's Skippy's kite." She set her dimpled chin with a finality that communicated an end to that question.

"Whatever you say," he said, smiling.

She was washing her feet. Ned sat sheepishly in a deep armchair next to an oil stove. Now what the hell was he doing in here? He dismissed in an instant what the lecherous Blade would think. No way ... A picture portrait rested on an end table between the stove and his chair. The table was painted white, with chipped paint flaking off the sides. It was strewn with paperbacks, which were smudged, peeled and frayed. Ned noticed Ayn Rand, Plato, and Pasternak among the authors. The photograph on the table showed a picture of a much younger Earl Murdoch and a woman that looked a lot like Skippy, proudly holding up a baby. Behind them was the lodge with Earl holding up a "Sold" sign in front of a real estate sign.

"That your mom in the picture?" he yelled.

"Yes," she yelled back over the sound of running water. "Ma's dead, now. Died 'a cancer five years ago." She hopped into the room with a self-conscious, vulnerable smile. "Didn't want no doctor looking at stinky feet!" Her eyes cleared for a moment, and she smiled shyly. She flounced down on the bed like a little girl, and tentatively offered a foot. "Here. It's the good one. At least tell me I got one normal one before I let you see the other one."

She giggled, and Ned got caught in the warmth of her eyes again. He was very nearly drunk with a rip-roaring beer buzz, and little warning bells were going off in his mind that there were lines that one should not cross as a doctor. Being in this woman's cabin, and examining her as a patient was one of them. Not only that ... what about Katherine? He carefully touched her foot, cradling the heel in his palm. With his other hand he touched her instep, her arch, and moved out to the toes. Large, smooth, blue veins pulsed as they coursed up the foot into her leg. He playfully wiggled her fifth toe, "This one went wee, wee, wee all the way home. That's all I know."

They laughed together, but Skippy's face had assumed a stony frightened look. "I get kinda' embarrassed, okay? I want you to see my bad one."

The oil stove fan kicked in, and Ned felt the blast of warmth from the hot exhaust, chasing the chill out of the room. The bathroom light threw long, dark shadows across the room, and she removed the towel.

"You won't throw up or anything, will you?" she joked, but her voice became throaty and broke, betraying deep emotion.

He tried to smile reassuringly into her downcast eyes. A lot more was being revealed than just a foot.

She let the towel drop, showing the withered left foot. It was smaller than the right one. The forefoot and toes curved in, and the heel was twisted sideways. There were calluses on the outside of her foot, where decades of abnormal pressure had been countered. He didn't know how to describe the deformity. He couldn't remember what varus or valgus meant from the brief week of orthopedics in medical school. He examined the deformed foot, testing it, and feeling the stiff, twisted joints, the calluses ... Could he say anything intelligent? He was mystified. Suddenly a clear teardrop splashed down on his hand. He looked up in surprise to see silent tears, streaming down her cheeks.

"Son of a bitch," she bit at her lip and looked away bravely. "I guess I just realized that I've never let anyone look at it before." She sniffed, "Don't know what got into me, letting you see this." She barked a harsh laugh and jumped up, moving about the room with her little skippy gait. "It's me, see? It's the way I've always been. I shoot ducks, I hunt ... Hell, why that cord a wood stacked behind the lodge ... I chopped it! I'm normal."

Suddenly she stopped in front of Ned, and grasped his startled face with both of her hands. "I'm a normal woman, see?"

She kissed him hard on the lips, and he flinched, tasting blood, beer, and cigarette smoke. He became frightened and pulled away from her. He had come to see a withered foot, and now things could happen that they would both regret.

"Skippy, call me next week at the hospital. I know people that can help. I don't want anything to happen here out of the blue, us drunk, that would ruin a chance to help you." He pulled away from this startled, teary girl and lurched into the cold night air.

* * * *

223

"Doc." A hand gently shook his shoulder. "Doc, get up," the voice whispered.

In the darkness he could make out Blinky Walters' bony features. *Where the hell am I?* Blinky whispered to get dressed, and Ned grabbed his shoes and clothes from the armchair. The luminous dial on a clock said 4:30 in the morning. He was in a hunting cabin! Now, how in the hell? Holy shit, was it cold! Didn't anyone around here believe in heat? His breath fogged out in front of him as he fought into his clothes, gasping and struggling as fast as his shivering body would allow. Then he hurried outside, where he found Blinky and Carl Morgan cursing outside the station wagon.

"Damn that dog, Blinky. Goddamn him to hell!"

"Shet, Carl. I'd 'a never dreamed he'd do such a thing. I stuck him in his kennel in the back of the wagon. But I left the door ajar, jus' a crack, so's he could stick his head out and lap a little water if he needed it. He must'a fought his way out."

"Holy shit's all I got to say. Hooo-ley shit!" Neal's father kicked at the gravel at the driveway in frustration.

"What's the matter?" Ned asked. He searched through a duffel bag and pulled out a hunting jacket.

"See fer yerself."

As Ned opened the front door of Neal's new station wagon, an abominable smell swept out. The inside light went on, revealing that the entire front seat of the wagon was spattered with foul, greenish-black, Labrador diarrhea. Neal's new, powder-blue plaid upholstery was smeared with liquid stool. Sprawled out on the back seat like a decadent Roman Caesar, with his tail thumping contentedly, lay Magic.

"Oh, my God."

Teeth ground behind Ned, as Neal Morgan peered in over his shoulder. The four of them stared in dismay at the mess in utter silence. Magic's tail thumped even faster as he saw his master.

Carl Morgan spoke first, "I refuse to sit in dog shit on the way to duck hunting."

Blinky looked around wryly, "I see we got all chiefs here an' no injuns. Ned, can you just hurry an' get some wet towels."

Carl Morgan looked at him sourly for a moment, and then they both darted into the cabin, emerging with four dripping bath towels. Neal stood frozen, looking desperately at the ruins of his wife's new car.

"Come on, Neal," rasped Blinky. "I can't change what that damn Magic's done, but we don't want to lose the hunt, too." He crawled into the wagon and held out his hand for a towel.

They scrubbed like madmen, cleaning up the obvious clumps first, trying to fold the towel over them. Then they scrubbed at the spatters. Ned passed in a new towel, daintily taking back the soiled one. Blinky kept scrubbing until he'd used up all the cabin's towels.

"Quick, get some paper towels!" he sighed in exasperation. "Jesus, how much dog shet can a dog shet?"

He opened the rear passenger door, and Magic slunk out with his tail down and ears back in submission. The dog went around to the back of the wagon and waited forlornly until the tailgate was lowered. Then he hopped up into his kennel, curled into a ball, lay down and sighed. Carl Morgan lumbered out of the cabin, carrying their guns and duffel bags. He threw them in the back next to the kennel.

Blinky slammed the tailgate shut, throwing one last duffel bag to a startled Ned and Neal. "You docs, that's extra gear fer you. Neal, you know how cold it can get, sittin' in a blind."

As they climbed into the car, Blinky inquired, "What'd you do with those dirty towels, Carl? We can't leave a mess like that for Skippy and Earl."

Neal's father was sulking, and wouldn't answer. Ned now determined where Neal had gotten the habit of grinding his teeth at the folly of human beings. This newfound knowledge was interrupted by a blast of cold air as Blinky rolled down the window.

"Sorry, docs, it's the smell. It's absolutely the worst, ever. I'll put the heater on, full-blast, but we've just got to have some fresh air."

Neal reached down and pulled out a ragged item from the duffel bag. "Blinky ... these long underwear are wool. I'm allergic. They're ancient, full of moth holes, and phew! They stink!"

Carl was driving like a madman in the thick fog, and the station wagon lurched and skidded around the gravel corners of country roads. He wouldn't let up, though, or they'd be late for the hunt. The ducks flew, whether you were ready or not.

Blinky twisted to face them. "Itch or freeze ... it's your choice, Neal. I brought all the spare stuff I got, fer you an' the other doc."

Grumbling, Neal and Ned struggled out of their jeans, and pulled on long johns, wool socks, wool shirts, gloves, and cap. Ned reached into his own overnight bag, and brought out an orange, hunting cap. It was his only hunting possession, saved from a single quail hunt with friends in Ohio.

"What's that?" Blinky asked.

"It's a hunting cap."

"It's orange."

"So?"

Blinky stared at him in disbelief. "Orange'll ruin the hunt. The ducks'll see us for miles. Here, put this on." He fished in his jacket pocket, and pulled out a black stocking cap. It was wool, too. As Ned pulled it over his ears, he felt like he was going to be one huge itch.

"Don't we need orange for safety?"

Blinky mustered all his patience and said slowly, as if to a child: "Doc, we'll all be in the duck blind together. Only the ducks needs worry about who's shootin' who."

Utter madness, Ned thought.

* * * *

They were stumbling frantically through fog and darkness. Blinky's favorite hunting spot was about a mile off a remote dirt road. Ned was loaded down with twelve gauge shells, a shotgun, and a dozen mallard decoys in a gunnysack strapped to his back. Blinky was like a quick cat with night vision, sinuously dodging the spiked branches of thorny Russian olive trees that dotted the swampland. It was all Ned could do to fend off the thorns in the foggy blackness. There was a suggestion of light in the direction of what Ned surmised was going to be the eastern sunrise. Overhead, in the blackness, they could hear the eerie sound of wind whistling through wings and the lonesome cry of a hen mallard quacking insistently for companionship. Magic charged ahead, barking and baying as Ned and the rest frantically followed his cries to the hunt.

Soon, the only things that Ned could hear were his own gasping and the thunder of his heart hammering in his chest. He was drenched with sweat. He paused to listen for the others and to get his bearings. His lungs burned, and his thighs were like jelly. His calves screamed with cramping spasms. He glanced down at his bloodied hand, which he'd cut when he fell over sagebrush in the dark. Ahead, in the dark, he saw a small penlight flashing back in his direction.

"Over here, doc! Over here."

Ned struggled back to his feet. He crossed a swampy area with black mud that sucked at his boots. The thigh-high grass seemed like clutching fingers, dragging and tugging at his legs. He forced his way through the swamp grass and climbed up onto a small, sandy knoll. Gasping for breath, he trudged over it onto a finger of land that projected into a lake. More ghost-like willows and Russian olive trees dotted the shoreline. An impenetrable wall of cattails raised up to block the border of the lake. Blinky had tromped out a small channel, and he was dragging out a load of decoys, struggling in the muddy water in chest waders. Ned could hear the sounds of mud sucking as rime ice cracked and creaked resonantly around the pond's edge. The black Labrador was tearing up and down the shoreline, fighting through the bulrushes, and swimming back and forth around Blinky. Magic looked up and whined excitedly, his tail wagging and splashing water around him.

Carl motioned Ned closer. "Pass me that bag of dekes, Ned. Where's, Neal?"

"I didn't see him," He puffed. "Hell, Carl, we're supposed to be young and in shape. You guys are old. How come I'm the sucking so much wind?"

Carl laughed. "Hunting's our life. You stand in an operating room, all day. Besides, there's a knack to moving through the brush and rough country. How many times you fall?"

Ned laughed, "How'd you know?"

"Good thing it's late in the year. The snakes are all hibernating." Carl stifled a chuckle, as Ned turned white.

Behind them, Neal puffed into view. His face was flushed, and he mopped the sweat from his forehead with a handkerchief. In the freezing morning, steam rose from his black damp hair as he held his hunting hat with his other hand.

"Must be out of shape," he gasped. "I got a stitch in my side that won't quit." He struggled to twist and throw off the bag of decoys strapped to his back. "It's all coming back, now ... I think I remember why I never went duck hunting again." He grinned in the darkness at Ned.

Slate gray eastern light filtered through the fog, surrounding them like a cocoon. They were "blinded up" in the cattails on the edge of the pond. Carl had tromped down two hollows, side by side. Blinky and Ned were crouched in the left blind, facing the lake. Carl and Neal were hidden in the right, father and son. Mallard decoys bobbed benignly in the water in front, strung out in wide patches, with an open patch of water in front of the blinds.

"You forgot to put some in front, Blinky. There's nothing in the middle."

"So's the ducks'll land there," Blinky answered, touching his nose.

Magic whined at Blinky's feet, trembling with anticipation. Ned trembled himself, shivering in the freezing cold. His sweat-soaked, woolly clothes were now frozen stiff, and the icy fog easily penetrated them. A freezing inversion had changed the weather on the lake, hardening the rim of thin ice around the edge. Above them, in the breaking dawn, Ned could hear the flapping wings of migrating ducks that were circling to land on the pond.

A flock landed, but Blinky restrained Ned, snaking a sinewy hand out and lowering his gun barrel. Magic fiercely whined in anticipation.

"It's not shootin' hours, yet, doc. We got five minutes yet 'til we're legal."

Ned continued to shake so violently with the cold that he thought of Bernie in DTs. Finally, Blinky gave a resigned sigh and pushed him out the back of the blind.

"Go on, ya' pup. Run around fer a second, an' beat yer arms. It'll warm ya' up."

Ned was all too happy to follow his advice. As he fought his way out of the cattails, another group of Mallards swooped in and landed among the decoys. Then they started in surprise, flying off and angrily quacking the alarm. For a moment, Ned could almost have sworn he heard Blinky grind his teeth. Ned ran in place, did jumping jacks, and beat his arms, twisting around like a mad Raggedy Ann doll.

Neal staggered out, catching his waders in the reeds, and joined him, bouncing around like a crazy marionette as they danced to generate body warmth.

"I don't understand it," Neal muttered. "That damn stitch I got in my side when I ran out here won't leave." Morgan bent over, and rubbed under his rib cage as he churned his legs in place. "There! When I bent over, it left." He straightened back up, and ran some more. Then a worried look crossed his face, and he massaged his right side again.

"Come on, docs, goddammit, come on!"

They pushed their way through the cattails back to their respective blinds. Blinky handed Ned his gun.

"Load up. Er ... you do know how to handle a gun, don't you?"

Ned nodded affirmatively. He fingered the safety, and showed Blinky as he shoved shells into the breech. Distant sounds of muffled gunfire echoed through the fog. Ned strained to hear something, but he could only make out the wind whispering in the cattails. More faraway, muffled crumps sounded. Suddenly, Blinky started calling on his wooden duck call. He started out with several long, plaintive calls, and gradually increased the tempo. Wind whistled and hissed through swooping wings overhead.

"Don't move, doc," he whispered. "Just freeze, 'til I tell ya' to shoot."

Blinky blew on the call again and again, and this time his call came out more excitedly. Ned stole a look. Blinky's cheeks were puffed out, and it sounded like his calls came from a deep rumble in his throat. Ned didn't move a muscle. The call changed to a rapid staccato of short quacks that ran together. Suddenly, streaking shadows, wings, and quacking sounds swooped right out of the fog in front of them.

"Take'em, doc! Take'em!"

Crashing gunfire exploded around Ned as flashbacks from muzzle blasts illuminated the darkness around the blind. Stunned for a moment, Ned was deafened, but he pulled the shotgun up and sighted a bird flying away. He squeezed, jerking at the trigger. Nothing happened. Shit! The safety was still on. He felt for it, pushed it in, and sighted down the barrel again only to see empty fog.

"I got one, dad. I got one! Goddamn! Did you see that shot?"

Ned looked out onto the lake. Five ducks floated on the water. Magic crashed out of the blind to swim out and retrieve one. The dog churned through the water, making a beeline for the closest one, grasped it in his mouth, and swam back, puffing through the bloody feathers.

"Fetch," Blinky sent him yet again.

Suddenly a single drake swooped out of the fog, his wings set for landing.

"Take'em, doc!"

Ned swung up, flipped his safety off, and he fired the over-and-under at the swooping bird. There was a blinding flash, and thundering recoil. Ned felt like his shoulder had been ripped out at the roots. He opened his eyes only to see the bird flying away. He flushed with the sting of embarrassment.

"Blinky, how can you shoot so well when you only got a left eye?"

"Never needed the right one, anyway doc. I'm left eye dominant. You need to pull that gunstock close to yer shoulder, see? Keep yer cheek next to the stock, fer sightin' with both eyes open. Crossing shots, lead 'em three lengths. Head on is head on." Blinky put a fatherly arm around his shoulder. "Don't feel so bad. It's yer first time. Everyone gets buck fever. You'll catch on."

Ned reloaded. Magic had retrieved the last duck for Blinky, and he sprayed them both as he shook off in an explosion of black fur and freezing water. Blinky grinned at Ned.

"Only a fool would have that dog, only a fool or a duck hunter!"

Again, Ned heard nothing; but Blinky suddenly hunched down again, repeating the calling pattern on his Championship Rosewood duck call. This time Ned was ready, and when the soft, staccato quacking ceased, he jumped up on Blinky's call. Great God almighty! Blinky'd called in a huge flock of at least fifty ducks! Ned blazed away, firing with the rest of them. They were all shooting over-and-under shotguns, except for Carl Morgan's side-by-side, double-barrel Parker. Five ducks floated in the water.

"Son of a bitch!" Ned cried in frustration. "I wasn't even close. And ... and it was such a big flock!" He jammed two shells in the barrel, snapping the breech shut in frustration.

"Ya' flock-shot, didn't ya', Ned? Did ya' pick out one and lead it, or did ya' fire at the bunch of them?"

Magic shook and again sprayed them with freezing water.

"Swing through a little more, doc. Yer pickin' a spot an' jerkin' the gun."

Ned groaned. "We've shot, what, ten ducks? What's the limit? Hell, you guys'll have our limit before I ever get the hang of it. Between shooting one-eyed doubles and telling me everything I'm doing wrong ... Blinky, if I wasn't so embarrassed, I'd take this damn wool hat off, and bow."

Blinky laughed. "Been doin' it all my life, doc. It's second nature. Don't worry though, between the four of us, the limit's twenty-eight. Seven ducks a man."

The fog hung on, turning the advancing dawn into a gray shroud. More ducks suddenly appeared like magic ghosts, squawked, and flapped away before any of them could get their guns up.

"Sometimes they do that, doc," Blinky smiled. "I think they can sense water in ways we don't understand. They'll come down through thick clouds onto a pond in the middle of nowhere. I seen it." Blinky touched his eye patch.

Another flock came in, summoned by Blinky's hypnotic, insistent, magical call. Thundering gunfire sounded again. Five ducks either lay flopping in the lake or floating belly-up in the water. Ned was near tears with frustration.

"Score one for Ned, boys," called out Carl Morgan. "Welcome to the fraternal order of fools and duck hunters."

Ned was hopeful, but he didn't want credit unless he was sure. "How do you know I got one?" he called out to Neal's father.

"Neal didn't shoot," Carl answered. He's holding his side, trying to get that damn cramp out."

The crinkles of a smile formed around the empty socket of Blinky's eye. Ned couldn't stop a smile, which, in spite of his efforts to control it, turned into a proud grin. Blinky clapped him on the shoulder. He heard a cough from Neal, but every fiber in his body was now concentrated on the field of fire around his blind. It was an electric sensation. He felt like some primordial part of his subconscious had just fought its way up to be recognized. He was a hunter! More ducks came in. He sighted one, led it, and fired. There was an explosion of feathers. See the second one! Lead it, hurry ... it's swinging to the right ... Lead ... fire! Blood and feathers. He was oblivious to the explosions and gunfire around him. His body was coursing with adrenaline, and his nerves were on a fine focus, answering the primeval urge to hunt and kill. Fire! Ducks, coming in ... Stay down ... stay down! Fire!

"Ned. We got to go. Something's wrong."

"Huh?" Ned swiveled, only to see a grimacing Neal Morgan, bent over, holding his side.

"We've got to go. I thought it was just a stitch, but it won't go away. You heard me coughing a while back? Shit! I got positive rebound. Goddammit, Ned, I think I got goddamn appendicitis."

Ned was incredulous. "Neal. You can't have appendicitis. Why you're ... you're the Chief! How can you have appendicitis out here, duck hunting? Are you sure it isn't gas or something? Maybe something you ate?"

"Ate? Shit!" Neal looked at his watch. "It's 8:45 in the morning. Think. I should be starving! We've been up since 4:30. The thought of food makes me sick."

Ned nodded and crawled out of the blind. "Here, lie down, and let me feel your belly."

Neal flopped down, and he pulled out his shirt. He lay back so that Ned could check him, but as he did, he grimaced and held his hand to protect his right side.

"Sonofabitch, it hurts!" His frightened and confused eyes looked up at Ned. "No rectal, asshole. Don't even think about it."

Ned laughed and wiggled his pink index finger under Neal's nose. "Don't worry, Sahib. If you think this innocent, gloveless digit is goin' up your dark bunghole, forget it! The Phantom never does a bare-fingered rectal!"

He started probing Neal's abdomen gently in the left upper quadrant. Deep inside he could feel the tip of Neal's spleen, then across to the liver under the right costal margin. "Only a fingerbreadth," he muttered. "No alcoholism ... at least none that's obvious."

"Fuck you. And ... and fuck the Phantom!"

He moved his hand down to the right lower quadrant, and Neal gasped in pain. His belly here was rigid. He shook Neal's pelvis, and Morgan gasped through grit teeth. Ned knelt down among the grassy dampness and placed his ear on Morgan's abdomen to listen.

"I don't have a stethoscope to listen with; Neal, but I can't hear a damn thing. No bowel sounds. I think you're right. I think you've got a hot appendix."

"You sure?" Carl Morgan looked down on them with Blinky. They were watching a doctor examine his patient.

"We're sure," said Ned. Neal was groaning.

Carl turned to Blinky. "We got to get my son out of here. Blinky, what do we have to do to get the hell out of here as fast as possible?"

The guide thought for a moment. "Carl, you and Neal start back to the car now. It's going to take Neal a little while to walk to the car. Besides, he'll need your help. Take yours and Neal's gun." He thrust out a leather stringer with seven ducks strapped on it. "Take these, too. I have to stay and pick up the decoys because if I don't an' the Feds come around and see untended decoys, I'll lose my guide's license. I won't carry the dekes out; I'll just hide 'em in the reeds and come back later. Ned, you stay an' help me."

Carl and Neal started out, trudging back towards the station wagon through the swamp grass, bull rushes, and fog. Carl carried both of their guns and the ducks, while Neal walked ahead bent over in pain. They disappeared over the sandy knoll. Blinky held up three more empty leather stringers filled with leather loops to put each duck's head through. He showed Ned how to string the ducks' heads through a slip noose, and then waded into the lake, gathering the floating decoys. More ducks tried to land right on top of him, and cursing at their luck, he shooed them away.

They started out together, loaded down with gear. On his chest Ned carried his gun, and a sack filled with decoys. In back Blinky had thrown a stringer of ducks over each of Ned's shoulders, fourteen in all. They were huge mallards, at least four pounds each, and by the time he'd gone a hundred yards the crushing dead weight made Ned's legs feel like burning jelly on match sticks, slogging through cement. Blinky had the last stringer, his own gun, and two decoy bags himself. It looked as though they'd make it in one trip, and not have to come back ... if Ned's arms and back held out.

Ned had started out at a fast trot, anxious over Morgan's condition, but Blinky restrained him.

"Ease up, son. You'll never make it at that pace."

Blinky had an easy loping gait, and Ned tried to imitate the way he glided over the ground between the clumps of sagebrush.

"You done good, son, real good fer yer first time. We had to leave one fer the coyotes, back there. We was one over the limit. I miscounted."

At this moment, though, Ned was not experiencing triumph, only pain. He gasped under the load, and couldn't answer. He tried to keep Blinky in sight, but eventually just followed his tracks in the dirt around the sage.

Finally within sight of the car, he collapsed to his knees, sucking in deep gulps of air, drenched in sweat. His lungs were on fire. Carl Morgan came back and helped him to his feet. Magic whined at Blinky, and then jumped up on the rear panel and shook off, spraying the back interior of the wagon with mud and dog hair. Then Magic crept into the kennel, sighed once, and curled into a tight black ball to go to sleep.

"It must be retrocecal," Neal absently muttered. "I've got a positive psoas sign. I can't straighten my legs anymore."

"We'll take care of you, Neal," Ned whispered. "Don't worry."

*   *   *   *

A silver-haired, unshaven man stood at the head of their circle. Neal lay on the bed with his legs drawn up with the pain, while Carl, Blinky, and Ned looked on attentively. The chubby old man wore a white doctor's coat, and a stethoscope was draped over his muddied, camouflage hunting pants. He looked around the group.

"His white count's 18- seven. Left shift. He has rebound, and no bowel sounds. His temperature's 100.4 degrees. We're pretty quick as far as the onset of symptoms ... only four hours ... so I don't think it's ruptured yet."

Neal clutched at his arm. "I gotta get home. I know exactly who I want for anesthesia, and exactly who will do the surgery." His face was flushed, and his glassy eyes flicked rapidly from face to face.

The old physician looked over his bifocals at him, and smiled reassuringly. "Son, if you go home, it doesn't matter who you get to do the surgery. It might as well be Jesus Christ himself, because if you drive for four hours with a ruptured appendix, that's who you're going to need! You're a surgeon. You know that."

Neal grimaced and nodded affirmatively. "Dammit, he's right. Dad, get Elly on the phone, quick. I don't have a choice." He looked up pleadingly at the doctor. "Sweet Jesus! I don't want to seem rude or insult you ... but, can you ... can you take out an appendix?"

Blinky spoke up, interrupting the doctor. "Listen here, Neal. I know you know all about surgery and seech. But I'll tell you right now ... Doc Edwards has taken care of everyone in this community for thirty years, an' he's damn good! Time fer you ta' be a patient, and shet yer mouth."

The grizzled old doctor laughed. "I think Blinky's said it all." He looked each of them in the eye again with a quiet confidence. "If you'll excuse me, I'll get out of this goose gear, and get the OR ready. Our scrub nurse said we could go in ten minutes." He looked down at Neal and smiled. "Damn inconsiderate of you, ruining my goose hunt!"

Carl handed Neal the phone. Now Neal's breathing was coming in rapid, little grunts, as if it hurt to take even a normal breath. The phone rang and rang, unanswered, and Neal slammed the receiver in frustration. "Shit! She's not home!"

Carl Morgan laid a reassuring hand on his son's shoulder. "Everything'll be fine, Neal. Everything'll be fine. I'll talk to Elly, later."

Tears of frustration formed in Neal's eyes. "Is this some stupid joke? I might not wake up. I could cool it ... Sonofabitch! I could cool it. I could cool it right here!" He grasped at Ned's sleeve. "Ned! I know you. You've got a knack for getting the right thing done. Be there, please? Be there. Don't let him close me up if it's ruptured, okay? No heroics."

Ned tried to reassure him. "Neal, you've got no choice. If you leave, you die. Here, you'll have a chance. I'll be there." He laughed reassuringly, "Besides, the Ghost Who Walks would never desert a friend in need."

A new face pushed into the circle. "Hi. I'm James Struthers, the nurse anesthetist ... and you're," he looked at the chart, "ah, you're Neal Morgan."

"Nurse anesthetist!" Morgan's eyes bulged, apoplectic.

"Yes."

"I want a spinal."

"I don't do spinals. When did you last eat?"

"Sonofabitch!"

Ned was on the phone in the hallway. He'd had the hospital operators back at the General track down Dr. Farnsworth at his home. He explained Neal's situation. "He's a G.P., Dr. Farnsworth. That's right ... and there's no anesthesiologist, just a nurse anesthetist. No. No question about it, it's hot. Yeah, that's what I told him, too."

Farnsworth's voice seemed optimistic to Ned. "Listen, Ned. As far as this Edwards fellow goes, I draw a complete blank. Zip. On the other hand, when someone's really bad, it doesn't matter where they practice, word gets around, you know? You hear about their mistakes. I have never heard of a bad result out of that little Marion Community Hospital. This guy Edwards must know his stuff. I know it's touchy, but if you can, help him. I trust you."

*   *   *   *

"What you're asking son, is illegal." Edwards stared down at Ned over bifocal glasses. "You don't have a medical license."

Ned turned beet red, and scuffed at his shoes. Edwards rubbed thoughtfully at his grizzled chin.

"This is an emergency, though, and if you think you can help, you're welcome. If you get in the way, I'll ask you to leave, and I expect your cooperation."

Ned inwardly sighed in relief, and nodded his assent.

They used the McBurney approach. It was the strangest feeling that Ned had ever had during his internship. His chief, Neal "Immaculate" Morgan, lay intubated and nude on the operating room table. His belly was prepped and the squared-off drapes revealed their "case." The scrub nurse automatically started to put in the retractors; but with a wink, Doc Edwards put them in Ned's hands and told him he needed his help. In less than thirty seconds Ned was staring at the open belly through a two-inch incision. With one careful probe and a deft twist, the cecum was delivered up out of the wound, and a swollen, inflamed appendix was staring back at them. Dr. Edwards carefully tied a purse-string stitch around the appendix's base, and with a deft snip, the appendix was dropped into the specimen bottle. Eight minutes. Phenol was touched to the stump, just before it disappeared under the closure of the purse-string stitch.

"It wasn't ruptured," Ned beamed.

Edwards just grunted. He used a running gut suture to close the peritoneum, followed by interrupted zero silk on the muscle layers. He then injected Marcaine into the wound.

"What was that for?" Ned asked.

"So when he wakes up, he doesn't feel pain."

The skin was closed with a running sub-cuticular stitch. In seventeen minutes' operating time, the dressing was on and Dr. Edwards was stripping off his scrubs.

"Jesus. That was the most amazing surgery I've ever seen," said Ned. "I mean, I know it was only an appy, but so fast, so sure ... You didn't need me. In fact, you didn't need anybody. Where'd you do your surgical residency?"

Dr. Edwards shook his head. "No residency, son. I had just an internship at St. Vincent's in Toledo. It was an old-fashioned rotating, the best kind ... And, yes, I did need you. I needed you so that now you, Neal, and the rest of your ornery troupe can sleep easy, knowing that everything went well." He gave Ned a wink.

Ned was still awestruck. "I don't get it. How can you be that good, after only just an internship? I still get scared just going into the OR.

Edwards looked across to Ned as they slid Neal off the OR table onto his hospital bed. Neal moaned and coughed up some phlegm, which the anesthetist suctioned out.

"Son, that extra training's nice. But when I finished my internship, there was a war on. Your learning curve gets pretty short in a war. Besides, some guys either have it or they don't. I've seen some of the most God-awful stuff done to people by board-certified university surgeons! What people that need a doctor don't realize is that when they go to a university training hospital, someone gets to learn on them. It doesn't work out, they can say, 'Heck, even at the U they couldn't help me.' But out here in the small town of Marion, I have nowhere to hide. I screw up on someone—they live here. I'll see them every day. I've got to do my best, every time, no learning on the job. When I came back from the Pacific theater, picking up a farmer with his hand ripped-off from a tractor's power take-off ... Well, I'd pretty much seen everything a horrible war could do; a tractor take-off was pretty easy."

Carl Morgan and Blinky Walters were waiting in the little hospital's recovery room. Blinky was pacing up and down nervously, waiting for their return. Even after Neal moaned and sat up to look around sleepily, Blinky looked worried.

"What's the matter, Blinky?" Ned asked. "The surgery went just fine."

"Hell, I expected that, doc. It's not that what worries me. I don't know how to break it to Neal."

Ned looked at him with a puzzled face.

"You know those damn ducks we threw in the back of the wagon? Hell, one of 'em revived, an' started floppin' around, quacking an' such. Ol' Magic fought his way outta' the kennel an' went after it. Shet, Ned, there's blood an' feathers all over the back 'a Neal's wagon!"

7

Wires and Dreams; Bones

NOVEMBER 10, 1971, 3:23 PM

Neal Morgan wasn't twenty minutes out of anesthesia when he propped himself up on his elbow, locked eyes with Ned, and said: "We're leaving."

"We can't," said Ned, "you just got operated on."

"Yeah, but I'm fine now. You're on call tomorrow, Ned. They expect me back, as well." Morgan coughed gingerly and spat some phlegm on a tissue.

Ned could see his grimace of pain, and he answered in exasperation, "Neal, this is bullshit. You just can't up and go! We're not leaving."

He turned to Neal's father for support, who in turn, looked blankly at Blinky Walters. The electric doors to the recovery room swung open, and Dr. Edwards strode around the corner. He'd pulled his clothes back on, and it was an interesting contrast, a white coat flapping over camouflage pants. He grinned at them, and wiped the grease from his lunch onto his sleeve.

243

"A late lunch is better than no lunch at all. How's our sterling patient?" He glanced at their sullen faces.

"Pretty ornery, doc," said Carl Morgan. "He says he wants to go home right now."

Morgan assumed his best authoritative air. He gestured towards Ned. "He's on call. I'm ... well, I'm the chief. I'm grateful for all you've done. In fact, I owe you my life. But we've got to go. Can you help us get home?"

Edwards' bewhiskered face grimaced down at Morgan over his bifocals. "Irregular to say the least. Not a total surprise, though. I had a guy in the Navy on the U.S.S. Oregon swab a ship deck two days after an appy. I don't recommend it, though." He looked around at them and grinned.

Morgan was beaming. "See? It's as good as done!"

"Not so fast, Mister hot-shot chief!" Edwards held up a restraining hand. He looked over to Ned. "You know how to give a shot, don't you? You know, IM pain meds?"

Ned looked surprised. "Uh ... sure. I know how to do a nurse's job, doctor," he said with a self-effacing grin.

"You won't stick him in the sciatic nerve, or anything?" Edwards' face smiled, but his eyes were hard.

"No," Ned smiled confidently back. "Just make sure the needle's big enough, and then Neal won't complain of the pain when I transect the entire nerve! I'll get the job done."

They chuckled, though Morgan's sullen scowl showed that he didn't think they were really that funny.

Edwards looked over his glasses at him. "If you sign an AMA form, I'll let you go. I'll try to be helpful as long as you acknowledge that it's 'against medical advice.' I don't condone your leaving, but I won't try to stop you. Your side-kick here is at least sort of legal to give you a shot, if you need one."

"I won't need one," Morgan said confidently, as though pointing out a certainty, something self-evident.

"Fine. In that case, hop on out of bed and get your clothes on."

Morgan tentatively swung his legs around over the side of the bed, and bravely pushed up with his arms. There was a muffled grunt as he gasped and doubled over at the bedside. Ned and Carl rushed up to support him. Edwards glared over his bifocals, "I can see you're obviously fine. I'll get the shot."

Waves of pain had turned Morgan's face chalk white, with beads of sweat congealing on his forehead. Ned helped get his feet into his pant legs, and Neal gingerly tried to buckle his belt. He couldn't quite make it, though, until he pulled the shirttails back out. At least then he could snap the buckle shut. While he struggled into his clothes, Blinky and Carl Morgan pulled the station wagon up to the hospital's entrance. With Ned helping him, Morgan carefully eased out of the wheelchair and into the back seat of the car. Doc Edwards came out to the wagon with an alcohol swab, a vial of morphine, and a syringe with a 21-gauge needle attached.

"Remember son, right in the butt, not in the nerve. On the side, you know." He winked, and turned to Carl Morgan. "You gentlemen be careful. Turn back if there's any doubt."

Carl Morgan looked up from the driver's seat to Edwards. "You sure about this, doc? If we all just refused to go, we might convince him to stay put."

But Edwards grinned back. "Carl, he'll be fine. The appendix wasn't ruptured, and I think that Ned will agree it's a secure closure." He waved his hands distractedly. "I'm not wild about this, but he can be just as miserable on the way home as he could be miserable here." He waved good-bye. "Have a safe trip."

"Boy, Earl an' Skippy're gonna be pissed!" Blinky grumbled. "They was gonna have dinner for us. Guess that's shot, fer' sure."

Neal Morgan grunted in pain as Carl accelerated and bounced out of the gravel driveway onto the road. Ned twisted his head to look behind at Doc Edwards, disappearing in the dust. He thought he glimpsed a beat-up, red pickup with a slender blond-haired figure jumping from the cab to look after them. He wistfully looked back at the receding form. His heart hammered in his throat. *What exactly had happened back there?* He knew the others didn't notice. They swerved to miss a jackrabbit, and sped west down Highway 24, homeward bound.

Lengthening shadows from passing sagebrush stretched towards them as they drove into the evening haze. Even Blinky was quiet. Neal was propped up on a pillow against the locked door, his drugged mind numb and long past the ability to grasp the implications of Labrador diarrhea, the oily duck and dried blood smells that permeated his wife's once-new car. A blood-red sun slowly slipped below the coastal range in the far distance, and as it did, Carl Morgan breathed a sigh of relief. He removed his sunglasses, rubbed at his bloodshot, bleary eyes, and stepped hard on the gas.

"At least that's done!" he muttered to a sleeping Blinky. "The sooner we get home the better."

Neal's eyes were glassy. His black hair was matted, stuck on a white forehead that was speckled with beads of perspiration. He shifted on his pillows, and Ned could hear him panting short, puppy-like breaths. Finally, holding his body rigid, he swiveled his head towards Ned. "I'm done being a goddamn hero. Give me the damn shot."

"You want me to pull down the side of your jeans?" Ned asked.

Morgan glared back. "Ned, I can't move. Jesus! It feels like there's a red hot poker in my belly."

"So how am I going to give you a shot?"

"In the arm. Make it a deltoid stick, not too deep," Neal grunted. "And please, miss the axillary nerve, asshole."

"Let me help you get your shirt off." Ned leaned over to help.

Morgan grimaced and held his arm even more tightly to his side. "Goddammit, Ned, can't you hear? I can't move. Jesus Christ, I didn't think the pain would be this bad!" He was as white as a sheet and panting.

"That local anesthetic Edwards injected in the wound must've worn off. Neal, how can I give you a shot if I can't take off your shirt?"

Neal looked up front. "Dad? Blinky? Anyone got a pocket-knife?"

Carl Morgan twisted to reach over the seat, handing Ned a small pocketknife with a bone handle pulled from a leather case that was attached to Blinky's belt. Ned was amazed at how sharp the blade had been honed. *It's sharper than a scalpel,* he thought. With three light swipes, he turned down a flap of Morgan's heavy, denim hunting shirt. He held up the syringe after wiping Morgan's arm with the swab. "You want it all, or just part? Doc gave us a syringe with the full 15 milligrams of Morphine."

"Jesus, Ned. How can you even ask? I weigh 210 pounds. Give me every goddamn drop in that syringe, and then let me lick it dry!"

Ned looked up at the road to make sure they weren't coming up on any bumps or turns. Then he stabbed in the needle, and pushed down on the plunger. There was a sudden hiss of inspiration from Morgan. Ned rubbed the alcohol swab across the shoulder where a little red dot appeared.

"Just like a nurse, huh? Maybe that's my true calling."

"Fine. Maybe I'll pinch your ass."

"The Phantom never lets anyone pinch his ass."

* * * *

What to do ... what to do? Ned was driving now. Neal's father had almost wrecked the car when he dozed-off, swerving off the shoulder of the road. An adrenaline rush from the near-accident wasn't the only thing keeping Ned alert behind the wheel. He glanced again at the brown envelope lying on the dash. They hadn't seen it until they changed drivers. Inside, on fine onionskin paper, was a striking pencil portrait of Ned, drawn from the memory of Skippy Murdoch.

"Damn, Ned. I do believe that girl's taken a shine to you," said Carl Morgan with a chuckle.

On the back of the envelope were her address and phone number.

Ned looked out the window at the darkened roadside, seeing the blurred shadows of moonlit trees go speeding past. He was not sleepy, but his mind was caught in a replay loop. Skippy, the club foot, Katherine, Skippy, the clumsy advance ... He liked thinking he attracted women and was flattered that someone as pretty as Skippy liked him. And yet, he was softly, warmly entangled in his feelings for Katherine to the extent that even considering something new seemed wrong, a perversion of their relationship. Then his mind shifted to another persona that had briefly shown itself ... the killer. There was that rising, primeval hunting instinct that had put him into a killing frenzy, an unnerving feeling on the edge of life and death, of hunter and prey that he'd never known before. He was twenty-six years old. How could he have learned so much and yet know so little about himself?

November 11, 1971, 1:30 AM

"You've got to help him, Ned. He's over at the Lakewood." It was Lunch Lefke's voice on the phone. "He's off the deep end, man. I mean, really off. Freddy's getting pissed and about to call the police. You've got to help him, man."

Then the phone in Ned's apartment clicked dead. The weary group of hunters had checked Morgan into the General and finally dropped Ned off at his apartment. He'd collapsed in his clothes onto the bed at 11:30, his alarm set for five AM. *Was this call real, or did I just dream it?* Ned wondered. He staggered down the hall to the bathroom to urinate, and then wandered in to check Blade's room. His bed was empty. Help the Blade, Lunch had said. Help the Blade. Like a sleepwalker he splashed water on his face, and then dragged a comb through his tousled, chestnut mop.

"Hi Blade." There was no response from the slumped, disheveled figure in dirty bloodstained whites. Blade was sitting on the floor outside the restroom at the Lakewood. Ned shook his shoulder.

"Blade, it's me, Ned. What'cha doin', buddy, here on the floor?"

Blade Blackston raised his head. His thickened eyelids fluttered, revealing unfocused, bloodshot whites with dilated pupils that drifted and then settled on Ned. Suddenly recognition flickered. He snickered, and then vacuously belched with spittle running indifferently off his lower lip. "It's Nedley Smedley, old boy. Nedley Smedley. Smedley. Only fren' I got." He seemed to perk up. "Why," he said, assuming an orator's pose, "I'm trolling for No's, Smedley."

"Trolling for 'No's?'"

"S'eazy ..." he slurred. He pawed at his white coat pocket, and took out a crumpled piece of paper. "Says here, I got twenty-three No's ... an' one Maybe Later." He threw his head back with a harsh laugh that sounded something like a hyena, then slumped and fell onto one elbow.

Ned shook his head. "I don't get it."

"S'eazy. Watch," Blade giggled and wiped the saliva off his chin. He pushed himself upright as a nurse came out of the ladies restroom, paused, and adjusted her skirt.

"S'ah, sa'hey, honey?" Blade struggled to steady his bobbing head.

She looked down at him in disgust and annoyance.

"S'hey, ma'am? Would you perhaps wanna fuck?"

"No."

"That's twenty-four!" Blade shrieked, making another mark on his list.

Ned leaned down and put a hand on Blackston's shoulder. "Blade, come on. Let's get out of here. You're drunk. In fact, you're past drunk. You've got Beth, old buddy. You don't need this shit." Ned tugged at his shoulder, trying to lift him up. "Come on, man."

But Blade grabbed his arm, swept a leg, and the next thing Ned knew, he'd been subjected to a lightning quick but gentle, single-leg wrestling takedown. "Bet that was as good a takedown as ol' Tipton ever threw." He looked across at Ned, and held his shoulder to steady himself. "Had Beth, you mean. Had Beth ... had Beth ... Never had Beth."

Ned looked back, surprised, and tried to say something; but Blade waved him off with a wavering hand, one finger raised in silence then sinking in desolation.

"Doan matter, Nedley, doan matter. I'll be back ... but I'll never open myself up to anyone again. Never, never, never." He waved the finger back and forth in front of Ned's nose. "She says," and here he put on a high falsetto, "'Why Vernon, you're really so sweet. But a serious relationship right now just isn't on my agenda.'" He smacked his fist against the other open palm for emphasis. "My fucking agenda! She tears my heart out with a fucking agenda!"

Tears brimmed in his bloodshot eyes and he tried to fight them back. Ashamed, he turned away from Ned, trying to force the cries down inside. Then he buried his face in his hands, his shoulders shuddering with the spasms.

"It's okay, Blade. It's okay to let it out."

"Cros', ol' Cros'. You got the gift. I could always count on you. God's finger on your forehead. He flashed a smile as he wiped the tears away. Then he twisted to tear his handkerchief out of his back pocket. He fell over clumsily, cursed, and finally gave up and wiped his nose with his hand. A pair of white-stockinged legs stopped in front of them.

"Sa'hey, hi hon'. You wouldn't wanna fuck, would you?"

"Hokay," she slurred back.

"Holy shit!"

November 24, 1971, 7:23 PM

After two days in the hospital on prophylactic antibiotics, Neal Morgan was ordered home by Farnsworth to recuperate. But within a week he was back, pale with occasional flickers of intellectual orneriness. He seemed the same old Neal, but somehow different at the same time; the crisp rounds and the mad dash up the flights of stairs were gone, and he now moved at a much more subdued pace.

Ned could feel the difference in himself as well, that his role had changed. He was still an intern, a toady, and not a "real doctor." But on the other hand, for a brief moment, Neal Morgan had been his patient, unconscious and under the knife, subservient and dependent upon his judgment. And that had permanently altered their attitudes toward each other. Morgan remained distant and cool towards Ned, a reflection of his distaste for that moment.

Meanwhile, Ned's feelings wavered between justification and guilty self-flagellation over the confused moment in Skippy Murdoch's cabin. What he chose to remember was that he'd had too much to drink, but that things had not gotten out of hand. *What actually had happened in that quasi doctor-patient moment,* he wondered? Ned felt that he had come out of this rotation a different person. The question was: was this new person someone he admired?

December 7, 1971, 2:12 PM

Ned was in the emergency room. Hazy, golden rays from the afternoon's setting sun streamed through the windows, stretching across the main ER holding area. They highlighted absolute chaos. A cordon of uniformed police stood over six prostrate, cursing motorcycle riders, belly-down, their hands cuffed behind their backs. Two patient litters were overturned in a wheels-up macabre posture, while trash and broken IV bottles dotted the floor. The cloth drapes separating two exam rooms dangled, torn halfway to the floor. The bikers lay stretched with their matted beards pancaked out in front like flattened beaver tails. Several sported knotted, bleeding welts, which were enlarging on their heads. They twisted and cursed, arms behind their backs, handcuffs chaffing, knuckles bloodied, lined up like sea gulls on a log. Police with nightsticks had subdued them.

One of the bikers was female. This "biker moll" lay on the only remaining upright litter, miraculously untouched in the shambles of the emergency room. She twisted and cursed, struggling with the arm and leg restraints that held her to the bed. A giant, red rose blossom of blood spread across the Kerlex gauze that was wrapped like a turban around her head.

These bikers had brought her in after a road accident. An LSD trip had ended badly when she discovered that her man's Harley Hog really couldn't fly. Fortunately, the cliff she thought she was launching herself from was actually an irrigation ditch—but hitting had it flipped her over the handlebars onto a rock.

The six bikers had roared into the ER entryway, blew past the sign-in desk, and threw her on a litter. "Find a fuckin' doctor, now!" they glared at Kathy. Ned had just begun his Neurosurgery rotation, and he'd come to answer the call. He pushed through the bikers, and introduced himself. A squad of hospital security quietly came up behind them.

"Don't fuck her up, man."

"I've got to at least look at her."

252

"You a real doctor or some jerk-off intern?"

Someone grabbed Ned from behind, spinning him around, and at that instant, the security guards jumped. The next thing Ned knew, he was in the middle of a brawling free-for-all. There were fists flying, metal-toed, black leather jackboots kicking, and he heard the ominous rattle of a chain. The frantic, confused melee spilled from one screened exam room to the next, as shrieking patients and scrambling nurses fled. In the middle, hanging onto the leg of the biker that had tried to kick him was Ned, while around him the grappling mob cursed and surged. In a sudden blur, a nightstick descended above Ned, striking the biker like a lightening bolt with the sickening crack of split nasal cartilage. Bloody snot from the broken nose splattered Ned. The man sagged to the floor, and Ned struggled free. There was a crescendo of wailing sirens outside, and a phalanx of city police with Billy clubs stormed the ER. There was one final, woody *thock!* This last gift from a police nightstick signaled the end of the riot, as whimpering, beaten bikers were clubbed to the ground.

Ned remained dazed in a corner. He wasn't sure, but he thought he'd been sucker-punched from behind by a glancing blow from brass knuckles. He stood up shakily, and gingerly twisted his neck. He reached up and carefully pawed at the rising lump of the side on his skull. *No blood,* he thought. *Not knocked out, but dinged ... Wasn't "dazed-but-still-conscious" what they called a Grade One concussion? Getting your bell rung?*

Nervous orderlies darted around, turning upright the over-turned trashcans, re-hanging the drapes, and sweeping up trash. Ned went over to the woman, who no longer struggled against her restraints. He saw an ugly, dark, bloody bulge under the dressing, the size of an orange, on the left side of her forehead. She seemed like she was sleeping.

"Ma'am? Ma'am?" Ned shook her shoulder.

Her eyes fluttered as she looked up sleepily.

"I'm going to take you right into x-ray, okay?"

His legs shook as he wheeled her across the hall. He wasn't sure if he was pushing the litter or hanging onto it. While he asked her questions about the accident, the x-ray technicians took skull films, a chest film, and an abdominal KUB. In between, he listened to her heart and lungs. Then, he pushed the litter back, and asked the radiology resident to give him a stat read on the films.

Ned started an IV and began to draw blood for routine labs. He was asking her name when she suddenly had a grand mal seizure, flopping like a fish on the litter, twisting in the restraints, and grunting through blue, frothy lips. Ned tried to hold her head still as he forced a twisted washcloth across her open jaw the way he'd seen Morgan do. A bite-block suddenly appeared in Kathy's hand, as she leaned across the patient's thrashing legs to keep her from jerking off the litter. The biker moll turned a deeper blue and suddenly the seizure stopped.

"What'cha got, Crosby?"

It was Peter "Bobber" Castleford from the trauma team. Castleford was now his supervising, first-year resident on neurosurgery. He wanted to become a neurosurgeon, and he had traded enough rotations that he would finish out the first year of residency on the service.

Ned explained the lady's history. Tattooed across her breasts were spider webs, a large red and black spider, a Harley motorcycle, and two names. Above the right nipple was stenciled "Blackjack's," with an arrow aimed at the nipple. Crafted on the left, in pink and blue flowery script, was "Shooter's."

The radiology resident stuck his head through the curtain. "Hey, Neurons! The skull, chest, belly ... they're all okay."

The patient's breathing was rapid, and her heart rate fluttered at 118. Ned read her blood pressure at 180 over 98. Her hematocrit was 38.

"It doesn't make sense," he muttered. "She's not shocky, but the pressure and pulse aren't right."

"First sign of increased intracranial pressure," Castleford answered. He swept a loose lock of blond hair from his porcelain-like forehead.

"Lady?" Ned shook her shoulder. "Ma'am?"

She didn't respond. Her eyelids fluttered for an instant, but she sighed and stayed silent.

"Here." Peter Castleford reached down. "Ma'am? Ma'am?" He grimaced as he drove the knuckle of his hand deep into her sternum.

"Goddamn, Doc!" She opened her eyes for a second, and then sank droozily back.

"What'd you see?" asked Castleford.

"What do you mean, what'd I see? She said, 'Goddamn, Doc!'" Ned mimicked the patient. "What'd I miss? She opened her eyes, and then closed them."

"What about the eyes?"

"Uh ... what about them?"

"Her left pupil's dilating," answered Castleford with a quiet smile. "Pupils usually blow on the same side of a subdural. She's bleeding into her head."

"But the radiologist said the skull films were normal."

"First rule of neurosurgery: Never trust anyone to read your films. Let's go see for ourselves."

As they hurried quickly from the room, Castleford called behind them for the ward clerk to page the neurosurgical chief—stat, of course—and then to call the OR and let them know they'd need a room set up for an emergency decompressive craniotomy. They swung into the darkened reading room.

"Where are those skull films?"

"What'dya need 'em for? They're okay." The bearded Radiology resident put down his Dictaphone. He was seated in the darkened room in front of a large fluorescent viewing box. He shuffled through the pile of freshly read x-rays.

"We'll see," said Castleford, confident as he crisply extracted the films with a flourish.

"Screw you! I read them ... they're fine."

Castleford held up a lateral skull film against the view box. His silhouetted nose bobbed in the dark. "If they're so fine, what's this?" His finger ran down the lateral exposure to a large line that ran around the temporal region of the skull.

"Temporal fissure. So excuse me! Interesting ... but normal." The cocky resident fingered his beard absently, like a wise old dog patiently dealing with a puppy.

Castleford held up the AP of the skull. "If it's so damn normal, how come it's pushed in about a half an inch?"

"Let me see that!" The wide-eyed radiologist grabbed at the film, his fingers tracing the edges of the depressed skull fracture. He turned white. "Sonofabitch!" he whispered, pulling at the scraggly edges of his beard.

Castleford smiled coldly down at him. "It was so big, you didn't see it. Try some humble pie, shadow man. Next time, don't be so damn sure of yourself!"

December 7, 1971, 4:27 PM

For obscure reasons, the bikers, even after having been beaten and handcuffed, refused to divulge the woman's name. As they were pushed into the police paddy wagon one called out, "You fuck her up ... we'll be back."

Now Jane "Moll" Doe was intubated and strapped in the sitting position on an adjustable operating room table. Green drapes sealed off everything except her skull. An ugly, blue-black, raw bulge on her scalp stared back at them. Half of her black mane had been shaved

WIRES AND DREAMS; BONES

away, exposing the injury. Draping towels were clipped to the skin, and in one brief moment, a large flap of her scalp was expertly turned down. Ned watched as the entire side of her scalp, from the crown down to the ear, was peeled away. Ned wondered how the Indians could ever stomach scalping someone; then he remembered that it had been the colonial English that started the practice.

The temporal artery and its tributaries lay at the base of the flap, just above the ear. Peter Castleford had done the approach. The chief neurosurgical resident, Roger Windisch, and the staff neurosurgeon, Xavier "Buzzy" Barraugh, had given Castleford the lead. They'd known him last year as an intern, and already knew that he'd soon join their neurosurgical residency. As Ned watched, he was reminded of the words of Doc Edwards. In perfect counterpoint to Castleford's deliberate speech were his quickness and manual dexterity. He had an uncanny knowledge of anatomy and a three-dimensional sense of spatial relationships. In less than five minutes, a huge temporal flap had been meticulously, and relatively bloodlessly, turned down. *The nose might bob,* Ned thought, *but Bobber "has it."*

Old, clotted blood was carefully irrigated away, exposing the fractured skull. A confident Roger Windisch took over. Gently, ever so gently, the chief resident used instruments to elevate the depressed pieces of bone. Fragmented spicules, like shards of shattered ivory, were sucked out with the neurosuction tip or delicately picked away with tweezers. Soon, the cranial fragments lay in pieces on the Mayo stand.

With hands carefully steadied, Roger made a longitudinal incision in the swollen, reddish-black dura, the membrane that pulsed up at them in their operative field, covering the brain. With utmost precision, he split it well away from the central vein, which, if lacerated, might spell instant death for the patient. The operating room was deathly silent; even George, their anesthesiologist, had ceased his idle chatter. Cushing pickups with small teeth were used to lift the dural flap. Beneath it lay a collection of clotted blood, the hematoma that was squeezing the neurological life out of this lady. Windisch gently and meticulously evacuated it with the neurosuction tip. The contused brain pulsed below with thoughts and a life of its own. The brain's ridges and convoluted folds had been distorted by intracranial pressure. They looked like rows of uncooked, hot dog wieners stuffed into a picnic basket. A small bleeder pulsed on the brain's surface, the source of this subdural hematoma.

"Careful ... careful." Dr. Barraugh's hands kept lifting involuntarily as he fought the impulse to take over the case from Roger.

The neurotip of the unipolar electrocautery approached by way of a steady hand, braced against the side of the remaining skull for stability.

"Piece of cake." Windisch's eyes and every fiber of his being were focused at that instant on the brain and its bleeding vessel.

"Careful, goddammit, Roger. Please, please be careful," said Dr. Barraugh, holding his hands up in prayer. There was an electric buzz and crackle, and smoke rose into the air.

"There."

The circulating nurse reached over and wiped the beads of perspiration from Windisch's forehead. Then she laughed and gave Dr. Barraugh a wipe, too.

"There? Shit! Did you see that smoke? You just cooked one of her dreams!" The lightness in Barraugh's eyes belied the acid barb.

"It was a bad dream. A nightmare."

"Any more bleeders?"

"Can't see any. You?"

"Nada. Zippo."

"Let's do a running on the dura, then an interrupted on the scalp. Leave a Penrose drain in the scalp, but recess it back so it's not right over the defect. We'll have to come back later and cover the hole in the skull with a stainless steel plate." Barraugh stripped off his gown and gloves. "Super job, Roger." He turned and smiled at Peter Castleford, firing an imaginary gun with his finger. "You, Killer, nice to have you back. You get your Berry Plan set up so Nixon won't draft you?"

"I got a conscientious objector deferment just so I can pray for my pals in Vietnam. I'm going to be a minister." Peter held up his hands in mock apology, "Just kidding, just kidding."

Buzz Barraugh shook his head in mock disgust and left the room.

"Got a dream, huh?" Ned had been standing quietly, like a preying mantis, for the entire case. Not once had his hands been near the wound, or even on the field. "Can I write orders, or do something?" he asked.

Windisch and Castleford were closing the dura. Their intent eyes never left the wound.

"Break scrub."

"Yes, sir."

They waited until he'd pulled open the chart. "Prophylactic antibiotics, Keflin for five days."

"Yessir."

"Decadron, 10 milligrams, IV, q twelve hours, times two days to cut down on cerebral edema. And restraints," Windisch added, almost as an afterthought. "We'll keep her paralyzed and asleep on phenobarbital for forty-eight hours. I can't have her thrashing around with that hole in her head. Anectine, per usual."

"Yessir."

Shit still ran downhill.

December 8, 1971, 2:35 AM

Ned was up with their biker craniotomy patient most of the night on the neurosurgical ward. Her vital signs went absolutely wacko. Her blood pressure skyrocketed to 222 over 140. They were afraid she might have a stroke, so they gave her intravenous reserpine and a diuretic. Then, her temperature climbed to 106.2 degrees. Ned and the evening nurse sponged her body down with cold alcohol. Suddenly, her pressure plummeted to 80 over zero with a pulse of 70. Then it shot back up to 190 over 95.

"Her regulatory system's been screwed up," he tiredly told the nurse who was helping. "The increased intracranial pressure from the cerebral swelling is messing up her body's control mechanisms."

The nurse had been working a double, and there was no response. At the head of the bed an Ohio respirator chugged and puffed its own reply.

Katherine came up to the ward with two cups of black coffee. Ned left Jane "Moll" Doe's side to meet her in the ward conference room. It was well past two in the morning, and an exhausted Crosby wondered why she was even still at the hospital? It was eerie, walking down the darkened ward, past mechanical respirators that were pushing life-giving breaths through the tracheostomies of comatose patients. In this surreal environment, he still felt a sense of disassociation from fatigue and a splitting headache from the concussion of the earlier blow to his head.

Katherine's eyes were frightened, and he noticed a tremor in her hands as she ran her fingernails into the Styrofoam coffee cup, etching random, meaningless patterns on its surface. The quiet, trademark smile that bathed him in affection was absent. Her dark eyes started like a frightened doe at his presence.

"Hi. You okay? Those bikers were something, huh?"

She didn't seem to hear him.

"I've heard from someone you know. Someone named Skippy Murdoch in Marion."

He flinched.

"She called the emergency room, trying to track you down."

Ned rubbed his hands over his glassy eyes. He was dying for sleep, and his head was pounding. *Skippy? Skippy who? What?* "So ... Katherine?"

She interrupted, "There's nothing to explain ... not really any need." She waved her hand abstractly in the air as she stared down at the coffee cup. "There's never been an obligation. I ... I just thought that we meant more ..."

"Kathy?" What the hell was this about?

"She said she wanted to follow up on what you'd seen in her cabin, and she's been trying to call you. But she doesn't know your home phone. So ... so I just gave her your damn phone number so you can talk."

Ned was groggily rubbing a bloodshot eye when he looked up and realized that Kathy had left. Gone! Just like that. He lay his aching head down on the table. *Just to sleep ... even for a few moments.*

December 9, 1971, 3:10 AM

Wasn't that Katherine's voice, calling him? Ned was so groggy that the phone had clicked dead before he could respond.

"They need you in the ER, stat."

He struggled from the bed in the night call room. Everett "No Problem" Jones, his fellow intern on neurosurgery, was gone for a week's vacation. Despite what were supposed to be the rules, Ned was looking at one week straight of being on call. One sleeve of his coat was inside out, and he couldn't get his arm though it. In exasperation he finally stopped, fished out the sleeve, and then descended the stairwell to the dreaded ER. Suddenly he cursed and turned around in disgust, realizing that he wasn't wearing shoes. When he finally arrived, his hair was, paradoxically, such a mess that it actually looked neat. Looking around the emergency room with sleep-puffed eyes and a grimy growth of beard, he extended his arms to anyone in a questioning shrug.

"Room seven," the ward clerk pointed. Ned knew that Kathy had rotated her shift to nights in an effort to avoid seeing him. He'd been unable to talk to her, and whatever Skippy had hinted at remained a mystery. He was sleep-deprived, at the hospital all week, and there'd been no phone call from Skippy either. But it had been Katherine who summoned him, and Ned could only surmise that she'd disappeared in an effort to avoid him.

It was three in the morning, and except for an orderly mopping the floor with antiseptic soap, the ER was virtually empty. Ned opened the door to room seven, and in the center, on a litter, sat an old man holding his head with his hands.

He looked over at Ned and grinned. "I'm a holdin' my head cause it don't feel right," he said.

Ned held out his hand to shake and introduce himself, but the patient declined.

"If you don't mind, I just feel like supporting myself."

Ned looked down at the chart. The patient was Lacey Bigelow ... ninety-two years old. He had the face of an ancient sage. Alert, gray eyes peered inquisitively from beneath scraggly, white eyebrows. Lacey's weathered skin was drawn like a fine parchment over his prominent cheekbones and a narrow, hooked nose. Splotches of brown sunspots dotted his thin scalp, where wisps of closely cropped white hair were neatly parted.

"Mr. Lacey, sir!" Ned warmed up to him. He liked his eyes. Ninety-two years old! "How can we help you, sir? Why are you here?"

"I was a changin' a light bulb, doctor."

Lacey's voice was quiet, yet commanding. He carefully enunciated his words, and Ned found himself hanging on every one.

"Don't know why it burned out ... Maybe because it was in that mildewy north corner of the house, I guess. Excuse me, doctor. I don't mean to ramble. But as I was changing it, I lost my balance on the second step of the ladder." He chuckled, "We old folks lose our balance a lot more than we care to admit! Well I commenced to hit the floor, and I felt a cracking sensation, and a little electric jolt ran down my body. You see, I landed on my head. From then on I felt like I needed to hold my head up in place. Things didn't feel right, so here I am!" He smiled across to Ned and then nodded towards the x-ray view box. "The emergency doctors took those films, and I guess they sent for you."

"You weren't knocked unconscious, were you?"

"Nope."

"Any numbness or tingling down the arms or legs, now?" Ned wandered over to the view box to look at the films.

"Nope."

"Hmmm. Mind if I ask a question?"

"Sure, sonny, I mean doctor, sir. Ask away." The gray eyes smiled and Lacey's Adam's apple bobbed with a swallow.

"How is it you were climbing a ladder to change a light bulb at two in the morning? I mean, isn't that a little unusual?"

"Not if you're ninety-two! You're too young to know, but we old folks don't need the sleep you young whippersnappers need. Me, I usually sleep about four hours a night, from two 'til six. Why, when you're my age you've got to keep the motion going."

"Keep the motion going?"

The man tentatively moved one hand expressively, holding the other under his chin. "Old folks' joints get stiff; you know, gotta' walk and move around. If the joints don't get you, the lower plumbing do. Hah! Don't walk enough, some pretty ornery bowel movements around the corner, sonny!" He chuckled. "Course, sometimes, no motion can imply motion. But that's another story."

Ned saw it. A flash of recognition seared his brain. Lacey Walters' first cervical vertebra, where the neck joined the skull, was broken. That explained the sharp crack, the electric jolt, and his feeling that he needed to hold his head stable. In textbooks they called it a Jefferson's fracture. Where the neck joined the skull, the first cervical vertebra was broken. If the spinal cord were injured along with the vertebra at this level, it would not be a partial neurological loss of function in arms and legs. It would be instant death.

"You ever been in a hospital before, Mr. Bigelow?"

"Never."

"Never? Not even sick?

"Nope."

"Just once?"

"God as my witness." A solemn hand came up.

Ned came over to him. "Please, just keep holding your head, sir. I need to get some help." He poked his head into the deserted landscape of the emergency room and yelled, "Anybody here?" After a moment Katherine came out of the nurses' office. She wouldn't meet his eyes, and her voice had an unaccustomed clinical detachment.

"Yes, doctor?"

"Kathy, please—I need a Philadelphia collar, stat. And I need the neuro resident. This man," he gestured towards Mr. Bigelow, "he's got an unstable broken neck."

"Neuro was called, doctor. There was no answer, and that's why we called you."

"Please, Kathy. Get me the collar, and get me some help. If this man makes one false move, even just a sneeze, he could die on the spot."

Mr. Bigelow's snow-white eyebrows assumed an agitated wiggle, and his eyes widened at hearing this report. Kathy returned with a plastizote, pre-formed cervical collar with Velcro straps to hold it in place. With Ned holding Mr. Bigelow's head stable, Kathy placed the collar around his neck. Lacey's eyes nervously looked back and forth between them, reading the concern in their faces.

"Looks like I done a good one, huh?"

Ned thought the collar seemed tight but secure. He laughed nervously, "Looks that way, sir. Yep, you done a good one."

All of a sudden, Lacey Bigelow's eyes rolled back. He retched out a half gasp that turned into a gurgle, and he fell backwards onto the litter. There was a vibrating tremor to his left hand, and then no limb movement at all. He began to turn blue. His eyes vibrated and rolled unnaturally back and forth between Ned and Katherine.

Without thinking, Ned ripped open the room's intubation set. He hooked the laryngoscope blade onto the light source and swung it open. Suddenly he paused above Mr. Bigelow's open mouth. "Christ," he muttered out loud, "If I lever his jaw open too much, I could damage the cord even more."

Bigelow's color worsened, turning a deep blue.

"What should I do?" He looked helplessly up towards Katherine. "Will I bring back a ninety-two-year-old man? Or will I bring back a quadriplegic who will curse me on a respirator for a week or two of the life that's left?"

Katherine looked back at him, wide-eyed and silent. Suddenly, some unknown instinct seemed to take over, and he gently inserted the blade. Ever so smoothly, he pried back the mandible, and cleanly slid the tube down the trachea. He grasped the ventilation bag from Kathy's trembling hands, and gave three quick breaths to aerate the

265

man. Mr. Bigelow's bluish color brightened. Ned carefully wrapped one-inch adhesive tape around the tube, and then around Mr. Bigelow's neck to stabilize it. He inflated the little protective cuff, and breathed again for the man. Mr. Bigelow's eyes blinked once, and he looked up at them.

Katherine pivoted on her heel, stuck her head out the door, and bawled to the ward clerk. "Ginger! You find that neuro resident, wherever he is. Find that damn resident, and get him here now! Wake up the whole hospital if you have to!"

When she returned, she saw Mr. Bigelow's hands vibrating through the same sequence of rhythmic twitch and tremor that they'd seen before. His feet started next. Ned continued to breathe for him with the bag. Suddenly, he stretched out one arm, then the other and experimentally wiggled his sinewy fingers. His eyes looked up at Ned through the brush pile of bushy, white eyebrows, and he made writing motions with his fingers.

"You want to write something?"

Lacey seemed to nod yes.

Ned turned to Katherine, "Kathy, do we have a chart and a writing tablet that Mr. Bigelow could write on?"

She ran to the nurse's station and returned with a pad and a pencil. Lying on the bed, with the tube still down his throat, Mr. Bigelow grasped the pad with trembling hands and his bony fingers scribbled. Then he thrust the pad over his head, back to Ned. In a scrawling, ragged script, Mr. Lacey Bigelow had written: "Thanks, doc. Sure thought I was a goner."

When Ned looked back at Lacey, he thought he could see tears in the man's eyes.

December 9, 1971, 3:46 AM

"Sorry I was late," said Peter Castleford. "I was helping the nurses do ice baths for that biker lady again. Her temp's back up to 105 degrees. What'cha got?"

Ned was surprised. "It's been two days since we operated. You think maybe she's got an infection?"

Castleford shook his head negatively while he scanned Mr. Bigelow's x-rays. "No, it's too soon. I think her brain's temperature control mechanism is still out of whack from the head injury." But then he grinned, "I CYA'ed it, anyway with a stat CBC, urine, and blood cultures. Her chest sounded good on the ventilator, and I don't think the temperature is coming from her lungs. So anyway, just to be safe, I changed the prophylactic antibiotics."

Ned put down Lacey's chart, on which he'd been writing orders. "Why didn't you call me? I could have helped."

Castleford shrugged. "I just happened to be finishing up on the ward when the nurses grabbed me. Besides, with Everett on vacation we can all pick up a little of the slack. Anyway, one thing just seemed to lead to another." Castleford let out a big breath, "Phew! Looks like you were busy. How'd you ever get the tube down without killing him?" He looked at the x-rays and then back at Ned. "In fact, why is he alive, at all?"

Ned told him what had happened, his voice breaking at times as he related his uncertain plunge into action. Having risked total paralysis of this man, he was apologetic, and a run of defensive words spilled out. "I didn't know what to do, Peter. There was no one here. One minute he was talking to us ... and the next minute it was either tube him or watch him die. It was that simple. I was afraid I'd be tubing a future quadriplegic." He stopped to calm himself. "You can see it seems to have worked out okay. What should we do?"

Castleford turned to Katherine. "Call the neurosurg floor, please. Have them send down the rotating Stryker bed, and the

Crutchfield tongs. We need to stabilize our friend here." He turned to Ned, "Cros', start shaving Mr. Bigelow's temporal areas while I explain to him what's going on."

While Ned shaved Lacey's head, Dr. Castleford told the patient about his broken neck, its instability, and the need to apply protective traction through stabilizing tongs. As he talked, the orderlies pushed in a huge, circular frame with a bed in the middle, and a cart with traction ropes, pulleys, and tongs. Mr. Bigelow wrote on his pad again, asking them when the tube could come out. Castleford read the note, and told him they'd extubate him as soon as the tongs were on and they had control of the fracture. Castleford used iodine to antiseptically scrub on each side of Lacey's head. He used a long needle to inject one percent Xylocaine with epinephrine, raising a large, white, vaso-constricted welt on either side of the scalp. He paused after each step, patiently explaining to Lacey what was going to happen next. With a number 11 scalpel blade, he stabbed on each side into the midpoint of the skull, drawing blood. Into each stab wound, he inserted the stainless steel, needlepoint end of the Crutchfield tongs. A rope was attached to the tongs and ran through a pulley off the end of the bed.

"Try five pounds of traction, Ned. He's not big man."

Ned gently added the weights. As the rope took up the tension, the tongs dug into Lacey's scalp.

"Perfect. Take a deep breath for me, Mr. Bigelow."

Lacey let out a deep sigh that hissed through the tube.

"I think its safe, Ned." He looked down at Lacey, "You want that tube out, sir?"

Mr. Bigelow blinked yes. Castleford used a syringe to suck the air out of the protective cuff, and then he gently pulled out the tube. Lacey coughed up some blood-tinged phlegm, and Kathy wiped it off his cheek.

Lacey looked like a confused, snow-headed apparition, head in tongs, bloody bandages on either side of his head, hanging in traction.

"My, oh my," he said, wide-eyed. "In all my ninety-two years, I didn't expect to see such things! Son, I don't know what happened. It seemed for a moment, like a lightning bolt hit my neck. The next thing I knew, you was breathing for me through that tube thing. My, oh my."

Ned beamed. "Sir. I just wanted to hear the rest of your story."

"What story?"

"Well, you know, you were telling us how stillness could mean motion. I wanted to see what you meant. We don't get too many ninety-two-year-old bits of wisdom here."

Mr. Bigelow chuckled. "Well, sonny. It's kinda' past my bedtime. In fact, it's way past. But you come by tomorrow, and you and I will have a little talk."

Ned and Dr. Castleford decided that, together, they'd push Mr. Bigelow up to the ward. As they rolled the Stryker rotating bed out into the emergency room, an uncharacteristic echo of their footsteps sounded through the empty emergency room. And, as she watched them depart, the emptiness was also echoed in the hollow look in Katherine's eyes.

December 10, 1971, 7:36 AM

"Jane 'Moll' Doe, Doctor Barraugh. We still don't know who she is. She's now three days post-decompressive craniotomy. We've stopped the phenobarb and anectine, and she's no longer paralyzed. Restraints, obviously, de rigeur."

The neurosurgical team paused in its rounds before this patient, who was posturing in de-cerebrate rigidity. Her brain was sending all sorts of unregulated messages to her body. Her arms were tightly held against her sides, fists clenched and twisted, palms out. In the meantime her thigh muscles spasmed and her toes pointed downward. Occasionally she would fight the ventilator, breathing on her own. In between breaths, her teeth chewed at the endotracheal tube and airway protector. Her eyes were puffed out black and blue. She looked like a raccoon in a huge, turban-like dressing with foam rubber protecting her head.

"That's good," Dr. Barraugh told Dr. Windisch. "She's coming out of it. If we had to keep her tubed any longer, we'd have to start thinking about a trach. Keep an eye on her, and when she consistently overrides the ventilator, pull the tube."

They moved to the next bed. In it lay Mr. Claude Juneau, a 53-year-old man silently writhing and twitching on soiled, twisted sheets. His motions never ceased. He had Huntington's chorea. Spittle oozed from his slack jaw, and vacant eyes stared past them. Dr. Barraugh explained the case to Ned.

"Huntington's chorea is a hereditary, sex-linked, degenerative condition of the brain. It affects males only, carried on the Y gene. It's a progressive, degenerative condition of the brain's basal ganglia and the cerebral cortex. Dementia, or senile mentation, is part of it. Mr. Juneau's had this disease now for about ten years. He is totally unaware of his surroundings, and, in fact, he's near death. The reason he's on our ward is because I have an NIH grant to study the brains of people with degenerative conditions, using a new machine from the university that does what's called computerized axial tomography. A CAT scan. I don't understand the technology, but a CAT scan takes pictures, like slices, through the brain. This guy Juneau was on the medical ward, being treated for pneumonia. We transferred him to our ward so Peter Castleford can do a trach and assist with pulmonary toilet. Then we'll take him by ambulance to the university, where they'll paralyze him with succinylcholine to stop the twitching, and do the scan."

Ned shuddered involuntarily. Whatever humanity Claude Juneau had left was trapped inside a writhing, tortuous prison of a body. Was his mind destroyed, he wondered? Or was he an alert, conscious prisoner inside living hell? He realized that you could go mad, asking that question, and decided it'd be better to be detached and at least try to learn from him. It may be the last useful thing he does on earth—to teach someone—he thought.

"Mr. Lacey Bigelow. A ninety-two-year-old ..."

"Ninety-two!" Buzz Barraugh looked down at Mr. Bigelow's smiling face. "Is that really true? Ninety-two?" He reached down to shake his bony, out-stretched hand.

Lacey gave him a firm grip back. "God as my witness. Born December 27, 1879."

Castleford and Ned related to Dr. Barraugh the night's events.

The latter scratched his head. "I would never have believed it. He must have slightly bruised the spinal cord, but not enough to cause permanent damage. It's amazing he survived the event." He smiled and looked down at Mr. Bigelow, jerking his thumb back towards Ned, "You know, Mr. Bigelow, I hear all kinds of lies about this intern. You never know what to believe, anymore. But in this case, I think some of the lies are true." He sighed then winked to Roger Windisch, "I guess it's better to be lucky than good."

December 11, 1971, 10:34 AM

They stood across from each other on either side of Claude Juneau's neck. Roger Windisch had mumbled something to Castleford while they were scrubbing, and then he left. Georgie had paralyzed Mr. Juneau with succinyl choline and quickly intubated him. Ned felt a wave of relief as the Huntington Chorea patient's incessant writhing suddenly stopped. Mr. Juneau was momentarily at peace.

"Roger says it's your reward."

"Huh?"

Castleford grinned, "The case is yours. I'll walk you through it. You deserve it. You've been on call for four straight nights, and I've never heard you complain. Lucky for all of us, it hasn't been too busy."

It hasn't been busy? A frazzled, exhausted Ned asked, "You sure you don't want to just do this real quick, Peter, and get it over with?"

"Stop being a martyr ... I know you'd kill for a case."

Ned laughed. Castleford was right. People in surgery liked to do things with their hands, to do something that would help or heal. He looked across the table at Castleford, who was already explaining the approach.

"Usually, we do this under local anesthesia. But with him twitching all over the place, I asked for George."

George stood up and gave them a formal bow. Ned looked up at the anesthesiologist, and then back at the neck, which started to loom larger and larger before his eyes.

Castleford continued, "Simple anatomy." He pointed with a gloved hand, "You can see his larynx."

Ned nodded, looking down at the Adam's apple.

"Just below, feel the cricoid cartilage."

Ned ran his gloved finger back and forth over the protruding bulge in the neck.

"Make your cut longitudinal, from the cricoid down to just above the suprasternal notch."

Ned did as he was told, using a number 15 scalpel blade. Blood oozed up, but he quickly sought the bleeders and confidently cauterized them. The concept of someone bleeding because he'd cut them no longer bothered him. Castleford used little pronged rakes to pull the skin away.

"See the trachea"?"

Pinkish, blue-white cartilage looked back at them. Ned nodded.

"There's no thyroid isthmus in this guy. Sometimes you have to ligate the bridging tissue just it to get it out of the way. Cut a circular hole in the cartilage, just below the second ring, oh ... say about three eighths of an inch in diameter." He grinned, "In case we go metric, that's one centimeter!"

Ned did as he was told, carefully using pick-ups to remove the cartilage. Underneath was George's tube.

"You popped my cuff, asshole," George grumbled from behind the drapes.

"Sorry, George, I didn't know." Ned looked up nervously. "What do I do now?"

"Well, since you ruined my tube, why don't you put in one of your own?"

George gave Mr. Juneau a quick breath of air, then extubated him. It was weird, Ned thought, watching the endotracheal tube slide right out from under his eyes. He picked up the curved, stainless steel, tracheostomy tube from the instrument stand, and inserted it down the hole. Then he tied the securing strings around Mr. Juneau's neck.

"There!" Castleford smiled. "And a job well-done!"

Ned laughed and raised an eyebrow. "Why praise such an easy thing?" He suspected this school-teacherish new mentor was patronizing him.

Castleford said with emphasis. "Ned ... Murphy's law. Anyone can screw up even easy things. Believe it or not, last year over at university, a resident killed a man doing a trach. Got into one of the thyroid arteries ... One thing led to another, and the next thing you know the guy codes and cools it. Big lawsuit, too. The more you do, the more proficient you become. But death isn't exactly supposed to be part of the learning curve! Every surgeon has to learn on someone. When I said nice job, I meant it!" Castleford smiled.

Ned applied the dressings, carefully adjusting them so they would not chafe or bind around Mr. Juneau's neck. George suctioned Mr. Juneau's lungs clear, and they moved him off the OR table over to his litter. As he walked away, Ned silently thought, *Thank you, Mr. Claude Juneau, for the chance to learn, and to maybe be able to help someone else more proficiently, another day. Thank you, whatever part of you is left inside.*

December 18, 1971, 3:10 PM

"Well sonny, you doctors are going to have to do something pretty soon, or you'll have a ninety-two-year-old grouch who hasn't had his BM in about three days!"

Ned couldn't help but laugh. Mr. Lacey Bigelow, facedown on the Stryker frame, looked like a rag doll stretched out in some weird erector set with tongs and traction hanging from his head. Ned and a floor nurse had just removed the clamshell after rotating him over from lying on his back. Ned sat down on a low stool, so that he could look up when he spoke and see Mr. Bigelow's face.

"They say tomorrow, Lacey, we'll put you in a halo jacket. That way, we can get you up and walking. The halo device is kind of like a steel ring that goes around the outside of your head, with four little pins that stick into the skull. Metal struts go down from the steel ring to attach to a plaster body jacket. It's awkward, but it'll hold your head stable and enable you to get around."

"Sounds like I'll be pretty stiff up top. You know we old folks got to move around ..." Lacey groaned, his scraggly white eyebrows furrowing.

"Lacey," Ned scolded, "you know we're doing the best we can. You broke your neck."

"Don't get all in an uproar, doc." Lacey waved his hand impatiently. "It's just that ... well, a man gets used to his habits. It's hard to adjust. I went through three wives, you know. I out-lived them all. Finally, it got too painful to bury any more, so I've been living by myself for these last eight years."

"Isn't it lonely?"

"Course, it's lonely, sonny," Lacey sighed. "But I got plenty to do. There's the daily crossword puzzle in each morning paper, then a walk to the post office at noon followed by checkers in the park with Ernie or Slim. Catch up on the evening news, and then I spend the evening writing in my diary or watching *Gun smoke* or *Perry Mason*. Plenty to keep a man occupied, sonny. Plenty to keep the motion going." Lacey grinned down at Ned through the opening in the Stryker frame.

Ned scratched his head. "Keep the motion going ... keep the motion going. What's all this 'keep the motion going,' Lacey?"

"Sonny, motion is life. Think about it. One day, I woke up, and my first wife, Lil, the love of my life, lay in bed next to me, silent, cold, and asleep forever. I come home from work to my second one, two years later, the same. She was lying on the kitchen floor. Hell, not even a hint of trouble. They said she had a bad heart. Now I let five years go by before I commence to remarry. I was retired then, and Lizzy and I hit it off real well. It lasted ten years ..." he sighed. "When we traveled, she even brought one of those little portable checkers sets, you know, with the little magnets so the pieces stayed on the board." Lacey's eyes watered a bit. "One day, though, the motion left her, too."

Ned remembered the riddle his patient had hinted at when they first met in the ER. "You said the other day that stillness implies motion. How's that?"

Lacey arched a fuzzy, white eyebrow, and gestured with his hand. The traction jiggled and Ned looked nervously at it for a moment.

"Well think about it, sonny. When you been watchin' things as long as I have, you see things that you missed when you were young and in a hurry.

"Such as?"

"Well, look at a ramp that goes from a dock down to the water at low tide. The weathered, sun-bleached pilings are exposed ... covered with shiny, black mussels and barnacles, and that ramp's just hanging there at an angle. Well heck, sonny, when you look at that hanging ramp, you just know that when the tide comes in, it's going to go up!"

"I see what you mean." Ned started to get up.

"You don't get off that easy, sonny." Lacey's sinewy fingers snagged his sleeve. "Think of one yourself."

Ned thought for a while, and scratched his head. "I can't."

"Come on ... come on." Lacey waved a bony finger impatiently. "You young whippersnappers are in too much of a hurry to take the time to think."

Suddenly Ned brightened. "How about a runner, Lacey? A sprinter, okay? It's the hundred-yard dash, see, and he's poised in the starting blocks. The gun is raised, his muscles are tensed, straining and ready to go ... but frozen, no motion. Every fiber in his body is waiting to explode. But while you see him frozen at the ready, you think of the motion to come."

"Well there you go, sonny. We'll turn you into a regular human being yet," Lacey chuckled. "While you're at it, you better figure out a way to move these here bowels a' mine. Right now the stillness is implying one hell of an explosion!"

December 20, 1971, 10:27 AM

"Hello." Their lady biker had awakened.

"Hi. I see you're awake."

"It looks that way. Do you mind if I ask—Just where in the hell am I? And what exactly am I doing here?'"

Ned laughed, and told her the story. She looked like an apparition from hell, a bizarre half-human, half-raccoon. Black and blue rings circled her eyes, while tinges of greenish yellow ran down her cheeks where the old blood was breaking up. Her swollen eyes had shrunk back to normal, but her left sclera had popped a capillary, turning the entire white of the eye a deep blood red. Crowning this was her huge, black mane—Mohawk-like, deranged on the right, with growing stubble on the left where they'd shaved her for the decompressive craniotomy. The healing scalp wound was an angry red. Puffy swelling had slowly subsided over the last ten days.

"Do you remember your name? They wouldn't tell us."

"Sure. Francesca Lambert. I'm Franny. Who's they?"

"Your friends." When she looked back blankly, Ned offered the only clues he had. "Uh ... somebody named Blackjack is tattooed on your right breast," he said, trying not to blush. "With 'Shooter' on the left."

She didn't look down at her breasts, but Ned thought he detected a flicker of recognition in her coal-black eyes. She ran her finger thoughtfully up and down her little, pert ski-jump nose as she looked out the window with her brow furrowed. Then she sighed and looked back at him.

"I seem to be unable to remember a lot of things. I know who I am, and that my parents live in Claremont, California. In fact," she held out her hand in an affected manner, "I remember going to Stevens College for Women, to get 'finished.'" She laughed and her black eyes flashed. "So how about it, doc? Got any grub in this joint?"

There was a thumping behind Ned, and he saw Francesca's eyes suddenly widen in amazement. Lacey Bigelow was using a walker for balance. There was a stainless steel halo ring glistening around his head, bolted to steel struts running down into his plaster body jacket. Little tufts of lamb's wool stuck out around his skinny arms and the neck hole, where extra padding was necessary. Lacey's snow-white wisps of hair and bushy eyebrows made him look like an ancient, wild mountain man. Together, these two patients might have passed as visitors from outer space. He paused from thumping around the ward to gaze down at them.

"Well, well, sonny. Looks like our sleeping beauty has awakened." He rigidly turned his plaster-encased torso from Ned to the lady. "Lacey Bigelow, at your service, ma'am. I'd bow, but I'd probably fall over and stab you with my halo."

She laughed and laughed at this courtly monster.

January 30, 1972, 11:23 PM

A raucous cheer arose from Ned's on-call room. He approached the door tentatively. He'd heard another EADR party had been planned, now becoming a tradition among the interns. He twisted the door handle and tried to squeeze into the packed room. The reek of beer and stale cigarette smoke engulfed him. Two side windows and the vent over the door had been cranked open for ventilation. Music blared from a transistor radio. The phone rang incessantly and interns jumped back and forth across the beds to answer it, shouting orders back to angry nurses.

"Two kings."

"Three deuces."

"Shit."

"Does anyone know if this is a straight?"

"Hell, read 'em and weep, you fud puckers, a flush!"

"Damn! Damn."

"Smedley, my man! Smedley, come join us." Blade jumped up from the half-dressed circle on the floor. He was flushed with excitement, and minus both shoes and shirt. Only his baggy, white intern pants remained. "Strip poker, Smedley."

Ned chuckled at Blade, who seemed to have recovered his zest for life and women. Blade winked as he pulled Ned close.

"I know you think I'm up to my old tricks ... but I'm not."

Ned studied his steel-blue eyes, which were deadly serious.

"I've learned my lesson from Beth. People do have feelings that should be respected."

Pawing hands grasped at his pants, and the Blade was pulled back into the circle. He gave Ned another wink.

"But I can't help it if they want me." The crowd cheered.

Ned glanced around the room. Sal DeLuca was curled in the corner in a fetal position, sound asleep on the bed. Peter Castleford seemed quiet and aloof, sipping on a soft drink next to Sal. He nodded his head towards Ned and tipped his can, jauntily. There were strange nurses from other wards that Ned had never seen before, curvaceous and smiling ... many quite interesting.

Jammed between the beds on the floor in a circle were the poker players. Giggling and drunk in his underwear sat David Hazelette-Warner. He'd been accused of stripping clothing without showing his hand. Next to him sat Eleanor, shuffling the cards. Her fingers slashed like rapiers as the deck snapped and fluttered. Cards darted out mechanically, and her eyes scanned the room's players. Her little pink tongue flicked in and out.

"Gentlemen, serious damage could be done by this hand. A member might be seen ... Not that that's anything we haven't seen before ..." She let a stony gaze linger for an instant on Ned. She was bra-less, and down to her panties. "Cards?" A trickle of sweat ran down between her breasts as she threw her head back to swallow some beer.

"Two."

"Gimme three."

"One."

"Goin' for the flush. He's goin' for the flush!"

"Fuck you!"

"I need a whole new hand. Five, please."

"Damage, gentlemen. Serious, serious damage. Anyone wants five, may soon show some skin."

"Three."

"Miss Katherine wants three."

Katherine! The room seemed to swim for a moment before Ned. He looked down. Her back was towards him, in the circle. Her shiny, auburn hair spilled out over her sweater. Several beer cans rested next to her bare feet. So she hadn't been losing that badly ... yet. He reached down and put a hand on her shoulder. She started at his touch, and for an instant, their eyes met. Then she blushed and looked away. He held out his open hand to her, and softly said, "Come?" She shook her head and took a swig of beer. He caught her eye again, and said, "Come ... please?" She refused to acknowledge his presence.

"Two kings, again. Christ!"

"Ha! Got you beat! Two pair."

"Shit!"

"Three nines!"

"Sonofabitch!"

"Well look at that. Miss Katherine's the winner. Looks like its sweater time."

Ned reached down again to pull Katherine up from the circle. He would not be denied. It was time to talk, to end the pain. Whatever it was that had been meaningful to Skippy, he hadn't a clue. But for him, Katherine had all the meaning. She was his center, his core, a focus for his heart that until now had been unspoken. And now was time to speak. He pulled her up from the floor, ignoring the catcalls, and they left the raucous party, slipping down the hall to Sal DeLuca's on-call room. He drew her inside, and they sat on Sal's bed tenderly holding each other, and rocking back and forth until dawn.

January 31, 1972, 3:01 PM

"You sure you got everything?"

"I didn't come with anything, sonny."

"Well, yeah ... uh, I guess that's true. I just wanted to check." Ned grinned nervously. "Just trying to keep your motion going."

"Yeah, yeah!" Lacey's white eyebrows impatiently wiggled. "Well, the nurse digging out that impacted constipation nearly moved me to tears." Mr. Bigelow's eyes twinkled. "Speaking of movement, that young lady with the broken head sure moved in a hurry back to her family in Claremont. Amazing how the bored rich think tinkering on the wild side is glamorous. Kind of reminds me where I read in the paper about that party some rich Manhattan socialites had for a Bronx gang. They thought it was unbelievably chic, that is, until the gang robbed everyone there. Got what their bleeding-heart asses deserved."

Ned shrugged. "Bad as things were, her accident seemed to awaken her to reality."

"Well," said Lacey, "should we try again?"

"Might as well."

Ned pushed Mr. Bigelow's wheelchair out the front door of the General, down the wheelchair ramp, and out into the driveway. They'd already tried once to send him home by taxi. But with the steel halo struts sticking above his head, he couldn't get into the cab. Peter Castleford had volunteered his beat-up, convertible TR-6, and he'd driven it into the circular driveway with the convertible top down. They carefully maneuvered Lacey into the passenger side, and hanging onto his struts, they lowered him into the seat. A grinning orderly jumped into the back, ready to help get Lacey situated back at home. After that, visiting nurses would look in daily. Meals-on-Wheels would come by, so he refused the social worker's offer to send him to a nursing home.

"No motion in those kind of places, sonny."

Ned leaned over the car door. "Uh, Mr. Walters, before you go, I got a little something for you. I'll be by to see that you use it." Ned fished into his white intern's jacket pocket, and pulled out a folded, miniature checkerboard made of bright shiny metal with the magnetic pieces stacked inside.

Lacey twisted his torso up to smile at Ned. "Why thank you, sonny. I really do appreciate this." He reached up and gratefully shook Ned's hand. "I got one last thought for you. All this talk about motion, you keep jabbering." Lacey twisted his trunk so that he could look Ned in the eye. "When does incessant motion imply stillness?"

Lacey paused, but Ned was mystified.

"Well, sonny, you go look at that Juneau fellow, and look in his eyes ... You'll know what I mean."

February 9, 1972, 5:47 AM

Ned was like an automaton that arrived early each morning on orthopedics. He went through the motions of keeping individual patient cards up to date, but he was lost. He spent a week in the throes of the depressing realization of how awesomely insignificant his knowledge of medicine was. Each decision was excruciatingly painful, and he agonized at night, worrying about hurting someone. His own naïveté never seemed to escape Farnsworth on rounds.

"I cannot hide my disapprobation at the peculation of your charges," Farnsworth sniffed to the chief resident.

The maze of treatment options for the injuries and fractures they saw on orthopedics led to chronic indecisiveness. Ned fell asleep at night with his head resting in Watson-Jones' textbook on orthopedic surgery.

"How should we treat this broken tibia, Ned?"

"I don't know."

"Well ... our options include: a long leg cast, non weight-bearing; partial weight-bearing in a PTB cast like that guy Sarmiento at USC recommends; open the damn thing and put on a plate; stick a rod down it; or put the leg in pins and plaster."

"I still don't know."

"Actually, Ned, any one of those options would work. You just have to know the rules of treatment for each ..."

This left him few outlets for solace. At the hospital he and Blade were a team, and made rounds together. Blackston wasn't worried too much about what he didn't know. He was worried about women, and he kept trying to convince Ned that he'd turned over a new leaf. Ned kept up the skepticism, asking Blade where was it that Miss Leaf slept? Blade grimaced.

Ned discovered the completely different demands of the orthopedic rotation. The confusing service went by like a speeding locomotive. For two months he cared for patients with broken bones and torn ligaments. He made his daily rounds through a maze of ropes, pulleys, suspended weights, and counter-traction, delicately holding splintered, fractured limbs in alignment—angles of force, muscular deformity, counter-deformity. It drove him crazy trying to make sense of which should be chosen: Split-Russell's traction, Buck's traction, Halo traction ... Just about the time it finally started to make sense, he reached the end of the rotation. In time, the patients' bones healed. But the frantic pace of the hospital didn't change, nor did the cries of pain from the injured.

This period was marked by several noteworthy events. Once a week he visited with Lacey Bigelow to play checkers. He nourished a deep affection for the old man. He couldn't let go of his feeling of protectiveness, because, for once, a situation in which he'd acted on impulse had turned out right! Ned wanted to keep a link with the lovable old codger. During those visits, Lacey's wrinkled, sun-spotted, bony fingers would carefully cradle a checker as he took his time, thoughtfully placing the vulnerable piece in an invitingly innocent trap. The deliberate, patient thoughtfulness drove Ned crazy, because he would always see the obvious trap and dodge it, only to fall into the real trap that was disguised beneath it. He got a kick out of Lacey's wry euphemisms, and he later wrote them down when he returned home. One day Lacey came home from the neurosurgical clinic unadorned with his rigid steel halo.

"I'm free again, sonny."

Ned's eyes brimmed with pleasure. He might be "only an intern," but he'd made his own decisions, the right decisions that had mattered. Lacey was a glowing ember of refuge from the cold sterility of the General.

Another noteworthy event was the setting of a little girl's fractured forearm in the emergency room. It was near the end of the orthopedic rotation, and Ned had gained some experience in setting broken bones. Katherine had called him, and they walked together into the fracture room of the ER. Little Shawna Pritchert lay on a litter. She seemed like a tomboy, with ragged jeans and a crooked baseball cap that hid sandy brown hair, cropped off in a pageboy. She clung to a beat-up baseball mitt with her good hand. Ned decided to nickname her "Skeeter." Shawna was eight years old, and she had soft dark lashes and big brown eyes that were wide and trusting. He sat down with her to explain about her broken radius.

"Skeeter ... it's broken, see? Look at the x-ray."

He held it up to the light, and they put their heads together to look at it.

"Can you see the break?" Ned pointed at the cracked, angled bone. He angled it over to the mother, too so she could see as well.

"Yes," she said. "I can see it."

"Now, Skeeter, if we just leave it like it is, your arm will be bent and crooked for the rest of your life. It won't work well. You don't want that, do you, 'cause you won't be able to play baseball?"

Her trusting gaze met his, and she firmly set her chin with resolve. "No. I don't want to grow up crooked."

"Skeeter, I've got to pull on it, real quick, to put it back in place. It'll hurt a little, and then it won't hurt much at all. It's what I've got to do to help you get better, okay?"

She looked over at her mom, and then back at Ned.

"Will it hurt a lot?" She held her arm away from him, protectively cradling it with her other hand.

"Skeeter, you'll cry for just a little, and then you'll be all better. You'll even get a new cast." Ned smiled cheerfully. "I'll be the first to sign it."

Her little brow furrowed and she pursed her lips. "Promise?"

"I promise."

She looked over at her mother again, and then at Katherine. Then she took a deep breath and sighed, lying back on the litter with her baseball cap falling off to the side. "I guess you can go ahead." She trustingly held out the crooked forearm towards Ned.

He hoped he wouldn't let her down.

He quickly injected some Xylocaine into the break to try to anesthetize it. Then, he grasped her wrist and forearm, like he'd been taught by the residents, and with a quick pull and a pronating twist, Ned set the bone. There was a muffled deep crunch and Skeeter screamed. Then she sobbed fiercely as tears ran freely down her cheeks.

"It hurts, Mommy, it hurts, it hurts ..."

Mrs. Pritchert cradled her daughter's head and kissed her cheek, while Ned furiously rolled cotton Webril and plaster onto the arm. Later, they put their heads together again to look at the post-reduction films. The arm bones looked perfect. The anesthetic had finally numbed up the pain, and Shawna looked at him again, locking her eyes with Ned's. She spoke in an authoritative manner that seemed far beyond her eight years of age.

"You said to help me that you had to hurt me, and you did. You said afterwards that the pain would be better, and it was true."

She put her good arm around his neck, and kissed his cheek. It was then that Ned realized this little girl had taught him one of life's truths: sometimes you have to hurt someone in order to help them.

March 4, 1972, 6:26 PM

"Well, well, well! Smedley, old boy! Glad to see you made it home." Blade jumped up from their decrepit little sofa with the floral sheet that covered up the stains. He pumped Ned's hand, his eyes alight with mischief. "Smedley, now that you're done saving lives and settin' bones, look what the cat drug in. A beautiful blond you've been hiding from me." Blade grinned viciously. "Duck hunting, my ass!"

Ned's eyes dilated and he felt a flush creep up his face. Jesus Christ, there was that girl from Marion, Skippy Murdoch! She was dressed to kill in an off-white silk blouse with two buttons opened to expose her lily-white throat. Golden hoops dangled from her sculptured ears, dancing and reflecting the evening light. What did she expect of him? She seemed a little scared, and could hardly meet Ned's eyes. She kept her hands steady on the armchair rest, but they trembled when she stood to shake his hand.

"Hello, Ned."

Blade Blackston cackled and threw his arm around his roommate's shoulder, exclaiming, "Say, you two. Damned if I don't have to go look up some chart work. I'll just slip away, if you don't mind, 'cause that Farnsworth'll eat me alive on rounds if I don't have the answers."

They both sat down as he waved and slipped out the door.

"I've made a fool of myself."

"Skippy ..."

"No, no ..." She held out a silencing hand. "Hear me out. That night at the cabin ... We were both a little drunk. Me, especially."

Ned nodded affirmatively. She poked her crippled foot out from under her skirt. "This thing ... this stupid foot, you can't believe how it's ruined my life. Skippy this, Skippy that! My very name's a reminder of this damn deformity!" She pounded her fist on the arms of the chair in frustration and anger. "I didn't show up for a college interview once, because I couldn't bear the shame of skipping in.

"So here you are, some hot young buck of a doc over from the city for a hunt. Here I was, moping around and feeling sorry for myself. Well, when I saw the care in your eyes, the way your hands wanted to do something to help, that maybe there was something that doctors could actually do to straighten it, and I guess I just went crazy. I've never even let anyone see it! I just didn't know what to do. So like a drunken idiot I screwed things up even more. Later, when I called the hospital, like you said to do, the operator transferred me to the emergency room where they said you were. But you weren't there! So I asked this nurse to get a'holt of you, to find out what to do about ... Well, I was so embarrassed to talk to a complete stranger that I just said it was about something significant. By the way," she queried. "What the heck kind of nurses do you have in your hospital? That lady gave me the phone number and hung up in a huff!"

Ned started laughing. It was complete! The enigma of miscommunication was solved. He leaned over and grasped her hand affectionately. There was a haunted, scared look in her eyes. He was going to make it disappear.

287

"Skippy, I can actually help. It so happens that I'm the orthopedic rotation right now. Tomorrow morning is the outpatient clinic. Be there at eight in the morning. I'll make sure you get in." He fidgeted a little. "Do you need a place to stay? You could maybe ... maybe sleep on the sofa, here."

She had slumped in relief, but now, at his suggestion, she laughed and waved him off. "No, no. Blinky drove me over in his pickup. We're staying at the Holiday Inn." She looked up and smiled at his poorly concealed astonishment. "It's not what you think," she said indignantly. "I got my own room. Him an' that stupid hound Magic's in the other."

March 8, 1972, 8:37 AM

They were in the operating room. Lying under the sterile drapes, asleep and intubated, was their case for the day: adult talipes equinovarus, or clubfoot. The withered foot was painted with brownish-orange Betadine antiseptic, and Georgie had intubated and anesthetized their patient for the day. Dr. Ned Crosby, who was assisting, as usual, had specifically requested George for the procedure. Skippy Murdoch lay supine on the table with a roll of towels stuffed under her left buttock to tilt her towards the right. This made the deformed foot fall inwards, to facilitate the surgical exposure.

"We'll use an anterolateral Ollier approach," the chief resident announced.

Ned thought he was watching the orthopedic version of Neal Morgan. One minute he was looking at a deformed, banana-like foot with a heel twisted inwards, and the next the whole thing had been flayed open, nerves, tendons, and arteries pulled out of the way, with the deformed joints sprung and dislocated to expose glistening, blue-white articular surface.

"It's the beauty of orthopedics, Ned," the chief resident explained. "Here, things make sense. Orthopedics is applied anatomy.

288

If you just have an understanding of anatomy and a sense for three-dimensional spatial relationships, you can do some miraculous things."

Ned looked up and nodded, pretending to understand.

"See how her heel is twisted in?"

Ned nodded again. Actually, it was pretty obvious—even he could see that!

"To correct this inside deformity, we'll base the resection of the wedge of bone on the outside. See?" A large, bone-cutting chisel, an osteotome, was hammered into the foot, across the deformed joint.

Wham! Wham! Wham! The osteotome drove though the joint, cutting a laterally based wedge of bone from the heel, the subtalar joint. The chief then pulled her heel bones back into place, and suddenly they were in perfect alignment!

He looked at Ned and smiled. "Now we'll take care of the twisted forefoot. It twists inward, doesn't it?"

Ned nodded dumbly, yes, again.

"So ... how should we base this wedge, Ned?"

"Er, if it twists in, the wedge should be on the outside."

"Right, genius."

Ned could see him smile though the mask. What was the big deal? It really did make sense. Kind of like that drunk in the emergency room with the cut eye. You just had to think spatially ... He started in dismay—the osteotome was being thrust at him.

"So if you understand it, do it."

"Holy shit."

"It's easy, Ned, really. The first cut is perpendicular to the heel's axis. The second is perpendicular to the forefoot's. That way, when you remove the wedge, the forefoot swings over, just right, closed into perfect alignment."

Wham! Wham! Wham!

"Holy shit! What'd you do?" the chief gasped...

Skippy Murdoch left the operating room table on Friday morning, March 8, 1972 in a plaster compression splint, with a foot that aimed dead-straight ahead, and that would fit in any shoe bought off the shelf from any store in Marion, New York City, or Paris.

* * * *

Ned reflected on this keystone event in his life. It always astounded him how seemingly random events eventually coalesced into a form that had purpose and meaning. Purely by chance, he'd met a barmaid on a hunting trip who had a deformed foot. Both of them had been naive and intoxicated, but somehow they'd muddled through a maze of moral and ethical pitfalls, any of which could have ruined one or both of their lives. Skippy crystallized her dream that somehow this horrid deformity, which had chained her to a barmaid's life in a rural community, could be corrected. And, through her inadvertent miscommunication with Katherine, she helped Ned to realize how very precious Katherine Lindstrom was to him.

Once Skippy's foot was surgically corrected, she applied to college, and ultimately was accepted at Washington State University's School of Veterinary Medicine, a very prestigious position. She ultimately became a professor and an innovative animal surgeon. Ned and Katherine were the Godparents of her first child.

And for Ned's part, when he completed that final hammer stroke on the osteotome, pulled out the wedge of bone, and looked down at a perfectly corrected foot, he realized that he had found his life's work.

8

Swamis

N ed fingered the diary. He was getting towards the end, and the vignettes were getting shorter. Of course he realized that, as the internship sped by, there had been less that shocked him, less worth writing down. Also, because of his experience on the orthopedic service, he lost interest in recording the detail of the remaining rotations. He'd found a home. There were several episodes that stood out, though, and he was anxious to read them.

One thing that wasn't present in the diary was the mundane, the crushing load of an intern's everyday life. He remembered how he dreaded the orthopedic clinic. It was filled each day with the crippled and arthritic. Even now it made him shudder, remembering all those seemingly forgotten older people on crutches and canes, or worse, stuck for the rest of their lives in wheelchairs. He'd wished that he could have written down his impressions then, because barely a year later a new operation, the total joint procedure, swept the country and ended the needless suffering of these unfortunate people.

* * * *

April 1, 1972, 8:20 AM

Dr. Sylvia Brigham, chief medical resident, led the interns through morning rounds. Their team consisted of Blade, Ned, David Hazelette-Warner, and the infamous Ramamurti "Hepatitis" Singh. Harriet Swathmore and Farley Vaughan were the first-year medical residents. Harriet was eight months pregnant, and taking a leave of absence. Ned introduced himself and Blade Blackston, and Dr. Singh dipped his turban in a bow, "I have heard of you."

Ned surveyed the team: the rotund Mrs. Swathmore; a noodle-thin, acne-plagued Vaughan, who was actually picking his nose in front of them; and the turbaned intern. He rolled his eyes at Blade and leaned over to whisper. "Looks like you and I get to do a lot of work."

Dr. Sylvia Brigham was, herself, on a roll. She was near the end of her rotation at the General, and she'd already been accepted into a prestigious endocrine fellowship for internal medicine at the university. Teaching new interns—particularly detested surgical types like Ned and Blade—wasn't exactly what she had in mind as her grand finale.

"Keep your cards in order, please," she snipped. "Ned, this next patient's yours."

They stopped in front of a patient's bed. Under the sheets was a twisted, deformed man with festering skin. Angry-red, weepy scales covered his body. His arms were frozen out front, extended as though praying. His elbows were flexed, and his scabby, stiff fingers stuck awry in a variety of crooked angles.

"Mr. Nelson Grimes. Age, thirty-seven. Severe, psoriatic arthritis, all joints involved ... Bedridden. Pneumococcal pneumonia, secondary to being bedridden ... Sacral decubiti, and excoriation in the perineum." Her litany droned on monotonously. "He's on penicillin, one gram IV, q six hours, pulmonary toilet with nasotracheal suctioning, and of course, nursing care for the decubiti, as well. Prednisone is for the psoriasis."

"Can he sit up?" Ned asked.

"No."

"If he could sit up, wouldn't it change everything? Pulmonary problems, decubiti, the works?" Ned ventured.

Dr. Brigham glared at him, her steely, closely set eyes boring through her thick glasses. "Doctor Crosby, now if he could sit up, he wouldn't be here, would he? Our prednisone will suppress the psoriatic arthritis, and we'll get physical therapy to work on his legs. Then, we'll get him up."

"Why not get an ortho consult?" Blade innocently offered. "Maybe a surgical release of the hip flexors, and then Mr. Grimes could sit up?"

Dr. Brigham bristled back, "You'll learn on medicine, doctor, that surgery occurs when someone on medicine fails. On our service, we won't fail!" She sniffed, "There's a lot less surgical steel flashing in this hospital, because of us!"

Ned retreated into reflective silence. Two things he'd learned so far: asking for help wasn't failure, and never argue with a chief.

In the next bed lay a black man with an iced towel draped over his head. Blade Blackston pulled out a three-by-five card, but Dr. Brigham waved him off.

"My personal patient, Doctor Blackston, Warren Childress."

"Warren!" Ned exclaimed. "Not Warren from supply? Hey, how are you, old buddy? Heck, I haven't seen you for months!"

Warren turned his head, and pulled off the wet towel. He held out his hand, and they shook. "Docta Crosby, good to see you, too. I didn't quite see you there, at first. Jus' fight'n a headache. Gots 'em all the time." Warren looked strange to Ned. His nose and chin were thickened, as were his hands.

Ned smiled and pumped his hand. "Warren, I still got my wallet and the five bucks you rescued for me. I haven't forgotten. Anything we can do to help? You ask, and you got it."

"So what's wrong with Warren?" Blade asked.

"You are referring to my private patient." Sylvia Brigham said testily. She slowly looked around the room for effect, emphasizing their dog-shit status as interns. "Warren has a pituitary tumor. We're going to cure him. As you know, he's very special to this hospital. No offense meant; I just want him to get the best care possible." There was an awkward silence.

Ned spoke up first, "Uh ... what's best for Warren is what any of us would want. Isn't that right, Blade?"

"Ditto."

They moved on to the next bed, but the Blade muttered under his breath to Ned, "Course, turd interns like us, we don't know nothin' but how to cut on people, right Smedley?"

Rounds continued until they arrived at the back of the medical ward, where a group of sealed rooms separated the Ward patients from these rooms. Dr. Brigham donned a gown and mask, and the rest of them followed suit.

"The hepatitis service, doctors. Some might say the private preserve of Doctor Singh."

Ramamurti smiled broadly at them, and bobbed his turbaned head.

"Doctor Singh," Brigham gestured with her hand, "please lead the way."

Singh opened the door, and as they entered the ward Dr. Brigham continued the banter.

"Doctor Singh lost his brother to hepatitis in northern India. It was for this reason he chose this rotation. With eleven months on the hepatitis service, he's finishing not one, but two excellent research papers."

Singh smiled, and she raised an eyebrow towards the rest of them.

"Doctor Singh's work has been outstanding. You can, and all should learn from him."

Singh opened the first door, and they entered. His eyes grew distant as he collected his thoughts and scanned the patient's chart.

"Wendy Turek," he said. "Age twenty-three. Here for three weeks. She has infectious hepatitis from eating shellfish. In fact," he beamed, "she's the only person on our ward with infectious hepatitis!" He grinned through his mask at them. "Bilirubin is now coming down at 11.7. It was as high as 19. LDH and SGOT, one standard deviation above normal. Soon ready to go ..." Dr. Singh suddenly seemed to turn white. He blurted out, "Excuse me please ... Dr. Brigham, excuse me," and he bolted from the isolation rooms.

Dr. Brigham watched in dismay as Singh stripped off his gown and mask, and sprinted out of the ward. She stared vacantly though her glasses, and distractedly waved her arms in exasperation.

"Well, for heaven's sake! I ... I guess we'll just finish rounds on our own."

She turned to Blade, and then gestured towards Wendy Turek, whose yellow eyes and jaundiced face stared back.

"Doctor Blackston, Miss Turek is your patient. Doctor Singh is taking his week's vacation, starting tomorrow, and these patients will need your and Doctor Crosby's attention."

Blade sighed as they entered the next isolation room.

"In this next room is Robert J. Washington." She gazed at their faces. "He's a heroin addict, forty-seven years of age. Serum hepatitis is the predominant disease on this ward, with most of the addicts in this city sharing needles. It's cheaper, of course. His bilirubin is 21,

LDH is 683, and his SGOT is off the scale. His liver, in essence, is shot. He has an intermittent fever, up to 101.8 degrees. Slight left shift, and of course, nutritional anemia ..."

The outer door opened and they turned to stare as Singh strode back into the room. Dr. Brigham turned a caustic gaze his way. "Doctor Singh! I ... I don't understand your behavior, running off in the middle of rounds." She glared over at him. "Please explain your actions, right now!"

Dr. Singh cowered. "Sorry, Miss ... er, Doctor Brigham." Then, curiously, he beamed; "A minute ago, I felt bad. However, I am much better now." He looked shyly around the room. "You demand an explanation, so I must tell you. Ramamurti passed a worm."

He reached into his white coat pocket and pulled out some balled-up tissue paper. As he unrolled it, there was a gasp and then a muffled thud as Sylvia Brigham fainted. Ramamurti looked around the room in bewilderment.

"I do not understand. I just wanted to blow my nose ..."

April 2, 1972, 8:20 PM

"Doctor? Oh, Doctor Crosby?"

Ned was seated in the darkened conference room on Four West, reviewing laboratory data on his patients. A single desk lamp lit up the charts that were strewn across the tabletop.

A nurse from the evening shift accompanied a middle-aged woman through the doorway. In spite of the room's darkness, Ned could see the mask of depression hidden beneath her pancaked make-up. On closer inspection, he also saw that her big, blond beehive hairdo was actually a wig, with wisps of brunette hair poking underneath. Ned stuck out his hand, and introduced himself.

"Doctor? How is Mr. Grimes?"

Ned smiled. "I'm sorry. I told you my name. I didn't get yours."

They remained standing awkwardly for a moment of pregnant silence.

"Well," she stammered. "I'm ... I'm ..."

Ned couldn't hear her so he leaned closer and cocked his ear to indicate that he hadn't heard.

She sighed, "Mrs. Grimes. The ex-Mrs. Grimes ... That is, I was, until you know ... that is, until it happened."

"What was 'it', ma'am?" Ned pulled out a chair, offering it to her. They sat down.

"Well, you know ..." She gestured nervously around with her hands. "Well ... when he got all scaly, and stiff." She shuddered, and in her eyes a mixture of guilt and depression flickered. "God, it was awful." Her hands fluttered again, jangling some brass bangles on her wrists. "Well how can you explain to the children that Daddy's messed his scaly, bloody sheets again, because he just can't move!"

When Ned didn't answer, she nervously continued.

"So I did the only thing left that a sane woman could do. I moved out, got a job, rented an apartment, and filed for divorce." Her mascara smeared eyes darted nervously around the room. They settled on Ned, pleading for some sign of understanding, of absolution.

"Look, I just want to know how he is, okay? Don't bother with the judgments, the accusations ... just tell me about Nelson. Any progress? No progress? Some progress? Just let me know how Mr. Grimes is, and I'll leave."

"He's awake ..." Ned started to gesture with his hand towards the darkened ward, but her clutching hand shot out in a vise-like grip.

"Oh God, no! Do you really think I could handle that? Or, him? How do you think he'd feel? Mr. All-Everything in high school ... And now, me coming in to look at a divorced, bedridden cripple? In fact, how do you think I stand this, myself?" she hissed. "It's hard enough, just coming here."

She sniffed and Ned sensed that the floodgates were ready to open. He really didn't want to deal with that, so he changed the subject.

"How long had he been bedridden?" he asked. "You know, when did this severe arthritis start?"

She shook out a wrinkled handkerchief, blew her nose, and then straightened the beehive wig. "Doctor, it was unbelievable. It was like everything just seemed to happen at once. Three years ago he was a draftsman for an architectural firm, and he wanted to become an architect. He said he was fed up with drawing lousy blueprints for people who clearly didn't know what they were doing. So he studied all night and worked all day, meanwhile feeding two kids and putting bread on our table. But of course, Nelson flunked the tests to go to architecture school." She looked back and forth between the night nurse and Ned. "Actually, he didn't really flunk, he just ... just didn't do well enough that anyone would help him with a scholarship. The architects in the firm where he worked thought he was arrogant. That was two years ago, and that's when the red spots on his skin started to grow. They got bigger, and weepier, and then they so big they all sort of grew together. Pretty soon ... well," she shuddered, "you can see the result."

Ned put his arm gently on her shoulder, "Listen, Mrs. Grimes, I just don't know anything I could say that could make you feel better. The things that you and Mr. Grimes have had to endure are beyond my experience. I've only just come onto this medical service, but I will really do everything I can."

April 2, 1972, 8:59 PM

"Was that the bitch?"

"Huh? I mean, excuse me?"

Ned had approached Nelson Grimes' bed in the dark. Grime's frozen body was turned away, and the wrinkled sheets were pulled up over his shoulders. Ned turned on the light on the nightstand.

"You mean, was that your wife ... er, I mean your ex-wife?" he responded. "Yeah, Mr. Grimes, it was her ... How'd you know?"

"I know her walk, doc. She comes in here in sneakers, I guess she'll come and go without my knowing it. Don't tell her though, okay? It's the only thing I got to look forward to: knowing she still feels guilty, runnin' out on me ... taking the kids." Nelson sighed, but then he held up the stubs of his frozen, scabbed fingers. "'Course, if she looked like me, I can't really say I wouldn't walk out on her either." He sucked in a breath. "She still wearin' that stupid wig an' glasses, like she's in a disguise?"

"Yeah."

Ned leaned over as Grimes coughed up some green mucous, and he wiped it away with a tissue.

"Tell me, Mr. Grimes, if there was something you could have, within the limits of this disease, something that could improve you, what would you want?"

Grimes sucked in a breath, and chewed on his scabbed lip. His eyes drifted out the window, and then he let out the breath with a deep rattle in his chest. He stiffly turned, his gaze falling back on Ned. "You know, if I could, I'd kill myself. I'm froze-up, though, and even if I could, I'd have to look hard to find the courage." Suddenly, his eyes grew hard, and his jaw squared. "But if I had the chance, I might try it."

Ned scolded, "Mr. Grimes, I said, within the limits of your disease; accepting that this psoriasis won't go away, and that you might have many more years to live than you want. What would you want, if we could give it to you?"

Grimes' eyes grew far away again, and he suddenly snorted, a grimacing smile creeping over his cracked lips. "By God, Doc, if I could, I'd like to sit. With my legs all drawn up and frozen, I keep falling over. The nurses have given up on me, doc. They've given up. I can see the disgust even in their eyes. So now I'm lying in bed stiff all the time. You think I don't feel the pain of that hole in my back from the bed sore? You think I don't feel it eatin' away at me? How do you think I feel when I mess on myself, and can't help it?" His eyes looked fiercely back at Ned's. "Maybe I could sit in one of those little 'lectric wheelchairs with hand controls, you know. And by damn, I'd find out where my kids are, and I'd go see 'em!"

Ned reached over to wipe a little more spittle off Mr. Grime's chin, and then he turned off the light. As he closed up the man's chart, he noticed an x-ray order for hip films, which had been flagged for the nurses to remove the next morning.

April 4, 1972, 1:25 AM

There was a light, insistent tapping at the door. Ned was sleeping in Sal DeLuca's on-call room. Blade was in their on-call room with Anita Gandrelli—just talking, he had glibly claimed. Ned almost believed it. As far as he knew, no one had been in the Blade's bed since Beth had rejected him. Blackston was insisting that his celibacy was proof that he was going to think about the "other half" of a relationship. He was wearing Ned out with these proclamations, but he was also wearing down Ned's disbelief. Ever the prudent friend though, Ned had decided to leave them alone, in case Blade had a momentary relapse.

He'd let himself into Sal DeLuca's room and conked out; but he was awakened from vivid dreams by the staccato knocking on the door. He'd been flying above a crowd, and everyone was pointing up at him in excited admiration. He thought he could see Katherine looking up at him, and he swooped lower, looking for her. The staccato tapping became machine gun fire, as tracers were directed his way. What? Why the hell was someone shooting? He was falling!

"Sal, Sal!" The tapping persisted.

Ned stumbled out of bed and clawed the door handle in his scrubs, rubbing the sleep from his eyes. He fumbled with the lock, and twisted the door open.

"Sal's not here. He's in on an emergency lap."

He looked down, startled. A little hand came up to cover a surprised, pink mouth as Eleanor Hazelette-Warner turned and ran away.

April 6, 1972, 9:10 AM

"A Salem sump, N-G suctioning, sir. Coffee ground-colored, guiac-positive emesis this morning at two AM ... so I snaked him. The IV is running at 150 per hour, D5 and half normal saline."

They were on another morning of teaching rounds.

"Anything else, doctor?"

"Er, excuse me, Dr. Farnsworth. I forgot to mention that there's 40 milliequivalents of potassium in the IV, too." David Hazelette-Warner's shuffled the mass of crumpled three-by-five cards like a confused bridge hand.

Farnsworth grunted non-committally. "What else?"

Hazelette-Warner stabbed at another card. "He's getting Maalox, two tablespoons every two-to-four hours, and that new ulcer medication called Librax."

"Very good, Dr. Warner."

"Er ... that's Hazelette-Warner, sir."

Farnsworth harrumphed, and a flicker of irritation fluttered on his left eyebrow. He did not like to be corrected in front of students. As he looked around at the students, the disgruntled eyebrow crawled back down and settled.

"Doctor Crosby?"

"Yes, sir?"

"Doctor Hazelette-Warner had just told us this man vomited coffee ground-colored material in the emergency room this morning."

"Yes, sir."

"What if he'd vomited up fresh blood? I mean, Doctor Crosby, what's this 'coffee ground' stuff? Tell the medical students here," he gestured expansively to their surrounding flock, "what the differential is."

"Well, sir, I'll try to speak to the surgical side, because I've only just started on this medicine rotation, so I'll do the best I can."

Farnsworth interrupted him with an impatient wave of his hand. "Stop this waffling, doctor! You're less than two months away from being a licensed physician. What should you be thinking about when a patient presents with coffee ground emesis? And what should you be thinking when they vomit up fresh blood?" Farnsworth glared over his bow tie.

Christ, Ned thought, now I got two questions to answer. He collected himself, and gave it his best shot. "Coffee ground emesis usually means a bleeding peptic ulcer, sir. It's low in the stomach, er, I mean, duodenum. The gastric acid juices break down the fresh blood, and turn it brown ... hence, 'coffee ground' emesis." Ned took a deep breath and continued, "Things to worry about include: bleeding-out ... uh, I mean hypotensive shock, and also, a gastric perforation with resultant bowel contamination and peritonitis."

Farnsworth interrupted. "You have, Doctor Warner, listened to his abdomen, haven't you?"

Hazelette-Warner grimaced at the repeated truncation of his name, but pressed on: "Yes sir, of course. He's tender in the epigastrium, as you'd expect. But no rebound, and very good bowel sounds."

"Rectal exam?"

"Negative, sir."

Farnsworth glared around at the group. "Examinations aren't negative! Only attitudes!" The bow tie quivered. "Your findings, please, doctor."

Things were going badly. Even Hazelette-Warner's bird's nest hairdo seemed to wither.

"The rectal exam revealed no abnormalities, sir. There were no palpable masses or perforations, and his prostate appeared to be normal."

Little dots of perspiration speckled his forehead, and dark, damp rings descended his short sleeves under each armpit.

"His hematocrit, doctor?"

"Er ..." Hazelette-Warner ran through his mass of cards again. "It's, it's 31, sir."

"Thirty-one, sir ... I assume you've typed and crossed him for blood, haven't you?"

He beamed, "Yes, sir. Four units of whole blood. Typed and crossed when he came in."

"Very good, doctor. Now ... Doctor Crosby," he turned expansively back towards Ned, like a tiger after a nap, returning to fresh kill, "where were we ...? We still haven't finished with the vomited blood." The bow tie quivered expectantly. "Fresh, red, bloody vomit." He gestured questioningly towards the students. "Yes?" The eyebrow arched.

"Fresh blood would come from either an esophageal laceration, like from an accident, or if the patient swallowed something sharp. Or, or ... a nosebleed, the patient swallowing some of the blood into the stomach, and then vomiting it back up." Ned looked around anxiously, his mind ticking off the possibilities. "And last, at least the last thing I can think of, would be bleeding from esophageal varices in an alcoholic with portal hypertension and a cirrhotic liver."

"And how would you find that answer, doctor?"

"A physical exam of the liver, a stat chem-screen and liver profile, or a serum amylase would tell you what his pancreas is doing as well."

The bow tie settled back to a satisfied hum. "Interesting answers, Doctor Crosby ... Interesting, ameliorative. Certainly, you have an awareness of the problems in bleeding ulcers, but not necessarily a comprehensive awareness. Nevertheless, Sylvia, you are to be commended for your service. It looks like you've schooled your staff well."

Sylvia Brigham preened. "Thank you, Doctor Farnsworth. We've had some of the very best interns each year since you've been the chief of staff."

Blade smirked and made shoveling motions behind the students to Ned.

Farnsworth let the meretricious fawning slide, and wheeled with the students. Then he gave his patented lurch stop. "My, my, my! We've forgotten Warren Childress. Sylvia ..." he gestured again, like a conductor, "please."

Like dogs on heel, they trooped down to the other end of the ward, where Warren Childress lay. The cold towel was again across his eyes and forehead.

"Headache again, Warren?"

Childress pulled away the towel, and sat up in bed. "Yes, sir. Oh, hi Docta Farnsworth, hi everybody." He smiled to the group.

In the light, Ned could see that his features seemed to have worsened since he'd last seen him. His forehead seemed flattened with frontal bossing, and his chin was more protuberant. His thickened hands seemed even meatier as he rubbed at his whiskers.

"It's the headaches, docta. I gots to put a towel over my eyes. Can't you do something for the headaches?"

Lloyd Farnsworth put a reassuring hand on his shoulder. "As soon as the doctors make sure it's safe, and have defined what's going on inside your head, Warren. Then we'll have the tumor removed." He turned to Sylvia Brigham. "No visual changes, Doctor Brigham?"

"None, sir."

"Let's be quick, then." He looked around sternly. "Find out what kind of tumor is in there, and then consult neurosurgery to get it out. Remember, Dr. Brigham, no visual field loss."

"Yes sir."

This time Farnsworth left for good, and Dr. Brigham turned to the group. "Good job, team. And," she leveled her gaze at Ned, "well done, surgical 'terns. Keep in mind that our bleeding ulcer patient is going to get better, and not need a hemigastrectomy. No damn dumping syndromes because of a surgical failure! Now that he's under our care, we'll preserve the whole man." She clapped her hands, imperiously shooing them away. "Busy, busy."

They separated to do the scutwork, to check on lab data and record that data in the chart. The medical students had crowded into the conference room, each assigned by Dr. Brigham to examine one patient. Everyone was fighting for a chart, trying to get his or her job done. Ned protectively grabbed his own patient charts, and left the room. There was no place to sit, so he sat on the floor outside the chief resident's office.

David Hazelette-Warner ran by, carrying a vial of freshly drawn blood. He thrust it into an orderly's hand, and whispered furiously that the man should run, not walk, but run that vial down to the lab for a stat type and cross. He noticed Ned on the floor, and he sheepishly shrugged, "CYA'ed it, Ned."

Ned tried to smile, and Hazelette-Warner saw the effort.

"Well," he said querulously, "I couldn't admit to Farnsworth in front of everybody that I forgot to type and cross a bleeding ulcer patient, could I?"

Inside the chief of medicine's office, Ned could hear Sylvia Brigham talking excitedly on the phone.

"Right ... right! I know, Doctor Zimmerman, I know. But if we can get four more 24-hour urines, before and after the hormone challenges, our research project will be done. That's right! Yes, definitely the tumor's an atypical eosinophilic adenoma. Can you believe it?" she squealed in a somewhat porcine manner. "Yes ... yes, I'm going to try one ACTH challenge. The numbers? They're incredible! Visual changes? Christ, I haven't checked. He's always got a damn towel over his eyes. That's right, just four more days, and then we'll consult the damn cutters."

Ned pushed himself up from the floor, and strode quietly down the hall to Warren Childress' bed. "Hi, Warren."

"Oh! Hi, Docta' Crosby. Didn't quite see you there ..."

April 6, 1972, 8:21 PM

They sat together in the University Hospital's darkened conference room looking at roentgenograms on an x-ray view box. Ned had driven across town to "Mecca," where Neal Morgan was completing his last chief's rotation. Lit up on the screen was a skull film, seen from the lateral projection.

Morgan sucked in his breath, and then whistled. "Sweet Jesus! That tumor must be the size of a golf ball! Do you realize what this must be doing to his optic nerve?"

"I know. I'm guessing he probably has a forty percent lateral field deficit, bilaterally." Ned looked at Morgan glumly.

"You realize, that makes the risks of getting it out without making him blind a lot higher, don't you?"

"On the other hand, if you don't take it out, they'll keep experimenting on him and he'll go blind, anyway, won't he?" Ned asked.

"What kind of assholes would do this? What are they waiting for? Why hasn't Neurosurgery been consulted? They should have seen this patient within one day of the diagnosis!"

"It's been over a month."

"Jesus Christ!" Morgan's eyes went cold with rage. "Ned, you know I've had to eat a lot of humble pie in front of you. More than I'll ever publicly admit." His eyes grew distant, as he looked heavenward. "I'll never forget Mrs. Fanning as long as I live. It took a sledgehammer to get my attention, but I finally learned—you don't do things you aren't qualified for. Asking for help is not a bad thing."

Ned shrugged. "I guess it's some research project. She says Warren's her private patient, and we can't get near him. She's forgotten to check the visual fields. She won't let anyone else take care of him." Ned looked uncomfortable as he met Morgan's gaze. "Look, I'm not even a doctor yet. For all I know, I could get kicked out of the program if they find out about this. I really didn't know what to do, Neal. That's why I came to you." He pulled down the x-ray film. "I'd better return these before someone finds out that they're missing."

Morgan snatched it from his hand. "Not before it's copied." He went to the door, and called in a rather cherubic-looking university intern. "Run this down to radiology, stat, get it copied, and bring the original back to Ned." He grinned back at Ned. "Shit runs downhill here too, Ned, even in Mecca."

The diminishing sounds of the intern's footsteps echoed down the hall.

Morgan turned to Ned and grinned, "This political bullshit's got nothing to do with you, okay? Your only responsibility is to the patient. Tell Warren that if he waits, he'll lose his sight. If he wants the neurosurgical service over here to take care of him, I'll set it up. It's his decision. If he wants the tumor out, contact me, and I'll figure out a way to get him out without involving you. I'll personally assist on the surgery, the day he sets foot in this hospital!" Morgan had a grim look in his eyes.

They shook hands, and after Ned collected the skull film, he left.

April 8, 1972, 11:31 PM

Blade Blackston was dancing merrily around the table at the Lakewood, a turban made from a sheet wrapped around his head. Recumbent on the chipped and carved wooden table, surrounded by empty beer glasses and cigarette butts, lay an obtundant David Hazelette-Warner. His frizzy hair was stringy with sweat, his wire rim glasses were askew, and a froth of vomit dribbled down the corner of his mouth. A crowd of laughing interns and nurses surrounded the table. An artificial flower had been stuck in Hazelette-Warner's buttoned fly. It had been bent, wilted at half-mast. His hands were clasped as if in prayer.

"Now, ah ... er, Mr. Troll" Blade mimicked Doctor Farnsworth's high pitched voice, and bobbed his Adam's Apple, "How long have you felt this way, er ... that is, 'lower than a snake's belly in a rut?'"

The crowd cheered his performance. He twirled his stethoscope, theatrically applying it behind his back, under an armpit, dancing around the table, and swirling with the turban.

"I feel more like snake shit, sir," Hazelette-Warner slobbered.

"Ah, propitious!" Blade exclaimed, wiggling his eyebrows. "Now we're getting closer to lugubrious, repressed, deep-seated, ano-sexual aggression." He suddenly thrust out his chest and pursed his lips, imitating Sylvia Brigham's falsetto, wiping on a pair of glasses. "Do you have a dog that's been to Greece, recently?"

There was more howling and spilled beer.

"Did you check his potassium?" Someone in the crowd yelled out.

Blade dropped down to a hunchback posture and stiffly swung his arms sideways, "Yeth, Maasther ... I thecked it twithe."

"You bloody fool!" the wag yelled, "Everyone knows it's the Borderline Potassium Syndrome. If you'd kept checking it, he wouldn't have any potassium left, and you could have treated him!"

There was more hooting and yelling, interrupted by the sounds of deep abdominal regurgitation as acrid, mephitic bile rushed from the lips of David Hazelette-Warner in a projectile fashion. With a gasp and cries of disgust, "medical rounds" at the Lakewood bar were disbanded.

April 9, 1972, 9:12 AM

"I just don't understand it," whined a frustrated Sylvia Brigham. She nervously chewed on the tip of her pencil. How could he just up and leave?" She looked around at the group.

They sat together in the conference room, the entire team, with the nurses on the periphery. Warren Childress' chart was in front of them. Dr. Brigham gazed down at it.

"Can anyone shed any light on this?"

A nurse from the evening shift spoke up at the back of the room. "Warren had his usual evening visit with Lenny, his best friend from down in central supply. Then he came up front to the desk with his street clothes on and politely asked for an AMA form. I asked why, and Warren said he had a very sick relative he had to see. He said he didn't want to cause anyone trouble, so he offered to sign out, AMA." She shrugged. "I couldn't talk him out of it."

Sylvia Brigham limply closed the chart, sighed, and pushed it away from her. "Damn. All that research, down the tubes." She strained to recover her composure. "Well, I guess that's it! We'll just have to hope that he comes back. I've called his home, but no one answers." She made an exasperated flapping gesture with her hands, and stood. "So let's make rounds."

Ned stared expressionlessly at the floor as they filed out, not daring to make eye contact with anyone.

They pushed the chart cart ahead of the group, stopping at each bed. Numbers were read, vital signs, temperatures, and improving or deteriorating laboratory values were given. The interns reported cardiac enzymes, blood gases, wedge pressures, CVPs ... ad nauseum. Ned enjoyed the intellectual aspects of the medical rotation, but there was no action! He couldn't physically do anything to help a patient. He could only guess at a diagnosis, push drugs, medicines, or nasal oxygen, and then he could pray.

The out-patient clinic was filled each day with depressed patients in their fifties. They would complain to him, "I'm so tired, all the time. What's wrong with me, doctor?" There was no treatment that he could offer. They sucked his soul dry and wore him down. He could see why doctors in private practice started giving lots of B-1 2 shots. If there was nothing they could do, then they could pretend the shot did something.

They trooped up to Nelson Grimes' bed. The extra pulmonary care Ned had given, and a change in antibiotics had paid off. Grimes' color was better. This was borne out by his blood gases, which showed 98 percent oxygenation. His sputum was clear, and even his decubiti were starting to heal.

"No progress on sitting or the hip motion, Doctor Crosby?"

"Here's why," Ned offered.

He held up hip x-rays, and the group clustered together to see them. The pelvic x-ray revealed a mass of bone extending from the pelvis down to each hip. Nelson Grimes' disease had spontaneously fused his hips, but in a poor, deformed position.

"All the therapy in the world won't help a fused joint," Ned said.

Sylvia Brigham mournfully interrupted. "I guess, then, we just have to accept this condition, and be grateful we were able to heal Mr. Grimes' pneumonia."

Grimes looked up at them and his eyes grew wide and hopeless.

"Not necessarily," said Ned, who was steeled for a fight.

"Ned, er, Doctor Crosby. Fused hips are fused hips. Mr. Grimes will never move his hips again."

Ned smiled graciously. "Doctor Brigham, I don't know much about it. I'm just an intern. But I showed Mr. Grimes' x-rays to the chief resident on orthopedics. He said that a Girdlestone procedure would restore motion, and allow Mr. Grimes to sit again."

"Hallelujah!" Grimes yelled.

All eyes incredulously turned to him, as if a potted plant had just spoken.

"A surgical procedure?" Dr. Brigham glared.

"Just point me in the general direction!" Grimes offered.

Now all their eyes were on Ned, who laid low, waxing apologetic.

"Dr. Brigham, I really don't know anything about it. I just asked for advice, was all. They said they could help." Beneath his passive demeanor, his heart was pounding.

"Doctor Crosby ..."

Nelson Grimes interrupted the dueling: "Ma'am, with all due respect, let those surgeons at me so they can get me the hell outta here!" His stiff joints flapped under the sheets.

The group now stared awkwardly at each other, and then at Grimes. The nurses went over to steady him so he wouldn't fall out of bed. In effect, Nelson Grimes had just fired them. He was transferred to the orthopedic floor on the spot.

May 30, 1972, 6:20 PM

Sick medical patients came and went, recovered or died. The patients arrived in various forms: blue, yellow, bloated, wheezing, gasping, or choking. Once, when Ned was late for the outpatient clinic, he pulled aside the curtain to examine his first patient only to see the lifeless eyes of a dead man slumped in a chair, staring back.

As the weeks went by, he learned to listen with the stethoscope for murmurs, gallops, clicks, rubs, arrhythmia's, rales, rasps, and the presence or absence of thrills. He became learned in the art of percussion. There was always skin color to check: pink–oxygenated, blue–anoxic, yellow–jaundice, gray–cancerous, and mottled–septic. Above all there was the almighty Lab.

Like ravenous beasts of prey, they waited for the morning lab work to arrive. It told of the responses to treatment, misdiagnoses, who was right, and who was wrong. Gleeful cackles or moans might follow the arrival of the lab data. Amidst the chaos, Ned found time for Katherine. There was the physical intimacy, but even more exciting was discovering who she really was beneath the sunny smile.

It was none too soon when the next end-of-another-damn-rotation party finally rolled around. For all of them there was excitement and a sense of anticipation, because after this last party they were almost "real doctors."

Ned moved briskly down the hall, returning from a medical consult in the emergency room. Katherine would be waiting for him at home. He darted through the crowded hallway, deftly avoiding a cadre of portly old ladies with shopping bags, crutch-walking patients, and a man cruising along in an electric wheelchair. As he slipped by them, he suddenly stopped and wheeled in a way reminiscent of Dr. Farnsworth. He looked back in amazement at the man in the motorized chair. It was Nelson Grimes! Nelson's grimace was his attempt to smile up at Ned. His twisted scabbed fingers clawed around the hand control of an electric joystick.

"Guess you know where I'm goin', don't you?" Grimes confided to Ned.

Ned smiled down at him. "You called and told them you had your operation?"

Grimes nodded affirmatively.

"I hope you warned them, didn't you? Somebody unprepared could be pretty surprised, looking at you."

Grimes shot a worried look at Ned. "How you think I look?"

"From my standpoint, pretty damn good, considering where we started." Ned gave him an encouraging thumbs up.

Grimes grimaced in his attempt to smile again. "I did call the bitch, er, Meg. That is, the nurse did. She held up the phone for me, anyway. So ..." his eyes drifted towards outside the hospital. "There's a little park about a block from the General. If I'm there, they can see me from a distance an' come up if they want. Meg said if the kids're too scared, she won't make 'em come. I said I'd understand. What'dya think, doc? Am I being stupid or selfish? Should I just forget about this foolishness, or should I do it? Hell, maybe I should go back up to the Ward, and let 'em remember me the way I was, you know ... back when I was good." He fidgeted nervously in the wheelchair.

Ned knelt down until he was eye level with Nelson Grimes. He grabbed his arms to focus his attention. He felt like a new Ned, even-keeled with no indecision, and he spoke with conviction. "If you don't go, you'll have thrown away everything you and I went through, for nothing. If you're scared they won't come, don't be. Hell, Nelson, I'll wheel you out there, myself!"

Grimes waved him off, "No, no, doc. I've been working to be independent. The State Welfare paid almost fifteen hundred dollars for this little electric buggy. Just take me down the main ramp in front of the hospital; I'll get to the park from there."

Ned followed him along in the hallway towards the front of the General. The electric wheelchair's motor whined and hummed, the little gears grinding and pushing on out the door.

The main entrance always struck Ned as incongruous, because it was through the emergency room, not here, that the hundreds of sick and injured passed to and from the hospital. The front of the old building, with its big columns and elaborate, carved archways, was just for show. To him, the ER entry was the hospital's true opening, where the real action began.

They passed through the doors, which Ned held open, and then Grimes drove the wheelchair under the archway to the main ramp down to the street.

He sucked in a ragged breath through scabbed lips, and whispered, "Oh, God."

The sounds of running children's feet echoed in the archway.

* * * *

Ned set down the diary for a moment. To him, this episode with Mr. Grimes was one of many examples of the effects on people when inner frustration and rage have no release. Chained to a job he despised, with no way out, Mr. Grimes' body found its own way out. He had seen this time and again over the course of twenty-five years' practice. Even more interesting, he wondered, what would have been the outcome of a course of low-dose methotrexate and ultraviolet light, coupled with modern arthritic treatment? The horrible, red psoriatic scabs were caused by rapidly dividing skin cells. Methotrexate, a cancer drug that kills rapidly dividing cells, and ultraviolet light, which stimulates skin cell growth, were an effective ways to control psoraisis in today's medical world. The frozen joints, though, were another story.

There was another problem here: the hidden experimentation on Warren. The whole idea of double-blind experiments in treatment was abhorrent to Ned. How could a doctor give unknown medicine or placebo to sick patients, not knowing if they were in any way affecting the disease or cancer? And even worse, without their consent... In today's world the doctor and the institution would be subject to criminal charges—not to mention a lawsuit.

9

R-One

JUNE 21, 1972, 4:35 PM

I t was the final week of the internship! A wave of emotions swept the interns: exaltation, relief, macho camaraderie, despair, anxiety, apprehension, and confusion. They'd taken the toughest the General had to offer, and survived ... All except for one of them.

This red brick hospital, a depression-era WPA project built in the 1930' s, wasn't air-conditioned. The interns' on-call rooms faced west, where the unprotected afternoon sun baked their quarters with blistering heat. However, the architects of that time had foreseen the problem, and each on-call room had a window above the door. A crank on a sturdy steel pull rod would open the on call room for cross ventilation, allowing an evening breeze to circulate the air. They found David Hazelette-Warner hanging from this steel cross-strut.

His approach had been methodical. He left a detailed letter, outlining his current list of patients, their diagnoses, what the treatment was, complete with any potential problems. As a prelude to this act, he'd taken ten quaaludes. Then he'd drunk an eight-ounce bottle of poisonous methyl alcohol mixed with orange juice—one last "eye-opener," as the letter said. Finally, he carefully climbed up on a chair, secured a hemp rope to the crossbar, put his head through the noose, and calmly, in a blind stupor, kicked off. Crumpled in a wastebasket in the corner they found his letter of rejection for an internal medicine residency in Boston. Written across it, in big angry letters, was Eleanor's brisk statement, "I'm going!"

"That was no gesture, man," Blade whispered to Ned at the service. "That guy punched his ticket one-way to the end of the line."

"Shhhh," Ned whispered.

Dr. Farnsworth stood in front of the hospital chapel to address them. He was dressed in a dark suit, and seemed smaller in stature than when bearing down on them in his intimidating white coat during teaching rounds. He harrumphed to clear his throat, and his grim gaze swept round, scanning their faces.

The residents had been pulled in to cover patients at the hospital, since every intern was at this service. They were crowded in the pews. Farnsworth told them that they should have a chance to grieve together, to say good-bye.

There was no casket, because Hazelette-Warner's note had expressly forbidden the "ghoulish trappings" of a modern funeral. Instead there was a simple floral arrangement on a table at the head of the room.

Farnsworth wiped his scarred, glabrous forehead with a white handkerchief. "My fellow doctors," he said, "this is a difficult time for all of us. David Hazelette-Warner was unique, as is everyone in this room. There are times when it is very difficult to decipher a catastrophe such as this. And, sometimes, there are no dulcifying words to offer." He seemed to catch each of their eyes in a portentous pause. "Each of us is groping for a way to understand what has happened, to find some meaning where there may be none. The Buddhists say that when we are born, the breaths of life that we are given are counted." He chuckled, "Each night, at bedtime, I hold my breath, just a little bit, to save up a few more."

A nervous titter rippled the group.

"Anyway, my fellow doctors, I've never found that death has any meaning other than this: It is a part of life. And surely, as you all know, it will visit us all. As doctors, we shouldn't attempt to prevent timely death; but rather, we should strive to alleviate needless suffering. This is what David Hazelette-Warner did in his rich, brief life. He cared for and helped many, many people. To the drug addicts, the prostitutes, the bikers, and alcoholics who end up at the General, Doctor Hazelette-Warner mattered very much. The spreading ripple effect of his kindness to these people may not be known for many years. Many rich and selfish people will live gluttonous, lengthy lives and never add anything of value to the world. David added kindness. And so, as we go back to our duties, to the cries of pain, the diseases, the whining, the blood, and the vomit, remember that David finished his part in life with the last breath that the Creator had given him. Rest in peace, Doctor David Hazelette-Warner. Amen."

"Amen," they answered back. But as they filed out together there was not one of them who did not avoid Eleanor as though she were a leper.

June 23, 1972, 11:47AM

"Doctor Crosby ..."

There was an expectant silence.

"Yes, sir?"

Dr. Lloyd Farnsworth sat behind his cluttered mahogany desk. His hands were folded, as always, cathedral-like as he gazed across at Ned, who, in turn, nervously squirmed in his chair. Farnsworth started again, a congenial smile on his face.

"Dr. Crosby, you may recall that I told you to come see me when you were ready to look into a residency. Here we are, one week away from the end ... er, ah, or the beginning, and I've heard nothing. I don't mean to be nosy. I'd just like to help someone who deserves it.

319

The chief resident on orthopedics speculated to me that you already had a program lined up. Is that true?"

Ned sighed. "Dr. Farnsworth, I really appreciate your asking. The truth of the matter is … that I do love orthopedics. I'm intrigued. But it took me so long to find that out, that I was too late to apply to their program this year. I love surgical care, and I like doing something immediate, something definitive … something that helps people." Ned's hand went up to smooth his dark curly hair, but he wound up rubbing it in perplexity. "I really don't know. I don't want to make a mistake, rushing into a program I'd later hate. I saw how hard it was on Harold Tipton, and how people resented him when he made what was, for him, the right decision."

"Yes … er, yes." Farnsworth nervously drummed his fingernails on the tabletop. "Why not do a year of general surgical residency? It's a good year, a learning year. I could make it the springboard to orthopedics if that's what you want! Your roommate, Doctor Blackston is joining us. I can make sure there's a spot for you."

Ned smiled, thinking of the Blade's apparent involvement with the statuesque Anita Gandrelli. Things seemed quite serious. The group of them had been drinking at the Lakewood when she had suddenly blubbered out of the blue, "I just can't imagine settling down with anyone but a surgeon!"

With that, Blade leapt up on the table amid the glasses and bottles and told the whole room: "Guess who's been accepted into the general surgical residency?"

His buddies oohed and aahed with their usual mixture of admiration and envy. But Anita glowed, looking like she'd just grabbed the brass ring. Ned thought there was no question that Blackston would make a terrific surgeon. The one thing Ned couldn't understand was why, in the list of new ob-gyn residents, he had seen Dave Lefke's name. Now that was an error, wasn't it? He turned his attention back to Doctor Farnsworth, and pulled a crumpled letter from of his coat pocket. He waved it limply at him.

"Here's a letter I got, just yesterday, from that doctor in Marion. You remember that fellow, Edwards? He's written me, asking if I was tired of being a student, and how about coming out to the real world and seeing what it's like to roll up my sleeves and take care of people."

As Ned stuffed it back into his pocket, Farnsworth chuckled and said: "Is that what the Phantom would want you to do?"

Ned gasped in astonishment. Was that actually a twinkle he saw in Farnsworth's eye?

"You know, Doctor Crosby, Neal Morgan's been accepted into the open heart program down in Houston. When he finishes, we've offered him his own Thoracic Surgery Department here at the General. Imagine the opportunity! Neal Morgan has spoken very highly of you."

Ned nodded in assent, "That's really great for Neal. It doesn't surprise me at all. He's tough, but also a fine doctor and a good leader who will get work out of any team he leads." He looked up at Farnsworth. "One thing about the Phantom, you know," he said almost sheepishly. "He's been my decisive alter ego. He doesn't have major contradictions. I want a role in life where I can excel, be the very best, yet the idea of achieving this through a bruising pyramid program leaves me completely cold."

Farnsworth mused, "Well, there is some ambivalence running through all of us. We wouldn't be human otherwise." He raised an academic finger. "However, regarding Doctor Edwards' offer—working with him would indeed be less of a rat-race, but do you really think you can live with the consequences of bad decisions made by an inexperienced doctor who is practically alone, out there in the boondocks of Marion? Think about it, Ned. Think about what you've seen here in just this year."

As Ned sat there wrestling with his thoughts, he was astonished to see Farnsworth jump up from behind his desk.

"Why do you think my hands move in this insufferable flutter?" he challenged. "Isn't it unnatural? See my right hand." It quivered spastically at his side. "See my left." He moved into an aggressive karate stance. The left arm flashed in a blur, moving through space on a sharply defined path, twisting in the finishing move of a kata, breaking into two fragments the plaque on his desk, awarded to the Resident of the Year for 1953. "A meaningless piece of wood, a gesture to a man robbed of his talent, his gift."

He turned a caustic eye down on a startled Ned, who was still nervously scrambling to pick up pieces of the destroyed plaque.

"I turned to ancient philosophies to try to find some meaning for the loss. How could my life, my talent be so suddenly robbed by a lunatic? I believe you have the gift, as I did. For lack of accurate description, call it an instinct, a knack, God-given and not to be wasted. The new procedures that await you, Ned, the difference that you could make to untold thousands, cannot be wasted. Take the year of General Surgical residency in our program, and then be sure of your path."

Ned was awestruck by Dr. Farnsworth's emotion. He hadn't realized that such feelings could run beneath the administrator's sagacious and scabrous exterior. He didn't know what to say, except: "You'll let me think about this, won't you? You wouldn't get mad at me if I just leave for a moment, and come back in five minutes and change my mind and ask for a position? I really do want to do something to help people." He grinned at Farnsworth impishly.

"Ned, don't worry about people getting mad at you. That's half your problem. Sometimes each of us has to follow our instincts to do what is right, and your instincts are impeccable." Farnsworth chuckled and pursed his lips. "A good, caring doctor is a diamond in the rough. Your performance as an intern was one of the strongest on record here at the General." He smiled graciously. "If I could convince you to stay, we'd love to have you."

They laughed, and Ned, sensing that the interview was over, stood up. He stuck out his hand and they shook.

"A crazy experience, sir ... A really crazy experience. I wouldn't trade it for a million dollars. But then, I wouldn't repeat it for a million, either!"

They laughed together again, and Ned let himself out. As he left Dr. Farnsworth's office, he paused outside the door, thoughtfully fingering the letter from Dr. Edwards in Marion. *One thing I do know,* he thought, *sometimes you have to hurt someone to help someone. Which means ...* He tossed Dr. Edwards' letter in the wastebasket. He would ask Katherine if she thought this was the right career decision, if she would join him forever.

June 30, 1972, 7:05 AM

"You adjusts the buttons, doctas ... you adjusts the buttons!"

Ned and Blade smiled at each other as Warren explained to a new group of dismayed green interns why the baggy whites were all the same size. Blade appeared to be checking out the legs of one of the new interns, quickly commenting that they didn't come close to Anita's. Warren gave his patented big, gold-toothed grin as he caught Ned's eye.

"You doctas needs advice, you just ask those two behind you. They's some a' the best!"

The new interns clustered around Ned and Blade. Ned couldn't understand why they seemed so young. Their faces were youthful, tanned, and healthy. A new intern with curly, blond hair and wire-rimmed glasses whispered to one of the others about Ned's facial tic and his gaunt features. Then he ceremoniously pulled out a gold pocket watch and announced to the group in an affected, nasal, Eastern accent that they'd best be sure to be on time for Doctah Faaanswuth.

"Not to worry, not to worry." Blade Blackston held up a restraining hand. He whispered to Ned, "I'll cut this Boston Brahmin schmuck down to size." Then he turned to the group. "You new interns want some advice, just ask. Don't be going-off, half-cocked, with all your book learning and kill someone! If you want, I can tell you which rotations are good, and which stink."

"Excuse me," said the rosy-cheeked Brahmin, "but I think yoah in errah. You may 'a been intuhns, but we'ah not! The term intuhn is now deemed to be ahchaic! We," he said, circling his fingers to indicate his group, "everyone in this group is considered an R-One." He pointed at Ned and Blade; "You are R-Twos. Residents in ye'ah one, residents in ye'ah two. Comprehende?"

Blackston almost fell over himself laughing. "Boy is Farnsworth going to have fun with this one." Blade never missed a beat. "R-Ones, R-Twos ... Listen, hotshot; you can call yourself anything you want! But the one thing that never changes is the number one rule of this institution. And that rule is: Shit flows downhill!"

Blade smiled at Ned, and as they wheeled away, he called over his shoulder, "By the way, R-One, you're twenty minutes late for Farnsworth's lecture!"

"Damn!"

Scurrying feet sounded down the hall.

* * * *

A sleepy Ned Crosby closed the diary. It was three o'clock in the morning. He stretched and twisted stiffly. It was all there in the diary; he'd just needed to see it. Forget the insurance plans, forget the administrators, forget the managed care, and forget the bottom-line of some slick accountant who'd figured out how to shave the dollars from a patient into his own pocket— caring was still the cornerstone of medicine. They might try, but they would never turn him into an assembly-line employee, a "care provider." Lloyd

Farnsworth had hurt those he loved, trying to help train them to become better doctors. He was a caring doctor. It was the ultimate truth, the sum of his life and his Hippocratic oath.

Epilogue

David "Lunch" Lefke

Lunch had, in fact, entered the OB-Gyn residency. He became a successful Beverly Hills obstetrician. His practice blossomed as his patients spread the word about how caring and gentle he was. They said he was so smooth, so gentle, in fact, that many times they hardly felt him examine them at all. But in California, any baby born with any defect automatically meant a lawsuit. So, eventually, Lunch branched off into fertility medicine and successfully pioneered the arthroscopic harvest of ovarian eggs for in vitro fertilization.

Everett "No Problem" Jones

Everett never recovered psychologically from the tragedy of Albert McNulty. Watching something as simple as a skin graft turn lethal led him to shy away from any specialty involving procedures. He became a Family Practitioner. He joined a 54-physician, Multi-Specialty Clinic in Seattle, Washington, where he married, fathered three children—all girls. As soon as he could, he retired from medicine to run a fly-fishing camp for trout and salmon at Lake Iliama, Alaska.

Vernon "Blade" Blackston

Blade entered the surgical residency offered at the General. And, he married Anita Gandrelli. His work ethic, drive, and surgical skills enabled him to survive the cutthroat pyramid program. Sixteen residents entered, and, four years later, Blade and one other resident finished their chief year. But the brutal on-call every other night took its toll. Blade's marriage did not survive past the third year, when a portly and pregnant Anita opened the door to his on-call room carrying some homemade minestrone soup, only to find that she needed an extra bowl for the additional occupant. After the burns healed, Blade entered the Thoracic Surgery Fellowship and joined Neal Morgan in establishing the Thoracic Surgery and Heart Program at the General.

Eleanor Hazelette-Warner

Eleanor finished her internal medicine residency at Mass General, and completed an Endocrine Fellowship, frequently publishing research articles in the New England Journal of Medicine. This was in spite of the fact that she became a single mother, delivering, that first year, a dark-complected son with thick, curly hair. The child was named David Hazelette-Warner Jr., and she raised him using a series of expensive European nannies through aid of the trust fund set up by the Warner family for their grandson. She joined a posh Manhattan practice, but was asked to leave three years later, due to a series of tumultuous affairs with married physicians and the CEO of the clinic. She eventually married a commercial real estate tycoon, quit practice, and now lives in Paris.

Ned Crosby

Ned was accepted into and completed an orthopedic residency. He distinguished himself in his surgical and clinical skills, but declined an offer to join the teaching staff. He and his wife,

Katherine, responded to the continual prodding of Doc Edwards and set up practice at Marion County Hospital. His successful practice and family grew, but he barely survived a climbing trip in the Bugaboo mountain range in the Purcells in British Columbia, which cost Blade Blackston his life.